THE BLOOD MARROW

THE BLOOD MARROW

KIERA SHEN GABEL

HAPPY DAGGER
PUBLISHING

To the young girl who always dreamed of telling stories, and to my parents, who always believed I could.

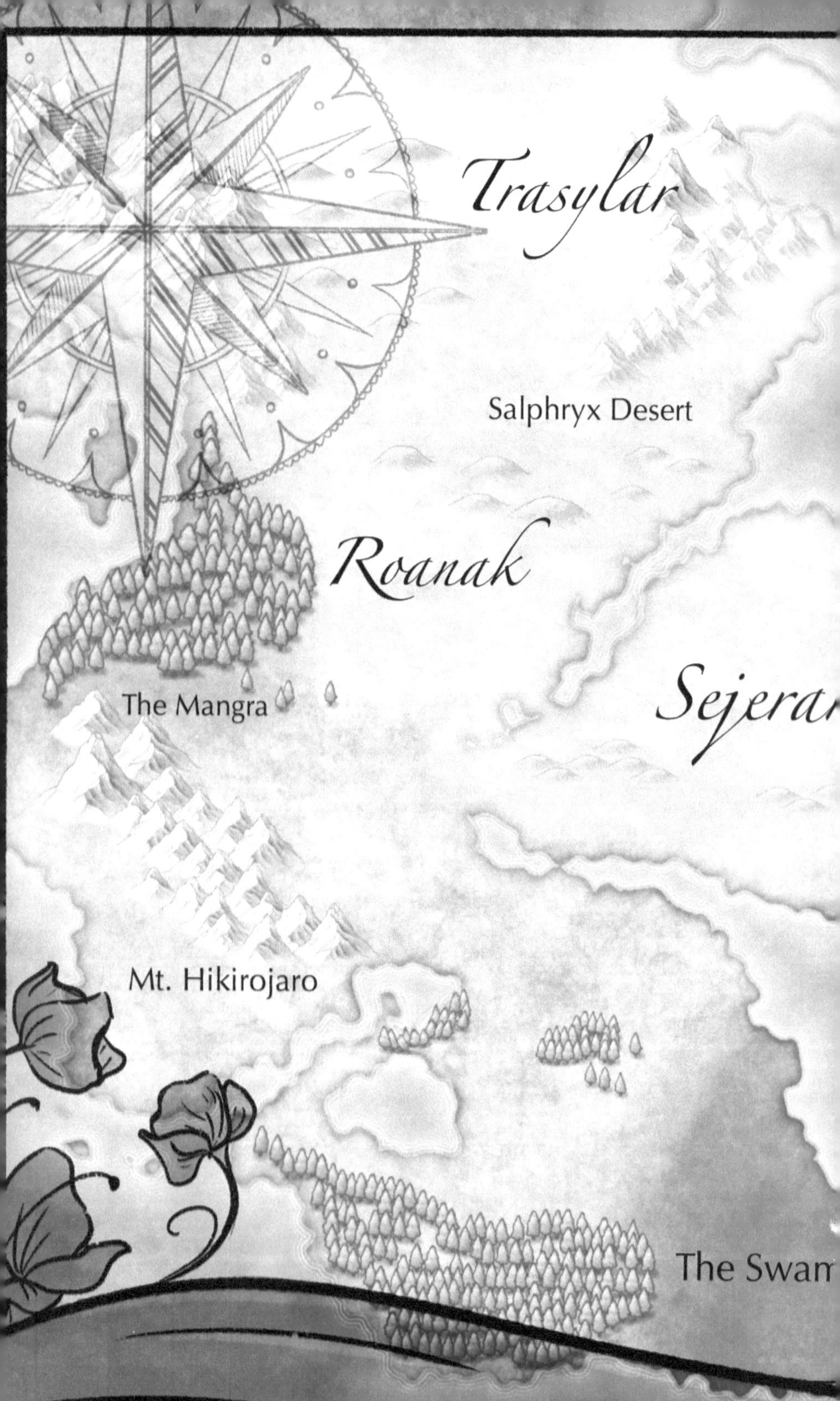

Trasylar
Salphryx Desert
Roanak
Sejera
The Mangra
Mt. Hikirojaro
The Swam

Winter Palace
High Range
Sierra
Imperia
Dark Sea
Cryencia
N
W
E
S

Prologue

They came without warning.

From high above the ballroom, the domed glass ceiling shattered, the sound cutting through the music and the conversations like a blade.

Everything came to a stop, and everyone slowly turned their noses to the sky. Dark figures perched on the ceiling beams, each with a long sword strapped to their back. There were at least six of them, but more began to file through the opening in the windows.

Around me, the masses of noble guests screamed and shouldered their way off the dance floor, pushing over the orchestra and bumping into tables and chairs. I glanced around, searching for my father, but couldn't find him over the sea of feathered hats and lush dresses.

"Get down!" the captain of the guard shouted.

My heartbeat raced as they carried me off in the wave of hysteria consuming the ballroom.

The six men released ropes from the ceiling and jostled their way down onto the floor.

Terrified screams echoed throughout the room, and I froze. Women around me cowered, tears blossoming in their eyes. Swords sliced through open air in warning.

Finally, I spotted my father's red uniform in the crowd. "Father!"

His eyes met mine, and he shoved his way toward me. "Iris!" he exclaimed. "You must get out of here!"

"What's going on?" I shouted over the chaos. "Who are these people?"

Behind me, another attacker drew a deadly sword, its blade shining in the moonlight. The other five joined in and threatened to slash their way through the terrified party guests. Only when my father shook me by the shoulders did I snap back to attention.

"They are a great threat to our nation," he said, then he called out to the nearest guard. "Take the princess to her quarters and keep her safe."

The guard took me by the arm and pulled us through the crowd.

"What do they want with us?" I asked him. "Are they from Trasylar? Is this a declaration of war?"

"I don't know, Your Highness," the guard said. "Please, come this way."

He was young, around my age. And he was terrified.

Another agonizing scream sounded, and I looked over my shoulder. The guard was no longer ushering me along, and I watched as he collapsed to the ground. Fear took hold of my breath and I stood in horror. A gleaming dagger stuck out of his lower back and blood trickled out from the wound.

I pressed myself against the back of an overturned table before the attacker could spot me. Concealed by the tablecloth, I felt myself shivering. The guard struggled to breathe next to me, and I took his hand in mine, providing what little comfort I could give.

"Help will come," I whispered to him. "Hang on a little longer."

Footsteps thundered around me as the last of the guests fled, leaving behind their expensive belongings. Even as I watched them run, I couldn't find the courage to leave my hiding place.

"Stop this madness!" I heard my father say, his voice quivering.

One man turned toward him. "We are here to collect what is ours," he said.

My father's long cape dragged on the marble floor as he approached them. I wanted to help, to tell him not to get too close, but fear kept me paralyzed.

"You will never have it," my father said, pounding his fist on a nearby table. "That I will make sure of!"

The man laughed. It was a deep, bone chilling laugh. "The Blood Marrow is ours. Our leader has grown impatient."

Across the ballroom, I heard a chandelier crash to the floor. My father shuffled to his feet. "I am the Emperor of Imperia," my father said. "I do not take orders from your *leader*."

"We know it's here," the attacker seethed.

I heard the sharp buzz of a sword leave its sheath, and I covered my mouth.

My father let out a shout as the sword sliced through his chest and he buckled to the ground.

"Guards!" my father bellowed.

"You will die where you stand," the man said, "and we will take what is rightfully ours."

"No!"

Before the man could strike my father again, I caught a glimpse of shimmering metal armor in the doorway. Reinforcements.

Palace guards rushed into the tattered ballroom, swords and spears in hand. In the back, I saw a familiar lock of golden hair and relief crashed over me.

Sorin Wingate, member of the Royal Guard, and my closest friend.

He spotted me instantly, and he raced over. "Iris," he said, his voice hurried. "What's happening?"

"We're under attack," I told him.

His blue eyes scanned me for injuries. "Are you hurt?"

"I'm fine," I said. "But he needs medical attention immediately." I gestured to the wounded guard, who groaned in agony.

Sorin nodded, and a few of his soldiers rushed over to help.

I set a hand on his arm to steady myself and allowed Sorin to pull me away from the table.

The Royal Guard seemed to have scared the attackers, and they scrambled back to the ropes dangling from the ceiling.

My father stood in a defensive circle of guards, glaring as he watched them go. To my relief, the protective armor under his tunic had blocked most of the blow.

I half expected my father to order a hunt, but he didn't. Instead, he staggered, yelling to his guards, "Get this cleaned up!"

The cloaked attackers cut down the remaining chandeliers and watched as they exploded on the marble floor. Then they disappeared into the night.

No casualties, nothing stolen. There was nothing amiss, aside from a few overturned tables and a shattered ceiling. I thought little of it—I only focused on the fact we had survived.

But soon I would realize they did not come to kill innocents or loot the palace. They came for one thing and one thing only. And they would do anything in the world to get it.

Chapter 1

*F*ive months later.

    The palace is quiet today, as it has been for the past one hundred and fifty-one days. The only place I find any source of life is in the courtyard, where the soldiers are just beginning their training as first light spreads across the grounds.

I draw a breath and adjust the helmet on my head so I can peer out through the slit in the middle. Before me, soldiers spar against one another and move with lightning-fast speed. The sound of clashing metal fills my ears and excitement rattles through me.

Before I can reach for a sword on the rack, hands lift the helmet from my head, tangling my hair in a mess above my head.

"Hey," I protest, whipping around to face the idiot who blew my cover.

"You know you aren't supposed to be here, let alone dressed in uniform," Sorin says, tucking the helmet under his arm. "Your father's going to kill me for this."

"It's *fine*," I say. "He doesn't have to find out."

Sorin raises his eyebrows. "He's the emperor," he says, "he knows everything that goes on in these walls."

I roll my eyes and make a grab for the helmet, but he holds it out of reach.

"I wasn't actually going to fight," I say, reluctantly unstrapping the armor so that it falls in a heap at my feet. "I just wanted to see what it was like."

Sorin shakes his head, amused. "You don't even like to go outside," he says.

I shrug. "With everything going on, I figure it's not a bad idea to learn the basics," I say. "Considering the attack a few months ago and now the rising tensions with Trasylar, we can never be too prepared."

Sorin picks up the armor from the ground and slings it over his shoulder. "You've got a point," he says. "Even so, you better get out of here before the emperor finds out and decides to skewer me himself."

I watch Sorin turn back toward the soldier's quarters where he's likely locking up his spare uniform so I can't steal it again.

Frustrated, I focus my attention back on the soldiers in the court-yard and I flinch as the tip of a sword strikes a soldier in the chest. It bounces off his breastplate, but the soldier is knocked back into the grass.

His helmet rolls off, and I recognize one of my half-brothers, Kaito.

"You got lucky that time," Kaito says, glaring up at his opponent.

His twin brother, Rai, laughs and points his sword at Kaito's throat. "I win again," he says. "This isn't much of a challenge any-more."

I watch Kaito jump to his feet and throw his sword to the ground. He lunges at his brother, arms outstretched.

Surprised, Rai stands still as Kaito seizes him by the shoulders and pummels him to the ground. He shoves Rai's cheek into the ground and plants a firm boot on his back.

"What was that you were saying?" Kaito says, smirking.

Beside me, a figure approaches, and I turn to see my father.

"They're improving," my father says, following my gaze. "Soon, they'll be ready to lead their own soldiers."

I fight the urge to laugh. The two of them are just barely fifteen and could hardly lead a group of men into battle. They would probably kill each other before they even left the palace grounds.

"And you, Iris," my father says. "You have an important role to play as well."

I raise my eyebrows.

"Tensions are high," he says, "as I am sure you are aware. My sons are preparing to take on their roles in this fight. I need you to be prepared to take on yours."

"And what is my role in this?" I ask.

My father folds his arms over his chest. "You must choose a suitor," he says. "A noble prince who will provide us with a powerful alliance and prove to benefit our nation."

I snap my attention toward him again.

"Marriage?" I ask, trying to keep my temper in check. "That's ridiculous."

"Ridiculous?" my father repeats. "It is the duty of a princess."

"You haven't let me leave the palace in years," I say. "What makes you so eager to marry me off *now*?"

He looks down. "After what happened five months ago," he says, "I have realized our kingdom may not be the safest place for you. But if you married a prince of another nation, more protected than ours, then perhaps you would be safer."

"Is that the only reason?"

I draw my eyes away, frustration clawing at me. Rai and Kaito resume their sparring, striking each other with their blades.

"Our country is in a dire need of alliances," my father insists. "You and I both know that war threatens us with every passing day."

"There are many other ways to deal with the tensions with Trasylar," I say.

"Refusing to marry means you neglect your duties as the princess," my father says. "If you wish to honor your mother's memory, you *will* go through with this."

My ears grow hot and anger heats my blood. "'Honor her memory?'" I seethe. "You mean like you did when you married Amara a few months after Mom died?"

"That was a political necessity," my father says, his voice barely audible. "I loved your mother with everything in my being. Not a day goes by that I do not think of her and wish she were here."

The way he wears Amara on his arm like a trophy makes me think otherwise.

"She would want you to be safe and to bring honor to your country." He pauses for a moment. "You must understand the necessity. If not for me, then for the nation. For the millions who will die if this war comes to pass."

"Millions will die," I say, "because there has been no talk of peace." *And you refuse to even consider it,* I think silently.

"Your duty as a princess is to serve the nation *and* the crown," my father says. "I will not remind you again."

He quickly leaves the courtyard, slamming the doors slamming shut behind him. I'm left standing alone against the wall.

"One day, I'm going to fight like them," a voice says. "I'm going to be the best fighter Imperia has ever seen."

Startled, I look down and see the youngest of my half-brothers, Will. His presence always seems to ease my temper.

Will's eyes lock on the soldiers, awe and admiration painted on his face. "I can't wait until I can start training, too!"

His words feel like a stab in the gut. Suddenly, dread fills my stomach. Imagining him anywhere near a battlefield makes me nauseous.

"Don't rush into it," I say. "Besides, there won't be a war, so there's no need for you to fight."

Will frowns. "My brothers are going to fight," he says. "I want to fight, too."

"Even they shouldn't be fighting," I say, trying to shake away the horrifying images of Will on the battlefield. "You're all too young. Most soldiers are at least eighteen."

"I'll be the best *and* the youngest Imperial soldier," Will says proudly, lifting his chin. "You'll see."

No, I won't, I say silently. *Because I will not let Father throw you into a war. Because I care too much to let you be taken from me.*

Something catches Will's eye, and his face lights up. He tears his gaze away from the fighting soldiers and runs along the palace wall, ducking under the bushes.

"Will, what is it?" I ask, following him.

He disappears into the green brush and a moment later, he reappears with a small white kitten in his arms. The creature is nothing but a scrap of fur, its pelt caked with dirt and mud.

"Look," he says, "isn't it cute? Do you think I can keep him?"

The way he holds the small animal with such care and compassion makes me smile. When I see him like this, I can't imagine him fighting in a war. It doesn't even seem like a possibility.

Before I can respond, Amara appears from around the corner. She spots us and her eyes fall to the cat nestled in Will's arms.

"What is *that*?" Amara says, stopping in front of him.

"Mother, isn't it adorable?" Will says. "It doesn't have a home. Can I keep him, *please*?"

Amara scoffs at the animal as if it offends her, and she frowns. "Absolutely not," she says. "I will not have that *thing* running around the palace. Get rid of it at once."

I step forward to argue with her. "It's just a cat," I say. "Let him keep it."

Amara shakes her head. "I want it gone. It's filthy and has no place in the palace."

Will seems to shrink under his mother's stare and reluctantly sets the cat on the grass.

We watch as it skitters away, bones visible under its thin layer of flesh.

"Come," Amara says. "It's time for your studies."

She takes Will's hand and leads him out of the courtyard.

He looks back, and I see the longing in his eyes.When I'm certain that Amara is gone, I make my way past the dueling soldiers and duck under swords until I reach the bushes. Crouching down, I look under the twisting branches.

Out of the corner of my eye, I see a blur of white and turn to find the kitten crouched under the leaves. As I observe the small creature, I see exactly why Will wanted to help it. The cat's left ear is torn, and as it slowly walks toward me, I see it's limping.

This cat would never survive in the wild, and Will knew that.

I collect the cat in my arms, surprised at its calm nature.

"I'm going to leave you in Will's room as a surprise, but you have to be good… Be good, alright?" I whisper as I tuck it within the folds of my dress. "We don't need to give Amara any reason to find out about you."

Later, as I leave Will's room, the sound of hushed voices echoing down the hallway makes me stop just short of the door. I press myself against the wall, and in the corridor I hear the voice of the captain of the guard. With him, I realize, is my father.

"Are you absolutely positive?" I hear my father say.

"Yes, Your Majesty," the captain says. "They grow more powerful by the day. Many citizens of Sejeran and war refugees from Trasylar have joined their ranks."

I press my eyebrows together and strain my ears, eager not to miss a thing.

My father's frustrated huff sounds. "What is their motive?" he says. "I don't want them running around inside our borders."

"My men have said many things," the captain replies, the sound of his heavy footsteps bouncing off the walls. "Their true intentions remain unclear."

I catch one last exchange before they're out of earshot, and it sends chills down my spine.

"I have not forgotten who they are," my father says quietly. "They thirst for power and will do whatever it takes to get it. We must clear them from our lands before they destroy the very fabric of our nation. With the problems they are causing in the south and Trasylar in the west, war is inevitable."

I stumble out into the hallway, using the walls to hold myself upright. Slowly, I make my way to my room. My breath comes in labored puffs, and my stomach turns to lead as I replay my father's words over and over and over.

War is inevitable.

Chapter 2

The flickering lights of the Imperial City taunt me through the darkness. From the ledge of my balcony, I can see for miles in every direction. Imperia spreads before me, the rolling hills to the deep valleys of the rice fields. But it's the city that has always drawn my eye. I watch the lights of cars racing down the streets and I can almost hear the folk music playing in the city square.

"Miss," a voice sounds from behind me.

Reluctantly, I pull myself away from the view of the city and peer out through the doorway.

"Yes?" I respond, spotting my maid, Myra.

She clasps her hands in front of her apron and smiles. "You have a visitor," she says.

I pretend to act surprised, but I know who it is.

"You may let him in," I say, nodding my thanks.

Myra shuffles over to the doors and peeks her head out, scanning the halls before allowing my visitor passage.

Sorin steps in wearing a full suit of chain link armor. "Good evening, Princess," he says, mocking a bow. "Is everything alright?"

I swallow, and my eyes search my room as if my father could be listening.

"I heard my father speaking with the captain today," I say, my voice quivering.

Sorin pauses. "What did he say?"

I sit on the edge of my bed and stare down at the floor. "He says there are new threats," I tell him, "which may make war a genuine possibility." The words taste foul in my mouth, and I don't want to believe them. I don't want to think about what war could mean for the nation. About what it could mean for soldiers like Sorin, and even Will.

Sorin leans against the bedpost. He's stiffer than usual.

"I've heard this as well in our daily war briefs," he admits. "They're not an enormous threat, at least we don't think so."

"We know little about them," he says. "But they're a band of rogues, which can be an issue. My captain told me they are unhappy with the leaders of the nations."

"Why's that?" I ask, sitting up.

He shakes his head. "I wish I knew," he says. "All I know is that they're called the Order. From what I've heard, they aren't too fond of the fighting in the North. They claim it's just another power play staged by the bigger nations. They may even try to interfere."

I want to ask him more questions, but Sorin's gaze tells me he doesn't know anything else.

Sorin must sense the frustrated expression still lingering on my face. "Did something else happen?" he asks.

I plaster on a smile and shake my head. "No, everything's fine."

Sorin lifts an eyebrow. "I don't have much time before my unit changes shifts," he says. "I'd rather skip the part where I interrogate you."

I feign annoyance, but I know his intentions are good. He always does this.

"Why am I upset, aside from potential terrorists inside our borders? Well, my father still wants me to get married," I say at last, trying to sound as casual as possible. "Only this time, he wants me to marry *now*. Like soon."

His expression falls. "Oh," he says.

I try not to focus on the deflated expression on his face.

"So, what's new with you, Lieutenant?" I ask before he has the chance to say more.

"Yeah, go ahead, change the subject," he says, giving me a crooked smile. "That always seems to work." Then his expression softens. "Your father hates when you're upset like this. He's going to send you to the infirmary one of these days."

I scowl. "There's nothing wrong with me. Besides, my father is too busy worrying about how he's going to seduce the foreign leaders into an alliance. My emotional affairs are the last thing on his mind."

Sorin snorts, unamused. "Hilarious, Your Highness."

"Rather than princess, maybe I should lobby to be the court's royal jester instead," I say.

He laughs. "Well, I should go soon," he says, lifting his helmet back onto his head. "Nightfall tomorrow?"

I smile to myself, pleased that he remembers.

Sorin and I have spent nearly every full moon together by the riverside since we were kids. The custom started when Sorin told me that the full moon was his favorite lunar phase because it lights up the land and makes everything glow. *It's like magic*, he had said.

"I wouldn't miss it," I say. "Provided my father lets me out of his sight for more than a minute."

"So dramatic! I'm sure he means well," Sorin offers. "Your safety is of utmost importance to him."

"And to me, of course," Sorin adds. "So don't get into too much trouble, alright?"

I usher him toward the door and laugh.

"I *never* get into trouble."

As soon as the sun dips below the horizon the following day, I slip out of the palace through one of the servant pathways and make my way into the gardens. I duck behind shrubs and roses and watch as the soft blur of dusk casts itself over the palace grounds.

Sorin waits for me behind one of the stalky bonsai trees on the edge of the garden. We walk the perimeter of the grounds in order to distance ourselves as much as possible from the guards' watchful eyes.

As we walk, Sorin stumbles forwards. He uses the tree trunk to steady himself and lets out a shaky breath.

"Everything okay?" I ask.

"Yes, of course," he says, shaking his head.

A strange silence hangs in the air as I watch Sorin step gingerly over the rocks on the riverbank. We've traveled this path a million times before. I could do it in my sleep. Something feels off, but I push the feeling away.

"I hope to visit the city one day," I say, breaking the silence.

Sorin follows my gaze across the river. "I've been there a few times," he remarks. "It's loud and crowded, but it's spectacular all the same. There's every type of cuisine imaginable and the parties are never-ending. You would love it."

I envision his version of the city, and a warm feeling washes over me. "Will would like it, too," I say. "He's always been one for parties."

"I'll take you someday," Sorin says. The unspoken implication of, *with your father's permission,* hangs in the silence. "And Will, provided that he doesn't drop kick me again."

I laugh. "That was an accident," I say. "You were hiding under a bush and spooked him. And remember, he was only five."

"Still hurt," Sorin argues, rubbing his nose as if he could still feel the impact.

The gong sounds far off behind us, signaling the new hour. Hidden by the enormous blossoming willow tree at the side of the river, Sorin leans in close, his mouth gently hovering near my ear.

"What are you—?" I start.

"Shhh," he says. "I have something I need to give you."

My breath catches, confusion rippling through me.

"I found this while on patrol," he says, his voice low. "I don't really know what to make of it, but I thought perhaps you might."

I feel something metallic, about the size of a compass, land in my hand. Quickly, he pulls away and straightens his uniform.

"Don't let anyone catch you with it," he murmurs, his fiery eyes scanning the garden. "I can't explain it, but I know there's something strange about it."

"Where did you find it?" I inquire, my fingers wrapping around the cool metal. "And is this why you were acting so awkward before?"

What is he getting himself into? I think to myself.

Without answering my question, Sorin continues scanning for eavesdroppers. "Put it away," he says, spotting the top of another guard's hat a few yards away.

Quickly, I stuff the object into one of the small pockets in my dress, hoping no one will notice the large bulge in the pink fabric.

"Sorry this was so abrupt," he apologizes, dipping his head. "I had to give it to you now. I think it's important, so keep it close, alright?"

"I don't understand, Sorin. Where did you get this, and what does it have to do with me?"

Again, he shakes his head. His voice is barely audible. "I don't know what it is, but I found it tucked away in the East Tower."

"Sorin, what were you doing in there?" I hiss. "You know it's restricted."

No one has stepped foot in that wing of the palace. Not since my mother died.

"I know, I know," Sorin replies, a shadow crossing over his face. "But that's not important right now."

"Then what's so important that you're giving me this?" I ask.

"I just think it's important that you have it," he insists.

Still skeptical, I trace small circles over the cool artifact in my pocket.

Sorin draws a breath and closes his eyes for a moment. "There's something else I need to tell you." He pauses. "I want you to know they're re-stationing me to the Winter Palace. We leave at dawn. I was afraid I wouldn't catch you in time to give it to you. And to say goodbye."

"Wait," I protest. "You're going to the front lines?"

A sour feeling of betrayal spreads over me.

His gaze drops to the floor, and I feel myself shaking. "I'm sorry I didn't tell you sooner," he says.

"How could you do this to me, Sorin?" I say, my voice breaking.

"Iris, I'm sorry," he says, his voice full of emotion. "But this is out of my control. I'm not in charge of where I get stationed. And the number of Trasylarian soldiers in the North is increasing by the hour. We need as many men defending that region as we can spare."

"You can't go," I say, almost as if it's a threat. "What if you..."

Almost entirely on its own, my hand flies to the pendant on my necklace. It used to be my mother's.

I can't lose Sorin, too, I think to myself.

"They're slaughtering innocents," Sorin says. "I can't just stand by and let that happen. You remember learning about the native genocides in class, don't you?"

"What does that have to do with this?" I ask, frustrated. "Of course I learned about it. It's the first thing we learned about in history class when we were kids."

"Then you understand how crucial it is that we do not let it happen again," he says softly. "The Trasylarians won't stop with the North. They will take over the entire country, wiping us from the maps, just like our ancestors."

I don't speak, not wanting to let him go.

"No one knew who led the massacres back then," Sorin says. "But this time, we *know* who our enemy is. We can stop them."

This war is going to take everything from me, I think as dread swallows me whole. Now, when I envision the front lines, I see Sorin alongside Will, fighting through snow and blood to his last breath.

"You're certain there's no way around this?" I demand.

Sorin looks away. "You and I both know there isn't. But the Trasylarian king is old, and he will not live much longer. When he passes, I expect the fighting to cease."

"Message me when you've reached the North, so I know you're safe," I say. "Please. I need to know you're safe."

"Take care of yourself for me, alright?" he says. "I'll be fine."

"You don't know that," I say.

Instead of replying, he takes me in his arms. I open my mouth to speak, but I let his warmth and comfort surround me just a little longer.

He closes his eyes. "Iris," he says. "I don't know how long I'll be away."

"You'll come home," I say.

Sorin doesn't meet my gaze. "I know how close you are with Will," he says. "Don't let him get sent to the front. I've seen the way he watches his brothers during training. He thinks he wants to fight like them, but you, of all people, know that he isn't meant to be a soldier."

"What's this got to do with Will?" I ask, frustrated that he's trying to change the subject.

"It's just..." Sorin's voice trails off. "It's just that I may not make it back. And I don't want you to face that twice."

I swallow. A brutal mix of anger and fear and longing tug at my chest. I've never been interested in any of my father's chosen suitors because a small part of me clutches onto the idea that Sorin is always there.

Instead of finding the words to tell him this, I say, "Don't you dare die on me."

I want to say more, but the second gong rings out, signaling the guard rotation.

And just like that, he's ripped away from me

The moon is high and clouds rumble overhead, casting a dark shadow over the palace. The wind is icy on my face as I stare out from my balcony, trying not to imagine Sorin embarking on the dangerous journey north. I try to think of anything but that. But the images keep coming. I see him in the North, his unit sent like lambs to the slaughter. He's among beasts; ruthless men willing to kill anything with a heartbeat. Dirt and grime coats his body and blood paints his hair red.

Fear keeps me awake all night, tossing and turning, until I give up on any hope of sleeping. The infamous Northern border seems to jeer at me through the darkness.

It taunts me, reminding me that Sorin is gone.

Chapter 3

"**Y**our Majesty!"

The following morning, the palace messenger bursts through the doors of the ballroom, holding a lengthy report.

My father turns to face him. "Yes?"

I straighten in my seat at the breakfast table.

Pushing up his rounded spectacles, the messenger catches his breath and straightens his posture. "I have come to report that the King of Sejeran will not be attending the Lunar Ball," he says through short, labored breaths.

"What?" my father demands, taking a step toward the trembling messenger. "And why is that?"

"Our eyes report an ambush, Your Majesty," the messenger says, shrinking. "Some rogues caught him before he could cross the strait into Imperial territory."

Taking a deep breath, my father steadies himself.

"How is he now? Safe, I presume?" my father asks.

The messenger nods. "Yes, he is within the safety of his palace and sends his regards," he says. "However, his heirs are still willing to make the trip. They should arrive within the hour, Your Majesty, if you will still have them."

My father's gaze snaps back to the messenger, and he smiles. "Of course we will have them. Wonderful!" he says, clearing his throat. "Well, then let's complete the preparations as soon as possible."

The messenger bows and leaves the room quickly.

The sound of classical ballads drone throughout the room, and I'm reminded of how much I hate them. They remind me of everything wrong with the palace. The facades we all put on in order to pretend like everything is perfect.

Large strips of white tool hang from the ceiling. Elaborate bouquets of cyan colored orchids and small vines of jasmine sit in the center of the tables. Gowns and dark tunics populate the ballroom and I can already hear chatter coming from the guests.

I almost run into my father as I step over the threshold of the grand doors.

"Father," I say, fighting back a frown.

Sending Sorin to the front lines was no coincidence. How he found out about our friendship, I'm not sure. But it's clear he's trying to eliminate Sorin from the equation entirely.

I dig my nails into my palms to quell the anger bubbling in my stomach. Nothing I say to him will bring Sorin back now.

"Iris," he says. "I was just coming to look for you. I see Amara has dressed you well."

I bite my lip, trying not to let my annoyance show through. Amara had insisted I wear the gown she picked out.

"I expect you to spend dinner with our family and the princes tonight," my father says.

"And what if I don't like them?" I ask.

"The two heirs are exactly how a prince should be," my father says. "They're well mannered, courteous, and very scholarly. I think they'll impress you, if you give them a chance."

"Fine," I reply, with no intention of doing any such thing.

Crossing the ballroom, I find myself at a long table filled with every kind of food and drink imaginable. I survey the table and find an inviting platter filled with a rainbow assortment of macarons. I selectively take a purple one and decode the sweet lavender taste of the small delicacy.

"Those are my favorite," a female voice says from over my shoulder. "We can hardly ever find them back home."

Startled, I look back to see the smiling face of a girl. She must be around my age, although she's unfamiliar.

Her dark, rich skin and her curly black hair tell me she isn't native to Imperia, which leads me to believe that she has come from Sejeran.

"They are quite delicious. I'm Iris," I say, stepping aside from the platter so that the girl can access it.

"I'm well aware. It's an honor meeting you, Princess," she says as she takes a bite. "I've heard so much about you, but this is the first time I've actually been able to visit. It's truly beautiful here, from the architecture to the bamboo forests. I wish Sejeran was more like this."

I smile awkwardly, unsure of how to receive such a compliment. "You kind of get used to it, I guess," I respond. "I'm sure Sejeran is just as wonderful."

Her gaze lowers, and she shakes head. "I can assure you it's not," she whispers.

"What makes you say that?" I ask, intrigued.

"Well, I suppose it's not really a secret," she says, fiddling with the golden bracelets on her wrists. "Our economy has been plummeting ever since the fighting began, and our people aren't very well off. I'm not sure if I should tell you this, but seeing as we're both princesses, I suppose we should stick together."

Now it's my turn to look surprised. "You're the princess? How come you didn't tell me before?" I say, curtseying respectfully.

"It really doesn't make a difference," she says, flustered. "On another note, I love your dress!"

"Thank you," I reply, still distracted by the situation she described. "And I'm sorry to hear about Sejeran. I hope this alliance will improve the conditions greatly."

"I appreciate it, Your Highness," she says, giving me a warm smile.

I shake my head. "Please, let's not be so formal. Call me Iris."

She lets out what appears to be a breath of relief. "Jess," she says. "By the way, have you met my brothers yet?" She looks across the room to where my father, Amara, and the two princes sit, deep in conversation.

"No, although I will soon, I'm sure," I say, trying to sound enthusiastic.

"A shame," she says.

I laugh. "I have to ask, are they looking for a wife? Perhaps a princess from Imperia would be suitable?"

Jess bursts out laughing. "That's why we're here, isn't it? So you can get a husband?"

I hold my hands up in mock arrest. "You caught me."

She scowls playfully. "Well, if you want to take your chances with one of them, go ahead. Heck, take both of them. It'll relieve some of my stress. Keeping those two in line is more work than I signed up for."

I laugh along with her, the tightness in my chest dissipating.

All too quickly, the servers call everyone to their seats for dinner. I sigh, wishing our conversation could continue.

We walk together toward the table where both royal families sit, all engaged in conversation. My father stations himself at the head of the long dining table with Amara to his right and my three half brothers to his left.

My gaze falls on Jess's brothers, the Princes of Sejeran. They both have the same earth colored skin as Jess and the same silky black hair. One of them is significantly taller than the other and wears a deep green colored tunic, while the other wears a white tunic and thin rimmed glasses on his nose bridge.

"Gentleman," my father addressed. "Please, meet my daughter, Princess Iris."

At once, both princes look in my direction, seeming to project a blaring spotlight on my figure. My face grows warm.

"Welcome to Imperia," I greet, giving them a shallow curtsy before taking the seat next to Will.

"Lovely to see you again, Your Highness," Jess says politely to the Emperor before taking the seat to my right.

"That's an interesting outfit," Rai says as he nods to my dress disapprovingly. "This is a formal ball, not a nightclub."

I fight the urge to glare at him. "I'll have you know that your mother picked it out," I say as light heartedly as I can manage. "If you have an issue with my attire, take it up with her."

Kaito chuckles under his breath and receives a sharp jab in the ribs.

"Shut it," Rai hisses.

"I think it's pretty," Will says.

I give him a grateful smile.

Rai ignores him, as usual. "You know, if you spend less time with your head in the clouds and more time going to your classes, then maybe you'll be able to pick out your own clothes by the time you're twenty-five," Rai sneers.

I suck in a breath to keep myself from reaching across the table and splashing him in the face with the water pitcher.

A cruel delight flickers in his pale eyes that reminds me so much of my father. Rai is the spitting image of my father, both in appearance and personality. Perhaps that's why we never get along.

"Hey," Jess says across the table to Rai. "Are you always this chivalrous toward women? Perhaps my brothers could learn a thing or two." Her voice is sweet, but I sense the verbal daggers she's sending him. We fist bump under the table.

"That's gotta hurt," Kaito says under his breath.

I smirk to myself as Rai's face grows into a shade of dark pink.

One stern look from my father is all Rai needs to collect himself once more. "Princess," he says. "I assure you, this is all in good fun. No hard feelings, right I?" His icy eyes turn to me.

I shrug. "Whatever you say, dear brother."

Kaito, the one with a knack for causing trouble, tosses a bread roll at Rai, who catches it in midair before it has the chance to collide with his cheek. Miraculously, Rai keeps his cool.

"Your reflexes are improving," Kaito comments.

"And your aim is still worse than a blind pig's," Rai says. He sets the roll onto his empty plate with a cat-like movement.

I can't help but squirm in my seat. I can already feel the weight of my father's glare. Soon, four servers come to my rescue and approach our table, placing piping hot plates in front of each of us, beginning with the emperor.

I look down at my plate, which is filled with roasted duck, a side of white rice, steamed vegetables, and four large shrimp dumplings. I can tell my father wants to make a good impression, considering that duck is a luxury even we have difficulty finding.

My father raises his wineglass, and everyone mimics the gesture. "To our new friends, the nation of Sejeran. We welcome you to our home and thank you for making the long journey."

We all raise our glasses once more.

"Enjoy!" my father says, inviting everyone to eat. "If anything is not to your liking, please, I encourage you to speak up so that we can have the royal chef cook something more suitable."

The food is as delicious as it looks, and by the silence, everyone else feels the same way. No one bothers to speak until we have all devoured our plates.

"Well, darling, that was absolutely exquisite," Amara says, beaming.

Murmurs of agreement sound around the table.

"We were speaking with the princes," my father starts, looking over at me. "Both Prince Nasar and Prince Zayne would be delighted at the opportunity to spend some time with you tomorrow, Iris. And I see that you've already acquainted yourself with the princess."

A few taunting 'oohs' arise from Rai and Kaito, who seem to find the entire affair entertaining. I don't even have to look in their direction to imagine the smirks on their faces. They think it's all fun and games.

Just wait until it's your turn to get betrothed, I think to myself.

"I look forward to it," I reply. I'm already dreading the next day.

The two princes smile. "We were thinking of a walk in the gardens or dinner on the balcony," one of them says, I'm not sure which.

"Or perhaps a stroll through the library," Kaito pipes in, his voice full of mockery.

"I can't wait," I say, keeping a steady tone.

"I'll warn you again," Jess says in my ear. "They're a handful, those two. Although I'm sure you know what it's like." Her eyes motion to

Rai and Kaito, who look about ready to leap across the table at one another.

I let out a small laugh, and my father looks skeptically in our direction. "Oh, I sure do," I say.

"What are you looking at?" Rai asks through narrowed eyes.

In response, I flick a grain of rice at him. My aim is near perfect, and it lands right on the tip of his nose.

Jess looks down to hide her grin while Rai gives me a look so fierce it could burn a hole right through me. The two princes exchange glances, possibly rethinking their date proposals.

"I expect you to behave like a proper young lady, Iris," my father says, his face reddening. "I will not have you encouraging such outlandish behavior, especially in front of our guests."

"Apologies, Your Majesty," I drawl, mocking a bow.

Rai snickers across the table. My father doesn't even bat an eye at that.

"Their jests are quite charming, Your Majesty," one prince says, grinning. "It reminds me of when my siblings and I were children."

I turn toward the prince, my eyes narrow. "I am pleased you find this entertaining, *Prince*," I say. "And that I remind you of your childhood."

He looks surprised, and his face pales a little, but I'm not finished.

"You present yourself as the perfect little prince, a gentleman," I say. "But you are no better than any other pretentious bastards I've met. I am not so far below you, nor do I take lightly to being thought of as a child."

Stunned faces surround the dinner table. Jess's eyes grow wide and Rai crosses his arms, sneaking a glance at our father.

A sputter of what sounds like an apology flows from the prince's mouth, and despite my pride, guilt stabs at my stomach. He didn't deserve that. It's not his fault he's here, after all.

The Emperor's knuckles grow white as his grip on his cutlery tightens. "The night has grown late," he says quickly. "Why don't we all retire to our rooms?"

He surveys the table, but he reserves his glare for me alone.

Amara frowns. "I, for one, was quite enjoying the night," she says. "Why don't we remain a little longer, dear? It will look poor if we retire before our guests have left." She gestures to the ballroom, which still teems with nobility.

"Very well," my father says. He turns to me. "Iris, I expect your formal apology to Prince Nasar."

My gaze flickers back to the prince, who seems to have shrunk in his seat. "My sincerest apologies," I say, but I don't regret what I said. It's all true.

"You are excused," my father says before anyone has a chance to speak.

It seems his fuse is much shorter than usual, and I already lit the match. He's moments away from exploding.

"You will need your rest," he continues. "Tomorrow you will wake early for your walk in the garden with Prince Nasar, provided he pardons your disrespect."

Taking one last glance at Jess, who's on the verge of bursting out laughing, I push back my chair and stand up.

"Until tomorrow," I say to no one in particular.

"Good night, Princess," the princes say in unison.

"Good riddance," I hear Rai mutter bitterly.

"Adieu, Milady," Jess says.

Chapter 4

*A*fter the guests have filed out, a booming knock sounds at my door. Myra seems to shrink to half her size. She knows who's on the other side of the door. We both do.

"Miss, please don't upset him further," she says.

"I won't," I say, for her sake.

I walk to the door and turn the lock.

As soon as the lock clicks open, my father's red face pushes through the threshold and he slams the door shut behind him. If it were a few degrees cooler in the room, I'm sure I'd see visible steam fuming off of him.

"What the hell were you doing in there?" he says. "Our family must appear strong and united. Not only did you humiliate me, you humiliated the royal name. I was a fool to think that you would ever assume your role in aiding our nation in her time of great turmoil."

I stare into his gray eyes, which gleam with a dark, irrefutable hatred.

"It's very clear to me now that you will not appear in public so freely," he says, shaking his head. "If you're so intent on acting like a child, you will be treated as such."

I take a step back and swallow, my entire body shaking.

"What are you going to do?" I challenge. "Lock me up? Keep me confined to the palace? Last time I checked, you were already doing that."

"And for good reason!" he bellows. "You have no idea of the dangers outside of this palace. There are people out there who would kill you the first chance they got."

"You don't know that," I say.

"Believe me, I know more than you know." He takes a furious step closer, and I glance over at Myra, desperate for any trace of encouragement, but she fades into the curtains.

"Don't look at her when I'm talking to you, child!" my father shouts, advancing. "Is she the one filling your head with ideas of retaliation?"

I stand my ground and shift so that my body blocks Myra from view. "Of course not," I say. "No one's giving me ideas. I've simply grown up enough to see everything that's wrong with your ways."

"Oh?" he says. "And tell me, daughter, what exactly is wrong with my ways?"

"You remain complacent," I say. "You send soldiers to the border but not enough to actually do anything. You throw balls, but you don't negotiate with Trasylar, you only make presumptive alliances."

"Being an emperor means doing what is right for the nation," he says. "The choices I make are not easy."

"I know my mother would have hated it here, too," I say.

His eyes grow even colder. "You know nothing!" he shouts.

Without waiting for my reaction, he storms out of the room.

"If you dare come out before I decide you should, your new room will be in the cells," he shouts from the other side of the door.

Hot tears swell in my eyes, and a fury consumes me as I sink to the floor. The weight of my entire life pent up in the palace comes crashing down on me.

My father despises me. Sorin is marching to his death. Will could be next.

In the morning, I drag myself out of bed and set my jaw firm. I will not let him think he won.

Despite my father's threats, I push out of my room and pass quietly through the halls. Hunger drives me toward the kitchen, and I make sure to keep clear of any eyes willing to turn me into my father.

As I walk, I spot Will walking toward me, his eyes bright. I smile, but it fades as he draws closer.

He holds a white rag to his temple, and I squint to see blood trickling down his cheek.

"Will," I say, hurrying over to him. "What happened?"

His eyes brighten when he sees me, and he beams. "I'm training for battle!" he says. "This is my first battle scar."

I frantically examine the cut stemming from the center of his forehead down to the base of his ear.

"Battle training?" I say. "Already?"

Will nods eagerly. "Yes," he says. "With my brothers, like I told you. Rai did this, but it's okay, I'm learning a lot. Even Father says I'll be a great soldier one day."

His enthusiasm makes me even more afraid. Every day is one step closer to Will joining Sorin on the front lines. I can't lose him too.

Before I get the chance to tell Will to be careful, a hand closes around my arm and pulls me away from my brother.

My father's grip is as strong as steel.

"What are you doing out here?" my father demands. "I told you not to come out of your room."

I free my arm from his grip and take a step back, putting a safe distance between us.

"Look at him!" I shout. "You're putting him into battle training already? He's just a child."

"He is my son," he says, without even casting a glance toward Will. "And any son of mine will make a fine warrior. He will make his nation proud. Can you say the same?"

"This isn't about me, it's about Will," I say, gesturing. "He has a cut the size of a serpent on his face. How are you going to explain that?"

"He earned it honorably," my father argues.

"There is nothing honorable about this," I spit. "There is nothing honorable about the war you're trying to start with Trasylar. Neither country has anything to gain, while hundreds of men will die for it anyway. Your *son* could be one of them!"

I remember Sorin telling me about the Order, and what they believed to be the true motive of the conflict with Trasylar.

It is nothing but a power play.

"My son will fight for this nation!" my father says. "I want no more out of you!"

I look down at Will. His smile has faded.

"He could die," I say. "And you will do nothing to stop it."

"That's enough," my father says. He motions for his guards. "You will remain in your room. Only this time, I will not make the mistake of leaving you unattended."

"I don't need escorts," I shout.

The two guards at his side move toward me anyway, but I don't let them touch me. Instead, I turn and I run. I hear the metal of their armor grind against itself as they race after me, but it weighs them down. I reach my room, the sound of metal far behind, and quickly lock the door.

My heart races as I place a hand on the wall to steady myself. Anger like I've never felt before surges inside of me and the image of Will's bleeding face replays in my mind.

It's then I realize I have no say here, no influence. Nothing I say will save my brother from the destiny my father has planned for him.

But maybe there are people who can. People who are already putting plans in motion to stop this war before it begins.

The Order might be able to help me, I think to myself. *If I can just find them, maybe...*

I don't know the first thing about them, but that hardly dissuades me. Even if they give me the slightest chance in preventing Will from entering the war, it will be worth the risk. It would keep Sorin safe, too.

They're a threat, Sorin had said.

But he also mentioned they may stop the fighting in the North.

Clenching my jaw, I tear off my gown and replace it with the only pair of pants and simple shirt I own. I pull on a pair of boots and leave my heels in a messy heap on the floor.

Before I can take another step, the shimmer of my mother's necklace stops me. I pause and lift it from its box. I slowly drape it around my neck, holding the emerald pendant in my hand, as if it can give me the strength I need to go through with this.

I can't protect Will if I'm stuck inside these palace walls. But there *are* people outside of them who can.

I just have to find them.

I take small, hesitant steps toward the balcony.

Drawing a deep breath, I push open the doors and step out onto the ledge.

Am I really ready to leave everything behind?

Chapter 5

*M*etal clashes with the marble floor, and I jump to find Myra standing over Sorin's golden artifact.

"Myra," I say, starting toward her.

Her face is pale, and her arms remain outstretched, as if she were reaching for the fallen artifact. But her eyes aren't seeing. They focus on nothing, and a sinking feeling consumes me.

"Look," Myra whispers, and I follow her gaze to the floor.

I observe the details within the artifact clearly for the first time. The rim of the circular artifact is a rich golden-bronze, and the edges are worn from decades of tarnishing. The sharply cut onyx gem still glistens and sparkles in the light. It's so rich I feel as if it can almost see me.

Slowly, Myra staggers backwards; her face a mask of pure terror.

"What's wrong?" I ask.

I watch as she covers her face with her hands and shrinks down to the floor, her shoulders shaking.

"No..." she mutters. "No, no, no."

"Myra, what is it?" I ask, placing my hand on her shoulder.

A shimmer of a tear falls down her cheek.

"I'll call for help," I say. "Just rest here, I'll be right back."

Myra reaches out and seizes my sleeve, holding me in place. "No," she says forcefully. "That isn't necessary."

"Please, talk to me," I say, stealing a worried glance at the artifact on the floor.

"That," she says, pointing, "should *not* be here."

I creep toward it and turn it over, as if it's hot to the touch, and reveal the etching on the inky stone.

What made her react like this? I wonder silently, scanning the artifact for answers.

Myra's face is red now, tears stain her cheeks. She stares at the artifact in my hand as if it could explode at any moment.

The sound of hammering footsteps reminds me of what I set out to do.

Myra flinches and turns toward the door, then glances back at me with wide eyes. "Go," she ushers. "You must go now."

"I don't understand," I say, lifting the artifact. "What is this, and why did Sorin have it?"

Myra pushes my hands away, and the artifact skids across the floor. "Do not show that to me again. Please," she says, gasping for air. "Please spare me from that."

Fists pound on the door.

"Where will you go?" Myra asks, her eyes darting around nervously.

"I need to find someone," I say. It's not a lie, but it isn't the entire truth, either.

"Be safe and take this," she says after a moment. She lifts the silk scarf from around her neck and wraps it around mine with trembling fingers. "It's cold. You will need it."

"Thank you," I croak. "For everything."

"It's my duty," she replies humbly. "And my honor."

"Keep him safe for me, please," I say.

She smiles sadly, and she knows I'm talking about Will. "Always," she says, as our eyes meet.

Forcing myself to turn away, I take a deep breath and step onto the rail of the balcony, scanning the scene beneath me.

Without looking back, I swing my legs over the side of the balcony.

I'm too high to jump, but I slide along the curves of the roof, slowly making my way toward the ground.

Guards swarm around the perimeter of the palace grounds like hornets. Escaping without being detected will be nearly impossible. Almost.

A few years ago, Sorin discovered a hidden cave tucked away deep inside of the bamboo forest along the palace perimeter.

It's incredible, isn't it? he had said as he watched me marvel at the glistening rock formations and the sounds of rushing water.

My mind jumps to Will. He isn't ready to face whatever horrors my father will thrust upon him. I don't want to leave him.

I approach his window. His room is dark, but I can still make out the softness of his face, untouched by war. A child-like glow still radiates off of him and the small white cat lays curled beside him. I only wish he could stay like that forever.

Before I can move away, Will shifts and faces me, his eyes fluttering open. He sits up instantly and rushes to the window, freezing me in my tracks.

"Iris?" he says, pushing the window open. "Iris, what are you doing?"

I hear my voice catching in my throat. "Will. It's late. You should be asleep."

I can't help but notice the thick wad of bandages wrapped around the side of his face. A reminder of what is coming, should I fail to keep him safe.

"What are you doing on the roof?" he asks, disregarding my comment.

I rack my brain for some kind of excuse, but I know that no matter what I say, I'll end up hurting him. "I'm taking a trip to the city," I say, angling my head toward the lights on the horizon. "A quick trip, only a few days."

"What for?" he asks, his eyes wide.

"Sorin and I have a big surprise planned for you and the others," I say, continuing the lie. "So don't tell anyone, okay?"

Will's face brightens. "For me?"

"Yes."

Will pauses, marking my words, then nods. "Okay. Come back soon," he says. "And while you're in the city, can you get a jade figure?"

"Of course," I say, fighting the guilt rising inside of me.

Satisfied, Will closes the window and waves.

"Take care of yourself," I call. "Don't do anything dangerous, even if Father says to do it, okay?"

"Okay," he says.

"And don't let Rai and Kaito push you around," I add.

"I know, I know," he says. "I'll be fine. It's just a few days."

I want to say more, but I can't bring myself to speak. Before he can see through my lie, I disappear from his window. As I descend, my heart aches for him, and what I may be leaving him to face alone.

I'll come back for you, I promise.

I scurry down a golden eave of the roof, eager to reach safety. Crouching down, I launch myself down onto another platform. This time, the landing is rougher. The hard landing causes my ankle to collapse on itself, sending a shock of pain up my leg.

I lose my balance and fall forward into the night air.

Wind whips past my face and tangles in my hair as my body falls toward the ground below. I reach my hands out to brace my fall, and my body crashes into the stone path leading away from the palace.

Pain shoots through my bones, and I feel them cracking underneath my weight. As my head collides with the rock, I feel my consciousness knocked from my body.

Moments later, I buzz back into reality, and the metal clanking of armor sounds above me.

"Hey, she's awake!" one of them calls. His voice is muffled, and my vision blurs.

More guards race over. "That's not possible," another says. "She fell from the roof. She should be out cold."

"She should be dead."

Confusion plagues my mind as I peer through blurry vision. "What?" I say, my voice sounding far away. "I...I'm fine. I didn't fall from that high..."

"Her bones should be broken," the guard says.

His words make me focus on the strange electric buzz flowing through my body. My joints sing with a mixture of pain and soreness.

"The emperor is on his way," the guard says, placing a hand on my shoulder.

Realization hits me, and I remember what I set out to do. If my father catches me, he'll drag me back into the palace forever. Any hope of helping my brother will be lost forever.

I twist away from the guard's hand and force myself to my feet.

I turn and bolt toward the trees. Despite the shouts of protest arising from the guards and the pain striking through my limbs, I don't stop.

I feel swift in the chilly night, and my legs carry me faster than I've ever run before. The tingling sensation in my body covers up the pain that comes with each step and each breath of air. I duck through the circular opening in the garden wall and make my way through the sculpture garden.

With one last glance, I make sure none of the guards have spotted me and push through the brambles, my boots blocking most of the thorns. Slowly, I make it to the thick bamboo forest and retrace the steps that Sorin and I would take to reach the cavern.

I reach the massive wall of thick green vines and inch my way through. It opens up to a narrow cavern, and I walk along the stone and follow the sound of rushing water. The tunnel is a labyrinth, and for a moment, I worry there's no opening at all.

After what feels like hours, the glow of moonlight finally shines through the rocky mouth. I creep forward until the silver light envelops me completely.

The night air is sweet. I breathe it in and tell myself everything is going to be okay.

I wish I wasn't lying.

Chapter 6

The sound of dim folk music reaches my ears as I emerge. I find myself in the countryside near a small town on the riverbank. Small homes litter the hills, spread out enough so that each house has its own plot of farmland. Since many are rice farmers, the grounds are wet and marshy, making me grateful for my boots.

I make my way through the tall grass and the warm glow of the lanterns lures me toward the town. It's quiet, but not deserted. I pass villagers returning to their homes or going out to dinner after a long days' work in the fields. As I near the center of the village, I smell the sweet scent of fresh cider and follow it to a small tavern across the street.

Cautiously, I push open the door and a blast of music meets me as I cross the threshold. Men surround the bar, drinking generously filled mugs of beer and cider. They clink their glasses together and cider splashes, soaking their shirts and beards. One man lets out a hearty laugh and stumbles off of his stool. The crowd pays no attention and continues on with their animated conversations.

"What can I get you, miss?" the bartender says as I approach.

I glance at the man on my left and point at his mug. "I'll take one of those," I say.

The bartender raises an eyebrow, then pours me a tall glass of amber liquid. "There you are."

"Thank you," I say, handing him a few silver coins.

"Are you new in town?" he asks.

I nod. "I am."

"Welcome," he says, then pauses. "But I feel obliged to warn you: a girl as young as yourself shouldn't be wandering out so late. Gangs run this place after dark, and trust me, you don't want to run into them."

Gangs, I think to myself, chest tight. *My father has never mentioned that there are gangs in Imperia.*

"I understand," I say at last. "I promise to be careful."

He looks at the glimmer of jewels around my neck. "And I would keep that tucked safely away," he says. "They love their treasure."

"Oh, right," I say, covering the pendant of my mother's necklace with my shirt. I look back at the bartender, worried that he's recognized the royal emblem on my necklace. If he does, he doesn't show it.

Instead, he nods curtly and turns as a drunkard calls out to him for a refill from across the tavern.

Once he's gone, I stare expectantly at my drink, wondering what it tastes like. Holding the glass up to my mouth, I take a sip. The cider burns in my mouth, but I force it down. I remind myself that this simple glass of cider represents my freedom. Away from the palace, I can do whatever I like without my father's disapproving gaze watching my every step.

My mind grows fuzzy as I drain the glass.

I set my empty mug aside and slide off of the barstool, holding on two chairs and tables as I make my way toward the door. I'm almost sad to leave the liveliness of the tavern. By now, most of the villagers have retired indoors and I feel alone in the unfamiliar town.

My head lolls a little, and I lean against a nearby building to steady myself. I'm almost dosing until I suddenly hear shouting. Instinctively, I drop to the ground and shield myself behind a cart of melons.

I can feel the violent vibrations of footsteps and I spot three men clustering outside of a small home. Deadly swords cling to their backs.

The men shout again. "What's taking so long?" one of them complains.

Another man bursts out of the house with what looks like a sack of flour on his shoulder. He's big and burly and his bald head shines in the moonlight. As he comes into focus, I realize with terror that he's carrying a woman.

"Did they follow you?" the man asks, keeping his voice low.

Before any of his comrades can respond, the bald man collapses. The woman falls alongside him. My hands fly to my mouth as I spot the gleam of a knife lodged in his back.

My chest pounds louder than a blacksmith's hammer, but I remain pressed flat against the dirt where they can't see me.

"Appears they did," a new voice says. A tall man steps forward with a second blade resting in his palm. Two other figures accompany him, dressed in dark suits. The sharp tips of swords and daggers reflect the moonlight, and the scent of blood fills the air.

What's going on? I demand in my mind, confusion and fear overpowering my senses. *Are these the gangs the bartender was talking about?*

"Who are you working for?" one man shouts, turning a nervous eye to his fallen comrade.

A woman steps forward from the trio, her light, silvery hair gleaming in the light. "Leave the girl with us and we'll allow you to escape with your lives," she orders. Her thick accent tells me she's from Trasylar.

Every muscle in my body tenses.

"Look, lady," a man says.

Before he can speak further, the woman knocks him off his feet in a flash and drives the butt of her dagger into his temple. I can't tell if she knocked him out or killed him.

"Do I make myself clear?" she says.

The kidnappers shrink under her icy gaze and nod, fumbling over their words before scurrying away.

One of the suited men has a crossbow strapped to his back and picks up the unconscious woman. "She's out cold," he says.

"That much is obvious," the blond woman mutters. "Bring her back to the house. We'll head back to the city at first light."

She pushes past them and swings the door of the house open. One by one, they file inside. Curiously, I shuffle closer. Still using the tall grass as cover, I peer through the window.

A candle is lit, spreading a warm glow throughout the house. The man sets the woman back onto her bed and quickly retreats out into the darkness. For a moment, I lose them in the shadows.

"A spy, you reckon?" a voice calls from behind me.

I jump and spin around, coming face to face with the deadly tip of a dagger. My heart lurches.

"Doubtful," the woman says, her dagger still pointed at the space between my eyes.

The red-haired man nods in agreement. "She's much too noisy for that."

I swallow.

"Then what's her purpose for hiding out back here?" one of them questions, his eyes narrow.

The woman forces the blade to my skin and I flinch, my head knocking into the wooden wall of the house. My body freezes.

"Perhaps we should just kill her now," the woman says.

I feel myself shaking under the cold tip of the dagger. "Who are you?"

"We are the Order of Alabass," she says, lifting her chin. "Soon every kingdom will know our name."

My breath catches. The Order of Alabass.

The Order.

I found them.

"I've heard about you," I blurt.

"Oh?" the woman says, her dagger still pointed at my head. "Then you know we are not to be taken lightly."

"Yes," I say. "I also know you disapprove of the conflicts in the North."

"We are dedicated to those who can't help themselves," she says. "The fighting between Imperia and Trasylar is foolish, and thousands of innocents have died because of it. Of course, we disapprove."

"So, you're planning to stop it?" I ask, a little too hopeful.

She scoffs. "You make it sound so simple."

I take a deep breath. My next words may change everything.

"I want to help," I say.

The woman narrows her eyes. "And what makes you think we just recruit anyone we find on the streets?"

"I assure you I'm not just *anyone*," I say. "I'm the princess of this nation. I could be of great help."

She lifts an eyebrow and slowly lowers her weapon. Her sharp eyes remain glued to me, but she takes a step back, allowing me to push myself to my feet.

"Is that so?" she says. "Prove it, then. Prove to me you're the princess."

Hesitantly, I grab my necklace out from under my shirt and hold it in the light so they can see the royal crest engraved on the stone.

"It's my mother's," I say, almost defensively, as she stares at it skeptically.

"Woah," the man with curly hair says, peering at the gem. He lowers his head to get a closer look. His face is tan, and based on his accent, I figure he must be from Sejeran, like Jess. I wonder what he's doing here. "That must sell for millions on the market."

I shield it with my hands. "It's not for sale."

"How do we know you didn't steal it?" the red-haired man says, crossing his arms.

"You said it yourself," I say. "I'm too noisy to be a spy, let alone a thief."

"It could be a fake."

"It looks legit to me, Welsh," the other man says, his eyes still wide in amazement.

I clench my teeth, my eyes still glued to the dagger hovering in front of my chest. One swipe, and I'm dead.

"I promise it's real," I breathe.

The woman barks a laugh. "And why would a princess want to join our ranks?" she demands. "You and your family are the reason people are suffering."

"Just finish her already," the red-haired man says, stabbing his knife into the wall just above my head.

If she wanted me dead, she would have killed me by now, I tell myself.

"My father is wrong in his ways," I say. "If the war comes to pass, we *all* lose."

The woman crosses her arms. "Perhaps having a connection to the Emperor will come to benefit our cause," she says.

I draw a breath. "It will," I say. "And as you know, if no one steps in, war will be inevitable. But this war will come at a great cost. One I can't afford."

My brother's life, I think. *Sorin's life.*

A long moment passes and the three of them exchange glances. I hear the blood pounding in my ears. Strangely, the tingle of excitement sparks inside of me as well.

"If you want to work with us," she says. "You must prove yourself."

"How?" I ask.

"I'll explain on the way," the woman says, motioning for the three of us to follow her into the fields. Ahead of us lies a sleek, metal ship. It has strips of lights along the sides and there are sharp pointed wings attached to it.

"It's a shadow striker," Khan says, gliding his hand over the smooth wing of the ship. "A much more advanced model of the Imperial airships, wouldn't you agree?"

I nod, admiring the beauty of the metal beast.

"Prove that you have what it takes," she continues, "and we'll bring you back to our city. Should you fail, I will not hesitate to kill you."

Her words are like icicles, cutting sharp and true. But there is no turning back.

I have to see this through.

"Do you really think you can handle it?" the woman challenges.

I think of Will and Sorin and the danger they may face. And then I realize her question makes me angry.

Clenching my jaw, I nod.

"Yes. I can handle it."

Chapter 7

The shadow striker lifts us high above my homelands, I can't stop imagining what must be going on in the palace. Is my father searching for me? Is he worried? The thought of causing him any sort of inconvenience makes me smile a little.

Hundreds of questions swirl through my mind, but I keep silent, waiting for the woman to speak. Something tells me she isn't one to cross, and speaking out of turn would certainly accomplish that.

She raises her eyebrows, surveying me. "You certainly are curious," she comments.

I nod. "I am," I say. "If I am to join your ranks, I'll first need to understand exactly who and what you are."

This sort of information, I realize, is the kind of information I should have sought *before* I agreed to strap myself inside their ship. Here, they hold all the power.

But I'm doing this for my brother, and for Sorin. I'm not thinking about the dangers it puts me in.

She considers this. "We are an elite organization, as you know," she begins. "Our leader and his line have led us for centuries."

I try to hide the surprise on my face. They've been operating in the shadows for centuries, but the first time I've ever heard of them was just a few nights ago from Sorin.

"We are organized into regimes led by our commanders," she says. "I am one of them."

"So, address her properly," the curly-haired soldier says, looking up from a metal-like book on his lap. Light glows from one of the panels. I've never seen anything like it before. "Should you fail to address her as '*Commander* Perovka,' consider your life on the line."

I can't tell if he's being serious or not, but I don't take any chances.

"Members like Khan work *under* the commanders," Commander Perovka says, shooting him a look. "Usually, they're much better mannered. It's clear he isn't part of my regime."

Khan catches me staring, and points to the strange device on his lap. "It's a computer," he says. "You've probably never seen one before."

"What does it do?" I ask.

He shrugs. "All sorts of things," he says. "Someday, they'll be mass produced, but for now, the Order is the only organization that possesses this kind of technology. They've put in a great deal of effort into inventions like this to put us at an advantage, since the nations have much bigger forces than we do."

I marvel at it for a moment. Airships are common now in regions like Imperia and Trasylar, but the level of technology the Order possesses appears to surpass any of the nations.

"How did you build it?" I ask. "What else is there?"

Khan laughs. "I'm not the inventor," he says, "So I don't know exactly how to build these. But once you get to the city, you'll see just how different it is from Imperia."

I think for a moment, still in a mix of awe and confusion.

"What do you do, exactly?" I ask, turning my attention to Commander Perovka. "I saw you in the village, with the girl and those gang members."

"We accept missions designed to protect the citizens of the nations," she says. "When the nations' leaders turn their backs on their people, *we* are there for them. It's what we do."

I want to believe her, and I want to trust them. But I saw the way she dealt with the gang in the town, and I can't forget the way she held me at knifepoint.

"We are on a mission right now," she says. "You'll see exactly what our missions entail and if you can stomach it, then you will be one step closer to becoming one of us."

I start to ask her more, but she turns away dismissively and begins to sharpen the knives on her belt.

"We're going to Yorksha," Khan says.

"What for?" I say.

"Well," he says. "There have been small revolts in this region because their queen has enacted a rule forcing those under her rule to give up three quarters of their wages to her."

"Really?" I say, shocked. "That's horrible."

He nods. "And that's not all," he says. "Those who refuse, largely because they don't make enough to sustain themselves, let alone give most of it away, are severely punished. Some have even been killed as a result of their refusal to comply."

"How could the queen allow that?" I ask.

Khan shrugs. "She's the queen," he says simply. "That is how all the rulers are. They do what they like, because they think they are untouchable."

I think of my father and the petty war he's trying to start. As much as I hate to admit it, Khan has a point. Even my own family is guilty of this. Jess, I remember, told me about the poor conditions in Sejeran. I can only assume that their king is like all the rest.

"That's why we've come to help the people of Yorksha," he says. "The region is small enough—we can make a difference and go straight to the source."

"The source?" I echo.

Khan swallows, and I can see uncertainty in his eyes. "We're going to remove her."

My stomach drops. Remove her is just another way to say they're going to murder her, that much I know.

"Surely, there's a way to negotiate?" I ask.

He shakes his head and closes his computer. "We've tried," he says. "This is what we do when there is no other option. It's the nature of our work."

The striker lands on the roof of a tall, regal chapel in the center of Yorksha. I recognize it as Saint Irvin's Chapel. I've seen drawings of the ancient structure in the Imperial history books.

I watch as Commander Perovka opens the door of the vessel and places a black cloth mask over her nose and mouth.

"Five minutes. If I'm late, leave without me," she says, tucking a few steel knives into her suit. "We don't want to keep him waiting."

I crane my neck to watch as she descends into the chapel through what looks like a small door in one of the steeples.

"You disabled the cameras with that?" I ask, pointing to the computer on his lap.

He smiles proudly. "Yep, pretty neat, huh?"

Then, his face falls.

"As proof of the kill, the leader has requested her crown," he says. "If we're lucky, she'll put it in a bag."

My stomach grows queasy with each passing minute.

Four and a half minutes later, I spot the dark figure of Commander Perovka appear from the door again. She darts across the roof of the building in a blur, a brown leather satchel slung across her chest.

Moments later, four guards emerge from the door and charge after her, all armed with long, metal spears and chain linked breast plates.

"Stop!" they shout at her, dashing to keep up. One of them throws his spear like a javelin but misses by a large margin. "By the Royal Decree, all crimes against the crown are punishable by death! Surrender yourself and face your sins!"

Next to me, Khan leaps out from the ship as the soldiers gain on the commander. His crossbow is drawn.

"Get down!" he shouts to Commander Perovka.

Teeth-shuddering shots ring out.

Two bodies fall to the floor, arrows piercing between the cracks in their armor.

Terrified, I press myself against the far side of the ship. I can't get myself to turn away from the gore and the carnage that erupts before my eyes.

I have to appear strong. I have to act as if none of it bothers me. For Will, and for Sorin, I

remind myself.

Commander Perovka pulls out one of her daggers and charges at one of the two remaining guards, swiftly slitting his throat. The flame haired soldier, Welsh, joins the fight just as three more guards appear.

"Get to the striker, Commander!" Welsh shouts, ushering Commander Perovka away from the guards.

Hesitantly, she obeys.

As Welsh reaches for his sword, one guard impales him with the tip of his spear. He collapses to the ground, bleeding out from the newly formed hole in his abdomen. It's over in seconds. *He* is over in seconds.

Khan and Commander Perovka battle until all four remaining guards lay slumped on the ground. Blood splatters decorate the chapel's roof like a wine-stained tapestry.

Who are these people? I think to myself, observing their ruthless nature with a mix of awe and disgust. *Just what did I get myself into?*

The two of them climb back into the striker and clean their weapons with a rag. They act as if nothing happened, as if they hadn't just taken the lives of seven guards and the life of a queen.

As if their comrade didn't just die.

Then, I realize it isn't Welsh's body they dragged into the cabin. One guard, injured and bleeding, sprawls across the metal floor in agony.

Lady Perovka's eyes shine with a supernatural hunger. She holds out a thin dagger. "Kill him," she orders.

I don't move.

She frowns. "Kill him and prove that you have the stomach for the job."

Again, I do not reach for the weapon.

Commander Perovka tosses me the dagger. "Either he dies, or you both do. Choose, Princess."

Khan places a light hand on my shoulder. "He's not innocent," he says softly, although I see the regret in his eyes. "These men carried out the cruel orders of their queen. They've slaughtered hundreds, all because they were too poor to pay the unreasonable tariffs."

Even though he's trying to help, his words only make me feel worse. These guards swore their loyalty to the queen, just like the guards back in my palace. It isn't their fault, not really. They were just following orders.

"We always have a choice," Khan says, drawing back. "They could have chosen against it, but they followed through with the queen's demands."

I swallow hard, and the stench of metallic blood fills my nose. I close my eyes and grip the dagger tightly.

"Do it," the guard chokes out. "I would rather die by the hand of a princess than by these *terrorists.*"

I gasp. He recognizes me.

"Please," he whispers.

The desperate look in his eyes causes a shift within me. He knows he's going to die. The arrow lodged in his chest won't allow him to live much longer.

No.

I can't.

Closing my eyes, I motion to plunge the tip of the dagger into his chest, every piece of me breaking in the process. Before the metal tip of the dagger can pierce his flesh, I pause, my weapon hovering over his slowly rising and falling chest.

"I can't," I whisper.

"Very well," Commander Perovka says, unimpressed. "I suppose it *is* early. You will learn eventually."

She opens the floor hatch, and the guard falls into the sea below.

His body crashes into the rolling waves, swept away to be lost forever.

I wish I could disappear with him.

Chapter 8

I *stare out as dusk blooms over the horizon, making me think of home.* I would give anything to be back on the palace grounds, walking the length of the gardens with Sorin or watching Will play in the fields. Before the fighting threatened to take them away.

I watch the guard from the chapel fall into the sea over and over again. I remember the feeling of pure guilt and fear as I held the dagger just a hair length above his chest. I believe I was prepared to kill him.

How did I go from ballroom dinners to this?

Commander Perovka picks up a metal device as soon as we're a safe distance away from Yorksha. Then, she speaks into it. "Wang," she says. "We've headed back to the headquarters. Our mission was a success. I trust you can report the same." I detect a hint of competition in her voice.

"It's a phone," Khan whispers to me.

I look at him, confused. It's another technological wonder I've heard of.

"She can speak to anyone in our regime with it," he says. "It's pretty neat, huh?"

Who is she talking to? Is it their leader? I wonder.

As if he read my mind, Khan leans toward me and whispers, "She's calling one of the regime commanders. *My* regime commander."

"Good," Commander Perovka says after a while. "Varys will want the three of us to report to Headquarters."

She ends the call and leans back in her seat, looking slightly more relaxed.

I look away from the smears of scarlet on her cheeks. I can't even look down at my own hands.

"You were messier than usual, Taiana," Khan comments.

Commander Perovka doesn't turn to face him. "Speak for yourself. You were supposed to disarm the cameras in the left wing," she responds bitterly.

He winces. "I may have forgotten one."

"May have?" she repeats. "Your little mistake could have cost us the mission. I can't believe how poor Wang's judgment is when it comes to selecting his men."

The soldier frowns. "You question his judgment?"

"He's capable of making mistakes," she says. "He's made them before."

Khan bursts out laughing. "You may see it as a mistake, but he sees it as freedom."

Commander Perovka looks as if she wants to throw him out of the ship. "Ridiculous. You act like a child."

Khan rolls his eyes. "Are you at least going to tell me what he said? If I recall correctly, you're the reason my phone got lost in the river."

She pauses for a moment but meets his request. "His mission in Jarenco went smoothly as well. Nothing major to report."

"What was his mission?" I dare to ask.

Before Commander Perovka can dismiss me, Khan answers. "He was evacuating one of the border towns. As you probably know, soldiers from Trasylar and Imperia are both fighting for control over Jarenco up north. They deployed the commander there to evacuate the citizens."

"He's gotten them all out," Commander Perovka adds. "Thirty soldiers dead, though."

"Thirty?" Khan repeats with surprise.

Commander Perovka nods. "Child's play, really," she says.

My heart sinks. *Thirty dead? How many of those are Imperial Soldiers?* I think. *Sorin could be one of them.*

"Careful, Commander," Khan says, smiling. "You almost sound impressed."

She scowls. "That's enough from you, Khan. Make no mistake, I'll be reporting your juvenile behavior to your commander."

"Go right ahead," he says, amused.

As soon as their voices fade and all I can hear is the soft purr of the engine, I allow myself to drift off to sleep.

"We're here."

The rough landing jerks me from my sleep. They quickly hustle me out of the ship and place a dark mask over my eyes, shielding my vision.

Despite my discomfort, I comply with their customs and allow Khan to lead me forward.

"I'm sorry about this," he whispers to me. "This is solely precautionary."

We walk across soft earth, whether it's prairie or wetlands, I can't tell.

The three of us climb into a metal box, or at least, that is what I assume it is. Then it moves. I hear the clicking of buttons and I feel the ground below us fall slowly at first and then rapidly.

Some kind of automated elevator, I guess. Once we stop moving, the doors open, and Khan lifts the dark cloth off of my head.

The sight is incredible.

Straight ahead of me lies an entire city, stretching across miles and miles. It's teeming with life and reminds me so much of the Imperial City. Only this place feels denser somehow. It's full of bright, new technology that puts Khan's small computer to shame. It truly is the center of technology, and I wonder how it remained unnoticed for so long.

"Pretty incredible, isn't it?" Khan says.

All I can do is nod, my eyes glued to the sight spread before me.

Rock surrounds the city and large panes of glass hold back an entire sea of threatening water. Not even a drop of sunlight can make its way through the layers of muck and algae. With moonstones shining like stars against the darkness, the city is trapped in a state of eternal night.

I'm awe-struck.

Behind the glowing city is a massive structure made entirely out of white marble. It must be their headquarters.

The sound of an engine catches my attention, and a black shadow striker, similar to the one we arrived in, appears before us on a rock ledge. It hovers in front of us, and Commander Perovka leads us inside. She glances down at her watch.

"He's expecting us within the hour," she says to no one in particular.

I turn to look out the window as we fly through the mysterious underground city. Lights flicker down below, and I can see the tiny figures of people walking down the streets and driving along the bustling roads. It's an entire civilization hidden from any map that I know of.

The murkiness of the water alludes to the Dark Sea.

We land in front of the marble building, and I notice an entire row of guards standing outside the black gates.

Commander Perovka makes her way to the base of the steps. "Follow me," she says.

I look back at Khan, who gives me a small, supportive smile. "You better go quick," he murmurs.

I do as he says and trail behind her as we enter the building.

Inside, it's darker than I expect, with black marble floors and cherry wood pillars holding up the ceiling. As we walk in, I see a desk with a small woman sitting behind a computer, typing vigorously.

"How may I help you, Commander Perovka?" she asks, stopping her work.

"Where is he?"

The woman glances at me and then back to Commander Perovka. "He's upstairs," the woman responds.

Nodding her thanks, Commander Perovka leads me inside the tall glass elevator. My heart rate increases as I watch the numbers on the elevator go from one to eight.

I don't know what to expect, but I know this meeting could change everything.

I glance up at Commander Perovka and examine her sharp features and bright, attentive eyes. She doesn't miss a thing and stands with better posture than any royal I've ever seen. If it wasn't for her human features, I could have easily mistaken her for a machine. The satchel is still slung across her shoulder, but the blood from her face is gone.

The queen's crown, I think, staring at her leather bag.

The elevator opens, and she escorts me down a long hallway, the dark orange glow swallowing us whole. We stop at a set of double doors, and Lady Perovka straightens.

"The leader is a very powerful man," she says. "He commands your respect...and I suggest you give it to him."

I nod. "I understand."

I hold my breath as her knuckles rap on the door.

There is no going back.

Chapter 9

"**C**ome in," *a gruff voice says from inside the room.*

Commander Perovka turns the knob and, with one hand firmly against my back, she forces me forward. I wonder if she can feel me shaking.

The room is spacious, and the entire back wall is a window overlooking the city. A long wooden table lined with leather armchairs sits in the middle of the room.

Commander Perovka stands up tall and crosses her arm over her heart, holding her hand in a fist. On her smallest finger is a smooth iron band. She bows her head low.

"Lord Varys," she says.

I draw my eyes across the table. The leader looms at the head, his broad shoulders spanning the length of a crane's wing. His goatee comes to a sharp point a few inches past his chin and his eyes seem to glow a rich golden color in the orange ambience.

I can't help but notice the deep scar across his cheek. Just thinking about how he may have gotten it makes me shudder.

Two men dressed in black stand at his side, their faces concealed behind dark black cloth. If not for the gleam of their eyes, I would have mistaken them for statues.

"Commander," he acknowledges. "You may sit."

Commander Perovka takes the opposite end of the table from the leader and motions for me to join her. All I want is to sprint out of the room, to return home, but fear keeps me glued in place.

"I see we have a new recruit," the leader says, eyeing me.

"Indeed," Commander Perovka responds. "She held up well enough."

A small, perplexing smile rests on the leader' face. "State your name," he orders.

"Iris Wu," I say, trying to keep my voice level.

The leader' grin turns into some variation of a knowing smirk. I can't quite decipher it. "Well done, Taiana. You brought us the Princess of Imperia."

Commander Perovka turns to me and holds out her hand. "The necklace," she says.

I hesitate, but the look in her eyes tells me she's going to get it whether I give it to her willingly or not. I lift the heavy necklace of diamonds off my neck and fold it into her palm, telling myself that my mother would have wanted this. She would have wanted me to do whatever it took to protect Will.

Biting my tongue, I watch Commander Perovka's fingers curl around the jewels.

She crosses the room and drops the necklace in front of the leader before setting her satchel on the table. Pride shines on her face.

"A little souvenir from our friends in Yorksha," Commander Perovka offers.

As she withdraws her hand from the bag, I notice the red stains speckled across her fingertips. A nose wrinkling odor wafts through the room.

As proof, the leader wants her crown, I remember, thinking back to what Khan told me.

Realization hits me. I swallow hard and suddenly I'm grateful my stomach is empty. The queen's skull rests in the bag.

"Well done," the leader praises, examining the revolting contents of the bag.

"Her reign of terror is over. I trust you sent a squad to help the citizens recover?"

Commander Perovka nods. "I did."

The leader raises an eyebrow at me. "Well, she's still conscious. I suppose that's a good sign. I believe you will acclimate to our ways nicely."

"I'm not here to kill people," I force out.

The leader smiles. "And I do not expect that of you," he says. "You have come for a reason unique to you, and I will honor that."

I let out a breath.

"Are you willing to pledge allegiance to our cause, Miss Wu?" he says.

"Some clarification on that cause would make my decision easier," I say.

"Very well," the leader says, twirling a small throwing knife around his fingers. "My great-grandfather was exiled unjustly from Trasylar centuries ago. He saw the faults in their monarch and he was punished gravely for it.

"And so, he founded the Order of Alabass. Our goal has always been to provide those who are lost with a purpose, and to harbor outcasts like my forefathers. Everyone here, which I'm sure you will discover, comes from nothing. But now, with the help of the organization, they are powerful, intelligent, and meaningful individuals. We bring peace and justice to those who need us."

"But enough about that," he says, waving a hand. "Tell me why *you* are here."

I glance at Commander Perovka, who eyes me with a sharp glare, her chin angled down. "I'm here on account of preventing a war between Imperia and Trasylar."

The leader pauses for a moment. "I have put forth a great deal of time and resources into that matter," he replies. "However, our plans are not yet complete. A mission of this caliber takes time. But I assure you, I will put things into motion before the fighting spreads."

"I'll do whatever it takes to stop it," I say desperately. "Because like you, I agree the emperor only wants to show off his strength. He doesn't care about the lives that will be lost."

He doesn't even care about the life of his own son.

The leader smiles approvingly. "Very well, Miss Wu," he says. "I will have you join our ranks, and when the time is right, we will prevent the bloody conflict we all foresee. You have my word. But I would like yours as well."

"You have it," I say.

"Do you agree to serve myself and the Order of Alabass no matter the dangers it may place on your own being?"

I know the risk is great, but the only image in my mind is of Will and Sorin, side by side, charging into battle.

"I do," I say confidently.

"Wonderful," he says. "I will soon assign you to a regime, but first I must brief you on the expectations. Here, we are a family, a tight-knit group of individuals working toward a common goal. You will learn to rely on your comrades with your life, while also constantly watching your back.

"I will place you in a compact unit by which you will complete a series of missions. This is for your own safety and will enable you to receive the most out of your training period. I expect you to train daily and study our ways. Does this sound manageable, Miss Wu?"

"Yes."

"Good," he replies. "I was never one for books. I believe experience is the most inspirational and effective teacher. Expect to be sent out into the field within the first few days of your training."

I nod in understanding.

"Now, while it would be preferable to have all three of my regime commanders present, I suppose it can't be helped." He smiles again. "Come forth. It is time for the initiation rite."

I stand slowly and approach him, still trembling.

He takes out a silver ring from his pocket, similar to the one Commander Perovka wears.

"I, Varys Strovka," he says, standing out of his chair, "appoint a new member to the Order of Alabass. Iris Wu, Princess of Imperia, accept this ring as a token of your official initiation and induction into our family."

I hold out my palm, and he hands me a small silver band with intricate markings engraved around the edges. I slip it onto my finger and instantly pain shoots up my arm. Sharp, thorn-like shards of metal dig into the soft flesh of my finger.

I try to pry the ring off of my finger, but the more I pull, the deeper the thorns dig. Blood oozes from my finger and pools up on the table. I bite my lip to keep myself from screaming.

"It will be over soon," Varys soothes, resting a heavy hand on my shoulder. "It's critical that we ensure the formation of a blood pact to bond you to the Order and our family. The blood is a powerful symbol of your courage and loyalty to the organization, to me, and to your new brethren. From this point forth, you will live by the Order," he says, lifting the weight of his hand, "and you will die by the Order."

My finger grows numb and the thorns retract back into the silver band.

"You will begin at the entry position of a soldier," the leader says. "As you gain experience, you will move up the ranks within your regime. I have high expectations for you, Miss Wu. Do not disappoint me."

"I won't."

I can't.

The doorknob clicks, and a tall young man with vibrant green eyes and inky dark hair emerges. He walks in, nods to the leader, and takes a seat.

"You're late, Wang," Commander Perovka says, a smirk tugging at her lips.

His presence sends chills up my spine. He's the commander from Jarenco; the man who single-handedly struck down thirty soldiers. He can't be much older than me, yet he's already a ruthless killer. And he doesn't have a single scratch on him.

From above his shirt collar, I see swirls of black ink creeping around his neck. As my eyes focus, I realize it's a dragon tattoo that snakes around his neck and dips back down under his shirt. I assume the rest of it is on his back.

Despite my fear, I can't help but admire how striking he is. My eyes drift to his sharp jawline and lean figure, but I force myself to focus my attention back on the room.

"You did well, son," the leader says, his golden eyes resting on the newcomer.

Son.

Commander Wang nods in acknowledgement and looks over at me. He frowns. "Who's this?" he says. Then, he seems to realize exactly who I am and his eyes grow cold.

"Our newest member. She shows great promise," the leader says. "The Princess of Imperia."

Commander Wang fixes me with a hard glare, one that makes me want to dissolve into my chair. "You can't possibly be serious," he says, anger ebbing into his voice. "A *royal?* Have you forgotten that they are the very people we stand against?"

The leader waves his comment away with a large hand. "We oppose those who do wrong," he says, probably not wanting to entertain the idea of him possibly having made a mistake. "Miss Wu has chosen a different path."

"That remains to be seen," Commander Wang says.

"Besides, Miss Wu's ambitions parallel seamlessly with our own," the leader says. "I would be a fool to deny her. I'm certain that she will be a wonderful addition to our family."

Family. I shudder.

"My regime is dwindling as it is," Commander Wang continues. "I can't risk the threat of an Imperial spy."

If it wasn't for the assertive aura he gives off, I would've expected Commander Wang to be strangled to death for the way he speaks to the leader. But then again, the leader is his father.

The leader sighs. "I understand the direness of the situation, which is why I have appointed Miss Wu to your regime. You have my permission to dispose of her should you discover she has ulterior motives for being here."

My stomach drops. *'Dispose of her.'*

Still dissatisfied but unwilling to argue further, Commander Wang remains silent. His sharp features turn toward me.

"Now tell me, son, how do you suppose we go about our new plan?" the leader prompts, changing the subject.

"Had you not sent me on your foolish errands, preparations would be nearly complete," Commander Wang says, his voice impatient.

The leader grunts, unsure of how to react to Commander Wang's sour tone. "I'm well aware, believe me. But now we can put forth all our efforts into this mission. I assume you gathered the intel from the southern nations?"

Before Commander Wang can answer, the leader looks over at me. "Miss Wu, you are dismissed. This conversation is of no concern to you. Two of my soldiers will escort you to your quarters."

I nod and stand without being asked a second time.

"Remember, you live by the Order, you die by the Order," the leader repeats, his voice following me out through the doors.

A cold rush of relief showers over me once I leave the room. I can finally breathe again.

Khan and the secretary stand waiting for me, and I almost crash into them.

"Miss Wu," the secretary says. "Please, follow us to your quarters. You will stay with the other soldiers and begin your training at dawn tomorrow."

"Don't worry," Khan says, smiling. "Training is easy once you get the basics down, and they've assigned me to help you."

He takes out a kerchief from his pocket and hands it to me. Reluctantly, I take it and wrap it around my throbbing finger.

"The Elites are pretty intimidating, huh?" he says.

"Who?" I ask.

He shrugs. "You know, the men standing next to the leader? They're a part of *his* regime and answer only to him. If I'm being honest, they give me the creeps."

I think back to the two droid-like men standing on the side of the leader and I nod in agreement with Khan's assessment.

"They don't do anything unless our leader commands them to," he says. "I've never spoken to one or seen them outside of their duties."

"So much for being a tight-knit family, huh?" I say.

"Yeah, I know," Khan says. "But besides them, the rest of us are pretty cool. Don't be too hurt if people are cold at first. While most of us try to forget our pasts, we can never shake it completely. Trust isn't something we give out lightly."

"I can tell," I say, thinking back to yesterday when they held me at knifepoint. It feels like ages ago.

As we walk through the busy streets, I observe the city of the Order up close. The members wear dark suits, but occasionally we pass people with more casual outfits. Every single person seems to carry a weapon of some sort.

No one is unarmed.

"Not everyone here is a soldier," Khan says as we walk down the street. He motions to the street vendors and food carts. "We take in refugees from every nation, and many of them aren't ready to jump on the opportunity to fight."

"Are they allowed to leave?" I ask.

Khan focuses on the people passing by. "With clearance, yes," he says. "Soldiers have more flexibility when it comes to leaving, since we're always out on missions."

We walk a few more blocks, and I take in the bright lights of the underground city. Something tells me I'm going to become very familiar with this place.

"Here are the soldier's apartments," he says as we walk inside. "As you've probably noticed, we're nothing like the soldiers that you're accustomed to within the palace. No metal armor here, just a few daggers and an irrational will to live." He taps his temple and smiles.

I acknowledge his attempt at lightening the mood but can't bring myself to match his enthusiasm. Everything is too new, too fresh, like a raw wound unsure if it'll heal completely or scar over. I want to like it here. I want to believe I'm doing the right thing.

"If I'm an entry level soldier, then what rank are you?" I ask him.

"I'm a squad leader," he says proudly. "It means I have the authority to lead squadrons and fall only one rank below the commanders. Before you can reach my position, you'll have to earn the silver insignia."

"And how do I do that?" I ask.

He laughs. "For someone of your stature, it may prove difficult. No offense," he says. "Typically, soldiers take anywhere from six months to five years before they earn their insignia."

I frown at his comment, but he has a point. "Still, what will it take?"

"Special recognition by the commander or the leader," he answers. "There's not one test that can earn you the insignia, so you'll have to prove yourself on the field."

"Sounds easy enough," I say sarcastically.

I don't have years to spare. Unfortunately, starting off on the wrong foot with the commander isn't going to help.

We head through the main lobby, the decor similar to the marble building. Lights illuminate the hallways, and we take the elevator up to the ninth floor.

"Here is your room, Miss Wu," the secretary says, handing me the keys. "Your daily schedule will be published promptly, and you are required to follow the regimen strictly."

Desperate for some time alone, I thank them and unlock the door.

"See you at breakfast," Khan says, giving me a smile before disappearing down the hallway.

I call back before closing the door. Only when I drop myself onto the couch do I realize how exhausted I am.

So many thoughts run through my head. I have so many questions. But there's only one that really matters.

Did I make the right choice?

Chapter 10

The cry of blaring alarms rips me from my sleep.

Picking myself up, I adjust to the darkness of the room, remembering that I'm still in the underground city. I gaze around my apartment and in front of the couch is an enormous wall of windows, similar to those in the conference room.

The furnishings all follow a similar gray, black, and tangerine color palette, save for the white rugs and lamps scattered throughout the flat. The kitchen is small but usable, and through a small doorway is a bedroom with an armoire. To the side of the couch is a large screen, which is where the alarm sound is coming from.

The blaring screen displays a message, delivering my schedule for the day. I'm required to meet on the first floor for breakfast at 5:00 a.m., which I discover leaves me only five minutes to get ready. Already in a panic, I skim the rest of my schedule, attempting to memorize it as best I can before heading out the door.

Because I can't find the elevators, I race down what seems like a hundred flights of stairs before I reach the cafeteria. It's nothing compared to the dining rooms of the palace. Instead, long cedarwood tables stretch across the stone floors. There's a shallow inlet in one wall where the cooks prepare breakfast.

I scan the room, and as I walk in, every head turns to look at me. Soldiers whisper to one another as I pass. Embarrassment floods my face and I keep my head down.

"Hey! Iris!" a voice shouts above the sea of heads.

I swivel to find the owner of the voice and see Khan waving from one of the back tables.

Eager to get out of the spotlight, I make my way toward him. The soldiers next to him slide over to make room, but it's clear they're not happy to see me.

"I officially welcome you to the soldier's quarters," Khan says, his eyes shining. "As one of us."

"Thanks," I say, my eyes scanning his burly and intimidating companions.

He motions to the three men sitting near us. "These lovely fellows here are my friends. They also happen to be in my unit."

'Lovely' is not the adjective I would use to describe his comrades. They all wear the same murderous expressions and look at me as if I'm a fawn strolling carelessly into a wolf's den. I refuse to make eye contact with any of them.

"This is Jaice Akerman," Khan says, motioning to the man to my left. "His specialties are combat and weaponry, although I've beaten him on several occasions. He also trains some of the new recruits, so you can expect to be working with him during your first few weeks."

Jaice looks to be about three or four years older than me and he's much taller. His blond hair is buzzed short on the sides, which reminds me of the guards back at the palace. Something tells me I don't want to get on his bad side.

Jaice makes no effort to introduce himself and instead fixes me with a disapproving glare. Sensing the hostility, Khan moves on.

"And this here is Crayln Mavros," he says. "He's really just a soft computer nerd on the inside, so don't let all the hair gel and sunglasses fool you."

I laugh a little at this.

"What exactly are you implying?" Crayln scowls, clearly offended. "I'm the head of the Cyber Division. 'Soft computer nerd' hardly describes me."

He's much smaller than Jaice, but just as intimidating.

"Pleasure to meet you, Princess," he says, his voice anything but welcoming. "We're not used to being blessed by royalty."

I manage a small smile. "The pleasure is mine."

"Last, there's Alistar Drakos. One of our most notorious spies," Khan says, holding out an arm.

Alistar's scarlet eyes watch me carefully, and his pale features make him look like a snake. He nods in acknowledgment but says nothing.

"And you already know me," Khan says. "But I'm Naveen. And guys, as you know, this is Princess Iris."

"But you can just call me Iris," I say.

"Sorry, yes, Iris," Naveen corrects. "Now that we're done with introductions, I'll explain how things work around here. These tables belong to the First Regime," Naveen continues, puffing his chest out proudly. "Then there's the Second Regime," he says, pointing to the table behind me. "And then the Third."

"So, it's like a hierarchy, then?" I ask.

One of them laughs. "Don't let Taiana hear you say that," Crayln says, pushing up his dark glasses. "Unless you have a death wish."

"If you haven't already picked up on it, she's a little uptight," Naveen adds, winking. She must be the commander I met outside of the palace—Taiana, as they refer to her, despite Naveen's prior warning.

"Yeah, she's made that pretty clear," I say.

"As the commander of the Second Regime, she answers only to the leader and to our commander," Naveen says.

Crayln smiles cruelly. "She can't stand that she answers to Commander Wang."

"You've got that right," Naveen says.

"We shouldn't be discussing the commanders like this," Alistar says quietly. "Especially not her. She's got ears everywhere." He looks around warily, his scarlet eyes darting around the room. "At least address her properly."

Naveen rolls his eyes. "What's the worst she could do? Wang would never let her lay a finger on me," he boasts.

"Well, not everyone's his pet," Crayln retorts.

"He's my best friend," Naveen says. "I'm not his pet."

Jaice snorts. "Yeah, right. Like he's capable of having friends."

"Anyway, I forgot to ask," Neveen says, shifting the topic from himself. "Are you hungry? You'll want to get in the breakfast line before it closes. We have to head out in ten minutes."

I look up, realizing that he's speaking to me. "I'm fine," I say, not wanting to face the battle that would be the breakfast line.

"Alright, suit yourself."

"Well, Nav, I heard Taiana had to save your ass yesterday," Crayln says mockingly. "Maybe the commander will have to demote you."

Naveen frowns. "She didn't save me. The way I remember it, I saved her."

"That's not what I heard!"

"Me neither!"

His friends howl with laughter.

"Yeah, yeah. Watch where you're getting your information from," Naveen says, crossing his arms and leaning back in his chair.

Their mindless bickering is almost endearing. It reminds me subtly of home and how Rai and Kaito would instigate each other until there was a full-on sparring match in the dining hall. Why I find memories of home comforting, I don't know.

I *chose* to leave.

"You look pale as a ghost," Jaice observes.

I wince.

"If you faint at the thought of a little blood," he says, as if he read my mind, "you'll be useless to the regime, and the commander will have no choice but to execute you."

"What?"

Naveen throws a pancake at his friend, hitting him square in the cheek. "Shut up. She'll be just fine. Look, he can be a little scary at first, but he's really not that bad."

Jaice scoffs. "This isn't some kind of joke. Being a part of the regime is serious work, and I doubt someone like her is cut out for it. She's one of *them*, for gods' sake. We should use her as ransom."

"What's that supposed to mean—'someone like her'?" I say.

Jaice shrugs. "Princesses aren't typically admitted into the Order, and for good reason," he replies, scanning the room. "Aren't you used to wearing dresses and having tea parties or something?"

Impulsively, I kick him hard from under the table, the rubber head of my boot coming in contact with the hollow bone of his shin.

He lets out a bark of surprise and glares at me. "What the hell?"

"Just a little something I picked up during all the tea parties," I say, trying to look innocent.

Crayln bursts out laughing, and Naveen struggles to contain himself. A wave of satisfaction washes over me, although I know it won't last.

"Yeah, yeah, very impressive," Jaice responds. "But I could throw you across the room with one arm, Princess."

"Alright, that's enough, you two," Naveen interjects. "Jaice, stop being an ass, and Iris, you'll learn to ignore everything he says."

"Yeah, ignore him," Crayln says. "He's never been good with the ladies, right?" He jabs Naveen in the ribs playfully, but clearly with too much force, causing him to topple over and fall to the floor.

"What was that for?" Naveen exclaims, grabbing Crayln's arm and pulling him down alongside him. "Might wanna take your glasses off for this one."

The two of them launch into a full on brawl, shaking the table as they kick and shove each other around. I scoot my chair back a safe distance as they continue to throw wild punches. I look around the room to see if anyone is going to stop them, but no one pays any attention.

"They do this often," Alistar explains calmly.

"And no one stops them?" I ask.

"Why should they? They'll work it out eventually," Jaice says.

I furrow my eyebrows but remain silent as the two men slug each other. Blood drips from Naveen's lip, and the space under Crayln's left eye shows signs of bruising. Behavior such as this would never be acceptable in the palace. Even Kaito and Rai would have been pulled apart before any real damage could be inflicted.

"That's all you got?" Crayln taunts, his lips curling into a wicked smile.

Naveen throws himself at his friend, knocking him over and sending them both crashing into the side of the table. They fall on top of two other soldiers and launch their food trays into the air, sending pancakes and sausages flying across the room.

This finally receives the attention of the crowd.

"Hey, watch it, you fool!" a soldier cries as he watches his breakfast get pushed to the ground.

"Shove off!"

"What a bunch of idiots."

"How did they survive this long?"

I feel a laugh rise in my throat and I try to hide my smile.

Maybe this won't be so bad, I think to myself.

A hand taps me on the shoulder.

I whip around to see Naveen, his face bloody. "Oh, sorry, I didn't hear you," I say.

"We've gotta go. Training starts soon," he says, wiping his face with his sleeve. "Today, Jaice will brief you on the art of combat."

I gather myself and follow Naveen out of the building. The sound of combat training is both exciting and nerve-racking. It makes me wish I had taken part in the training sessions back at the palace alongside my brothers, although I know that my father would have never allowed it.

We walk out into the city streets, and it's difficult to adjust my eyes. The clock reads 5:30, but judging by the amount of light in the city, it could easily be midnight.

"We'll travel on foot today," Naveen announces to the large group filling out of the building behind us. "Round up!"

A few of the soldiers who sat at our breakfast table join us, along with Jaice, Crayln, and Alastair. As soon as everyone is accounted for, Naveen motions for everyone to follow him.

"Alright, last one to the Needle is today's punching bag!" he shouts, then takes off in a full sprint down the street.

The rest of the soldiers dash after him, leaving me alone, standing aimlessly in front of the apartments.

"Hey!" I call after them. "Wait up!"

I have no choice but to dash after the crowd. I watch, frustrated, as they become smaller and smaller, disappearing behind a series of tall brick buildings. My legs can hardly carry me fast enough, and I don't know where I'm headed.

I come to a corner, and by this point, all the soldiers have disappeared from view. I stop to catch my breath, cursing to myself.

Looking around, I see a few people littering the streets. None of them look approachable, nor do they make any effort to interact with me as I heave on the sidewalk.

I walk down a couple blocks hoping that at least one of the others will come back.

"You, there," a voice calls.

I flinch and turn, coming face to face with a large, unrecognizable man dressed in all black with a sword resting loosely at his hip.

"You look familiar, sweetheart," he says, reaching out and clasping my chin.

My heart pounds in my chest, and all words seem to be lost.

"Ah," he says, his voice raspy and cold. "I remember now. You're the runaway princess. They plastered your face all over the Imperial Nation."

I struggle to get out of his grasp, but he holds firm and takes a step closer. "If I brought you in, I'd be a rich man. That fool of an emperor is offering millions for you."

"Let me go," I say, preparing to kick him.

Swiftly, he slams me against the brick wall of the building, forcing my jaw against the hard rock.

Pain shoots through me. He presses his forearm against my shoulder blades, trapping me. Desperately, I scan for any signs of help, but the street is empty.

"If I receive the Emperor's reward, I'd be set for life," he says. "What do you say, are you ready to go home?"

Despite the fear rising inside me, I clench my teeth and stand my ground.

I will not go back to that palace.

Chapter 11

His arm digs into my flesh, making me wince, and I clench my teeth to keep from crying out. I struggle, but I can't overpower him.

"Let go of me!" I shout, more forcefully this time.

He lets out a low laugh. "This is no place for someone like you," he says. "You're better off back in Imperia, and I'll be better off once I collect your bounty."

My jaw tightens with apprehension.

A flash of silver whizzes by my head and finds its target in the man's shoulder. Another passes, he releases his grip.

He slumps against the bricks, blood oozing from his shoulder and thigh. The man clutches his wounded leg, his face twisted in agony.

I look up to see where the knives came from, and another man comes walking from the other side of the street. He's familiar, and the moment I see the gleam of his eyes, I recognize the leader's son.

Commander Wang.

Fear grasps me all over again as I think back to the meeting. He talked about me as if I were nothing but vermin. Something to be cautious of.

He wants me dead.

What could have brought him to my rescue?

I swallow as he bends down next to the man laying on the cement. His gaze never drifts to me.

"C-Commander Wang!" the man gasps. "P-please, hear me out. It's all a great misunderstanding. I would never harm the princess."

Liar.

"Quit your groveling," Commander Wang says coldly. "Do you wish to displease the leader by attacking our newest member?"

The man gasps for breath. "No, never, my lord," he says. "I would never wish to displease the leader."

"Enough."

The man clamps his mouth shut, his eyes wide with fear.

"Someone will tend to your wounds," Commander Wang says, rising.

"Oh, thank you, thank you, my lord," he cries out, wincing as he attempted to stand. "Your mercy is most noble."

Commander Wang narrows his eyes. "I am not finished," he says, anger ebbing into his voice. "You are banished to the cells until I deem you fit to return to your duties."

"Yes, my lord," he says, deflated.

A black jet flies above our heads and lands smoothly on the road next to me. Four men file out, and a woman wearing a white doctor's coat leads them.

"My lord," she says.

"Take him," Commander Wang says, his back to the bloody man. "You know what to do."

The medics nod and haul the man up by the armpits and place him on a stretcher. They usher him into the jet and take off as fast as they came.

And just like that, I'm alone with the commander.

He glances at me briefly, his eyes hard and dispassionate. "You should be training with the others."

"I know," I stammer. "I got turned around. I'm sorry."

I draw in a breath, hoping I haven't made a completely bad first impression.

"You must abide by the schedule developed for you to succeed in the Order," he says. "And to ensure that things like this do not happen again."

I stand in place, preparing to respond, but he turns away before I can speak.

"One wrong step and you're dead," he calls over his shoulder.

I watch him until he disappears behind the street corner, in utter shock and horror. He means every word.

I ball my fists in frustration. *I need to learn how to fight.*

Eventually, I spot signs that direct me toward the training centers.

I follow them until I reach a large rock wall on the outskirts of the city. A tall platform rises many yards above the ground and a thin rope ladder hangs off the side.

I take hold of the rope and begin to climb.

As I near the platform, the sounds of shouting and fighting grow, confirming that I'm in the right place. Only a small portion of the platform rests on solid rock, with the rest of it suspended in the air. If someone were to fall off, they would fall to their death.

From the top of the platform, I can see the entire city. We're at eye level with most of the buildings in the area, and I scoot far away from the edge. Soldiers line the perimeter of the platform and sit, some with their legs dangling dangerously off the side and others facing the middle, where two soldiers are sparring. Others fight and practice within the safety of the cave created by the array of rocks.

Many of the female members wear their hair cropped short and piercings line their ears. All I can think about is how I definitely do not fit in.

"Well, she finally decided to show," a voice says.

I look over and see Jaice standing by a rack of weapons, a dagger laying dangerously in his palm. Next to him, Naveen and Crayln spar near the rocks, finishing what they started at breakfast. A white circle of chalk surrounds them to signify what I assume is a boundary.

"Hey!" Naveen calls. He breaks away from his match with Crayln, receiving a small, annoyed grunt, and approaches me. "Welcoming to day one of training."

"Sorry I'm late," I say. "I hope that the punching bag thing was just a bluff?"

He laughs. "It wasn't. But it's alright, we took it for you. Can't have you getting beaten to a pulp on your first day, now, can we?"

My eyes widen as I observe the enormous bruises and scratches along his back. "You didn't have to do that."

He shrugs, rolling his shoulders. "It's no big deal. These are mostly from Cray. None of the others could lay a hit."

"I know you're scared," Crayln calls mockingly. "But get back here so we can finish our match. Unless you'd rather forfeit and admit I'm stronger."

Naveen snorts, giving me an apologetic look before stalking back over to the fighting ring. "Not a chance. Bring it, pipsqueak."

I watch as the two launch into battle. They're brutal. Both of them bunch their muscles in preparation to leap at their opponent, not afraid to hold back. Naveen has the size advantage, but Crayln is quick and dodges every blow. Sweat pours down their faces, and they're practically drenched in a matter of moments.

Naveen finally lands a blow to Crayln's exposed abdomen. He plants his foot on Crayln's chest in triumph.

"I won again," Naveen says, grinning down at his defeated opponent.

Crayln shoves him off and the two of them reach for the towels near the weapons rack.

"I'll get you next time," Crayln promises. "One eye open at all times, Khan. It'll come when you least expect it."

As Crayln moves to his water jug, Naveen turns and walks over to me.

"So, do you think you're ready to learn to shoot?" he asks.

I follow his gaze to the crossbow in his hand and examine the intricate mechanics of the weapon.

"I suppose," I say, taking the spare he offers me.

"It's not too hard," Naveen says.

Jaice laughs behind me. "He says that because he's the sharpest shooter in the Order," he says. "Don't expect to get it on the first try."

Naveen frowns at him. "That's not helping," he says, shoving Jaice out of the way. Naveen points across the rocks at the targets plastered on the far wall. "See those? Aim to hit one. Don't worry about hitting the bullseye just yet, we'll work on that later."

I step next to him and watch as he lifts the crossbow to eye level. Peering through the small scope, Naveen draws in a deep breath. As he exhales, his index finger slowly squeezes the trigger. The arrow sails through the air.

My eyes widen as I watch it pierce the center of the red dot hundreds of feet away.

"See?" Naveen says. "Just like that, and you'll be fine."

He helps me load the arrow into the crossbow and guides the scope so that I can peer through it. The wall of rock is straight ahead of me with three canvas targets hanging off of it. I look for the one Naveen hit and then focus on the one to its left.

I take in a deep breath just as I'd seen him do. I use my index finger to squeeze the trigger. As I hold it, the arrow shoots from the crossbow and harmlessly bounces off of the rocks. I stumble back, surprised by the small kick.

I hear some of the other soldiers snickering. Jaice is one of them.

My ears grow hot.

"Don't worry," Naveen says, jogging over to collect the arrow. "And ignore the others. They were all just as bad."

I do my best to brush it off and the next five times go exactly the same way: the arrows hit the rocks and Naveen runs to retrieve it while the other soldiers around me laugh.

"I don't think this is my strong suit," I say to Naveen as he hands me the arrow.

"We'll keep practicing," he says, grinning. "I promise it'll get easier."

He runs toward the wall and takes one of the canvas targets down. He brings it a few yards closer and holds it in front of his chest.

I lower the crossbow, not liking what he's thinking.

"Come on," he says. "All you have to do is hit the board."

"No," I say. "I'll hit you."

Naveen shakes his head. "No, you won't," he says.

"She definitely *will*," Crayln says, appearing from behind the rocks. "You got a death wish or something, Nav?"

Naveen ignores him. "Iris, you can do this," he says. "Just try."

Biting my lip, I slowly move to load the arrow. I close my eyes and try to block out everything else until the only sound I can hear is the roaring of blood in my ears.

I raise the scope and peer through it, focusing on the white canvas in front of Naveen's chest.

I let out a long breath and release the arrow. I squeeze my eyes shut, unable to watch in case I miss and end up killing Naveen.

Heartbeats pass in silence.

"You did it!" Naveen exclaims.

"Barely," Crayln mutters.

I open my eyes and Naveen runs toward me with the target in his hand. My arrow sticks out of the top left corner only inches from the edge.

"You're crazy for doing that," I say. "I was inches away from landing it in your shoulder."

Naveen shrugs. "But hey, you didn't."

"Well, I think that's probably enough target practice for today," I say, my heart still racing.

"Good," Jaice says. "Because now it's time for combat training."

"What?" I say.

He crosses his arms and jerks his chin toward the extended platform where soldiers are sparring. Others watch intently from the edge.

"Does anyone ever fall off of there?" I ask, my stomach queasy just looking at it.

"Only if they're really stupid," Jaice says. "Scared of heights, Princess?"

"No," I blurt out. "But I wouldn't exactly fancy falling off of a platform like that, either."

"Only one way to get over your fear," he says, putting down his dagger. "Follow me."

He makes his way to the platform, and my heart drops.

"Wait," I call after him. "I've never fought a day in my life. Shooting a crossbow is one thing, but this? Can't we practice here on solid ground first?"

Jaice rolls his eyes. "The commander says you have to start combat training, so let's do it. It's all or nothing, sweetheart."

I hesitate.

"Simon! Riona! Clear off," Jaice calls to the two soldiers occupying the platform.

The girl turns and takes one look at Jaice before hurrying off the platform. The boy murmurs in protest, but thinks better than to argue with Jaice, who is undoubtedly bigger and stronger than him.

"You don't expect me to fight *you*, do you?" I ask, watching Jaice step onto the platform.

He's a foot taller than me and at least twice as wide. Maybe he wasn't bluffing when he said he could throw me across the room.

Perhaps I should have rethought my witty remarks during breakfast.

"See anyone else up here?" he asks, spreading his arms to make his point.

"Well," I say. "We could ask the others. Maybe Crayln or Alistar. Or someone else. Really, anyone else is fine."

Jaice throws his head back and laughs. Perhaps the thought of me bloodied and bruised on the floor is all it takes to make him smile. "Scared of me, Princess?"

Yes, I think to myself.

"I don't even know the basics of combat," I protest, walking off of the metal floorboards. "I'm not going to spar with the top fighter just to get my ass kicked."

Jaice rolls his eyes and walks over to me. He takes hold of my wrist and drags me onto the platform.

"Well, you'll never learn unless you try. They assign me newbies for a reason. So, if you want to learn how to throw a good punch, you're going to have to shut up and listen, got that?" Jaice says, not really waiting for a response.

He's infuriating, but he's right. I nod. I want to learn how to fight.

I have to.

"Alright," I say. "Teach me."

He smiles. "You're going to regret kicking me in the shin, Princess."

THE BLOOD MARROW

I wonder if I just made the biggest mistake of my life.

Chapter 12

Training with Jaice takes a harsh toll on my body, and progress is painfully slow. After only a few days of combat training up on the Needle, as the soldiers call it, I'm sore all over. I've gained a few scrapes and bruises, but by the time it's time to train again, they're gone, only to be replaced by new ones.

"Why can't Crayln teach me computer programming or something instead?" I complain, frustrated, as I wipe the blood from my nose. "I'm never going to get the hang of this. And it's painful as hell to try."

In response, Jaice sends me flying with a kick to the ribs. "Not with that attitude, you aren't."

"Shut it," I say, grimacing as I push myself up. "I need a water break."

Jaice rolls his eyes. "Again? There aren't any breaks in the middle of an actual fight, you know. Your opponent isn't going to lower their weapon and wait for you to recover."

I ignore him and walk to the edge of the platform and down my entire water bottle in one gulp.

It's well past the typical day hours for training, but Jaice insists I practice as much as I can to make up for being years behind the others. Between knife throwing, hand-to-hand combat, and target practice with Naveen, my schedule is packed. Although training occupies most of my day, I manage to slip out after hours and go to the library for my studies.

The downtown library has more books than I've ever seen in my life. There are preserved tales detailing the victories achieved by the leader and his predecessors, and how they've liberated hundreds from the fetters of the monarchs. I don't know what I'm looking for, exactly, but I have learned a decent amount about the entire history of this underground city—Dravkia.

"Head out of the clouds, Princess," Jaice says impatiently.

I shoot him a glare.

"Have you ever considered that beating me every day without providing any instructions on how to defend myself isn't the most effective training method?" I demand. "Every inch of me is black and blue and I can hardly get out of bed in the morning." Even as I stand facing him, my muscles ache and beg for me to let them rest.

"Look, Princess," he says, walking toward me. "I've trained dozens of recruits for the Order, all of whom are now well-established soldiers. There is nothing wrong with my teaching. If anything, I think you've been too sheltered and privileged to understand the value of hard work."

I scoff, but a small part of me knows he's right. I don't let him know that, though.

"Now get up," he instructs. "We're going to do this again and again until you get the move right."

I grit my teeth but rise anyway, determined to get to the library before it closes. "Fine. So, all I have to do is lock your arm in my elbow and flip you on your ass, right?"

"Yeah, something like that," he replies, standing across from me.

I take a deep breath and prepare myself.

He charges at me, and I watch as his left arm falls slightly behind the other. Anticipating his left hook, I duck at the last moment. A swoosh of air tickles my ear, but I evade his fist. Taking the opportunity, I step left and plant my foot to trip him, but he's swifter than I expect and kicks me away from him.

Pain shoots in my ribs, the skin tender from multiple targeted hits.

I'm done with this. I have to beat him.

"Come on, Princess," he mocks. "Stop dancing and fight."

I dart toward him and slide under his legs, grabbing one to set him off balance. The moment he glances down and attempts to free his leg, I push myself up and grab his arm. Using the momentum I gained from my running start, I twist my entire body and lift him off the ground. In a split second, my back hits the ground and so does his. I quickly roll over and plant a foot on his chest.

"Got ya," I say triumphantly.

He raises an eyebrow. With little effort, he lifts himself from under my foot and quickly our roles are reversed and I find myself pinned to the floor.

"Better," he says. "But not perfect."

He gets up and holds his hand out. I take it and allow him to help me to my feet, my entire body aching.

"That's enough for today," Jaice says, wiping his hands on his pants. "I think I'll have you spar with one of the others soon."I raise my eyebrows. "You really think I'm ready for that?"

He shrugs. "It's the only way you'll get better."

I sigh and follow him down the ladder, leaving the platform for the first time all day. We part ways, and I walk alone through the city, making my way to the library.

The building is enormous, almost the same size as Headquarters. Tall marble pillars line the sides and I make my way toward the doors under a shimmering archway. Inside, the smell of old parchment and leather fill my nose and the quiet hum of lights buzzes in my ears.

Among the shelves I find a book titled: *History of Dravkia: Medicines and Apothecary*. The book is over five hundred pages and details the origins, uses, and chemical properties of every natural herb and medicine known to humankind. Many are only used in small, secluded towns belonging to the tribes of the High Range Sierra or the native tribes of Sejeran.

I walk along the tall rows of bookshelves, running my finger over the spines. When I pull my hand away, dust lines my fingertips. No one has touched these books in ages.

I hear shuffling on the other side of the shelf, and I stop. I'm not alone.

"You there," a voice whispers through the shelf.

Peering through a hole in the books, I see a man in a hooded robe staring back at me.

"Who are you?" I ask, the hairs on my neck rising.

"Come with me." He stares at me for a moment, his gaze sending chills up my spine. "I have something you need," he says, his voice raspy like an ancient whisper.

Everything about the situation tells me to run, but a small spark of curiosity makes me stay.

Carefully, I walk around the shelf to where he stands. Before I get the chance to speak, he seizes my wrist with a grip as strong as steel.

I suck in a breath as he leads me out of the library, through the back door, and down a narrow alleyway.

"Where are we going?" I ask as I'm dragged down the dark streets.

The lights in the city are fading, and it's unearthly quiet. I think back to when Commander Wang prevented one of his soldiers from tuning me in. I doubt I would get that lucky again. Every part of me hopes this isn't another bounty hunter looking to drag me back to Imperia.

He snaps his head back to look at me. "You should not have come," he insists.

I blink, but do not respond.

The man's eyes narrow and his voice drops into a hiss. "You should *not* have come!"

Fear keeps me silent as we approach a run-down building on the outskirts of the city. He lifts a scrap of the wall and ushers me inside.

"What are you talking about?" I ask, but he doesn't hear me.

Warm candlelight flickers, illuminating the small room that can't be much bigger than my old closet back at the palace. Scrolls and paper litter the floor and the desk, along with tall bottles filled with ominous liquids.

The man retracts his hood to reveal a tangle of gray hair and pale, hollow eyes. Fine wrinkles border the crevices of his face.

In the candlelight, I glimpse a scar, or possibly a burn, that has permanently disfigured his right ear. He covers it as soon as he detects my gaze.

"Iris Wu," he says, shuffling through his shelves for a scrap of parchment.

"How do you know who I am?" I ask, taking a step back.

He rummages around his mess of parchments, only half hearing me. "They call me Simu. Officially, I am the supplies keeper. Unofficially, however, I have many more esteemed talents." His eyes fall on me at last as he holds up a tattered, yellow stained sheet of paper. Black ink spreads across the parchment in smooth, almost illegible handwriting. "But that is unimportant."

"What's that?" I ask carefully.

"This is a scroll written in Imperia's native tongue," he says.

I reach out for the paper dangling between his bony fingers. "But that's impossible," I say. "Hardly anyone speaks in the native tongue."

Simu shifts and sits on the floor, surrounded by his papers and wax candles. "It's the last thing I could salvage from your mother's village."

"My...my mother?" I say, stumbling in disbelief.

I quickly scan the piece of parchment in my hands. The writing, as Simu had said, is in the native tongue. To me, it just looks like swirls on paper.

"Indeed," Simu says.

"How did you get this?" I ask, my hands shaking.

"It was my village once, too," he says simply. "It was my home." Then, a shadow crosses his face and he frowns. He falls into an unsettling silence.

Furrowing my brow, I step a little closer. "Are you alright? What happened to her?"

"*They* came," he says, his voice strained. "Everything changed that night."

"Who?" I ask. "Who did you see?"

But Simu is no longer listening.

"Come for me," he mutters under his breath, tucking his knees to his chest. "Leave them alone. Leave her alone. Take me." Simu's eyes grow wide and his pupils dilate threefold. His breaths come in puffs and his hands drop to the floor.

I want to speak, to snap him out of whatever trance he's in, but no words escape from my mouth. He shuffles around on the floor, searching desperately.

"It's here somewhere," Simu murmurs, his eyes shooting around the small room. "Help her! You can't take her!" He whips around to me, screaming as if he's cornered by a pack of wolves. "There aren't many of us left! Have mercy..."

"Let me help," I say, reaching to comfort him.

He lashes out and takes my wrist in his bony hand, shoving me through the opening in the metal wall. "Out! Get out!"

Startled, I stare back at him, my heart racing.

From under one of the messy stacks of paper, he draws out a knife. "Get out of here!"

He lunges for me, slashing the blade in the air. My heart leaps. "Out!" Another slash. My ears ring with the shriek of the second slash of steel hitting the metal door. Without another warning, I sprint.

"Your kind isn't welcome here," he snarls.

I dash down the dark streets, completely lost, but determined to escape this strange man.

Eventually, I collapse on the sidewalk, unable to continue running. I heave and catch my breath, my chest aching.

That man, I think to myself, shaking, *He must have been lying. The native tribes are spread so thin and there are hardly any of them left. It would be impossible for my mother to have been one of them.*

My mind whirls as I try to make sense of Simu's words. He tried to kill me. I shouldn't be thinking logically about him at all. Yet, I still wonder what the letter said, and what he knows about my mother.

"Iris? Iris!" a voice calls out, tearing me from my thoughts.

I lift my head to see Naveen running toward me, followed closely by Jaice. Their two figures blur together as my eyes struggle to remain open.

"Hey," Naveen says, crouching down next to me. "What happened? Are you alright?"

I'm shaking, but I swallow and pick myself up. "I'm fine. Just a bit tired," I lie. "What are you guys doing here?"

"We were looking for you," Naveen replies, worry showing on his face. "You didn't show up for dinner."

"Oh," I say. "Well, thank you. But I'm okay."

Jaice eyes me, and his expression tells me he knows I'm lying. Thankfully, he doesn't press. "Let's get you home," he says.

The three of us walk back to our apartments in silence. The moment my head hits the pillow, my eyelids close and I drift off into sleep with Simu's words echoing in my mind.

Your kind isn't welcome here.

You should not have come.

What could he have possibly meant by that?

Chapter 13

The next morning, Naveen comes knocking on my door well before we're scheduled to be in the cafeteria.

"Yes?" I answer groggily, opening the door.

His smiling face appears in the doorway, and he looks even more ecstatic than usual. "I hope you're well rested, because today we're taking you out on your first real mission."

I feign a smile, my head still foggy with sleep. "Great."

"Aren't you excited?" he exclaims, handing me a bag. "I packed for you, just a few things you'll need."

I take the bag gratefully. "Thanks. When do we leave?"

He thinks for a moment.

"Ten o'clock."

Groaning, I shut the door. He's at least five hours early, if not earlier.

"C'mon! Open up!" he complains from the other side of the door.

Ignoring him, I walk back to my bedroom and fall back asleep.

Another knock comes a few hours later and this time, I force myself to get dressed. I pull on my boots and the leather jacket hanging in my armoire. I open up the bag Naveen gave me and find a change of clothes, a few snacks, a water bottle, and a dagger. The dagger's handle is a cold silver with three sapphires along the grip. The blade is paper thin and wicked sharp. It enchants me, but I hope I won't have to use it.

After gathering my things, I leave my room to meet Naveen in the lobby.

"Morning, sleepyhead," he says, smiling.

"Why were you awake at four in the morning?" I ask.

He laughs. "I get up at that hour every day," he says. "Soon, you will too. As you advance in the rankings, you get bombarded with a ton of additional duties."

"Sounds lovely," I reply.

His expression softens, and he lowers his voice. "I know you probably don't want to talk about it, but what happened last night?" he asks.

I turn away and shrug. "I wasn't feeling well." I try to push the memory from my mind, but Simu's voice is strong. "Jaice's training hasn't been easy, either."

Despite the rational part of me warning me against it, I know I have to return to the old man's lair. I need answers. Answers that I'm beginning to believe only Simu can provide.

Naveen bites his lip but shifts the conversation. "Anyway," he says, motioning for me to follow him outside. "Jaice and Crayln will join us soon."

"Alright. No Taiana this time?" I try to force a smile, but it doesn't quite appear.

"Nope," Naveen replies. "The commanders only take on the most important missions. We're playing mailman today. It'll be a good introductory task for you."

Crayln and Jaice appear out of the building with small bags of their own. "Are we ready?" they both ask in unison.

"Yes," Naveen replies. "Let's head to the station. A striker is waiting for us at the surface."

I follow Naveen and the others to a large facility right up against the rock wall of the city. We catch a train that takes us up at lightning speed.

"An underground base is cool and all, but doesn't it get tiring having to take a train each time you want to leave?" I ask.

The others merely shrug. "I suppose we could've taken the elevator," Jaice says. "And besides, the pros of Dravkia being underground far outweigh the cons. For one, no one knows where we are."

I don't argue and instead peer out of the window at the blurred moonstones along the tunnel. Soon, a bright light pours through and I know we've reached the surface. Marshy green water surrounds us, and tall cypress trees tower overhead. On the bank, there's a strip of asphalt lined with strikers. Behind it rests an enormous metal beast, a ship like I've never seen before.

"All right, the people we're looking for are in Valenca," Naveen explains as we exit the train and board the ship. "We'll have to be extremely careful. No one can know we're there."

"So, what do we have to do once we get there?" I prompt.

Naveen scans the paper in his hands. "We'll land at midnight and hopefully the cover of the darkness will work to our advantage. We're looking for a villa with a sun crest. It's in the heart of the city."

Crayln curses. "I hate that place," he says bitterly.

"Why's that?" I ask.

A rare fire dances in his eyes. "I was born in Valenca," he says. "And to put it plainly, it wasn't great. I never knew my parents, and I grew up in an orphanage with a ton of other boys."

He taps his fingers on the computer resting in his lap, the memories resurfacing.

Crayln tries to shrug it off, but I can tell it isn't easy for him. "I was smaller than the others, so naturally, they liked to kick me around," he says. Then, he looks up. "Don't take this the wrong way, I'm not looking for pity. That was a long time ago, and I'm much stronger than I was before."

"It seems like the Order really helped you," I say.

He smiles. "Yeah," he says. "It changed my life. And now, I want to do the same for others. That's why I joined."

"Alright, that's enough of the sappy stuff," Jaice says, patting Crayln on the back. "Let's focus on how we're going to get this done undetected."

Naveen nods in agreement. "At least we have a bit of a bargaining chip," he says, smiling mischievously.

"Why are you looking at me like that?" I say.

"If we run into their authorities," Naveen says, "we can offer you up as a bargain. Almost every country has posters with your face on them and a handsome reward underneath."

"You wouldn't dare," I say, although I'm too sure.

He chuckles. "Kidding, kidding. Sort of."

I frown at him, but he just laughs louder.

"We're here," Jaice says as we approach the landing pad. He gathers his materials, a sword at his side and various other weapons concealed under his suit.

"Glasses on," Naveen says, unfolding his own. "We need to be as unidentifiable as possible."

I take the black sunglasses and place them over my eyes. The city grows into an even darker shade of midnight, and I have to squint to make out the fine details of the road and buildings around me.

"Let's move," Naveen says.

We file out of the striker and onto the roof of a tall building in the middle of the town. I look up, and the moon is a sliver of white in the sky.

"There," Naveen says, pointing to a spot in the distance. "That's where we're going."

"Alright, I'll set up here and disarm the cameras," Crayln says, taking out his computer. "They're going to know there's been a breach in their system, but we should have a good five minutes."

Naveen nods. "I'll signal you when we're close. For now, we'll wear these and stay hidden."

He hands the three of us dark cloaks with hoods that conceal our faces. We camouflage almost seamlessly into the night.

"Perfect. Jaice, Iris, follow me," Naveen says, and we slowly climb down the stairs on the side of the building.

I hold my breath to prevent myself from making any extra noise. We pad quietly along a series of villas, keeping close to the sides and blending into the shadows.

I watch as we pass the houses, each with a different marking engraved on the wall. They range from swirls and patterns to cats and flowers. Eventually, we find the one marked with the sun stamp. The villa is silent. Whoever is inside is fast asleep, completely unsuspecting.

Naveen makes a signal, sending a message to Crayln through his watch.

"Okay, he's disabled the mics and cameras in the area," Naveen whispers softly. He motions for us to round the back of the house.

Jaice helps launch me up to the top of the small villa, and Naveen appears moments later. We're close to a small window on the side of the house and I pause, waiting for instruction.

Naveen hands me a small object wrapped in a black silk cloth. "Take this," he says, "And leave it under the woman's pillow. Don't unwrap it."

My eyes widen. "Me? I can't do that," I say. "I'll keep watch. You do it."

He shakes his head. "No. This is an excellent opportunity to dip your toe in the water."

I bite my lip.

"We only have four minutes left," Naveen reminds me.

"Fine," I say, snatching the small object from him.

Taking a deep breath, I pull the black mask over my nose and mouth and slip through the small opening of the window. It's dark inside, save for a small candlelight burning. Slowly, I tiptoe down the hall until I come across a bedroom door. I push it open and peek in.

It's the room of a young child. A small bed rests in the corner and toys litter the floor. The boy, who must be only five years of age, is fast asleep. His youthful innocence makes my heart ache. He reminds me so much of Will it hurts. I remember the way I left him: the softness of his face and the small kitten cradled in his arms.

I back away from his door and search for another. Eventually, I come across the room containing a larger bed and a woman sleeping within the tangle of covers.

She's middle-aged, with slight wrinkles in the creases of her eyes and around her mouth. Remembering my mission, I hold the object up to the candlelight.

Curiously, I peel back a little corner of the black cloth and the sliver of the object I see is all too familiar. With horror, I drop the object to the floor, and it releases a loud clamor throughout the house.

My hand flies to my mouth in shock.

The woman is still sleeping, but I hear footsteps behind me.

A hand taps my shoulder, and I jump to see Naveen, looking for some kind of explanation.

Sorry, I mouth silently.

Still shaking, I bend down to pick up the object, covering it again so Naveen can't tell I unwrapped it. I slip it under the woman's pillow.

Once we leave the room, Naveen takes hold of my hand and ushers us out the window in the hallway. I struggle to keep up as he practically shoves me off the roof.

Jaice is outside keeping watch, but the moment he spots us, we dash away from the villa as fast as we can. I follow Naveen as he leads us back to the building where Crayln is waiting.

I expect him to scold me, or to report me to the commander for jeopardizing the mission. If he does, my plans for preventing the war and protecting my brother will be over before they have a chance to truly begin.

To my surprise, he doesn't speak of it.

I take a moment to admire the scenery of the town, hoping for a distraction. We run across an ancient cobblestone bridge that rests above a beautiful river. The air is crisp and fresh, and I realize this is the first time I've been above the surface in over a week, although it has felt like months.

"Keep up, Princess," Jaice calls.

I run faster and we finally reach the building. We climb back up the small, wired ladder until we reach the stone ledge.

Crayln is already in the striker when we arrive, and Naveen races ahead to start the engine. I can hardly listen to what they're saying. The image of the artifact remains vivid in my mind. I know those symbols. The artifact Sorin gave me is an exact replica of the one I left under the pillow of some unsuspecting sleeping woman.

"What exactly did we drop off?" I ask wearily.

"A stone. A black diamond, to be specific," Naveen replies. "They're our signature symbol—the object we left tonight is a warning." I furrowed my brows. "A warning?"

"We give diamonds to high-listed offenders of the Order," Jaice says.

"That woman is in charge of distributing funds for Cryencia," Naveen says. "Our intelligence reported that she's been keeping large quantities of it for herself and for the king. None of the funds are going toward rebuilding old towns or helping their people."

"So, she gets a diamond?" I ask, still confused.

"They're called the Eyes of Alabass," Crayln adds. "After the founder of the Order, Alabaster Strovka. You may have heard of him. He's our leader's great-grandfather."

My eyes turn back to the floor and the image of the Eye flashes in my mind again.

"Why send a warning at all?" I ask. "Won't they just try to escape?"

Naveen shrugs. "The Eyes are more than decorative jewels," he says. "They hold tracking devices inside of them. It allows us to keep tabs on them and ensure they understand our message clearly."

Cold shivers run through my body. Sorin found an Eye of Alabass in the East Tower. No one has occupied that space in years. Not since my mother.

Dread fills my stomach.

Sorin believed my mother might have had a connection with the artifact. Could the Eye have been sent to her?

It becomes almost impossible to breathe.

I think back to my maid, Myra, who acted as if the stone was a touch of death. *This* is why she reacted the way she did. She knew what it signified. But how?

"Iris, are you okay?" Naveen asks, concern hanging in his voice. "You look like you're about to retch."

"I..." I say, my voice trailing off. "I'm fine."

"We only resort to this when we have to," he says gently. "When there's no other way to get the message across."

I ignore his attempt to comfort me. There's nothing he could say that will alleviate the guilt I feel. My mind spins with thoughts and scenarios and questions, all circling around my mother.

I need to know the truth.

Did my mother fall victim to the Order?

Chapter 14

"*Everyone has a role in their unit,*" Naveen explains. "I think that for now, 'supplier' will do just fine."

I look at him, unimpressed. "Supplier?"

Naveen shrugs. "Each mission requires specific materials. I took on your role last time and got the Eye. But now I think that you're fully capable of doing it on your own."

"How do I know what to get?" I ask. "And where am I to get all the supplies?"

"The Order's official supplier has a workshop down on 49th," he says, pointing down the street. "It doesn't look like much from the outside, but he's got an entire shop in the basement with practically everything and anything we'll need for future missions."

I swallow. I know that place and I know the supplier. Last time I was there, Simu tried to kill me.

My muscles are tense as I near the workshop, flashes of my last encounter still vivid in my mind. Above the sounds of cars and horns blaring from the streets, I hear my heart ready to leap out of my chest.

To my surprise, Simu is in a much better mood compared to when I last saw him. I find him sitting in the same small room, still surrounded by the flickering glow of waxy candles and a mess of yellowing parchment. But the wild rage and fire in his eyes is gone.

"You have returned," Simu comments.

I stand across from him, my hand feeling for the dagger in my pocket. "Yes," I say. "I hope you're not going to kill me for it."

He seems to ignore my remark and continues shuffling through his shelves.

"I've come for the materials for our next mission. Naveen says that you would know what that means," I say.

"Tea?"

I raise an eyebrow as he disregards my request and pours tea out of a small, ancient tea kettle. He pours two cups and hands one to me. I'm about to refuse, thinking there's a high possibility of it being poisoned, but the aromatic scent of the Imperial mountains is too inviting to resist.

"Imperial tea?" I ask, taking the teacup. "How did you get it here?"

Simu smiles, his eyes focused on the milky liquid in his own cup.

The tea tastes so familiar, and for a moment, I feel the weight of homesickness. It doesn't last long.

"Your next mission," he begins, "will require a set of specific cloth capable of blocking out the harsh grit of the desert."

I lift an eyebrow. "We're going to the desert?"

He nods. "Yes. And you will need to be careful. The desert is a wondrous place, filled with ancient secrets followed by timeless curses. You must proceed with care."

Simu motions for me to follow him down a small set of stairs concealed behind a hefty bookshelf. It's cool and dark as we descend the spiral staircase, a small candle lighting our way.

"Is this your workshop?" I ask as the lights flicker on.

The room, as Naveen said, seems to hold everything we could ever need. There are racks of weapons, ranging from small daggers to long swords and even some spears. In one corner, there are small trinkets and scraps of metal, along with parts of computers and radios.

"Indeed," Simu says, digging through a bin of cloth. "I've spent years collecting all of this. Most of it is older than both you and I."

I marvel at the antiques that litter his workshop and run my fingers over a rich, copper machine. It's unlike anything I've ever seen.

"Ah," Simu says, pulling out five white robes. "These will allow you to travel through the desert safely. It's Imperial silk, which, as you know, is one of the strongest materials in existence. I suspect it could withstand a sandstorm."

I take the silk in my arms, and it's as light as air. I remember the soft feel of the fabric from back home.

"Thank you," I say, folding each robe in my arms.

He nods. "You wish to ask more, do you not?"

Curiosity gets the better of me. "What can you tell me about my mother?" I ask softly, not wanting to trigger whatever fit he had the previous night.

Without responding, he drops a pile of dusty books in front of me. "You must first learn of my people. Of *our* people," he says. "The history of the Kuyang people dates back centuries. If you wish to uncover everything, you must start at the beginning."

"I don't see how learning about a dying civilization will tell me anything about my mother," I protest, the words coming out harsher than I intend.

His voice is calm, and much kinder than I deserve. "There is more to the story than you have been told," he says. "You must figure it out for yourself."

I allow his words to sink in. "Did you know her?" He ignores me. "Read these and return to me in two days' time."

"Did she have anything to do with the Order?" I ask. "We found an Eye in our palace. Are they...are they the reason she's dead?" The last words come out as a whisper.

As I say the words, I feel a cold chill wash over me.

"Read," he says, and turns away.

Frustrated, I take the small pile of books and brush the dust off the covers.

"We will speak soon," Simu promises.

After a long day of training, I make my way back to the apartments and set the books on my desk. I watch them carefully, as if they could explode at any moment. Simu believes they hold the answers to my questions. I am not so sure.

Impatience overpowers me as I read through the pages upon pages of history. I feel like I'm back in the palace, studying at my desk under the watchful eyes of my teacher.

The bore of studying makes me itch for answers. The warriors of the Old Age, while valiant and admirable, can't tell me what happened to my mother. They can't save my nation from the destruction that a war would cause.

As I read through one of the last books that specializes in ancient tribal warfare and medicine, something catches my attention. The language is all in the long forgotten native tongue, but there are vivid pictures on every page. As I look closer, I realize they're drawings.

Fading and blotchy with age, it's difficult to decipher the images. I see monstrous creatures resembling tigers but three times the size of one. On the next page, there are paintings of deer, pursued by an entire battalion of warriors.

The last page sends a shiver down my spine. A wounded man, bloodied and unconscious, lies on the forest floor. Judging by the markings on his skin, he's some kind of chief. Warriors sit along his body, appearing to have returned from battle. Further away, a warrior lays dead, a devastating hole occupying the space where his heart should be. I grimace when my eyes trail to his leg, which is almost entirely skinned, as if it's been disintegrated or burned. A healer kneels next to a fallen warrior, holding a small porcelain dish filled with a violet liquid.

My fingertips brush lightly over the worn painting, and I desperately wish that I could understand the small caption beneath it. What is the healer giving to him? Which war is the image depicting?

In the next image, the same chief who was previously on the brink of death, looks entirely healed. His fallen comrades, however, remain in their eternal sleep, torn and tattered, bones and skin showing.

I tremble as I close the book, trying to shove the gory images out of my mind.

Then, it hits me.

Simu is not the only one who knows about my mother. If she was affiliated with the Order, the leader would know. One of the higher-ups would know.

The leader must have records stored away. He has to. But the thought of my mother falling victim to anyone makes me sick all over again and I can't bring myself to leave my room.

The following morning, I gather my training gear and throw a pack over my shoulder before racing down the stairs. There's really only one person I can go to for help.

I knock three times and step back, waiting for Naveen.

"Morning, Iris," he says, smiling, not looking one bit tired. "Is this payback for waking you so early?"

"Not exactly," I say, too tired for jokes.

"What can I help you with?"

I bite my lip, still unsure if I can trust him.

"May I come in? I have a favor to ask of you," I say.

Surprise lights up his face, but he nods. "Of course."

I walk into his apartment, which is furnished almost exactly like my own, and we sit down on his couch opposite of each other.

"Alright, talk to me," he says, pouring two cups of coffee.

"I need you to promise me you won't tell anyone about this," I say, keeping my voice barely audible.

He raises an eyebrow and turns on the coffee pot. It creates a loud whirring noise as it springs to life and produces searing hot liquid. It's so loud I can hardly hear him.

"If you want to talk in private, here is certainly not the place," he says, leaning close to me. "The noise of the coffee pot should drown us out, but we can't discuss anything of importance here. You never know who's listening."

"Where, then? It's important," I insist.

He thinks for a moment. "Meet me at the Fall. Noon."

Reluctantly, I nod.

Chapter 15

The Fall is located in the outskirts of the southern end of the city. It's hidden behind a large stone forest that gives way to an enormous underground lake. The rushing water from the fall will mask our conversation well.

I spot Naveen standing behind the blur of water and make my way toward him.

"Hey," he says, and we head deeper into the cave. "Even though this place probably isn't bugged, we still need to be careful."

I nod.

"So, what can I help with?" he offers, taking a seat against the cave wall. "Nothing illegal, I hope."

I snort in amusement.

"Does the Order keep records of everyone they come in contact with?" I ask.

"I'm intrigued," he says, smiling.

"So that's a yes," I say, taking a seat next to him. "I need your help in gaining access to them."

"You know what, committing an illegal act sounds much more appealing," he says. "And at least with that, there's the chance we'll escape with our heads."

"Please be serious," I say. "This is important."

He sighs. "Look," he says. "Someone of my rank will have no way of accessing them. Who are you looking for, exactly?"

"Evelyn Wu," I say.

He raises an eyebrow. "Your mother?"

I nod.

"Do you know when she may have been in contact with us?" Naveen asks.

"About eighteen years ago," I answer. "She received an Eye, just like the woman from Valenca." I hear my voice break as I choke out the last few words.

"I'm sorry," he says after a moment.

I shake my head. "It's alright," I lie. "Who, exactly, will have access to the records?"

"I don't think I should tell you," he says, folding his arms over his chest. "The look on your face tells me you'll get yourself into a boat load of trouble."

"I won't," I protest. "Just, hypothetically. If I were to find these records, where would I start?"

He smiles, defeated. "Iris, you have to *promise* me you won't do anything stupid."

"I promise," I say. Although, if it means finding more information on my mother, I'm not sure I'll be able to keep my word.

"Well, the most I can do is take you to the commander," he says. "If anyone would give them to us, it's him."

I frown at the mere mention of him. I know he already despises me. He'll look for any reason to get rid of me, and if he thinks I'm snooping around, he won't have to look far.

"Are you sure that's a good idea?" I say.

"I take it you don't like him very much," Naveen says, cracking a smile. "Your face is paler than the moonstones."

"We didn't exactly hit it off," I admit. "But it's not a big deal. If he can provide the records, I'm willing to meet with him."

"That's the spirit," Naveen says. "But let me warn you, it's very possible that he won't give them to you. After all, they're highly classified, and not just anyone can see them."

"Yeah, I figured," I say, not wanting to think about that possibility.

Naveen nods. "Alright, then. Hopefully we can catch him at the station before he heads out on his next mission."

I follow Naveen out of the Fall, and we make our way down the street toward the station.

We stand before a large stone building with glass windowpanes lining the sides. As we walk under the marble archway, we're met with hundreds of soldiers trying to catch their trains. It's busy, and I scan the floor for the commander, but I don't see him.

"Everyone looks the same in these suits," I observe. "How are we going to find him?"

Naveen laughs. "You'll get used to it," he says.

I notice that the two of us stand out like a rose in the winter snow, with our black T-shirts and dirty pants clashing with the pristine pressed suits of the others.

"I messaged him and he agreed to meet with us in one of the security rooms," Naveen says. "But we have to make it quick. He isn't exactly in a great mood today."

I follow Naveen through the station, which feels like a maze. Eventually, we reach the commander's door.

Naveen knocks.

"Come in," the deep, recognizable voice of the commander orders.

I stand behind Naveen as we enter the small room, which consists of a table and a single light. It looks like an interrogation room.

It's dark, but I can still make out the sharp, intimidating features of the commander. He sits back in his chair with one ankle crossed over his knee and his hair combed back neatly.

"Good to see you," Naveen says, smiling.

The commander does not return his friendliness and instead replies, "Khan. Do not think for a moment that I did not receive an entire report detailing your juvenile behavior in Imperia."

Taiana wasn't bluffing, I think silently.

Startled, Naveen bows his head. "My bad."

"Make it short," Commander Wang says.

Naveen clears his throat. "We'd like to request access to a specific record," he says, his voice having lost the casual spark it had a moment ago.

"We?" Commander Wang raises an eyebrow and frowns at me.

Naveen hesitates. "Myself and Miss Wu," he says.

"You're dismissed," the commander says, without even glancing at Naveen. "I want to hear it from her."

I swallow, but I'm determined not to let him get the better of me.

Naveen salutes him respectfully and shoots me a look that tells me not to lose my cool. The door clicks behind him.

"Sit."

I do as he says and press my spine to the back of the chair.

"Now," Commander Wang says. "Tell me, soldier, what is it you want?"

I avert my eyes and explain. "I'm looking for the records of someone who may have been affiliated with the Order. Her name is Evelyn Wu."

He frowns and looks at me through narrow, cat-like eyes. "You demand I give you access to the Order's most classified records?"

"I only want to see hers," I protest. "I won't share the information with anyone. At the very least, can you confirm if you even have a record for her?"

"Absolutely not," he says, his voice tight.

"And why's that?" I challenge him, my body reacting faster than my mind.

His eyes flicker dangerously. "Your royal title means nothing here. Why should you, who's been here for merely two weeks, be given access to these documents? Why should I impart such trust in you?"

As the words come out of his mouth, I feel my mind blanking. I don't want to admit it, but he has a point. Why should he trust me with the records? Because I'm a foolish girl searching for her mother? That answer will never do.

Because I can't think of anything clever to say, I shift the subject. "Why do you hate me?" I ask.

"I do not hate you," he replies, although I know he's lying. "But I do not trust you, either. You fail to understand that these records are not mine to give out like candy. They hold information that, in the wrong hands, could unleash an entirely new brand of chaos."

Frustrated, I force myself to remain seated. "I need to see it," I insist.

He stands up and leans forward so his face is only inches from mine. "Do I look like I'm offering?"

"I'm one of your soldiers now, too. Haven't I earned even a little bit of your respect?" I say, struggling to keep my rage in check.

He scoffs. "You are so far from earning even a morsel of it," he snaps. "Good day. And tread carefully in my city."

Without waiting for my response, he stands and heads for the door. With one last eye piercing glare, he leaves me in the dimly lit interrogation room.

"Asshole," I shout, although I don't think he hears me.

I slam my fist into the table and wait a few moments, hoping that he's long gone, before I join Naveen outside. He bites his lip. "I'm guessing it didn't go well?"

"He's unbearable," I say, gritting my teeth. "How do you all worship him like he's some kind of god?"

"A god? Definitely not," Naveen says. "But to me, he's a friend."

"How?" I ask, astonished. "How can you be friends with someone like him? He's so...vile."

Naveen shrugs as we walk back through the station. "It's a long story."

"I've got nothing else to do," I reply.

He shakes his head but gives in. "Well, long story short: he saved my life. We were only ten, but I remember it as if it were yesterday. I was just some kid in the streets of Caira, scavenging, stealing, looking for whatever food I could find. One day, I stole from the wrong family, and they placed an enormous bounty over my head."

I raise my eyebrows but remain silent, enticed by his story.

"Anyway, with everyone in town after me, I was captured pretty quickly," Naveen continues. "They took me to the town square and tied me to a wooden post where everyone could see me. It was humiliating, but that was hardly the worst part. They planned to kill me, but not before lashing me until my back was raw."

He pauses for a moment, a shadow crossing his eyes.

"I'm so sorry," I whisper. "You don't have to continue if you don't want to."

"No, no," he says. "It's okay. Well, as I lay slumped against the post, my back bleeding, I saw Commander Wang. He was young, too. Twelve, maybe? But he was the bravest person I'd ever seen. And I lived in a town crawling with thugs and gang leaders, mind you. The only thing on him was a switchblade, but that hardly mattered. He could've gotten the job done with a butter knife.

"He took down the head of the family in a flash. Before I knew it, the man was on the ground. In less than five minutes, he took down the rest of them."

"He was only twelve?" I ask, my mind flashing to Will.

Naveen nods. "And he's only sharpened and improved his skills since," he says, pride in his voice. "Believe it or not, we were really close. But things have changed a little as he's climbed through the ranks. I owe him everything, though. He took me back and gave me the opportunity to start a new life. I couldn't ask for anything more.

"Without the Order, I would still be scavenging on the dirty streets of Caira. To be honest, I probably would've been dead by now. But here, I feel truly alive."

I think for a moment and let his words sink in.

Slowly, I begin to understand him. In just a few weeks, I've experienced more than I ever thought possible. Maybe this is what freedom is like.

Chapter 16

"*Do you really think I'm ready?*" I ask, wiping sweat from my brow.

Jaice shrugs. "Do *you* think you're ready?"

I scan the platform for my opponent, Raelyn Okorie. She's one of the lower ranked soldiers, and according to Jaice, she'll give me a fair match.

"I am," I say, trying not to let my nerves show.

I watch Raelyn as she wraps her arms with tape and chats with her friends, a smug smile dancing on her lips. Her toned arms and muscled shoulders tell me she's much stronger than I am. She has the height, weight, and strength advantage, but I'm used to that since I train with Jaice.

"Speed is going to be your biggest asset," Jaice says, doing his best to prepare me for my match. "Her skills are sharp, but she's slow. Hit her before she hits you and turn her strength against her."

"Got it," I say, trying to ignore my fluttering heart rate. "And if I'm not faster than her?"

He laughs, as if he finds joy in the thought of me getting pummeled to the ground. "Then you'll lose, I suppose. But you better not, because that will reflect on my teaching, which I know for a fact isn't flawed."

I roll my eyes. "You know, I thought I'd beaten some of that ego out of you."

"Yeah, right, like you could even land a hit," he taunts, crossing his arms.

"Hey, I've beaten you multiple times!" I say, shoving him playfully.

"I was going easy on you," Jaice says. "I can't have my student losing faith within the first few weeks."

Before I can reply, the bell rings, signaling for the fighters to get ready. Taking a deep breath, I step over the white line marking the boundaries of the fighting ring.

"I've never fought a princess before," Raelyn says, rolling her shoulders. "Want me to go easy on you?" She brushes a dark lock of hair behind her ear before stepping into the ring.

"No need. If anything, you'll be the one begging for my mercy," I say, lifting my chin. If there's one thing I've learned from Jaice's lessons, it's how to talk smack.

Unfortunately, Raelyn doesn't take it the way I hoped. She pins me with a glare and balls her hands into fists.

"You're going to wish you never stepped foot out of that palace, Princess," she growls.

Crap.

The second bell rings, beginning the fight. She wastes no time and lunges for me, attempting to pick me up by the abdomen.

Quickly, I sidestep and drive a knee into her side, just like Jaice has done to me over a hundred times. By this point, the move has become second nature.

She staggers back, but that doesn't seem to dampen her fire. She rushes forwards again, this time anticipating my dodge, and sweeps my legs from underneath me.

I land on the floor, my head banging against the ground. Grunting, I roll out of the way, watching her elbow just barely miss my head.

Spinning to my feet, I circle her, keeping my distance.

"Running away already, Princess?" she jeers, stepping in for a jab to my ribs.

Before she can make contact, I fasten my hands around her arm and turn my body. Using her momentum against her, I throw her off balance and drop kick her, a move that's been extremely difficult for me to pull off.

"That's it!" I hear Jaice shout from the sidelines.

As I approach her, preparing to hold her down, she leaps up, hands free, and has me in a dangerous head lock.

I gasp and attempt to twist out of her grip, but her arm overpowers me. I feel the airways to my lungs struggling against the pressure of her grip.

I close my eyes and think back to the moves Jaice has taught me.

Swiftly, I plant my feet as if they're stuck in concrete and trip her. She stumbles and drags me down with her, but her grip loosens enough for me to wriggle out.

In her moment of confusion, I reach over and clasp her arms behind her back and put a knee to her spine. Using all the strength I have, I hold her for the full ten seconds and at the sound of the third bell, I release her arms and rise.

Jaice smiles proudly and claps me on the back. "Well done, Princess," he says. "I wasn't sure if you had it in you."

"Better watch your back from here on out," I say, smiling.

"Alright, let's not get too ahead of ourselves," he says. "You've still got a lot of training to do before you can take me down."

"Fair," I say.

I walk over to Raelyn, who's dusting herself off. "Good match," I say, extending out my hand.

She looks up at me and then at my outstretched hand. "I'm sure for you, it was." She turns away, heading back to where her friends sit snickering on the edge.

"Don't let her get to you," Crayln says, appearing from the weapons rack. "She's always like that. Some say it's because she can't seem to get a date."

"Not everything has to do with someone's love life," I remind him.

He smirks, pushing up his sunglasses and flashing me a grin. "That's not as true as it seems. For example, you're grumpy because you're lonely."

I scowl. "I am neither of those things."

Crayln elbows Jaice and leans against his shoulder. "C'mon, you gotta admit, she's a little cold sometimes."

Jaice shakes him off. "Like an icicle," he says with an eyebrow raised.

"Man," Crayln complains. "Where's Naveen? *He* understands my humor."

As if summoned, Naveen appears from the side of the platform, breathing hard. "Guys!"

he calls. "The details of the new mission finally came in."

We all cluster around him as he catches his breath. "I'll explain once we're in private, but get ready because we're going to Trasylar. Iris, bring the robes you got from Simu."

"Aw man," Crayln protested. "We just got back from Valenca."

"Trasylar?" I exclaim.

Naveen nods. "We'll be going on neutral grounds, so don't worry. Besides, we've got to take on as many missions as we can if we're going to make any difference."

"You've got a point," Crayln admits.

"Well, we should get going, then," Jaice says, throwing his training bag over his shoulder.

"Pack first," Naveen says. "Sounds like we'll be there for a few days. Oh, and I need someone to find Alistar."

"I know where he is," Crayln says, perking up. "I saw him with his new lady friend."

We all roll our eyes.

"No, seriously!" he says. "I saw them having lunch at the bakery downtown."

"Someday, you'll find a girl of your own and *then* you'll get your nose out of everyone else's love life," Naveen says, pretending to be exasperated.

I laugh and we climb down the ladder of the Needle and head back to the apartments to pack.

As I settle on the ship, I watch as we fly over the vast, swampy terrain below. Slung across my back is a small bag filled with water and small nutrient packets, along with my dagger. Something tells me I'm going to need it.

"Alright, so the mission is in Ancia Dera. The Golden City, as many call it," Naveen says. "As you're probably aware, it's the only town in the Salphryx Desert, and for good reason. The conditions there can be brutal, so be prepared."

"Simu gave me these," I offer, handing each of them one of the long gowns of Imperial silk.

"We have to wear these?" Crayln asks, looking at the robe skeptically.

"It'll keep you safe, idiot," Naveen says, disappearing into a blanket of white. "And we'll need to make sure to conserve our water."

He shoots Crayln a stern look.

Crayln quickly caps his water bottle and holds his hands up in surrender. "Okay, okay, I'm putting it away."

Naveen sighs. "You'll be the death of us."

"What's the job?" I dare to ask.

"We're to return a missing boy to his family," Naveen says. "According to our notes, he's been taken by local thugs, and he's been missing for the past three days."

"Sounds easy enough," Jaice says, leaning back in his chair.

Alistar shifts uncomfortably. "I wouldn't be so sure," he says. "I've done some research, and these thugs are stronger than you'd think. We can't underestimate them."

I look out the window, watching as land and sea pass underneath us. The flight is long, but it gives me time to rest before the mission truly begins.

"We're here!" Naveen exclaims, jumping up from his seat. "Alright, let's get this done before the sandstorm."

"Sandstorm?" we all exclaim in unison.

"We've still got a couple of hours before it hits," he reassures us. "The robes should hold, right Iris?"

I shrug. "Simu said they should, but I'm not entirely sure that I'd like to test that theory."

Naveen laughs and pushes the doors open.

"Only one way to find out."

Chapter 17

I step out onto the searing golden sand and a dry heat blows against my face. Pulling up the white cloth, I do my best to squint through the harsh winds. Ahead of us lies a city, and as Naveen mentioned, it's entirely made of sandstone.

Each building has intricate, ancient carvings and beautiful pillars of golden yellow stone. A large archway marks the entrance of the town, along with two statues of sleek, golden felines. At the base of the city lies an oasis, drawing travelers from every end of the desert. Tall palms line the water, and people set up camps and tents along the bank.

We approach the entrance and I see open-air markets along the dirt road and the people of the town bustling within. The place is lively, like no town I've ever seen before. Music sings from the alleyways and a flutist sits on the side of the road with a small woven basket at his feet. Kids run past us, chasing small sand cats through the crowd. Fruit stands and artisan craft stalls line the street and locals dance in the town center.

"There are so many people," Crayln complains. "How are we supposed to find the boy?"

"Alistar's gone to search for information," Naveen says. "You've all seen the photo, so you should be able to recognize him."

I look around our group, and sure enough, Alistar is gone. I hadn't even noticed him slip away.

We split up into groups of two to more efficiently search the town. Naveen and Crayln take on the east side, while Jaice and I take the west.

"We should've brought a tracker along," Jaice says.

I nod in agreement. Another one of the specialty categories for soldiers is tracking. Unfortunately, none of us are a part of that group.

"At least we have Alistar," I offer. Jaice and I continue through the town, trying to keep a low profile. It isn't easy considering that Jaice is paler than the sandstone and I'm clearly from the eastern lands. We pull the cloth high over our faces and keep our heads low.

"Jade sculptures! Hand crafted by our very own artisans here in Ancia Dera!" one of the stall vendors shouts out.

"Tapestries and rugs on sale!"

"Figs and lemons! Freshly grown at the oasis!"

There's so much to take in and I have to keep my head in constant motion in order to see everything. The markets are so vivid and full of color I almost forget about the mission.

"Could that be him?" Jaice whispers to me, pointing to a small boy at the other end of the street.

He's strapped to the back of a man four or five times bigger than him and has a cloth wrapped over his head, concealing his face.

"It could be," I say, taken aback by the sight. "Either way, we've got to help him."

As I start toward them, Jaice catches my arm. "Think for a moment, Princess. Before exposing us all and spoiling the mission, *think*. Going after that kid without knowing if he's the one we're looking for could end poorly."

"We'll never know if it's him if we don't help," I say, pulling my arm away. "Come on, they're going to get away."

Without waiting for a response, I push my way through the dense crowd of people and toward the sinister-looking men. They seem to stand guard, and sure enough, one of their gang members emerges from one of the small shops with a bag of valuables.

"Got it, Boss," I hear one of them say.

They take off in an instant, and I sprint after them, ignoring Jaice's shouts of protest. I follow them as they turn down a long, deserted alleyway. We come to a small square, with high walls surrounding us on all sides.

"Hey!" I shout. "Stop!"

At the sound of my voice, the three men come to a halt and tower over me. The one in the middle, with the boy strung to his back, glares at me with dark, beady eyes.

"This is no place for a pretty little girl like yourself," he says.

"Let him go," I demand, ready to reach into my pocket to retrieve my dagger.

The three of them look at each other and howl like a pack of hyenas.

"No, I don't think I will," he says, stepping forward. "We don't take orders from anyone, especially not from foreigners. Now turn around and pretend like this never happened."

Gripping the cool handle of my dagger, I take a deep breath and unsheathe it. "Let him go. I will not ask again," I say, the sharp blade glistening in the light.

"Your little toothpick doesn't threaten me," he says, his hands balling into fists. "Last chance to escape with your skin still attached to your body." A wicked smile grows on his face, and I cringe at the thought of his threat.

"Big talk. Can you back it up?" a challenge sounds from behind me. Sure enough, Jaice walks up next to me, rivaling the three men for height and strength. He unsheathes his swords.

"Come and see, boy," the man says, his voice gruff.

"Iris, get back to the town," Jaice warns, gripping his swords so tightly that his knuckles turn white. "Find Nav and the others."

"No," I say, stepping up next to him. "This was my idea. I'm not going to let you take all the credit."

"Don't be ridiculous! You beat *one* soldier in training and you think you're ready for real life combat?" he says in disbelief. "Get out of here before you get yourself killed."

Adrenaline pumps through my body and my feet remain planted on the ground.

I'm not fleeing.

I'm not afraid.

I stomp my foot defiantly. "Jaice, I'm not letting you fight my battles. We take them down together or we die together. Either way, I'm not going to run."

He lets out an exasperated yet defeated sigh. "Fine. But just don't die."

I smile. "Got it."

We look over to the three men and the one in the middle flings the boy behind him, rolling his shoulders.

"Isn't that sweet," he mocks. "But your brave words aren't going to help you."

My muscles tense, but before we can move into action, the three men standing before us collapse. I peer closer and notice thin darts sticking out of their necks.

I look up to see Crayln, Naveen, and Alistar, each with a dart gun in hand.

"You're welcome," Crayln says, smirking as he slides off of the roof to join us in the plaza.

I snort. "We could've handled it."

"I doubt that," Alistar says. "Some witnesses told me they saw these three leaving the bar on the east side just a few moments ago. They left it a bloody mess."

"What happened?"

Alistar shrugs and I can barely make out his expression through the cloth covering his face. "A fight. Or a robbery. Either way, they aren't people you want to mess with, especially if you're outnumbered."

I sigh and look over to where the three of them lay in a heap. Padding over carefully, I walk up to the boy, still bound by rope.

Using my dagger, I cut the binds, and the boy's eyes spread wide.

"We're just here to help," I say calmly. "You're safe now."

He's breathing fast, and I can tell that he wants to run. I slowly remove part of his mask and instantly recognize the boy Naveen showed us.

"It's him," I call over my shoulder.

The four of them come rushing over, which seems to terrify the boy even more.

"You're right," Naveen exclaims, pulling out the photo to compare. "Nice work, rookie. Alright, who wants to carry him back?"

I scowl and debate slapping him. "Are you kidding? He was just hauled around the entire town by a group of thugs and now you want to do the same thing? He's clearly afraid."

Naveen considers this. "Okay, what do you propose?"

I think for a moment.

"Hey, there," I say to the boy. "Are you hungry? How about we take you down to the market and you can pick out anything you want? Then we can get you home. Does that sound okay?"

To my relief, he nods.

"Alright, you're paying for lunch, then?" Crayln says, slapping me on the back.

I shove him. "You've gotta pull your weight somehow."

Crayln lets out a howl of laughter. "Feisty today, are we?"

"Shut up, you two," Jaice says, leading us back to the market. "Or we'll leave you here."

I shoot Crayln a glare, and he smirks. How irritating.

I feel a tug at my arm, and I look down to see the boy picking up a large orange from one of the fruit stands.

"Is that what you would like?" I ask him.

He nods.

Naveen ends up paying for the orange along with a few other pieces of fruit that the five of us share.

"Guess I can't have my team starving on me in the middle of the desert, huh," he says as he hands us each a piece of citrus. "Save it for the road, though. We've gotta get the kid back."

"I have to go investigate something else," Alistar says. "Don't worry, I'll find you guys soon."

He turns and disappears into the crowd before anyone has a chance to protest.

"Alright, where's his house?" Jaice asks.

Naveen points to one of the largest homes in the village up on a large sand dune. "There. His parents own the town. It's surprising that they can't find him, considering that they have eyes everywhere."

"Well, it's possible that those thugs were guarding him pretty well," I say darkly, thinking of the scene Alistar described.

It takes almost forty minutes to walk from the market all the way up the dune to the boy's house. By the time we reach the front gate, we're all dripping with sweat.

"These long robes are not helping," Crayln pants as he steps under the shade of a palm tree. "I'm considering ripping them off."

"Please don't," the four of us say together.

"Yeah, no one needs to see that," Naveen says, snorting.

Crayln rolls his eyes. "I'll have you know that the ladies back in my hometown would be swooning."

Ignoring him, Naveen presses the small button on the keypad outside of the grand gate. After a moment, the gate opens, and a man comes strolling out of the manor. He walks down the sandstone steps and his elegant white silks blow in the wind.

"Sir Osama," Naveen greets, straightening himself up and taking the boy's hand from my own. "We are here to return your son."

The boy runs to his father, and Sir Osama pulls him into a strong embrace. A warm feeling of pride washes over me.

Naveen smiles beside me. "This," he says. "This is what makes everything worth it."

Chapter 18

We leave the reunited family and find our way back into the heart of the town.

"Man, I'm starving," Crayln says, clutching his stomach dramatically. "Let's get something to eat."

Jaice raises an eyebrow. "We just ate."

"Yeah, I had an *apple,*" Crayln says. "I'm hungry for real food."

"Well, I need to look for Alistar," Naveen says. "I'll meet you all back on the ship. Make sure to grab me something good."

Crayln turns to me. "Are you coming, Iris?"

I shake my head. "I'm not hungry. I'll see you back on the ship, too."

Crayln shrugs. "Suit yourself."

He leads Jaice down into the market, scouting out restaurants and food stalls. I take this chance to take in the unfamiliar scene. Now that I'm out of the palace, I'm desperate to explore.

I approach a stall filled with herbs and spices. Behind the stall is a small tent, its entryway covered with a deep purple fabric.

"What can I help you with, miss?" the stall owner asks. She's a short woman with deep copper skin dripping with golden jewelry. Her majestic robes match the color of the tent, while her headscarf is a lighter shade of lavender.

"I'm just looking," I say, scanning the assortment she has laid out.

"Well," she says. "I never like a customer to leave empty-handed. Please, come inside. At least let me offer you one of my guidebooks. I give them out for free to all of my customers."

"Really, it's alright. I have no way of repaying you."

"No worries," the woman says, motioning me toward the tent. "Teaching others about the botanical mysteries of the desert is one of my deepest passions. That's what has kept me here for so many years."

I follow her into the tent, and to my surprise, it's much more spacious than it seems. I take a seat on one of the cushions on the floor.

The woman stands across from me and grabs a woven basket from her shelf. "Here, take this," she says, handing me a small booklet. "It includes many spices and plants and explains the uses of them. Many of the plants found here in the Salphryx Desert are used as medical drugs or as dyes that the artisans use for their rugs and tapestries. They really are quite extraordinary."

Not wanting to appear rude, I accept the gift and give her my thanks.

"You're very welcome, dear," she says. "If you have questions, come visit me again and let me know. And if there's anything not listed in the book, I'm sure I can help you."

I smile, and then the photos from Simu's book flash in my mind. There was a purple liquid, presumably made from native plants, that was used to heal the wounded warriors.

"Actually," I say, "I have one question."

The woman smiles widely. "Please, ask away."

"Do you know much about ancient Imperial medicine?" I ask.

She thinks for a long moment and flips through another one of her books. "I have studied the plants in all five nations," she says. "Which specific one do you seek information on?"

"It's purple," I say. "At least, when turned into a liquid."

The woman walks over to her small bookshelf and pulls out what must be some kind of ancient text. The book's bindings are falling apart, and the parchment paper looks like it's about to disintegrate. She carefully turns the pages, her eyes scanning ravenously.

"There's a small passage here," she says, her finger running through the lines. "That depicts an ancient medical substance matching your description."

My heart leaps. "What's it called?"

"It's called Marrow," she replies. Her eyes scan the pages curiously. "Although, it appears to be referenced more in Imperial mythology than in reality. In fact, I have never heard of it before."

Marrow. The word is familiar. I remember with horror that my father spoke of it a few times. But this isn't the same thing, is it?

"What does it do?" I ask.

The woman flips the page. "According to the text, the Marrow was created by the Kuyang tribe as a healing tonic. They believed it held extraordinary healing properties. It could ward off death."

"That's impossible. Which means it must be just a myth?" I ask.

She nods. "I have yet to hear about it elsewhere," she says. "It says here it was used as a plea to the spirits. The Kuyang hoped the tonic they created would heal their fallen, but there is no living proof of this. Only the highest in their ranks were granted the honor of the Marrow."

I bite my lip. Simu's book didn't seem like any sort of fairy tale. But I can't be certain that the purple substance in the book is the Marrow that the woman speaks of.

"Are you alright, dear?" she asks, scanning my face with worried eyes. "As I've mentioned, it is highly likely that it is just a made-up story, with the purpose of giving hope to the sick. I wouldn't let it worry you."

I sigh. "I know," I say, although my curiosity is far from quenched. "Thank you for your help."

"My pleasure."

As I turn to leave, a shadow appears in the tent's mouth. The figure belongs to an old woman, shorter than the stall owner and at least twice her age. Gray hair falls in braids down her back. "You speak of the ancient miracle?" she rasps, rushing over to me. She seizes my arm in an iron grip.

I gasp in shock. "Who are you?" I stammer, slowly trying to pry my arm out of her grasp.

Her eyes focus on me. Something about her holds me captive, and everything else seems to fade.

"Leave us," the old woman says.

"Yes, as you wish," the stall owner says.

The old woman's eyes narrow, but her grip remains excruciatingly painful. "No one may listen but you who seeks the miracle. You want the truth, do you not?"

My heart pounds. *Miracle?*

The old woman drops my arm and settles on the floor.

"Now, tell me what you want with the miracle," she says in an accusatory tone.

I panic, the harshness in her tone taking me aback. "I don't understand what you're asking," I say. "This is the first time I've heard of it by name."

She looks unconvinced. "Who sent you here? Who sent you to find it?"

I swallow. "No one," I say. "I'm not here to find anything, I swear. It was pictured in one of my history books, that's all."

The old woman laughs and smiles wickedly. "And tell me, why don't you seek it?" she asks. "Anyone who knows about it surely seeks it, no?"

I shake my head. "The woman said that it was a myth."

This provokes a loud howl of laughter from the woman, but her eyes remain colder than ice. "My daughter is foolish," she says. "But I have dedicated a lifetime of work and research to proving the mere existence of the miracle."

"Have you found it?" I ask, unsure of why I entertain her fantasy. A medicine capable of providing invulnerability is impossible. How could she have spent so many years searching?

"You dare mock me, girl?" she snarls.

"Of course not," I blurt. "But if it's real, how come we don't use it in our hospitals? It would be revolutionary."

She shakes her head. "Discoveries are a work of time and luck," she says. "It can't be rushed. And besides, I wouldn't want a bunch of wealthy kings searching for what should be mine.

"My family has been in the business for some time," she says. "Decades ago, my husband came across the legend of the Marrow—or the Blood Marrow, as many call it."

My body goes rigid. My mother was killed because she got in the way of the search. I can hardly think straight as I draw connections and conclusions between the old woman's words and what I've learned with Simu.

During the terrorist attack on our palace, the attackers had spoken to my father. They demanded he give them what was rightfully theirs.

They wanted the Blood Marrow.

Does this old woman know the men who attacked the palace? Just how many people are searching for this miracle?

"Along with his men, he searched endlessly for it," the old woman says. "Now, my husband is gone and my son searches still. I believe he is close, if not having already found it."

The old woman sits in silence for a long moment, and I hold my breath.

This can't be real.

I think back to my conversations with Simu. He mentioned how unnamed groups had wiped out the native tribes until none remained. Perhaps their miracle fell alongside them, if it's even real. Thinking about it makes my skin prickle.

"You look familiar," she says, looking me up and down, trying to remember.

I shift uncomfortably.

"Who are your parents?"

I don't answer. Something tells me this won't end well.

Without needing a response, she straightens. "You are Evelyn Wu's daughter," she whispers to herself, although I'm barely able to make out her words. "You are Kuyang."

"Did you know my mother?" I ask.

As if possessed, she snaps to attention and her eyes grow wide. Her mouth curls into a malevolent grin and she stands up with astounding speed.

I shoot up too, slamming my head into one of the tent posts.

"It's you," she says. "We've been searching for *you*."

And with that, she lunges.

Taken off guard, she knocks me to the ground and I struggle under her weight. With her left hand, she draws out a sharp blade from under the thick sleeves of her robes.

The fire in her eyes dances dangerously as she threatens the knife against my throat.

Despite her small size, I can't throw her off of me, no matter how much I try. My breaths are labored and sweat pours down my face.

"What are you doing?" I cry, as I feel the sharp blade of the knife graze the thin, vulnerable flesh of my throat.

Pain spikes through me like a rocket, and I scream out.

"Seems that my luck has yet to run out," the woman laughs. "My son will be jealous, surely. But no matter, I'm sure there will be enough to share."

She muffles my screams with her hand, and I feel blood trickling down my neck. The exposed skin and flesh tingles and sings with every passing moment. The blood slows, but that doesn't stop the woman from pressing her blade deeper into my throat.

Panicking, my eyes dart around the tent, searching for anything I can use to defend myself. My dagger is in my pocket, but as I reach for it, she snatches it and throws it across the tent.

"You have the wrong person," I say. "I have nothing that I can give you. I left the palace and severed ties with the royal fortune."

My pleas seem to only fuel her determination. "You have everything I need," she says.

From the corner of my eye, I spot the shimmer of a clay pot filled with desert cacti. Before she can sense my movement, I reach out my one free hand and grab hold of it. Her eyes trail to my hand, but it's too late, and I smash the terracotta into her temple.

I kick her away from me and push myself up, gasping for breath. My hand flies to the pulsing pain in my neck, and I trace the deep flesh wound. Blood covers my hand and I look over to where the woman lays, still conscious.

I prop her against the wall, staring into her eyes.

"Tell me what you want with me," I demand.

She cackles but reveals nothing. Her eyes twinkle. "I should thank you, girl. I haven't had fun like that in years."

My glare only hardens.

"Know that you have been warned, and that you will never be safe," she says, blood running down her face. "A target rests on your back and we will never rest until you are dead and we have our miracle."

I feel as if icy claws are being dragged down my spine as I listen to her twisted words. "Why do they want me dead? *Who* wants me dead?"

"Why do you think?" she says, coughing. "People will do anything for a taste of this miracle."

Footsteps sound, and I whip around to see the rest of my mission squad standing at the entrance of the tent. Jaice has the woman from the stall in a headlock, while Alistar has a sword in hand. Naveen's eyes are wide as he rushes over to me.

The old woman gasps, and she scrambles to her feet. Before I can stop her, she turns and bolts out of the stall.

"Stop her!" I shout.

I trip over pillows and curtains as I reach the back entrance of the tent. When I push aside the fabric, the old woman has disappeared into the crowded market street. Hot sand blows against my face, and I'm breathing hard.

A hand touches my shoulder, and I flinch, finding Naveen.

"Iris, what happened? Are you hurt—"

I cut him off. "Stay away," I say, my voice trembling. "I need to be alone right now."

I push through them and step out of the tent, my heart still racing. I keep walking, despite Naveen calling after me.

I'm still trembling as I close myself inside the ship, slumping against the wall. I just escaped death, and everything about the old woman continues to haunt me. She believes in the Blood Marrow, and she wanted to kill me because of it.

I look out the small windows and see a sandstorm brewing in the distance. As small particles fly against the glass, I watch the townspeople pack up the market and head indoors for safety. People scramble as the winds pick up and blow their tents into the endless desert.

No matter what happens, I have to get stronger. I won't be able to protect Will and Sorin if I'm dead. I have to train until killing me becomes impossible.

A foolish thought.

Nothing is impossible.

Chapter 19

The flight back to Dravkia passes in silence.

The moment I step foot back in the city, I head straight for Simu. I tell him everything from the moment I entered the tent to the death of the old woman.

Simu looks haunted as he processes my story. "It's my fault," he says after a moment. "I failed to prepare you for this. I was ignorant and hoped you would have a longer period of peace."

"Simu, what was she talking about?" I ask, desperation rising in my voice. "Why are there people out to kill me?"

He shakes his head in dismay. "Even I do not possess all the answers. But I know the Blood Marrow is very real, and our ancestors have used it for centuries. I have never seen it for myself, however. The Imperial Tribes kept it hidden, and by the time I was born, they had stopped using it altogether. It was just too tempting for jealous, power-hungry men who would stop at nothing to get it."

"If it was so powerful, why did they stop using it?" I ask. "Why not share it with the world, if it's regarded as a miracle?"

He shakes his head. "It was a gift for our people and our people alone," he says. "But man's greed threatened to tear it all apart. And it did."

"There was an attack on the Imperial Palace a few moons ago," I say. "The emperor kept it quiet, but the men were searching for the Blood Marrow."

"Yes. I heard of that," he says, his voice soft.

"Simu, my mother was *killed* because of this," I say, desperation rising in my voice. "Please, please help me understand."

"Let me tell you a story," Simu says.

When I don't speak, he draws a deep breath.

"I grew up in one of the last remaining Kuyang villages, along with your mother. By the time I completed my sixth birthday, there were only two camps left.

"One day, I was playing in the fields with my brothers. We were racing straw boats in the river when a dark shadow crossed the water and the ducks took flight. An entire battalion came to our lands and lit our homes aflame. Before we knew it, they were rounding us up like cattle."

I swallow hard but can't find my voice.

"My mother ushered some of my siblings and I onto a boat," he continues, his eyes glossy. "We escaped with our lives and nothing more."

When he finishes his story, he takes a long sip of his tea and closes his eyes.

"I'm so sorry," I whisper. "I really am."

"You may have learned of these massacres in your studies back home," he says. "But the history books do not provide an explanation. I predict the Marrow had everything to do with it. It was our ancestor's worst fear coming to pass."

My fingers run through the dust littering the new stack of books that rest in my lap.

"How do *I* fit into this, exactly?" I ask. "It's not like I know where to find the Marrow, I'm of no help to them."

Simu's eyes grow dark. "I am doing everything I can to find the answer to this," he says.

"Is there anything I can do?"

"For now, I advise you to remain with your friends. Do not stray far, certainly not in foreign lands where the power of the Order is weaker," Simu says.

"But they can't help me understand this," I argue, but Simu is already ushering me out of his small lair.

I fiddle with the loose strands of thread on the hem of my shirt as I walk down the sidewalk. As much as I want to trust that Simu will figure everything out, I have many doubts.

For the following week, I train alone. Despite Naveen's best efforts, I turn him away. There are too many things I have to figure out on my own, and I don't want to drag any of them into this. Not that they would believe me, anyway.

The enormous marble arch outside of Headquarters looms above me. I take a deep breath and prepare myself for whatever form of punishment may be coming. This morning, I received a message calling me to Headquarters to speak with the regime commander. I can only assume that I'm to be punished for skipping the organized group training sessions.

Knocking on the door, I hear the voice of Commander Wang sound from inside.

"Come in."

Pushing the door open, I find myself in a spacious, but dark, office room. There's a cherry wood desk near one of the large windows filled with paperwork. Tall bookshelves line the walls stacked with old leather-bound books.

"Sit," he says, motioning to the chair positioned in front of his desk.

Still looking around, I slowly walk over to the desk and sit in silence. The last time I spoke with the commander, it didn't end well.

"I hear you're skipping your training sessions," he says, his voice dispassionate as per usual. "So, tell me, what are you doing instead of training?"

"I train more effectively alone," I say simply, doing my best not to appear intimidated.

He frowns. "While that may be true, you don't have the liberty of veering off from your schedule. None of my soldiers do."

"Look, I'm sorry," I say, still sour from our last encounter at the station. "Can I go now?"

"As much as I wish to end our conversation as soon as possible, I need to brief you on your next mission," he says.

"A new mission? I thought I was in trouble."

"You are," he says, his voice tight. "But this isn't elementary school—I'm not going to keep you here in my office all day until your parents come to pick you up."

If it wasn't for his unamused expression, I would have laughed.

"This time," he continues, "I have assigned you to a different unit, seeing as though you're avoiding your current one."

He hands me a folder with the contents of the mission. "Tonight, you will follow squad leader Wryt to the Royal Palace, where the goal is to spoil the official meeting between the Emperor of the Imperial Nation and the King of Sejeran. You are to prevent them from forming a much-anticipated alliance. Khan's team will rendezvous with yours shortly after you both complete your missions."

My shock must be visible, because Commander Wang suddenly stops speaking.

"M-My father will be there?" I say.

"Yes," Commander Wang says. "However, there will be absolutely no verbal interaction between either of the rulers and my soldiers."

A small breath of relief escapes me.

"Your mission leader will instruct you accordingly. You are dismissed," Commander Wang says.

"Understood," I say quietly, standing from my chair.

As I head for the door, I take one last glance at the commander and find him with his back turned, facing the windows overlooking the city.

My head spins as I race down the marble steps leading away from Headquarters. I'm going to see my father again. The thought is terrifying. Will he be upset by my absence, or has he already moved on? If he sees me, what will that mean for my position within the Order?

No, he can't see me.

If he does, everything will be jeopardized. If he takes me back to the palace, years will pass, my brother will be conscripted, and I'll remain powerless to stop it.

After dinner when I reach the striker, Taiana is standing outside, sharpening her blades.

"The princess is tagging along?" she says to no one in particular. "You've got to be kidding me! She'll blow our cover."

Commander Wang shrugs. "The leader has his reasons. Where's Wryt?"

She frowns but doesn't argue further. "He's fallen ill," she says simply. "They have assigned me to take over as head of this mission. Besides, no one's skills are as sharp as mine when it comes to missions like these."

"Your team should leave immediately," he says in response. "The sun sets in five hours. It's crucial you arrive before then."

"I know, I know," she says, then pauses.

"Good luck," he says to us.

"Princess, let's go," Taiana shouts, taking my elbow and pulling me into the ship.

"Ow, let go," I protest.

"You shouldn't even be here," she growls. "The leader must have finally lost his mind. Maybe I'll just leave you with your father. It'll save me some trouble on the way home."

"What's your issue with me?" I say. "You're the one who agreed to bring me here in the first place."

"I realize now it was a grave mistake," she says.

I let out a breath. It's going to be a long flight.

"Wear this," Taiana says to me as we reach the royal lands. "You can change in the back."

I take the bag she hands me and do as she says. After stepping into the formal black dress, I place a mask over my face, which covers my eyes and nose. Last, I tie my hair into a tight bun.

"Good," Taiana says, having changed into her own rose-colored gown. She turns to address the squad. "The princess and I will directly infiltrate the party and report back our findings. As we've discussed, there are four exits in the main ballroom. You two will take the one on the left wing when I give you the go-ahead." Her fingers run across the blueprints of the palace, and I decide not to think about how she got them.

"What are we waiting for?" I ask. "How do we know when to give the signal?"

"I'll be the one giving the signal," she says. "You just need to worry about evading suspicion. Namely, you're to act as the lookout."

I nod, but I'm not thrilled being kept in the dark.

"Okay, here's how it's going to go," she says impatiently, reaching into her pocket. "Our target for tonight is the King's royal advisor. I will pour the contents of this vial into his drink, and it will make him want to vomit. When he gets up to leave for the washroom, that's when I will signal them to enter."

"Why are we targeting the advisor?" I ask.

"The King of Sejeran is one of our greatest threats," Taiana says. "Take a look around. His country is in ruins and poverty. We've had more members join us from Sejeran than any other nation because of how horrible the living conditions are. But taking out the king is too obvious and too catastrophic. His advisor is an equal threat to us, and he is the one pushing for an alliance with Imperia.

"We tried to get the job done a few months ago, but we were unsuccessful," Taiana continues.

I remember the ambush on the king that prevented him from attending my father's ball. That must have been the Order's doing.

"This time, we have a plan," she says. "We will not fail again."

"Can't we negotiate?" I ask. "Does someone really have to die tonight?"

"Do you think we haven't tried that?" Taiana says, crossing her arms. "Nothing we say will work, and if Sejeran becomes allies with Imperia, we'll have an even bigger issue on hand."

I tense but say nothing.

"Alright, land here," Taiana says.

We're still a few miles from the grand palace of the king, but a sleek black car is waiting for us.

I stare out the window, taking in the town before me. Mothers and children lay outside their humble homes, bathing in buckets of rainwater or cooking food over a small flame. Men desperately try to sell any goods they might own, while others openly resort to theft.

"Don't you see?" Taiana says. "These are the faces of the people we are helping. These are the faces of people who have been kicked to the curb by their king."

The car stops outside of the enormous palace. A grand fountain comes into view, and massive archways and onion bulb tops decorate the palace. Copper and gold designs decorate the walls, shining like a king's crown. Two tall palm trees sit on opposite sides of the main archway and two guards stand in long tunics with bayonets strung across their backs.

"Good evening," Taiana says politely as she presents our invitation. It's forged, of course, but the guards don't notice.

They nod. "Enjoy your night."

I suck in a breath as I walk past them, avoiding eye contact. We walk down a long,

open-air corridor until we reach the main ballroom. The venue is beautiful, with cream-colored tapestries hanging from the ceiling and vivid, lush desert plants spread across the floor.

"Lie low for now," Taiana says to me, brushing a strand of hair out of her face. "And remember: you are not to make contact with your father or anyone else while we're there."

"I know."

"Good," she says. "See the clock? Once it reaches eight, I should have completed my part. When you hear the chimes, come find me. I'll be standing by the east exit. Do not be late."

"Got it," I say, scanning the crowded ballroom with a pit growing in my stomach.

My father is here, I think to myself. *What would I even say to him now?*

I sigh and make my way to the back wall, hiding behind the crowd. And then I see him.

He sits atop a makeshift throne next to the King of Sejeran, a frown on his face appearing to be set in stone.

My heart sinks. Images flash through my mind. I hear his fist pounding on the door. I see the fire in his eyes, and I remember the fear he instilled in me.

Then a hand taps my shoulder, and I jump.

Chapter 20

"*Iris,*" *a familiar voice says.* "Is it really you? Everyone's been searching for you."

I turn to find Jess, a look of relief plastered on her face. She wears an elegant gown of emerald green and pale yellow, the colors of her nation.

"Jess!" I exclaim, but then hush my voice. "How did you know it was me?" A new fear clutches my chest. If Jess recognized me this easily, there's no telling who else could see right through my mask.

"Uh, because you're my friend?" she says, still smiling. "Did you come to visit me?"

"You can't let anyone know I'm here," I say.

"What? Why not?" she asks. "Your father's here. I'm sure he'd be glad to know that you're alive."

I shake my head apologetically. "It's complicated. *Really* complicated."

She bites her lip. Taking my hand, she brings us over to a small table in the corner of the room. "I've got time," she says.

I search her face, wondering if it's worth the risk of telling her everything. But the only thing I think of is that I'm here to murder her father's royal advisor.

Jess takes my hand gently. "Iris," she says softly. "Whatever you're going through, I'll listen, I'll understand. We're in this together, remember?"

"Jess," I force out. "What I tell you could put you in danger. Like... a lot of danger."

"Help me understand," she says. "You're safe here. Whatever or whoever is forcing you to stay silent won't hurt you here." She motions to the palace guards stationed at each exit.

You don't know how wrong you are, I want to say.

"Come with me," I say quietly, taking her hand as I stand up from the table. "I can't tell you here."

"Where are we going?" she whispers, as I navigate us through the crowd.

"We need to go somewhere private," I tell her.

She thinks for a moment. "Alright, then let's go to my room. It's in the South wing, far from the ballroom. There should be hardly anyone around."

"That's perfect," I say, and allow her to lead the way.

We walk up the staircase and down multiple corridors until we reach Jess' room.

"Welcome to my humble abode," she says, falling onto the bed. She kicks off her shoes and lets out a small sigh of relief. "You won't believe how uncomfortable those are."

I sit down on the lounge across from her bed and take a deep breath, examining the intricate patterns of the rug below my feet. She quickly shoves a few parchment scrolls into a drawer.

"Are those poems?" I ask, noticing the structure of the sonnets.

She nods. "Yes," she says. "But they aren't any good. It's just something I like to do in my free time."

"May I read one?"

"Maybe later," she says. "First, I want to know why you ran away."

I look down at my hands, still debating whether I should tell her.

"I couldn't stand by while my brother fell victim to the war my father is hell bent on starting," I say.

Without waiting for her to even respond, I tell her everything. Well, almost everything. There are bits and pieces I leave out, including whatever ties my mother may have with the Order and, of course, I leave out the fact we're here as assassins.

"You're serious?" she says. "You've joined a group of rogues?"

"It's not as bad as you make it sound," I say, although I'm not entirely sure if I believe myself. "They have good ideals. They save people from terrible situations, many have come from Sejeran."

Jess goes silent for a moment, fidgeting with her golden bracelets. "They're right to leave," she says. "I know I told you a little at the ball, but things are getting even worse. My mother has tried to convince my father to implement new policies, but he and his court are convinced nothing is wrong."

"I wish there was something we could do to change his mind," I say.

She sighs. "He's unbearable these days," she says. "No one can speak to him, this is the first time he's appeared in public since the ambush. But nevermind that, what are *you* doing here, Iris?"

"I can't say," I tell her, looking away. "I'm so sorry, Jess. I wish I could stop it." That part is true. I wish I had even a little bit of sway over Taiana and the others so I could convince them to think of something else, but I don't.

"Stop *what*?" she presses.

I shake my head. "It will be okay, I promise," I say. "Please, trust me on this." I don't deserve her trust or her kindness.

Jess looks like she's about to argue, but she nods slowly. "Okay, Iris," she says. "I trust you."

I offer her a small smile, and my fingers trail across a golden embroidered paper sitting on her table. Carefully written calligraphy decorates the satin pages.

"Oh, more of my poems," she says, following my gaze. "They're a nice escape from all of this." Jess stands and takes the poems in her hand and delicately sets them on her bookshelf.

"I'm sure they're lovely," I offer, trying to lighten the atmosphere.

"And just to confirm," Jess says, still visibly bothered. "You're looking for information on a mythical power that makes a person invincible?"

"More or less," I say. "I know it sounds crazy."

Jess purses her lips. "Why are you looking for it?"

"I was almost killed because of it," I reply, thinking back to the desert. "I need to know what it is."

Her eyes flash with concern. "Well," she says pensively. "If there's a book or a scroll that would have information on it, we would have it in Sejeran."

I lift an eyebrow. "Really? Even though it's from Imperia?"

She nods. "Yes. My family has access to one of the oldest libraries in all the nations, with ancient texts from all five nations. It's restricted, of course, and it's far out in the desert. But I know where to find it."

"I can't ask you to do that," I say, leaning forward.

"Iris," she says, "If people are trying to kill you because of this, the least I can do is help you figure out why. I know it will be dangerous, but I'm willing to help. As a fellow princess... and as your friend."

My heart aches. I hate how kind she's being.

But I also know she's going to go whether I want her to or not.

"Alright," I say. "But let me come with you."

"You can't," she says. "Your ship leaves tonight, doesn't it? The journey to the library will be at least three days. And besides, only members of the royal line have access to it. I'll need to do it alone."

"Jess, that's crazy," I argue. "Three days alone in the desert is dangerous enough as it is. If any of these...*people* find out that you know about the Marrow, they'll kill you, too."

She smiles. "Then I won't let them find out."

"Your stubbornness is admirable," I say, smiling. "But seriously, be careful. And if anything seems off–drop it, okay?"

"You have my word," she says.

The clock chimes, and I leap up from the bedside. "I have to go," I say. "Tell me you'll be careful. And please, don't tell anyone about this. I don't want them coming after you."

"I won't," she assures me. "I'll be fine. Is there any way for me to get in contact with you?"

I think for a moment. I can't risk her writing to Dravkia, nor to the Imperial palace. That leaves one place, one ally that I can trust. I scribble down an address on a scrap piece of paper and hand it to her.

With that, I give her a brief hug and we say our goodbyes.

"Don't get yourself killed," she calls after me as I race down the stairs.

Taiana is already waiting for me at the east exit and when she sees me, her arms crossed over her chest. "Is this your idea of 'on time'?" she snaps.

"Sorry," I say, following her through the door, ducking to avoid the stares of the guards. "I had to use the lady's room."

When we're far enough from the doors, she turns to me. "I didn't realize you were so well acquainted with the princess."

I pause.

"I'm an assassin," she says sharply as we made our way back to the car. "Therefore, I'm well versed in the art of human behavior. I knew you'd leave the ballroom with her before even you did."

"She's an old friend," I say, trying to play it cool. "We were just catching up."

Taiana narrows her eyes, leaning against the car door. "What exactly did you say to the princess?"

"I didn't tell her anything about the operation, if that's what you're asking," I say, guilt tugging at me. "We're just two princesses catching up on the affairs of our nations."

"You know how much we detest royalty," she says. "Especially the Sejeran family."

"Jess isn't like her father," I say.

Taiana doesn't look one bit convinced. The two other members of our team appear, rushing out of the palace and nearly slamming into the car.

"Let's go!" they shout.

The driver peels out of the palace driveway, and we speed through the front gates, kicking up dust and sand in our wake.

I twist around to look for a sign of pursuers, but no one follows.

"Another success," one of the men says, smiling. "I've got to hand it to you, Taiana. That plan was brilliant. And hilarious."

Her head turns at the sound of her name, and I watch as she wrinkles her nose. "Stop acting so informally," she says.

The man scoffs. "My bad, sis," he says, smirking. "I'll remember that for next time."

"You're unbearable," she says. "If I really wanted to, I could drop you off on the side of the road right here and you could walk back to Dravkia."

Her brother laughs.

"Anyway," his companion voices, breaking the silence, "the running story is that the king's advisor choked on an ibis bone during the celebratory feast. We staged it well, so I'm sure the physicians will agree with our assessment."

"Well done," Taiana says, gazing out of the window. "Varys will be pleased."

I let out a breath as we enter the swamps.

I clench my jaw. I should never have told Jess about the Order. I should never have let her help me.

If she gets hurt because of me, I'll never be able to forgive myself.

Chapter 21

We rendezvous with Naveen and his team halfway back to Dravkia. As soon as we enter the swamps, a black striker sits waiting for us.

Despite my best efforts to move to the far back of the vessel and sit alone, Naveen snags the empty space next to me.

"You can't avoid us forever," Naveen says, offering me a smile.

I sigh, but I know he's right. "Sorry," I say. "I just needed some space to figure everything out. A lot has happened."

He shrugs. "No hard feelings," he says. "We were just really worried for you. Oh, this is for you." Naveen shuffles around in his duffle bag until he pulls out a thin folder. "Don't go parading it around or anything, though."

He hands it to me, and I open it.

I have to squint my eyes to see the lettering through the darkness, but eventually I make out the name: Evelyn Wu.

I let out an audible gasp. "You found it?"

"Shhh," he says, peering at the others. "I had to pull a *lot* of strings to get this. And believe me, the commander won't be too thrilled if he finds out about it, so keep it quiet."

I nod gratefully and read through the pages.

When I finish, I wish I hadn't read it at all. Up until this point, I hadn't fully accepted the fact my mother had any relation to the Order, no matter what Simu or anyone else said.

But now, here it is.

Clear as day.

My mother, the former Empress of Imperia, was a soldier in the Order of Alabass.

She was a loyal member, it seems, until she had me. Members of the Order rarely have relationships with people outside of it, let alone children. It's just too risky. So why did she do it?

The worst part of her file is the word that follows her status: *Deceased.*

I can feel Naveen watching me closely.

"Are you alright?"

"I just don't understand," I say. "They killed her because she had a family? Did it pose too much of a risk?"

Naveen shrugs apologetically. "Your guess is as good as mine. Only in recent years has the ban on outside relationships loosened. Back then, it was forbidden and punishable by death."

A cold sweat covers my hands. "Then why would she have a family if she knew the consequences?"

"I don't know," Naveen admits. "I wish I could tell you."

My hands quiver as I hold the papers. "Take them, please," I say, handing him back the folder. "I can't look at it any longer."

"I understand," he says, tucking the folder back into his bag. "Sorry if that makes you feel worse. I thought it could help, maybe provide a little clarity."

I sigh. "Thank you. I appreciate it, really."

"I'm sure the leader knows more," Naveen offers.

I bark a laugh. "Like I'm going to talk to *him* about my personal problems," I say, shaking my head. "What does it matter, anyway? No matter what reasons she had, the ending is the same. She's dead. We know that much, so pursuing her intentions is pointless."

"I don't like seeing you this upset," Naveen says. "I didn't mean for this to happen."

"It's better I found out now, before I attempted anything stupid in order to get these files,"

I conclude. "I still can't believe you stole them from the commander."

Naveen shrugs, grinning, and we exit the ship.

As much as I want to push my mother out of my mind, she remains like an itch that I can't quite reach. She had her reasons for joining the Order and she had her reasons for breaking the rules.

I'm determined to figure out what they were.

I join the others the next morning for training on the Needle for the first time in weeks.

"Hey, Princess," Jaice calls. "Nice to see you finally showing up for practice. I'm betting you're a bit rusty. What do you say to a sparring match?"

"I've been practicing every day, I'll have you know," I reply.

Today, we work on target practice. Jaice hands me a few throwing knives and I aim them at a small white dot painted on a wooden board. The first one misses, but the following three hit the target.

"See?" I say. "I've been practicing."

Jaice smiles and throws knives of his own. They all hit their respective targets. "Knife throwing is the easy part," he says. "Let's hop in the ring and see how much your hand-to-hand has improved."

"I'll be testing that, Akerman," a voice says from across the platform.

My spirits drop and I turn toward Taiana. Her arms are crossed over her chest, and she's wearing combat clothes. It's impossible to miss the knives strapped to her ribs.

Even Naveen and Crayln break away from their sparring match, watching Taiana curiously. Alistar joins them, sheathing his throwing knives.

"Apparently, you think you can do as you please and skip training," she says, pinning me with a sharp glare. "Not to mention the way you jeopardized our mission in Sejeran."

"I told you," I say, "I didn't tell the princess *anything* about the mission."

Taiana scoffs, but she doesn't leave. "I've been assigned to ensure you show up from here on out," she says.

"She's here now, Commander," Jaice says. "I'll take it from here."

"No," Taiana says, stalking toward us. "Today she will be fighting me."

I swallow, and from the corner of my vision, I watch as soldiers clear off of the extended platform. They create a small arena, and I know who's going to be fighting in the center.

"Very well," I say, lifting my chin. "I accept."

Taiana laughs. "I wasn't asking," she says, taking her place in the center of the ring.

I move to join her, stealing a quick look at Jaice and the others.

Jaice nods slightly.

"You've got this," Crayln says. "Don't let us down. Remember, the First Regime *always* comes out on top."

Naveen smacks him lightly on the back of the head. "Don't make her nervous."

Too late, I think, but I keep walking.

"Today," Taiana calls out to the gathered audience, "will be a demonstration of two things: the finest hand-to-hand combat maneuvers and the punishment for disobedience."

I hear Raelyn and her friends laugh on the edge.

Just as I think things can't get any worse, a new figure appears on the Platform. The commander watches us with his arms folded over his chest.

This is his doing, I think. *He sent Taiana to teach me a lesson.*

I clench my teeth and I almost wish he had challenged me himself.

"Ready?" one soldier calls.

"Oh, we're ready," Taiana says, confidence written all over her smug face.

I crouch into a fighting stance, but she remains tall, awaiting my strike. I don't waste a moment, and I dart toward her, preparing to throw her off balance.

Before I can kick her legs out from under her, she seizes my throat and takes us both down to the floor. Gasping, I grab her wrist but she doesn't loosen her grip.

"Easy," she hisses in my ear.

As I fight for air, I drive my knee into her side, and her grip loosens. I twist away from her, but she lunges and tackles me again.

Her sharp nails dig into my shoulders, drawing blood. I struggle under her grip.

"You're pathetic," Taiana says. "You expect to call yourself a member of the Order, but you fight like you're still in the palace."

"I'm not pathetic," I snap.

She glances up for a moment, and I follow her eyes to where Commander Wang was standing just moments ago.

He's gone.

"Not even your commander has faith in you," she snarls.

I clench my teeth and drive my fist into her jaw. Pain flashes through my knuckles, but I leap to my feet.

Fire flares in her pale eyes and she draws one of her knives.

"Stop!" I hear Jaice yell. "That's not fair!"

She doesn't answer, and instead she slices open my cheek and I stagger back. Warm blood trickles down my cheek.

"What the..." I stammer, reaching up to my face.

"You're weak," Taiana says.

She charges again and throws a punch to my temple, knocking me to the mat. I grunt as my head collides with the ground.

I flip myself over, my face still stinging from her blade. She stomps her foot onto the small of my back and leans toward me, pressing the cool blade of her dagger to my neck.

She's going to kill me, I think, panic rising in my chest.

"I never should have brought you here," Taiana says. "You're a liability to our cause. I don't understand why leadership *insists* on keeping you around."

Past the anger in her voice, I detect a hint of jealousy. But I don't have time to think about it further. Footsteps sound around me and I hear angry shouting coming from Jaice and Naveen.

"What the hell?" Jaice says, crouching over me. "Weapons aren't allowed in the ring. You could've done much more damage than *this.*"

"Get off of her!" I hear Crayln shout.

"I do as I please," Taiana says, but she rises to her feet. "The girl was to be taught a lesson. I hope all of you understand what happens when you go against orders."

Naveen covers my cheek with a cloth. "Iris, are you okay?" he asks.

I groan, taking the cloth gratefully. "I'll be fine," I say.

"That wasn't okay," Naveen says, turning on Taiana. "You aren't *our* commander—you have no authority to do that."

She scoffs. "*Your* commander assigned me to oversee the princess' training today in any way I see fit," she retorts. "If you have an issue with it, take it up with him."

Naveen moves toward her, but I hold him back.

"It's not worth it," I say. "Besides, I kind of deserve this."

Taiana sneers before disappearing down the ladder. I let out a long breath of relief.

Naveen helps me to my feet.

"Next time," Jaice says, nodding slowly. "You'll get her next time. I'll make sure of it."

I manage a smile. "Sounds like there's a lot of training in my future."

Jaice's face is serious. "You can't be bested that easily if you wish to survive here," he says.

"I beat Raelyn last time," I say. "I'm not *that* bad."

Jaice doesn't look convinced. "If you can't stand up to Taiana, she'll walk all over you," he says. "You can't afford that."

I know he's right.

"Well," Naveen says. "I have something that might raise your spirits."

I raise an eyebrow. "Really?"

Naveen's smile returns and he nods. "Yep. Yesterday, I convinced the commander to sign a permit for us all to take the day off. We'll have to be back by twilight, though, since we're getting assigned a new mission soon."

"Another mission already?" I ask.

"I thought you'd be used to it by now," Naveen says, amused. "Things are moving quickly now. The leader has been working on a big project and it's almost time to follow through with it."

"What's it about?" Crayln asks. Naveen looks around and lowers his voice. "I can't disclose the details yet, but many of our missions have been a part of this project."

"Aw, man," Crayln complains. "What's the point of having a guy on the inside if he won't talk?"

Naveen gives him a playful swat at the head. "If the commander thinks you should know, he'll tell you."

"I think I'll sit this trip out," Alistar says, pushing up his sunglasses. "I've got some things I have to check up on today."

"Are you sure, Al?" Jaice asks. "I feel like you're never around anymore."

Alistar smiles apologetically. "I do better hidden in the shadows anyway," he says. "Besides, apparently I'm needed now more than ever. I can't take a day off."

With that, he climbs down the platform, and we watch as he disappears into the city.

"Think we'll ever really know what he does?" Crayln asks to no one in particular.

Naveen sighs. "We all have our secrets, I suppose."

With that, Naveen picks up his bag from the edge of the platform and clears his throat. "All right, we should head out soon. Iris, how's your cut?"

I remove the cloth I've been holding to my face and let him examine the cut. Naveen peers at my face, his eyes wide.

"Wow," he says. "You heal incredibly fast."

I shrug, touching the cut along my cheek. When I inspect my finger, there's only a faint trace of red blood.

"Well, looks like I'm good to go, then," I say.

Naveen nods. "Let's head out!"

Crayln, Jaice, and I follow him down the ladder and we make our way through the city. Naveen stops at the apartments to grab some supplies, and I pack a bag with a pair of spare clothes and my dagger.

On our way to the station, I run into Simu. He's just returned from Imperia.

"Simu!" I call, catching his attention.

He spins and rushes toward me, a haunted look in his eyes. Simu's eyes scan the station and he swallows.

"He knows," Simu hisses, taking my arm and pulling us into a secluded corner of the station.

"Who knows?" I demand, feeling my arms beginning to tremble. "*What* do they know?"

A series of curses flows under Simu's breath as he drops his hand.

"Varys," he says.

"Varys knows about the Marrow."

Chapter 22

"What?"

"Listen very carefully," Simu says, his voice dangerously low. "I visited the ruins of the Imperial tribes and found a journal. It wasn't in the greatest condition, but I could decipher it well enough."

I look around the station warily. Some of the other soldiers are staring. "Is it safe to discuss this here?" I ask.

As if he's seeing the crowd for the first time, Simu blinks. "No," he affirmed. "I will tell you more when I can, but just be aware that he knows. He and his family have known for a long time."

He runs an anxious hand through his hair.

"And he wants it."

"Does that mean he..." my voice catches in my throat, but Simu knows what I'm thinking. The old woman in Ancia Dera. Was she his...*mother?*

My son searches still, she had said.

"Simu," I say. "I thought the Order was supposed to be *good.* I thought they wanted peace." My heart tightens, and I realize how much of a fool I've been.

I came to the Order believing they could help me.

Now I realize they are the very thing that could put us all in danger.

"The Order isn't Varys," Simu says. "I'm sure they know nothing of this matter. It is Varys and his forefathers who are at fault for this."

"How did he do it, then?" I say. But I answer my own question. "The Elites. They answer only to him. They're the ones who attacked the palace."

"As far as I'm aware," Simu says, "you are in no immediate danger. I am Kuyang as well and so far, he has yet to come for me. But be wary, Iris."

"You can't possibly expect me to act like nothing happened," I say. "How can I go about like normal, knowing the leader is a *monster*? Everyone should know this. They would never stand with him if they did."

Simu shakes his head. "It is too dangerous," he says. "Until I gather more evidence, we can't make this public. I promise he will be brought to justice, but only when the time is right." Despite his words, I see a fire raging in his eyes. He watched his village burn to the ground, and now he knows who's at fault. I don't blame him for being angry.

I want to keep arguing, but nod instead. "Okay. I trust you."

"That is not all," he says, his voice barely audible.

"Iris!" someone shouts.

I turn to find Naveen and the others calling to me. "The train's going to leave any minute. We've gotta go."

I shoot Simu a worried glance.

"Go," he says. "Speak of this to no one."

"Tell me everything when I get back," I say, debating whether I should still attend Naveen's field trip, if it means delaying Simu's news.

"Stay in the public eye," Simu calls, before disappearing down a dark corridor. "Do not allow yourself to be alone with Varys or his son."

He leaves me in the middle of the station. Luckily, Naveen takes my arm and guides me to a seat on the train. None of them question my silence. All I can think about is the fact that Varys knows. He knows about the Blood Marrow and he *wants* it.

The more I think, the more things make sense. It's clear now that the motive behind the massacres was the Marrow. But I can't seem to figure out why they had to die. What use would they be dead?

The rumbling of the ship's engine tugs me back to reality, and my vision settles on the interior of the black vessel.

I look around at my friends, wondering if they know anything about their leader's true intentions. But I don't let myself speak. Simu told me it was too early to tell them, and I have to trust him.

"Are you kidnapping us or something, Nav?" Crayln asks, pushing up his sunglasses as the windows darken.

"Yes," Naveen says. "That's my master plan: kidnap my best friends."

Crayln scoffs at the sarcasm and then turns to me. "What did that old loon want with you?"

"He's helping me study," I say, trying to keep my voice from trembling. "The leader wants to make sure I know all the customs and regulations of the Order."

"But why him?" Crayln asks. "He's certifiably crazy."

"He's not that bad," I say.

Crayln doesn't look like he believes me, but he doesn't argue.

"Take those off, will you?" Jaice says, nodding to Crayln's dark sunglasses. "You look ridiculous. It's impossibly dark in here as it is, thanks to Nav and his secrecy."

"It will all be worth it," Naveen promises. Then he changes the subject and throws Crayln a grin. "So, Cray, what's up with you and Riona?"

The name sounds familiar, and I remember she's one of the top strategists in our regime. I've seen her during training, but I never knew Crayln had a thing for her.

Crayln grins, but color spreads across his face. "How'd you find out about that?" he asks. "Stalking me now, are we?"

"Come on," Jaice says. "We all saw it coming. And you two don't stop flirting with each other during training."

I guess I've missed a lot in the weeks I skipped out on group training.

Shrugging, Crayln says, "I supposed it can't be helped. I'm just too damn charming."

I laugh at this. "It's a wonder she's able to put up with you and your big mouth."

Crayln's eyes flash mischievously and opens his mouth to say something undoubtedly crude, but Naveen jumps up before he gets the chance.

"We're here!" he exclaims.

The ship lands, and the doors open, letting in light we have all been missing. Naveen is the first to step out.

"Ah," he says, taking a deep breath. "Here we are: the base of Mount Hikirojaro. Welcome to Roanak."

I step out of the ship and take a long look around. We're standing in front of a full-sized mountain. Although, it's still smaller than any of the mountains in the High Range Sierra. All around the base is lush green grass and vegetation, while a thick layer of fog masks the summit. There's a long stretch of lake near us and I spot glistening fish jumping through the streams. Small brown creatures with slick pelts glide through the lake on their backs and snack on the shimmering fish.

"You want to climb that?" Crayln asks, turning my attention back to the looming mountain.

Naveen nods. "Yep," he says. "I brought some special equipment. It'll allow us to travel at least five times faster than the average climber."

Crayln folds his arms. "This sounds like suicide."

I elbow him in the side. "Stop being such a downer," I say. "It looks like fun."

I'll do anything to take my mind off of Varys and what he's done, I think.

Naveen flashes us a toothy grin. "That's the spirit!" he exclaims, handing out harnesses and grappling hooks. "I used to come here all the time with the commander when we were younger. Just wait until we get to the peak!"

Along with harnesses, he hands out a small backpack to each of us. "Wear this, but don't open it. It's for when we get to the top."

We strap on the harnesses and I loop my arms through the backpack handles.

"How does this grappling hook work, exactly?" I ask.

"You shoot out the hook with the trigger here," Naveen says. "And then, you click this button and it pulls you up. It's a brilliant invention."

"Are you sure it'll hold?" Jaice asks, eyeing the hook.

Naveen nods. "I'm sure of it," he says confidently.

Jaice still doesn't look convinced, and rightfully so, but Naveen brushes past him and faces the mountain.

"Alright, let's do it. If we leave now, we can make it to the top by sunset," Naveen says gleefully. "That's when the view is best."

I watch carefully as he pulls the trigger and launches the grappling hook onto the rock ledge at least twenty feet above his head.

"See you at the top!" he shouts, joy lighting up his face.

He clicks a button, and instantly he shoots through the air. He uses his hands to grab onto the face of the mountain and his boots find small divots in the rock. We stand at the base watching him until he's so far up he disappears within the fog.

"Well, let's head after him," Jaice says, placing one foot up on the rock.

I take a deep breath and join Jaice on the face of the mountain, Crayln trailing behind. We aim our hooks and fire. They both anchor onto the rock, and I tug at the rope to make sure it's steady.

"Here goes nothing," I say, and force my finger down on the button.

My body instantly flies from the ground, and I shoot through the air. I almost smack into the face of the mountain, but I hook my hand around a chunk of rock and use my boots to stabilize myself.

Breathing heavily, I slowly turn to look down at the fields below. I'm not very high, but I've never done anything close to this in my entire life. My heart feels like it could beat out of my chest, but the adrenaline rush is too great and I continue climbing. Soon, I fall into a rhythm of shoot, hook, and fly.

The experience is exhilarating. Jaice and Crayln are at my side, and we travel as fast as we can in order to catch up to Naveen. However, he's nowhere in our line of sight and we know we have to keep pushing.

After an hour or so of climbing, my arms are exhausted, but I can't stop. Hanging off the side of the mountain isn't something I want to entertain, so I continue on until I reach a flat clearing in the mountain.

The three of us collapse the moment we reach it and lay heaving on the edge. Snow covers the cliff, and the cold sensation is refreshing.

"Wow, okay," I pant. "I've never done anything so physically demanding in my life."

The others grunt in agreement, stretching their arms.

"What a surprise!" a voice chimes. "You know, I didn't think that you three would have the strength to make it to this point."

Naveen sits on a large boulder, arms crossed and a smug look on his face.

"Not so easy, though, is it?" he asks.

Crayln scoffs and puffs his chest. "Never underestimate us."

Naveen laughs and looks out from his vantage point on the ledge. "Damn," he says, his eyes sweeping over the vast cloudscapes around us. "This view never gets old."

I follow his gaze in awe. The sun is slowly sinking behind the canopy of clouds and casts pink streaks across the sky. "It's incredible," I breathe.

Moments like this remind me of why I left the palace. I needed to be free. I can't remember the last time the mood has felt so light.

"I want to thank you all," Naveen says, turning to face us. "This day has been amazing already. It really takes me back."

Jaice walks over and pats him on the back. "Well, I'm sure the view's even nicer at the top. Race you!"

We all rush to pick up our gear and take off, scaling up the mountain as if we'd done it a thousand times. I muster as much strength as I can and pull myself up, bounding up the rocks.

I don't stop to look back until I reach the summit, only milliseconds behind Jaice and Naveen.

"I won!" Jaice bellows from the peak.

"I let you win," Naveen claims, playfully shoving him into a snowbank.

Jaice is up in moments and launches himself at Naveen with full force. The two of them tumble in the snow, soon to be covered in white powder.

"Hey, not here," I say. "We don't need anyone falling off of the mountain."

"Sorry, Mom," Naveen says, smirking.

I roll my eyes but can't help but smile.

"Wait a minute, where's Cray?" Jaice says, swiveling his neck.

We dash over to the cliff side and peer down the mountain. Through the thick clouds, I spot him at least fifty feet below us.

"Cray!" Jaice shouts. "Are you good?"

"Just give me a minute," Crayln says, his breaths labored.

Naveen looks worried. "I'll go down and get him," he says, buckling his harness. "Stay right there!"

"I'm not some damsel in distress, you idiot!" Crayln calls. "I just need to catch my breath. Not all of us are descended from mountain goats!"

Naveen ignores him and swings his legs over the cliff. I watch him, holding my breath as he slides down the snowy face and finally launches his hook to catch himself.

"Got ya," he says, hooking his own harness to Crayln's. "Alright, milady, hold on tight."

I laugh, exchanging an amused look with Jaice as we watch. Crayln is clearly debating if he should punch Naveen in the face, but eventually decides against it, remembering they're dangling hundreds of feet in the air.

Naveen takes the shot, and the grappling hook comes shooting up at me. I leap away from the ledge just in time for the two of them to come hurling over the side.

"I didn't need your help!" Crayln insists, shoving Naveen off of him.

Laughing, Naveen shakes snow from his dark curls. "Fine," he says in mock defeat. "Next time, I'll let you fall."

With wild eyes, Crayln leaps at him and they tumble through the snow, kicking and shoving.

I'm used to their skirmishes at this point. And they're a constant reminder of Rai and Kaito, the two twins who I never thought I would miss. Yet, as I see a part of them in Crayln and Naveen, a comforting feeling spreads through me.

"Are you guys done yet?" I say.

They both lay in a heaving heap in the snow, neither of them able to move. "Truce?" Naveen offers.

"It's because you don't want to injure my pretty face, isn't it?" Crayln jeers.

"Riona would probably come for me if I did, right?" Naveen says as he chucks a snowball at Crayln. It lands between his eyes, stunning him.

Jaice intervenes before Crayln can create a snowball of his own. "Nav," he says, distracting them. "Didn't you have something in mind for when we got to the top?"

"Oh, right!" Naveen says, getting up to brush the snow off of his pants. "They're in the backpacks."

My attention turns to the sack still slung across my shoulder and I open it to find a bunch of small pieces of wood and cloth.

"What are they for?" I ask him.

Smiling proudly, Naveen takes out his own pack. "Watch," he says as he gets to work assembling the pieces.

The rest of us mimic him and soon enough, we have four fully constructed hang gliders. Mine is violet with a yellow and white gradient, and I wonder if Naveen chose it to match the flower I'm named after. Cheesy, but I admire the effort.

"Oh no," Crayln began. "I don't like where this is going."

Jaice raises his eyebrows skeptically. "I hate to admit it," he says, "but I'm with Cray on this one. This looks incredibly dangerous."

I swallow and peer down the steep slope of the mountain. Suddenly, the sharp, jagged rocks and the thousands of feet separating us from the ground seem much more daunting. One wrong move, one unlucky gust of wind, and we could be blown straight into the rocks.

"It's one of the best things you'll ever do in your life," Naveen assures us, showing off his own scarlet glider.

I think about arguing, but the spark in Naveen's eyes keeps me quiet.

"Why is mine orange?" Crayln asks, wrinkling his nose.

"Don't be so ungrateful," I say lightly.

"Easy for you to say," he says, motioning to my beautifully colored glider. "Nav knows that orange is my least favorite color."

"Must've slipped my mind," Naveen says, shrugging. "You won't even see it once you're in the air."

Crayln sighs, looking defeated. His attempt at stalling the flight doesn't work. "And the Crayln torture continues," he murmurs.

Naveen walks up to the edge, confidence radiating off of him. He raises the hang glider above his head and puts his upper body through the metal rail. All I can see are the backs of his legs and the triangle shape of the red cloth.

"Follow my lead!" he calls back to us.

I hear Crayln take a deep breath, and before Naveen can take off, Crayln sprints off the side of the mountain.

Chapter 23

"*C*ray!" *Naveen shouts, gliding after him. "Where the hell do you think you're going?"*

A harsh wind gusts past us, and Naveen and Crayln disappear from view as ice and snow swirl around us.

"That idiot is going to get himself killed," Jaice says.

"We need to go after him," I say.

Jaice wastes no time and launches himself off the mountain. I draw a breath and jump after him, the numbness of my legs fading as crisp air swirls around me. The small crystalline shards in the wind scrape my face, but as I glide through the mountains, I feel like a bird diving at top speed without restraint.

The ride down is much faster than the climb up and I have much less time to think.

As I descend through the thick clouds, I see the faint green of the fields below us. Jaice is close behind me and I turn to him, gripping the metal bar as tightly as I can to avoid losing balance.

"How do we land this thing?" I cry out to him, watching as the lake draws closer and closer.

"Pull up on the bar when we get closer to the ground!" he shouts through the air. "Straighten out the glider as much as you can to slow it down."

I nod, doing my best to follow his instructions.

The ground grows closer, and I brace myself, doing just as he says. Using all the strength I have, I pull up on the metal bar and slowly adjust the glider's position. Instead of diving like a falcon, I glide horizontally through the sky like an eagle.

Relief floods through me as my glider slows. The lush fields are just a few feet away. I'm so close to them I can touch the flowers.

"When you slow down enough, you're just gonna have to jump out!" Jaice shouts. "We'll do it on three."

I look at him as if he's half crazy, but there isn't any other option. Either we ride the gliders into the ground, or we tumble out.

"Okay!" I yell back.

"One."

"Two."

I squeeze my eyes shut and then force them open. "Three!" I leap out from above the metal bar and release my grip. My body free falls for a split second before I hit the hard ground and tumble through the stalky grass. My head slams into the grass, but aside from a few bruises, I'm perfectly fine.

"That was amazing!" I shout, adrenaline still coursing through me. "Now I understand why Naveen loves it so much."

Jaice clears his throat and nods. "I think I swallowed a bug," he says distastefully.

I laugh as he spits into the grass. "Thanks," I say to him, flicking mud off of my pants. "For helping me out back there. I probably would've ended up landing face first in the dirt had you not said anything."

"It's what friends do," he says, ruffling my already messy hair. "Can't have you dying on me, Princess."

The former me would roll my eyes at the name, but I've learned to tolerate it.

"Did you see where Naveen and Crayln landed?" I ask him as I scan the fields. Our striker is the only thing I can see for miles, aside from the looming mountain ranges.

"There," Jaice says, making his way through the tall grasses to where Crayln and Naveen's gliders lay.

I follow him nervously, praying that they're alright.

In the mess of splintered wood and torn fabric, Crayln and Naveen struggle to their feet.

"You guys alright?" Jaice calls, jogging over to them. "What happened?"

Crayln supports Naveen on his shoulder and winces.

"We're fine," Naveen says, but the agony on his face tells a different story.

His pants are covered in dirt and ripped at the knees. Blood drips from his knee.

"Nav, you're bleeding," Jaice says.

"Damn, I think it's broken," Naveen says as he tests his weight on it. Instantly, he falls back on Crayln's shoulder. "Okay, I'm not going to lie. It hurts like hell."

"This is my fault," Crayln says. "I'm really sorry, man."

Jaice takes over for Crayln and supports Naveen as he pulls him away from the wreckage.

"What do we do?" I ask. "We should get him medical attention as soon as possible."

"I'll be fine," Naveen says. "Really, it's alright. I don't want to dampen the mood."

Jaice rolls his eyes. "Don't worry about dampening the mood, idiot," he says. "Worry about how we're going to fix that leg of yours."

Naveen sighs. "There's a village just south of the river," he says. "I've been there a few times in the past."

"Then that's where we'll go," I say, leading the way back through the field.

The striker sits at the base of the mountain, and the four of us climb in.

"So, who's going to fly the ship?" I ask, looking around.

Jaice sets Naveen down in the back, and I know he's doing his best to conceal the pain.

"Well, Nav can't, that's for sure," Crayln says. "And I don't know how to, so it's

probably not a good idea."

"Jaice?" I ask.

He looks skeptically at the cockpit and frowns. "I'm more of a feet-on-the-ground type of guy," he says.

"Do you seriously trust me flying this thing?" I ask.

Naveen laughs. "Looks like it's up to you, Iris," he says. "I'll help from back here."

Jaice takes the co-pilot seat before I can protest, and Crayln remains in the back with

Naveen.

Great.

"Alright, fine," I say. "But I'll need help."

Naveen instructs me on how to start the engine, and to my relief, the metal beast roars to life.

"Good," Naveen says, before delivering his next set of instructions.

The striker rolls forward at my command and picks up more and more speed. We race through the grassy fields and I pull up on the handles. The ship lifts into the air and I feel the thud of the wheels clicking back into place underneath the body.

"We need to go higher," Jaice says, peering out the window and gripping onto the seat.

"On it," I say through gritted teeth, using all of my strength to pull on the lever. The daunting mountains lay before us, and I know that if I don't get us high enough, we'll run directly into their rocky faces.

"You see the mountains, right?" Jaice says, panic seeping into his voice. "Pull up!"

"I am!" I roar over the barking engine. "It's not working!"

"Oh gods, you're going to kill us," I hear Crayln say.

Together, Jaice and I grip the handlebars and just before the nose of the place can crash into the mountain, we fly over the summit.

I let out a breath of relief.

"That was close," I say.

Jaice's eyes are still wide, but he nods. "Too close."

"I think I just lost ten years of my life," Crayln says.

"See the river below?" Naveen says. "Just keep following it south and you'll see the town on your left."

I veer the ship down closer to the water and glide along the river.

"Um, Nav?" I call over my shoulder. "How do I land this thing?"

Naveen grunts as he tries to push himself up enough to peer out of the windows. He thinks for a moment and then delivers new instructions.

I do as he says, and once the town is in close range, I slowly pull the lever toward me. We descend toward the grassy plains, and I hold my breath as I engage the wheels.

The landing is bumpy and, for a moment, I think the ship will tumble over, but luckily it remains upright. I pull down on the brake as we approach the outskirts of the town until we come to a complete stop. My heart is still pounding by the time we climb out of the ship, but I can't help but feel a small tingle of triumph.

Jaice hauls Naveen over his shoulder, despite his protests, and we walk toward the village.

My hope dies a little as I take in the town for what it is. It's old, and many of the homes are falling apart. There is one dirt road running the length of the town, and horse-drawn carriages pass us as we walk. Compared to Dravkia, or even Imperia, the town feels eons behind in industrialization.

I approach a woman standing outside of a small tavern and ask for help.

"We don't have any professionals here," the woman says apologetically. "But the town medic is just down that row of houses. The last one on the left."

I give her my gratitude and we rush Naveen to the door of the medic's house. Before my knuckles hit the charred wood, the door swings open.

"What do you want?" a tall, bearded man asks, accusation heavy in his voice.

Taken aback, I jump, but clear my throat. "It's our friend," I say. "He needs medical assistance. Can you please help us?"

The medic takes a long look at us, and then his eyes fall on Naveen.

"Come in," he says gruffly, turning into his house.

I hesitate but know this is the closest we can get to helping Naveen.

"Lay him here," the medic says, gesturing to a small space on the floor.

"There isn't an infirmary around here, is there?" Jaice asks hopefully as he lays Naveen down.

Looking slightly offended, the medic frowns. "If there was, you wouldn't be here, now would you?"

Jaice clamps his mouth shut and all we can do is sit and watch as the medic tends to our friend.

"He'll take a while to recover," the medic observes, as he dresses Naveen's external wounds. "For the time being, you three can remain here, as long as you don't pose too much of a bother to me."

"Thank you," Jaice says.

I can't push the feeling of apprehension rising in my stomach. *You're doing this for Naveen,* I remind myself.

We gather against the wall of the cabin and silence settles in the room. Naveen gives in to sleep, and the medic cleans his wounds and wraps a cloth around his leg.

I exchange a look with Jaice. We both know this isn't going to be enough.

"We need to get back to Dravkia," Jaice says, keeping his voice low. "The doctors there are much more qualified to treat Naveen."

"Is there any way we can get word to them?" I ask.

Jaice shakes his head. "If there was, I would have called them by now," he says. "This town has no radio towers or phones of any kind. A letter will take weeks at the least."

I think for a moment.

"What about the radio on the striker?"

Rubbing his neck, Jaice considers this. "I didn't think of that," he says. "It's worth a shot. But even that may not reach the city."

"Well, come on," I say. "We have to try."

"I'll keep watch over Nav," Crayln says. "Tell me if you reach them."

I nod and Jaice and I head out of the cabin and walk back to the field harboring our ship.

I hop into the cockpit and search for the intercom. Once I find it, I take the small microphone in my hand, turn it on, and wait for a response.

All I can hear is static.

"Told you," Jaice says, shaking his head.

"Wait a moment," I say, turning up the volume dial as far as it can go.

After a long moment, we hear the murmur of a voice. It sounds far away, muffled by the static, but it's still there.

"Hello?" I say into the microphone. "Hello, can you hear me?"

"Where the hell have you been?"

Despite the muffled sound, I make out the cold voice of Taiana.

"I order your squad to return to the city immediately. The leader is furious."

Jaice reaches for the microphone, and I pass it to him.

"Commander Perovka," he says clearly. "One of our own has been gravely injured and we're afraid that flying him back without medical support will be dangerous. Is there a patrol that can meet us here?"

There's a pause, and I worry we've lost the signal.

"The patrol will be at your location in four hours," she finally says. "Stay where you are."

"You're taking the Iron Wing?" Jaice says.

"It only makes sense," she says. "Another team is meeting me in Roanak for a mission, anyway."

"Thank you, thank you so much," Jaice says, but this time, the radio cuts out.

"Thank the gods she's in Roanak," I say. "I doubt the signal would have reached Dravkia."

Jaice nods, and relief crosses his face.

"What's the Iron Wing?" I ask him.

"It's the largest and fastest airship we have in our arsenal," Jaice answers. "It makes traveling long distances much easier, but it also eliminates the element of surprise."

"Good," I say. "It'll be easy to spot them, then."

I let out a long breath and jump down from the ship. Jaice and I walk over to the small stream just outside of the village and I find a large rock to sit on. He joins me and together we keep our gazes fixed on the horizon, waiting.

For a while, nothing fills the sky but wispy clouds and the occasional screeching hawk. As the hours pass, we grow more impatient.

Jaice stands and paces up and down the small bank. "They should be here by now."

"Give it time," I say, tossing a small stone into the stream.

It lands with a splash, and I look up just in time to see an airship in the distance.

As the massive ship emerges through the dense clouds, we jump up in anticipation. Wind rips through my hair as the ship makes its descent into the field in front of us and heat radiates from its core.

"They're here!"

A woman I've never seen before steps out, her red hair pulled back into a tight bun. Following her is another woman in a long doctor's coat, along with a few nurses. I recognize the doctor from my first day in Dravkia.

Jaice and I rush over to them. "Thank you for coming," I say. "He's right this way."

I turn to lead them to the medic's house, but a deep voice stops me in my tracks and makes the hair on my neck prickle.

"Stop right where you are, soldier."

Chapter 24

"*You are needed elsewhere,*" *Commander Wang says.* "I am certain Akerman can take it from here."

Everything tells me not to listen.

Do not allow yourself to be alone with Varys or his son, Simu had warned me.

Jaice and I exchange worried glances, but I have no choice.

"I'll see you back in the city," Jaice says to me. "Watch your back. If both commanders are going, that means this is serious. This mission will not be like the ones you've gone on before."

I watch as Jaice leads the group of medics into the town, leaving me alone with the commander.

"Get in," he says motioning to the Iron Wing.

I do as he says, my entire body tense. I become even more aware of the dagger strapped to my leg, prepared to use it if I have to.

"We're meeting the others in the Mangra," he says, although he doesn't look at me.

I have to stop myself from raising an eyebrow in confusion. The Mangra is the largest rainforest on the entire continent. What business can we possibly have there?

I hardly have time to adjust my seat belt before we're off the ground, shooting through the air at an ungodly speed. In a matter of seconds, the town is a speck of dust, and then it's completely out of sight.

"How fast is this thing?" I ask, forgetting that the man piloting the ship is my commander, who hates my very existence.

"Fast enough to get us to the Mangra by nightfall," he replies.

Desperate to avoid falling into an awkward silence, I ask, "Why are we going to the rainforest?"

"You ask a lot of questions," he comments, half to himself.

"I think I have a right to know," I snap, then instantly wish I hadn't. "Sorry. It's been a long day."

"We have a mission there, not really much of a surprise," he says. "The rainforest just happens to be a meeting place between us and some important suppliers."

"Suppliers of what?"

"Information," he says simply. "The leader has a special project that requires it." His voice is steady, and he chooses his words very carefully so as to not say anything that could give the project away.

This must be the project that Naveen spoke of, I think.

I avert my eyes to stop myself from staring at his sharp jawline and strong features. His voice alone is enough to make my heart rate increase.

He's the leader' son, I remind myself. *The leader who knows about the Marrow and could be plotting my death. Simu doesn't trust him, neither should I.*

I rest my head against the seat and look out of my window. We're high above the clouds and they pass at astounding speed. As darkness envelops the sky, I see the faint green vegetation of the rainforest. We fly closer to the canopy and in every direction, the forest touches the horizon and beyond. It's enormous and so full of life.

Commander Wang slows the ship just above the canopy and steps out of his seat. He presses a button, and the door of the Iron Wing slides open.

I realize with dread that he expects us to jump.

"Are you serious?" I say, stepping away from the opening door. "I'll break my legs in the canopy."

"You'll be fine," he says, fixing me with a hard glare. "The others are already here and waiting."

"I can hardly see the branches," I say. "How do I know where to jump?"

The commander seems to fight the urge to roll his eyes. "You'll know."

I purse my lips but refuse to let him see my fear. "Okay. But you first."

He scoffs at my tone, but shrugs. "Fine, but you better jump after me, or else I'll have no choice but to climb back up and drag you out."

"Deal."

Without wasting another moment, he jumps. I peer over the side of the ship to watch him land in the branches and skillfully lower himself down to the forest floor.

Not wanting him to think I backed out, I jump. My body crashes through the canopy and leaves obstruct my vision. Knots of tree trunks and branches slam into my arms and my back, causing the trees to shake and the birds to take flight.

I fully prepare myself to hit the solid floor of the forest as I collide with tree branches and tumble through leaves, but the final drop never happens.

Strong arms wrap around me and we land on a nearby tree branch, wide enough for him to set me down.

I look up to see the face of Commander Wang above me. His usual stone-faced expression is gone.

His eyes search me for injuries and my body throbs with pain, but thankfully, it's not broken. After regaining my senses, I sit up quickly, embarrassed.

"I don't know what happened," I say, dusting myself off.

He shakes his head dismissively. "It's my fault," he says, picking out a large jungle leaf from my hair. "I should have prepared you better for the jump. Are you hurt?"

"I'm fine," I say, balling my fists to conceal the shaking of my hands.

"Good," he says. "Come on." He stands and offers me a strong, gloved hand.

I take it carefully.

"The others aren't far," he says, checking the radar on his watch.

I follow him down the tree, stepping in the same crevices he does in order to prevent myself from slipping.

Lush vegetation surrounds us and bright coral-colored flowers decorate the ground. The chirping of tropical birds echoes in the canopy and above us, small monkeys scramble through the tree branches.

"Careful," Commander Wang says, his arm guiding me away from the plants.

My muscles tense at the touch of his hand on my shoulder, but I allow him to guide me through the forest.

"Those are poisonous," he says quickly, removing his arm. "Don't get too close."

I eye the shimmery red plants reaching out their claw-like thorns. I hear them hissing inside of my mind, intimidating me with their appearance alone.

We come to a small clearing in the forest and three other men and women wait in a small circle.

They turn at the sound of our footsteps and straighten. "Commander Wang," they greet, unrivaled loyalty shining in their eyes.

He nods to them. "Have you scouted the area?"

A woman steps forward from the group, and I recognize Taiana instantly.

"Of course," she says. "Don't doubt my soldiers, Wang."

I watch as he clenches his jaw, but he moves on. "Then let's head out."

Taiana's eyes rest on me and she smiles cruelly. "You just keep popping up, don't you? Sort of like a weed."

"Nice to see you, too," I say.

"Varys wants her back in the city," she says, looking at Commander Wang.

I gulp at the sound of that.

Commander Wang shrugs as he begins carving a path through the forest. "She's a part of my regime and I needed another soldier for this mission. He can wait."

"I don't understand why you chose *her* for this," Taiana says, falling in stride with Commander Wang. "Even that idiot Khan is more competent."

A shadow crosses Commander Wang's face at the sound of Naveen's name, sending chills through me. "He was not available," he says tightly. "She's here now, and we need to move."

I stray a few paces behind with the other soldiers, trying not to be bothered by the way Taiana speaks of me.

Taiana smiles. "I didn't mean to come off so harsh," she says to the commander, in a voice very unlike her usual self. "You know how hard it's been lately. Tensions are so high, with the political climate in Imperia and Trasylar. Not to mention the stress of the leader' *project.*"

Commander Wang continues walking, slashing the leafy palms as if they're made of rice paper.

"Lighten up," Taiana says. "Perhaps you should go out with us sometime. The bar on 17th is nice, you'd like it. Besides, you haven't stopped working since we graduated training."

It's odd, watching Taiana act like the teenager she is. She likes him, and for some reason, the thought makes my stomach churn. It's not jealousy, I tell myself. It's more like I can't imagine a woman as ruthless as her having a crush on anyone.

Commander Wang frowns at her. I often forget that he, too, is just barely eighteen.

"Even entertaining the idea of going out to party when there is so much going on is foolish," Commander Wang says, moving his arm out of Taiana's grip.

She doesn't seem to notice, and keeps a stupid grin plastered on her face. "Just once," she says. "It'll be fun. Just like old times."

"Fun is not a luxury I can afford. Neither can you," he snaps, failing to conceal his irritation. Before Taiana can speak, he stops. "Quiet."

The entire party stops in their tracks. I strain my ears but hear nothing but the sounds of animals and the swaying of leaves.

"Get down!" Commander Wang roars, drawing his swords.

Taiana stands, her dagger in hand. Slowly, the rest of us follow suit.

An arrow shoots through the air, its tip burrowing deep into the tree trunk above my head.

We're under attack.

Chapter 25

"**A**mbush," *Taiana curses.*

Before anyone can reply, at least ten men appear in the trees, armed with crossbows. They wear dark red cloth over their faces and ropes uncoil from high in the canopy.

Commander Wang scales a tree with astounding agility and doesn't waste a moment. He palms a few throwing knives and makes his way toward the attackers.

"What business do you have here?" he demands.

None of the newcomers make an effort to reply. Instead, they draw their weapons and lunge.

"Wang, take the left, I'll cover the right," Taiana shouts before disappearing through a thick wall of green leaves. More shouts arise and all I hear is the clashing of blades.

We're surrounded.

I realize I'm unarmed and dart over to one of the fallen men. Taking the crossbow in my hand, I rest a finger on the cool trigger and aim at the canopy above.

An arrow flies past my head and nicks my ear, causing me to suck in a sharp breath. Warm blood trickles down my cheek, and a familiar tingling sensation spreads from the tip of my ear to my cheek. I grunt but shove the pain aside and take aim. I pull the trigger and the stone-headed arrow shoots through the air. It hits one of my attackers in the shoulder. The force is enough to throw him off balance, and he tumbles down through the trees.

He scrambles to his feet, and I watch him retreat into the thick jungle.

Between the screams and clashing of steel, I can hardly think straight. Blood litters the forest floor and soon enough, more and more attackers retreat. Next to me, one of our own collapses, blood trickling out of the corner of his mouth.

I catch sight of an approaching figure in the corner of my eye. Whipping around, I come face to face with one of the masked attackers and the head of his arrow points directly at my nose.

"Surrender yourself," the man growls, his index finger ready to squeeze the trigger.

My breath is ragged and I can't find the strength to move.

"Commander!" someone cries out.

My head snaps to the center of the clearing where another man from our party lies on the ground. He's in a similar position as me, with an arrow pointing at his heart.

"Help me!" he shouts. "Please."

Commander Wang's eyes flicker between his comrade and me. He holds a throwing knife in his hand.

The tension between us is tight, and I know he only has time to save one of us. I squeeze my eyes shut, waiting for the cold metal to strike through the front of my skull.

A heartbeat passes and nothing stirs.

Metal slices through, and air and the commander's knife hits its target.

I wince, half believing that an arrow is stuck in my skull and I just can't process the pain, but my attacker slumps to the ground. His knees buckle and he lays dormant, a silver blade protruding from his chest.

Shuffling away, I wince as I spot the other man from our party. His attacker releases the arrow, hitting him in the stomach.

"No!" the commander shouts, palming another knife.

But it's too late.

A rush of guilt overcomes me as I stand and wipe blood from my face. The only reason I'm still standing is because my comrade is dead.

The commander was forced to choose, I think. *And for some unknown reason, he chose* me.

Taiana appears through the leaves moments later, sprayed with blood, but seemingly unharmed. She's breathing heavily, her eyes wide as she scans the battlefield.

"They're dead," she whispers, ghostly pale. "They're all dead." I don't have to ask to know that she's referring to her soldiers.

Commander Wang's eyes are dark and his face is a mask of shadows. He mutters something I don't catch and bends down to retrieve his knives.

"Wang, we have to move," Taiana says, urgency in her voice. "One of them called for help before I could get to him. They're close."

"Let them come," he says. "I want answers."

A shiver passes through me at the murderous tone of his voice. It's full of a deadly fire, and I'm not sure I want to bear witness to its wrath.

Taiana steps closer with purpose, confidently raising her chin. "We need to meet the suppliers at the river port. If we're late, we'll lose everything."

"Then go," Commander Wang says. "I'll meet you back in the city. I'm not finished here."

"You," Taiana directs at me, anger boiling behind her icy blue eyes. "Stay here and stay low. Make sure he doesn't do anything stupid. I can handle the suppliers on my own."

I nod. I won't give Commander Wang any reason to think he made the wrong choice in sparing my life.

Taiana takes one last worried look at the commander before pushing her way through the foliage. Her blond hair soon disappears, and I wait for the rest of the attackers.

"Killing them won't bring back your comrades," I say softly.

Commander Wang doesn't turn his head, focusing only on retrieving his knives. "When they hit one of us, they hit all of us," he says. "I won't let them get away with this."

My gaze sweeps across the forest and I walk over to one of the fallen men and pick up a dagger from the floor.

"What are you doing?"

"You don't expect me to fight unarmed, do you?" I say.

"No," he says. "I don't expect you to fight at all. Climb up in the canopy so they won't see you. And keep quiet."

He reaches out to take the dagger, but I hold it away from him. "You're not going to fight them alone," I say, although I'm confident he could. "We don't know how many of them there are."

His eyes are hard as diamonds, and any bit of his previous courtesy has dissolved. "Exactly. They will certainly outnumber us, and I can't fight them *and* protect you at the same time. You've only been training for a few weeks. Stay hidden."

"Then why am I here?" I demand.

He fixes me with a stern look before turning away.

Frustrated, I roll my eyes. "Like hell I will," I say. "I'll go up in the canopy, but I'm not staying silent. And I don't need you to protect me. I'm perfectly capable of doing that on my own."

He scoffs.

"You're ridiculous," is all he says, but he doesn't argue further.

The rustle of leaves sounds, and I shoot up the tree. The dagger sits tucked away in my back pocket, and I hoist myself up slowly, branch by branch.

I watch as Commander Wang draws the two swords strapped to his back and leans against the trunk of a giant rainforest palm. He looks even more menacing in the way his gloved hands grip the hilts of his swords.

Before I see them, I hear the release of arrows. Six.

Commander Wang wastes no time and aims his knives into the canopy. At first, I assume he's throwing blindly, but each knife reaches its target.

I grab for my weapon, but a strong hand clamps around my wrist before I can grab it. The figure shifts and then his mouth is hovering next to my ear.

"Thought you could hide?" he hisses.

I try to call out, but his gloved hand stretches over my mouth and muffles my voice. My eyes dart around, looking for anything that can give me the upper hand.

Determined to fight, I use all of my strength to force him forward, and he somersaults over my head, crashing to the ground. A small bit of satisfaction washes over me.

Unfortunately, his fallen body alerts the others around me and another drops onto my branch. This time, it's a woman with light hair and the same dark mask covering her face.

"She's up here!" she yells to the others.

I curse. Pulling out my dagger, I drive it into the flesh of her leg.

She shrieks in pain and aims her crossbow at my chest. Luckily, my training with Jaice has quickened my reflexes, and I duck just as the arrow splinters the bark inches above my head. There's no time to catch my breath, so I push myself up and kick her off of the branch.

Her body falls to the ground and lands with a devastating *thud*.

We can't lose, I think.

I resort to the close combat moves Jaice has drilled into me. I use my speed against them and throw my attackers off balance. For those with more stable footing, it's a game of strength and endurance.

A woman lands a forceful punch to my jaw, but I recover quickly and leap at her, throwing her out of the tree. An arrow passes by me and shreds the skin on my shoulder, causing me to yelp in pain. This time, blood pours angrily out of the wound.

I draw my weapon, but my attacker easily kicks it out of my hand. I'm done for. He loads another arrow into his crossbow and lines it up.

No matter how forcefully I tell myself to move, to dodge, to duck, I can't. I'm stuck, slumped against the tree trunk waiting to be shot.

Wincing, I watch as the man's finger squeezes the trigger. Before the arrow has a chance to release, he's kicked to the side and his arrow shoots harmlessly into the canopy.

My eyes flutter upwards, expecting to see the dark figure of Commander Wang. Instead, I see a masked man crouching above me. Despite the ragged clothing and the face covering, I recognize him immediately. I would recognize him anywhere.

Sorin.

Eyes widening, I gape, shock hindering my speech.

He's alive.

"We've come to bring you home," he says, his voice breaking with raw emotion. "Iris, we're going to take you home." His hands cup my face.

I'm stunned. I never thought I'd see him again. Especially not under these circumstances.

"What are you doing here? *How* are you here?" I manage to say.

"Your father reassigned me to his personal guard," he says. "I'll fill you in on everything else soon, I promise. But first, we have to get you out of here."

A rush of emotions overwhelms me. I want to throw my arms around him. I want to yell at him for the way he left.

"Come on," he says, reaching out a hand. "Let's go home."

I hesitate. There are so many things I want to say to him, but the only thing I can manage is, "I can't go back. Not yet."

Confusion plagues his face. "What are you talking about? These people *kidnapped* you, didn't they?"

"It's complicated," I say, dropping my eyes.

"Iris, we can talk all you want on the way, but now we have to get going," Sorin says, lightly grasping my shoulders. "Whatever they're threatening you with, I promise I won't let them hurt you. It's going to be okay."

"I can't go back," I repeat quietly. "I'm sorry."

Sorin pauses for a moment and as I stare into his eyes, the deathly sounds around us seem to fade.

"I missed you so much, Iris," he says as he wraps a tight piece of cloth around my gushing shoulder. "All I want is for you to be safe."

"Then don't take me back," I say. "I'm safe with them. We're going to stop the fighting."

"These people have no reason to help you," Sorin says. "If anything, it's just a bluff to keep you here. You remember what I told you, right? That they're a threat to Imperia. They're a threat to *you* especially."

I look away. He's right, in a sense. But their leader is the only true threat. Everyone else is in it for the right reasons. How can I explain this to him? How can I make him understand?

"Call off your soldiers, Sorin."

"Iris," he says softly, his hand brushing my cheek. "Things will get better. *We* can make things better. All I'm asking is for you to trust me now."

"I want to," I say. "And I do. But that's not enough to make me go back to my father."

"But why?" he says, his voice cracking with sorrow and hurt. "That man down there, his leader and his soldiers are ruthless, merciless creatures. Do you see the way he kills?"

"They don't kill without reason," I argue. "It's only when they truly have to. And your men attacked us first."

Sorin shakes his head in disbelief. "Iris, I don't get it."

"They can help me protect Will," I say. "And *you*. You said it yourself, they don't want a war. Isn't that a good thing?"

"None of us want a war," he says. "But they're going about it all wrong, Iris."

"They have information on my mother, too," I say, as if it'll convince him.

His eyes flash. "Your mother was...one of them?"

"It's more than that. I know it is," I say. "There's something more that you don't know about, that even *I* don't fully understand yet."

"Searching for dead people is a dangerous game, Iris," Sorin warns. "I don't want you to get hurt."

"I'll be careful," I say.

Sorin shakes his head. "Iris, if you don't come now, I can't guarantee your safety."

"What's that supposed to mean?" I fire sharply. "Are you going to let your men kill me if I refuse?"

"Lords, no!" he exclaims. "I just mean that wherever they take you, I won't be able to follow. I don't like leaving your safety in their hands."

"I can handle myself," I insist.

Before Sorin can reply, Commander Wang calls up to me. "What's going on?"

Around him, nothing stirs. Most of the attackers have fled, but a few unlucky ones lay motionless on the ground.

Sorin bristles beside me and stands, crossbow in hand.

"Don't shoot!" I shout to no one in particular.

Neither of them lower their weapons.

"Iris," Sorin says. "They are a threat. Killing him would do us all a great favor."

"Wait," I say, resting a hand on Sorin's outstretched arm. "Please."

"Are you kidding?" Sorin says, bewildered. "Have they twisted your mind so much that you would turn your back on the safety of your nation? Don't think for a moment that he wouldn't kill you if it furthered his own agenda."

I look warily at Commander Wang, who's smattered with blood, but remains tall and shows no signs of backing down.

"Get out of here," I shout down at him, but knowing the commander, running is never even an option.

"I'm taking the shot," Sorin says.

Panicking, I shove the crossbow out of his hand, and he staggers backwards, catching himself just in time.

"Iris, what the hell!" he shouts. But there isn't anger in his voice. There's pain. The pain of betrayal. "Iris..." he says, repeating my name over and over, as if it'll change my mind.

"Goodbye, Sorin," I say quietly, backing down toward the forest floor.

My heart aches as I watch him stare at me from the tree. His eyes are full of hurt, and the boy I've known since childhood is drifting farther and farther away. It breaks me.

But I can't go back. Not with him, not with anyone.

"We're finished here," the commander says.

He takes hold of my wrist and pulls me through the thick vines of the forest. My hand feels frail as it quivers uncontrollably in his, but he remains sturdy, and that's enough to keep me going.

"Who was that?" he asks, slowing his pace as we reach the Iron Wing.

I hesitate. "A member of the emperor's guard," I reply. "They wanted to take me back."

The commander lifts a curious eyebrow. "And you refused?"

"I came here for a reason," I say. "And I made a promise to keep my brother safe. I will not leave until that promise is fulfilled."

He looks away. "You should have gone with him."

"And why is that?" *Because you hate me,* I want to add.

Commander Wang turns to me, his gaze almost angry. "Because he was right. You aren't safe here."

"If I wanted safety, I would have stayed in the palace," I counter.

He looks like he wants to argue, but he turns away and reaches for one of the ropes hanging down from the airship.

I want nothing more than to leave this rainforest and all of its death behind.

I want to forget the sick feeling of guilt spreading through me as I imagine Sorin standing alone, watching as I walk away from him.

Chapter 26

Nothing is the same. Dravkia looks as it always has, but the familiar glow and electric excitement of the city is long gone.

Naveen is recovering slowly in the infirmary. The doctors keep telling us that injuries like his always take time to heal, and he'll be back with our squad in a few months.

The three of us visit Naveen as often as we can. Jaice spends most mornings with him after breakfast and Crayln and I take the night shifts before dinner. Naveen is still his usual self, but I can tell he's not pleased with being cooped up in the infirmary all day.

Simu left me photos before he left for a mission. I found the stack in his workshop upon my return along with a hastily written note. The photos capture the ruins and remains of the Kuyang tribes in southeast Imperia. I don't know what to make of them. In each photo, there's a body. A dead body.

In his note, he wrote six bone-chilling words.

Do not let him find the others.

I assume he means the rest of the Kuyang, those who escaped from their lands and now take refuge across the continents. How Simu expects me to help keep them hidden, I don't know.

Ever since our return from the Mangra, the leader has scheduled weekly meetings with me. According to him, it's to ensure my training is progressing adequately, but I know there's something more. The leader knows something about the Marrow that he isn't telling me, that much is clear.

"I trust that your training is coming along well," the leader says during one of our meetings.

I hate even being in the same room as him.

If he wanted you dead, he would have killed you by now, I remind myself over and over. It's the only thing keeping me still as I sit across from his desk.

"It's fine," I reply.

"I hear you performed well in the Mangra," he continues, fiddling with the silver rings on his fingers.

I shrug. "I would've died without the commander."

The leader laughs. "And how are your studies?"

"They're going well," I say, trying to sound uninterested. "I've learned a lot."

"Miss Wu, I think that's enough dancing around the real subject of interest," the leader says, a small smirk growing on his face.

"And what is that?

Suddenly, I become all too aware of the tinted windows and the heavy metal door keeping me trapped inside.

"It has come to my attention that one of my suppliers, Simu Gong, has been snooping into some business that does not concern him," the leader says, a black puff of smoke erupting from his mouth as he pulls away his cigar. "And that he has decided to share extremely classified information with you. It's perplexing. So please, enlighten me, Miss Wu."

"I don't know what you're referring to," I say. "But I can assure you I have only ever traded light conversation with him. Nothing more."

"Miss Wu," he says. "One of the first lessons that I hoped you would have learned by now is that lying to me is dangerous. I need to know what that old fool has told you for your own safety and the safety of the Order."

"He hasn't told me anything," I say, my voice stronger.

I know his amber eyes see right through me. "Very well," he says, his tone lighter. "I suppose it's only right that you receive the silver insignia for your loyalty to the Order and your bravery in the Mangra."

I cross my legs uncomfortably. He knows I'm lying. So, what is he playing at?

"I'm honored," I say, going along with his game.

The leader smiles and shuffles through a mess of papers on his desk. As he flips through his files, I notice ink snaking up his arms and curling around his fingers. Thin black tendrils seem to wrap around his neck in a thorn-like pattern.

"Recent reports say the emperor lowered the age for mandatory military service this morning," he says. "I figured this would be of interest to you, considering how invested you are in the Imperial-Trasylarian conflict."

My heart jumps at the sound of that. "What?" I say.

His eyes flick up at my outburst, and he closes the cabinet. "Indeed. I believe the emperor fears his numbers will hardly rival those of Trasylar's, and now he's ordered men as young as thirteen to attend training camps."

I freeze, feeling the blood roaring in my ears. Thirteen. Will has two months before he joins the war.

My fingers curl into a fist. "Tell me how I can stop it," I say, anger burning inside of me.

"I envision a future where both nations will coexist in harmony, same as you," the leader says wistfully. "I trust that you have heard of my new project, yes?"

I nod.

"Well," he says, "as my eyes in Trasylar have informed me, we are close. Very close.

The last operation will take place in the North in five days' time."

"This is the plan you mentioned, about how to prevent the war?" I ask, remembering the leader and Commander Wang discussing it the day I joined the Order.

The leader smiles and the sides of his mustache just barely touch the far sides of his cheeks. "Precisely."

"How is it going to work?" I ask.

"Your unit will receive mission details soon enough," he says.

I want to ask for more, but I decide against it. I let out a long breath of relief. If the plan works, my brother will be safe.

"Continue your training, Miss Wu," the leader says, presenting me with a silver emblem. "You're progressing beautifully."

My stomach churns at his comment, but I take the insignia and pin it to my jacket. I can't bring myself to feel happy, or even proud. I don't deserve it, and coming from the leader, it means nothing.

Jaice is waiting for me on the corner of the apartment buildings, a stack of papers in hand.

"Hey," I call.

He looks up. "New mission," he says, showing me the papers. "A big one, at that."

"In the North?"

"Yeah. From what I've gathered, we're taking almost two entire regimes, and Commander Wang's leading us."

This is what the leader was talking about.

"That sounds slightly terrifying," I tell him, a chill passing through me. If two entire regimes are needed, just what are we getting ourselves into?

"There aren't many details here, but we're heading to the Winter Palace, which is Imperia's northern stronghold," Jaice says, continuing to read from the report. "Both Trasylar and Imperia have been sending more troops to the border. They haven't moved far, but if we're headed there too, something tells me there's going to be blood, and lots of it."

I sigh. "Well, if we die, at least we'll die as one big, happy family."

Jaice allows himself a small chuckle at my feeble attempt at a joke. He tucks the paper into his pocket and turns toward the apartments. "Get some rest. We're training early tomorrow."

I'm not ready to follow him, so I head down the main street. The city is bustling and loud, with everyone's interest peaked at the spreading news of the mission. The glow of the moonstones reflects on the cement sidewalk, and I keep walking until I'm unfamiliar with my surroundings.

Continuing through the street, I sense the sweet fragrance of a bakery nearby and the savory smell of pizza wafts through the air. Despite the inviting smells, I'm not hungry. I can't remember the last time I've had a proper meal, but the thought of eating makes me want to throw up.

"It's late for you to be roaming around, soldier."

I turn. It's the first time I've seen Commander Wang since the rainforest, and it makes me nervous. Instead of his typical suit, he's wearing more casual clothes. A black jacket is pulled over a tightly fitted T-shirt and his hair is messy. I almost mistake him for a normal boy.

"I wasn't quite ready to retire to my room yet," I say quickly.

His gaze softens a little, and my eyes drop to the bouquet of flowers in his hand.

"I hope I'm not interrupting anything," I say, trying to keep the mood light.

The corner of his lips curl into a half smile. "You aren't," he says. "I'm on my way to the infirmary." He lifts the flowers, and I understand.

They're for Naveen.

"Oh," I say in surprise.

"Care to join me?" he asks. "I understand you two have grown quite close."

I hope he can't see how red I am. "Uh, sure," I say stupidly.

I trail a pace behind him as we head down the road and toward the infirmary. I can't figure out why he offered for me to join him. Maybe he's angry with me, wishing he saved his friend instead. Maybe this is his tactic to get revenge. Maybe he's taking me to a secluded area of the city to kill me. The leader would never know it was him. No one would.

As if he can read my thoughts, Commander Wang pauses and turns to face me. "Stop worrying," he says, almost as if it's an order. "I'm not going to harm you."

I remain a few paces behind him still, but my muscles relax.

"Contrary to what you may believe," he says. "I am not going to attack my own soldier in the shadows of my city."

I don't meet his eyes, almost feeling guilty for having made such an assumption. But then again, he's given me plenty of reasons to think that way.

We enter the infirmary and the crisp scent of rubbing alcohol and cleaning detergent fills the air, replacing the savory scents of dinner. The infirmary may be the only fully lit building in the entire city.

"We are here on account of Naveen Khan, of the First Regime," Commander Wang says to the woman at the desk.

She nods and salutes him respectfully before giving us Naveen's room number. She looks flustered and fumbles with her papers as we leave. I suppose the commander just has that effect on people.

The elevator is fast and takes us up to the seventeenth floor in a flash. I've visited Naveen every day since we returned, but I still haven't gotten used to the infirmary.

Commander Wang turns the knob of Naveen's door and I wait outside, giving them the privacy they need. From the way the commander steps hesitantly into the room, I can tell it's the first time he's visited.

I sit patiently, leaning against the wall and watching the slow ticking of the clock. I almost begin to doze off when the door opens again.

"How is he?" I ask, standing up.

"He's well," the commander says, his expression more relaxed than I've ever seen it. "We were close once."

I look up. "What happened?" I ask.

He pauses a moment and considers my question. "I pushed him away," he says. "I allowed my ambitions to override everything else in my life."

"Oh," is all I can find to say, shocked by his sudden vulnerability.

Commander Wang laughs to himself. "I don't know why I'm telling you this."

That makes two of us, I think to myself.

I peer through the glass windowpane looking into Naveen's room and I notice the commander's flowers resting in a small vase. They're beautiful white lotuses, and from what I remember, they grow everywhere in Sejeran.

"Are they his favorite?" I ask.

Commander Wang follows my gaze and nods. "From what I've gathered, yes."

I don't know what comes over me but curiosity pushes me forward. "And are they your favorite, as well?"

He lets out a small laugh. "No," he says.

"They're not my favorite either," I agree. "We always had them around the palace and eventually they blended in with everything else."

"Let me guess," he says, raising his eyebrows, "your favorite flowers are irises?"

"Real original," I say, fighting a smile. "Actually, I prefer roses."

After a moment, he says, "Thank you."

I open my mouth to ask what for, but he cuts in before me.

"You saved my life in the rainforest," he says.

Like that's the truth, I think to myself. He would have made it out alive whether I was there or not.

"You did the same for me, once," I say. "Twice, actually."

He shakes his head. "No," he says. "The difference is you did it by your own free will. I didn't do it for you out of the kindness of my heart. Varys wants you alive, and I have to follow orders."

I stand still, not sure of how to respond. My instincts were right, I suppose. His only rationale for keeping me alive is because of his father. He still doesn't trust me. But the feeling is mutual.

Commander Wang clears his throat. "But in the Mangra, you didn't have to stay. You could've let that guard friend of yours shoot me and you would've been free. So, for that, I owe you."

As if he'd allow himself to get shot.

"Going back to being locked up in the palace is hardly what I would call freedom," I say.

"Just because you do not wear shackles does not mean you aren't a prisoner here," Commander Wang says.

"I know," I say, swallowing. "But the Order at least gives me a chance to prevent the war, and as of now, I'll take what I can get."

According to Commander Wang, the leader wants me alive. That's enough. Perhaps Simu is wrong, perhaps the leader suspects nothing. Maybe it wasn't *his* journal Simu found in the ruins.

"The night is late," Commander Wang says, after a long pause. "You should return to your room before your commander realizes you've missed curfew."

I raise my eyebrow in confusion. "But *you're* my commander."

It could be a trick of the light, but I swear I see the faint line of a smirk appear on his face.

"Take care," he says with a small rasp in his deep voice that sends tingles through my body. "And congratulations." He nods to the silver glimmer on my jacket before I close the door, and I know it was his doing.

I ride the elevator alone, my face blushing furiously. The reflection in the glass displays a silly little girl and I can barely stomach it. I can't allow myself to veer off track, not for anyone. Especially not for the commander, who is loyal to his father above all else.

I sneak into the apartment, swinging through an open window on the first floor. It leads to an empty room, and I travel up the stairs unnoticed. While I can feel the watchful eyes of the cameras on my back, it's rare that anyone monitors them. Once I reach my room, I collapse onto my bed and kick off my boots.

I play back my strange yet intriguing encounter with the commander over and over in my head until sleep finds me.

Chapter 27

The days leading up to our departure are stacked with training. Jaice and I almost never leave the platform, and when we aren't fighting, we're sleeping.

"Good," Jaice says, wiping blood from where I kicked him in the lip. "You almost look ready to fight in the real world."

I cross my arms. "Did you forget that I just came back from fighting in the Mangra? That seemed pretty real to me."

He shakes his head and returns to the weight rack, beginning his daily set of reps. "This is going to be different," he says. "If we're unlucky, there will be arrows flying from all sides and they won't care who they hit. War is unforgiving. It's not something to be taken lightly."

"I know that. But this isn't war, not yet," I say, joining him on the floor with weights of my own. I pause for a moment. "Will it ever get easier?"

Jaice doesn't look up as he finishes his first set. "It's all repetition. Eventually, you'll lift these with ease and move on to heavier weights."

I roll my eyes. "I'm not talking about lifting," I say. "Fighting. Killing. Does that ever get easier?"

Jaice's eyes darken. "Yes, and no. You'll learn to get over the fear of pulling the trigger, but you'll never grow out of the guilt. That always remains with you."

I think back to all the lives that were lost in the Mangra. So many people died that day.

"Do you think the commander feels that way, too?" I ask.

Jaice takes a moment to respond. "I don't know for sure," he says. "I haven't exactly had a heart-to-heart with him. I know he can seem ruthless, but there's a reason you haven't seen him out and about much since the Mangra. He grieves in his own way."

I think back to when I saw him a few nights ago with flowers for Naveen. When I think of that version of him, it isn't hard to believe that there's a little compassion under his cold front.

"It's never easy," Jaice admits. "But there's always a purpose, always a reason. Think. If the commander hadn't killed all of those people in the rainforest, would you be here now?"

I swallow, focusing on the weights in my hands. "No," I say. "I wouldn't."

Jaice sighs. "I'm sorry you had to witness that," he says. "If I knew what was waiting for you there, I would've gone in your place."

"It's okay." I return my weights to the rack, my hands shaking. "I better go pack my things."

Jaice rests a hand on my shoulder. "It's going to be okay."

"I hope you're right."

The alarms sound at 3:00 in the morning. I join over a hundred soldiers who launch themselves from their barracks and file on to the Iron Wing.

I follow the others into the hollow deck, where rows of seats protrude from the metal walls. I'm shoulder to shoulder with the other soldiers, with hardly any breathing room. They sharpen their blades and sleep in what little space they can find.

Jaice and Crayln sit at my side, and the three of us refrain from speaking too much, most likely to hide the quivering in our voices.

The commander steps through the door into the soldier's quarters and calls everyone to attention. Whatever humanity he had a few days ago in the infirmary is long gone, replaced by his usual hostility.

"Soldiers," he says. "As you've been made aware, our mission lies in the Northern region of Imperia. At 0700, we will land on the outskirts of the Winter Palace.

"The battlefield will be dangerous, and casualties will be unavoidable. However, you have all sworn your lives and loyalty to the leader and the cause our organization represents. May you fight or fall with honor."

The grim tone of his speech isn't what I expect. The war generals back at the palace do everything they can to mask the dangers of battle, hoping to prevent their soldiers from getting cold feet.

But that isn't the case here, and I quickly understand why. The soldiers of the Order thirst for a battle like this, and their allegiance to their commander fills them with courage. None of them want to turn back.

"I have assigned you all to legions," Commander Wang continues, his piercing green eyes scanning the faces of his soldiers. "Legion One will be with me on the battlefield, while Legion Two will accompany Commander Perovka at the designated coordinates. Now, make your way to your legion commander and the details of your assignment will be disclosed. Dismissed."

The large screen above the door divides the soldiers into two groups. I scan for my name. Next to it reads: Legion One.

My breath catches.

I search for Jaice and Crayln on the screen. They're both in Ta-iana's legion.

Good, I think. *They'll be safe.*

"Let's switch places," Jaice says quickly. "They'll never know."

"They will," I say, my voice shaking. I'll be on the battlefield in less than four hours.

Jaice balls his fists. "Why the hell would he do this?" he says, glaring at the commander. "You've been through enough already. You shouldn't have to face the battlefield, too."

I place a hand on his arm to steady him. "You've trained me well," I assure him. "Let me prove it."

I'm scared out of my mind. But I can't sacrifice Jaice's life for mine. He's clearly the better candidate, but there must be a reason the commander chose me for his legion. He never acts without reason, and I have to trust his instinct.

Maybe he just wants to kill off the weak link.

"Good luck," I say to both of them.

"You, too," Jaice answers, looking as if he still wants to protest.

I take a deep breath before crossing the metal room to where my legion gathers. We're larger than the other, at least twice their number, yet I have a terrible feeling that by the end, it won't be so.

"Listen up," the commander says, once we were all accounted for. "We're going to be fighting against Imperial soldiers. They aren't anything we haven't handled before, but there will be a lot of them, and we're gravely outnumbered. That being said, we're going to need to rely on our heads just as much as our weapons."

My stomach drops. *We're fighting Imperial soldiers?*

This is the exact opposite of what I had in mind. The leader's idea of preventing a war is nothing more than massacring the armies.

I want to scream, but fear and shock hold my voice hostage in my throat.

"We'll crush those glorified servants," a soldier sneers. "They're soft from years of pampering from the royals. They'll never know what hit 'em."

The commander silences him with a sharp glare. "As I was saying," he says. "We need to corner them and force them into Trasylarian territory. Then, we will have the upper hand and a fighting chance. Understood?"

Everyone but me nods.

"Good," he says. "That is all. Rest up. We'll be landing shortly."

As the crow disperses, I ball my fists and march up to him.

He raises an eyebrow. "Soldier?"

"What the hell is this?" I demand, forgetting that he's my commanding officer. "We're setting out to *murder* the entire Imperial Army?"

Heads turn toward us, but I don't care who's listening. Rage boils my blood.

Commander Wang's countenance remains as cool as ever. "Our goal is to encourage a retreat," he says calmly. "Not a massacre."

I clench my teeth. "I'm not a fool," I say, and gesture to the airship. "This is a force designed for war."

Commander Wang takes me firmly by the elbow and drags me toward the control room. "We aren't doing this here," he says tightly. I struggle against his grip, but he doesn't budge.

"Iris!" I hear Jaice yell.

The metal door slides shut behind us, blocking out the curious stares of the legions.

"This isn't about you," he says, releasing me as he folds his arms. "The leader has been working on this project for *years.* Stop acting so entitled."

I narrow my eyes and heat floods my face. "Care to explain, then?"

He scoffs and narrows his eyes. "Explain *what,* exactly?"

"Explain why the hell we have to kill Imperial soldiers in order to prevent this war. A simple meeting with my father would probably be enough," I say.

He lets out a long sigh, his eyes swimming with annoyance. "Fine," he snaps. "I'll *explain* it to you so you get out of my hair.

"The leader needs to show a display of strength in order to gain the favor of the Trasylarians. A simple 'meeting' would never accomplish this. Therefore, we are ending the conflicts with force."

"The favor of the Trasylarians?" I repeat.

Commander Wang turns toward the windows and watches as the airship nears the borders of Imperia. "Their king is old and dying," he says. "And his sons are dead. Trasylar has no heir."

A shiver passes through me. "So, the leader wants to take the throne?"

"Oh look, you're finally catching on," he says.

"That's..." I say, but I'm at a loss for words. "I thought the Order stands against the monarchs?"

"We stand against the current monarchs," Commander Wang corrects. "They're oppressive and neglectful. The Order can lead reforms in Trasylar, and when the other nations notice, they will follow."

The thought of the leader ruling over an entire nation makes me sick. His power will grow, and he will tear apart the world looking for the Marrow, tearing through people like pages in a book. Like my mother. She got in his way, and he killed her for it.

"Now, get back out there and wait for landing," Commander Wang says. His tone tells me there is no room for argument.

I swallow, but I do as he says, desperate to get away.

I slip into the crowd, avoiding eyes and murmurs. Ignoring them, I angle my ears toward Taiana's legion, where she's discussing their portion of the operation.

"The Winter Palace is at these coordinates," she says, pointing to a place on the map. "We make a beeline for it the moment we land, with Commander Wang's troop distracting the fighting soldiers. That way, we should make it there swiftly and without confrontation."

Someone interjects, confused. "Are there guards stationed at the palace?"

"Only our own," she replies, although didn't look happy about being cut off. "We've been monitoring the palace ever since we received the green light from Trasylar. There shouldn't be any issues there. But be prepared to fight."

"What are we doing in the palace?" someone asks.

She smiles with a bloodthirsty hunger that makes my stomach churn. "We're burning it down."

My stomach drops.

"Hundreds will die," someone murmurs. It's Crayln.

"Not if we're smart about it, Mavros," she says simply. "In and out. Mission success. They will have time to evacuate, but it is crucial we destroy the Imperial Army's stronghold."

A disturbing silence falls over the room. My heart pounds. How many deaths will this cause? How many soldiers, on both sides, will die?

I remember Will. He's still a month and a half away from conscription. At least he won't be here in the North.

"It's going to work," Jaice says comfortingly.

"It's not that," I reply.

A shadow crossed his face. "Do you know them? The Imperial soldiers, I mean. Do you know any of them well?"

"Some," I say.

Jaice is at a loss for words, although I don't expect him to say anything. He isn't conflicted like I am. To him and to the others, this is just another mission.

"I never want to go back to the palace," I told him. "But that doesn't mean I want to watch those who are loyal to it die. I don't want to kill them."

"It's not too late to switch legions," he offers. "I'll march in and tell the commander right now."

I shake my head. "No, don't do that."

His eyes fall, and we sit in silence. The entire ship shares the same emotions. Apprehension. Worry. Excitement. Dread.

"We're here," the commander's voice says over the intercom. "Meet your commanders outside of the ship."

Taking a deep breath, I force myself to follow my legion.

Jaice's legion does as Taiana instructed, and as soon as they land in the powdery snowscape, they dart south to where the palace stands. It's fortified by strong stone barriers and deep trenches made to withstand battle. There's no turning back.

The vast frozen wasteland spreads before me, chilling me to the bone. The cries of battle blare in my ears. In the distance, I see them. Soldiers clashing and shredding each other like a pack of ravenous wolves. Behind them is the base of an enormous rocky mountain, much larger than the one we climbed.

"Who are they fighting?" someone asks as we make our way toward them.

"The Trasylarians, you idiot," another replies. "These two nations are causing an unnecessary amount of chaos. That's why we're here to stop them."

Dread bubbles in my stomach as the battlefield grows into focus. Blood splatters everywhere, and the winds carry the agonizing sounds of soldiers' last screams. The winds pick up, and shards of ice fly through the air, scraping my face hard enough to draw blood.

I pull my hood over my head, but it still doesn't prevent the deadly shards of ice from digging into my flesh. A trail of crimson drops follows us.

"Spread out!" I hear the commander yell from the front of our pack. "Encircle them all! Drive them across the bridge!"

We do as he says, and I watch as the left wing of our group exchanges rushed words with the Trasylarians. Immediately after the commander finishes, the captain of the Trasylarians howls out a retreat.

Confused, I watch as half of the battle tears away, replaced by our own soldiers who rush toward the Imperial army. After a moment, Imperia's front line breaks.

"Take the far end!" the commander instructs.

I follow one of my comrades, Raelyn, I recognize, as she runs closer to the fray. She draws a knife and aims at the closest Imperial soldier, bringing him down with one fatal shot to his neck.

"Come on!" she yells at me. "We've got to surround them from the back." Without waiting for a response, she takes my gloved hand and pulls us onto the ice bridge connecting Imperia to Trasylar.

I almost trip on fallen soldiers and broken armor.

Three Imperial soldiers surround us. Raelyn takes one of them out in the blink of an eye. I do everything I can to keep moving and to avoid the spray of arrows.

Before I can react, one soldier knocks me to the ground. The air leaves my chest, and the metal blade of the soldier's sword presses against the back of my head.

In a flash, the soldier is forced off of me, and a dagger hits him in the shoulder. The others lay fallen around Raelyn, who wipes blood from her lip.

She glances at me, and to my surprise, she reaches out a hand. "Come on," she says. "You weren't seriously going to let him beat you, were you?"

I don't respond, but I give her a grateful smile.

"You have to fight," she says to me, glancing over her shoulder to check for Imperial soldiers. "You signed up for this, remember?"

I bite down. "I don't want to kill them."

Soon, another wave of soldiers comes marching across the bridge, and chaos resumes.

"What now?" I call to her.

"Fight back, Princess," she says. "And try not to die."

"Easy enough," I say, fixing a firm grip on my weapon.

As the soldiers approach, one of them breaks off and charges toward me. With his sword outstretched, he aims for me. I duck under his arm and throw him into the snow. Before I can move out of the way, he kicks me in the chest, knocking the wind from my lungs.

I gasp but hold my ground. Twisting away from his sword, I seize his arm and send him sprawling. I take hold of his sword and slide it into my belt.

"If you're smart, you'll get the hell out of here," I tell him. "And tell the rest of your soldiers to do the same."

The soldier laughs. "We are not cowards."

"Look," I tell him, stepping closer. "You will all die here if you don't leave *now*. You're outnumbered. Can't you see I'm trying to help you?"

A cry rings out, and I direct my attention toward the sound.

Raelyn kneels in the snow, a river of crimson pouring out from a deep slash in her abdomen. The two soldiers around her bleed into the snow.

With horror, I rush over to her. "Raelyn!" I shout, trying to put pressure on her wounds. Soon, my entire hand is drenched in blood. "Raelyn, can you hear me?"

"I wouldn't be so worried about her," a newcomer says. "She's as good as dead. As will you be."

The metal clanking of armor tells me he's an Imperial soldier.

"I'm sorry," Raelyn whispers, blood trickling from the corner of her mouth.

With wide eyes, I keep my eyes pinned on my attacker. A long sword glistens in his hand, and his eyes gleam. He sees me as an easy target.

"Don't speak," I say to her. "Reserve your strength. Help will come."

She lets out a blood-filled laugh. "Do me a favor, Princess."

"Anything," I say.

"Win."

Chapter 28

The soldier advances, raising his sword to deliver a fatal blow.

Without thinking, I draw my dagger, putting myself between him and Raelyn, who breathes heavily at my side. She pushes herself up onto her hands and knees. A few paces away, another member of our regime struggles under the sword of an Imperial soldier.

"I'm going to help him!" Raelyn shouts to me, staggering to her feet. "Stand your ground."

I open my mouth to protest and point out that she's in no shape to fight, but Raelyn is already disappearing into the battlefield.

"I wouldn't be so worried about her," the Imperial soldier says to me as he steps closer.

I swallow and tighten my grip on my dagger.

Before he can take another step, the soldier collapses onto one knee, and his sword skids off the bridge. An arrow pins him to the ice.

I whip around to see the bloody face of Sorin. His crossbow points to the space previously occupied by my attacker. Making his way over, he takes me in a strong but brief embrace, and I fall against him before finding my footing.

"Sorin," I gasp, my head swiveling around the battlefield.

"Iris," he says, brushing the hair and blood from my face. "What are you doing here?"

"It seems like I just can't get rid of you," I say.

He smiles, but I know our reunion will be short-lived. Three more Imperial soldiers approach, all pointing their weapons at me.

"Stand down," Sorin rasps, spitting blood from his mouth, "she's with me."

One of the men narrows his eyes skeptically.

"Wait a minute," one of them says, eyeing me closer. His eyes grow wide. "She's—"

He never gets the last words out. Sorin charges at him and tackles him into the snow. In a flurry of fists and swords, I manage to duck every blow. Neither one of us wants to kill anyone, and I notice Sorin avoiding every vulnerable spot as he trades blows with his own soldier.

The two others round on me, and I bring one of them to the ground, knocking him out. The remaining soldier manages to slice his sword along my back, forcing me to my knees. Through searing pain, I plunge my dagger into his hand and he drops his sword.

He stares at me, wide-eyed and angry, but turns to run.

Sorin takes my shoulders a moment later and hauls me to my feet. "Are you hurt?"

I shake my head. "I'll be fine."

"Good," Sorin says. "Good."

I look over his shoulder at the soldier he fought with. An arrow sticks out of his chest, and I know he must be dead.

"Sorin…" I say, my voice faltering. "I'm so sorry."

He shakes his head, trying his best to conceal his guilt. "You have nothing to be sorry about, Iris."

"He was one of your soldiers," I say.

"We have to keep moving," Sorin says. "We'll get killed if we stay here."

I hesitate but allow him to lead me away. We dart through the fighting and scan for any kind of cover among the flying arrows.

I glance over to the Winter Palace. Smoke bellows from the towers and the walls begin to crumble. *They're succeeding.* The thought is both horrifying and relieving. At least that means Jaice and Crayln aren't running into trouble.

Sorin follows my gaze. "So, we can either get burnt to a crisp or take a sword in the heart. Lovely choices."

A blast erupts from inside of the Winter Palace, and bright light pierces my vision. Then, it's gone. The right side of the palace collapses immediately, and the other wings still burn from the raging flames.

A golden flare shoots into the air and crackles before fizzling out. Taiana's legion is done.

"Back to the ship!" I hear the faint voice of the commander roaring through the battlefield.

"I have to go," I say quickly, watching my comrades head back to the airship. They run with astounding speed, even as arrows follow them.

The sound of metal piercing flesh sounds behind me, and I turn to find Sorin clutching his leg. A blade sticks out of the flesh, and blood pools at his feet.

I start toward him, but the sound of heavy metal boots crunching on ice makes me stop.

A few paces away, standing on the bridge, is one of Sorin's own soldiers, the Imperial emblem shimmering on his breastplate. He's blurred by snow and wind, but he's stalking toward us.

"You're a disgrace," the soldier growls at us.

I freeze.

The fighting around me slows to a blur. The voice is all too familiar.

My throat burns as I wipe the hair from my eyes and focus on the approaching figure.

"Will," I croak.

His eyes are full of an unnatural hatred as he glances up at me. A sword is slung across his back and another dagger rests in his hand.

"I'll give you ten seconds to clear off the bridge before I throw this one," he says, his voice belonging to a man three times his age. Disgust is written all over his face, and it tears me apart.

"I heard what father did," I say. "Lowering the fighting age, forcing you into a position that you shouldn't have to be in. I can't imagine how frightening it's been for you, Will —"

Will sneers, cutting me off. "Who told you *that?*" he asks. "Father did nothing of the sort. I *chose* to enlist."

All I can hear is the pounding of my heart.

"What?" I manage, the weight of the battle coming back into focus.

The leader was lying. Why would he lie?

More and more soldiers pile onto the bridge, and a deafening crack echoes through the air, causing everyone to jump. The bridge is breaking.

"Is it so hard to believe?" he asks, his blond hair stained red. "You *left* me, remember? 'A trip to the city?' When, exactly, were you planning to tell me you left your family for these rogues? That you left *me*? For months!"

"It wasn't like that at all..." I try to tell him, but even I don't believe myself.

"Father said I would make him proud," Will says. "And I intended to do just that."

The ice underneath my feet splinters, and the cracks grow larger as more soldiers stampede across. I start toward Will, but his grip around his knife tightens.

"Will, don't!" I call. "I'm your sister. I never meant to hurt you. I only ever wanted for you to be safe."

"You say that," he says. "Yet you fight on the other side!"

I watch him aim the blade at my heart.

"I have no sister," he says.

My eyes squeeze shut, and I feel the rush of tears as Will's words shatter me. I brace myself for the blade, but the pain that follows is far worse. A heavy weapon is brought down over my head, and I crumple to the ground. The ice bridge shatters under my knees.

I'm going to fall.

The center of the bridge crumbles into the ravine below. Will follows the rest of his soldiers across the bridge and then he's gone.

Soldiers blur around me and the thunderous sound of footsteps fades into nothing more than the pitter patter of rain.

Out of the corner of my eye, I watch with dread as the shadowy figure of the airship lifts. There goes any chance of escape.

The brewing blizzard around us picks up speed, tearing at our clothes. I make my way over to Sorin, slowly inching across the ice.

Tears well in my eyes as our gaze locks. A moment of realization passes between us: We are going to die here.

"Sorin, I'm so sorry," I say. "For everything. For what happened in the Mangra."

He's hardly visible through the thick snow, but he's there, and smiling faintly.

"No," he says. "You did nothing wrong."

"Close your eyes," I whisper to him, counting down the seconds we have left. "It'll all be over soon." I rest my head on his chest and listen to the slow beating of his heart. With his remaining strength, he strokes my hair comfortingly.

"It's going to be okay," I say, matching his smile.

All I can hear is the shuffling of boots through snow and a series of shouts and screams in the background. Soon, the blizzard reaches full force, and snow piles at my sides and almost fully buries Sorin. My body is numb, and even the shallow thump of Sorin's heartbeat begins to dwindle.

Then, everything disappears completely.

Chapter 29

My consciousness returns slowly, and I don't believe I survived. I heard the bridge crumble. I saw the airship leave. So how am I breathing?

Every muscle and joint aches furiously, and there's a constant throbbing in my head. But the pain tells me I'm alive. Death wouldn't be so uninviting.

Blinking back into reality, bright light pours into my eyes, and I have to squint in order to take in the full view.

Snowy tundra spreads out for miles and woven in the arctic landscape is a beastly mountain range. The sun glistens high in the sky, but its warmth isn't powerful enough to keep me from shivering in the crisp, wintry air.

Then, I realize I'm moving. Muscles ripple underneath me, and I push myself away from the figure carrying me. I fall onto the hard, icy ground and a fresh wave of pain shocks through me and I wince.

"Finally awake, are you?"

I recognize the voice instantly. The commander is standing above me, folding his arms across his chest. There's a deep gash on his shoulder, and a few minor scrapes and bruises decorate his face.

"What happened?" I manage to say.

"Oh, this?" Commander Wang says, gesturing to his wounded shoulder. "It's nothing. A lucky hit, really."

I'm too exhausted to filter myself, so I roll my eyes. "No, I mean, what *happened?* The bridge...I heard it break, I *felt* it."

To my surprise, he has the audacity to smirk. "It did," he replies, reaching out a strong arm to help me up.

"Then..." I say, trailing off. "How am I still alive? I was on the bridge. I remember that."

He thinks for a moment and motions for me to follow him. "We need to find a way out of here," he says, gesturing to the vast landscape that surrounds us.

"We're lost?" I ask, a hint of worry ebbing into my voice.

"Not so much 'lost,' as turned around," he says, the calmness in his voice perplexing. "I have a vague idea of how to navigate these mountains, so we should be fine."

Still not convinced, I follow him anyway.

"Alright, talk," I say.

"Well," he says, rolling his shoulders and neck as if he had been sleeping for days. "Perovka's flair went off, and I realized all of my soldiers weren't accounted for. Those who I presumed were still alive, of course."

"What would make you think that I, of all people, was alive?" I ask.

Commander Wang laughs to himself. "I didn't," he says, his eyes twinkling. "But I went back to look for any survivors. That's when I saw you on the bridge. A nasty situation you got yourself into."

My heart drops, and I remember Sorin was there, too. I know I can't assume Commander Wang saved him as well. Especially not after Sorin was so willing to kill him in the Mangra.

"What happened to them?" I ask, almost dreading the answer.

"The blizzard blocked almost everything from view," he says, helping me climb up a steep slope. "I don't know what happened to them, or if they got out at all."

My silence tells him his answer isn't satisfactory.

"He's your friend?" he says, although it was less of a question than a statement. "That soldier, the one from the Mangra."

I nod, but don't elaborate.

As we walk, the memories of the battle come flooding back to me and I remember how angry I am at the commander. The memories. The memories of *Will*. He could be dead, and it would be my fault. The Order's fault.

My fault.

Before I can stop myself, I pause and turn to Commander Wang and shove him into the snowbank. Hatred surges beneath my skin. Hatred toward the Order, my father, the war. But most of all, hatred toward myself.

"I can't *believe* this," I spit as he blinks snow from his eyes. "I never should have gone through with this."

Commander Wang remains silent, watching me carefully as rage pours out of me like scorching lava.

"My brother could be dead right now," I say, my voice breaking. "He was never supposed to fight. And you all let it happen. I joined the Order and swore my oath to it in exchange for Will's protection. *Everything* I did for the Order was for him."

I dig my nails into my palms, using the rest of my strength to keep the tears out of my eyes.

"How could you do this?" I say, my voice barely audible.

Brushing the snow off of his pants, Commander Wang stands and looks me in the eye. His cool collectedness makes me itch for a fight.

"That was never my intention," he says, his voice level.

"But you did," I say, taking a dangerous step forward. "You set out to kill the Imperial soldiers. My brother was one of them."

Commander Wang's gaze remains steady. "I did what I had to for the sake of the mission."

I clench my jaw in frustration. "You should've left me to die, because the moment I get the chance, I'm going to kill you."

"I'd rather you didn't," he says, frowning.

"You should've thought about that before assigning me to the battlefield, before destroying the Imperial Army," I say. "Leave me here. I'll find my own way back."

Commander Wang is excellent at hiding his emotions, but at this moment, his mask slips just a little and the muscle in his jaw flutters impatiently. "Very well."

He brushes past me, but not before pressing something cold and metallic into my palm. I debate throwing it back at him, but keep still as he makes his way through the snow.

My hand closes around the metal so tightly that it draws warm, scarlet blood from my palm. I open my hand. A glistening chain rests inside of it.

It's made of diamonds, I realize. An impressive emerald falls in a teardrop along the rope of stones. The gems are now stained with red, but I recognize the necklace at once.

My mother's necklace.

I examine each gem, each twist of metal, and my mind wanders to my mother. She might have been like me, broken and with nowhere to turn but to the Order. That must be why she joined.

I need to get back to Dravkia. I need to speak with Simu and learn the truth of my mother, the Order, the leader, and how all of these pieces connect to the Blood Marrow.

I can't die here in the mountains.

Swallowing my pride, I drape the necklace over my head and peer across the landscape for Commander Wang, but he's long gone. I hang my head, but my eye catches a splotch of red. His shoulder, I remember.

A small sliver of guilt stabs at my gut. He saved me and somehow returned my mother's necklace, and I repaid him by reopening his wound. Still hesitant, I follow the trail of blood deeper into the mountains.

I walk for miles, and by the time my legs give out, the sun has set, and darkness washes over me. Perhaps I'll get what I want after all. Perhaps death by frostbite will be painless.

A deep, rumbling laugh sounds a few paces away and destroys my hopes of dying a peaceful death. I glance up in a flash and see Commander Wang leaning against the rocky face of the mountain.

"You found me," he comments.

"Appears so," I say dryly.

"We can camp here tonight," Commander Wang says, nodding to a small crevice in the mountain. "Can't say much about a fire, though. There aren't any trees for miles."

I lift an eyebrow. *Shouldn't he be angry with me?*

"I need you to give me a reason," I say, stopping just short of the cave's entrance.

"A reason for what, exactly?" he asks, turning to face me.

I clear my throat. "I need you to give me a reason why I should trust you," I say.

"The most prominent issue at hand is getting out of this frozen wasteland," he says. "Whether you trust me or not has no significance in that."

I open my mouth to argue, but he dips his head and disappears into the small cave. Despite my better judgment, I hurry in after him.

As the last sliver of dusk dips below the horizon, I lean against the cave wall, shivering. I'm exhausted from the battle and I close my eyes, trying to ignore the cold nipping at my limbs.

Never missing a thing, Commander Wang crosses the cave and drapes his jacket across my shoulders, settling down next to me.

My heartbeat flutters, and I almost protest, but something stops me. Instead, I offer him a grateful smile.

We're both too exhausted for a further exchange of words, so I allow sleep to find me.

I see my mother. She's smiling, staring at me with round, beautiful eyes. Her dark hair sways as she steps toward me, and I feel her warmth and her light. But the scene changes, and she's whisked away, replaced by black, haunting smoke.

And then there's nothing.

I call out to her, willing her to shift back into being, but she never does. My cries echo meaninglessly in my mind.

Sounds of screams fill my ears and then I'm back on the battlefield, only this time, it's my father who points a deadly blade between my eyes. His red face, twisted with anger, dares me to fight, to protest, to run. But I can't do anything. No matter how much I struggle to scream, my voice catches in my throat.

"A disgrace to the nation," he shouts.

My eyes fly open, and I gasp for air, a cold sweat covering my body. Heart racing, I look around desperately, trying to remember where I am. The hard walls of the cave and the harsh frigid winds remind me I'm in the mountains. *Lost* in the mountains.

Commander Wang awakes a moment later, his green eyes reflecting in the moonlight.

"What's wrong?" he asks, his eyes sharp and alert.

I shake my head. "It's nothing," I say quickly. "Sorry for waking you."

His eyes search mine, but they aren't scornful or full of judgment, like in the past. No. They're softer, kinder. Understanding. Something about the way he looks at me makes my face flush, despite the chill of the air. I try not to focus on how close he is, how our body heat mixes together to keep us both alive.

"Nightmare?" he guesses.

"One of many," I say quickly, turning away so he can't see the color in my face.

"You never quite get used to them," he says, clenching his jaw as he looks out into the night beside us.

I raise an eyebrow carefully. "They haunt you, too?"

He almost laughs. Almost. "Considering everything I've done," he responds, "it's only natural that they do."

"So that makes two of us, Commander," I reply, not meeting his eyes.

"I suppose," he agrees. "Try to get some rest. We have a lot of walking ahead of us."

Before closing his eyes, his gaze meets mine again.

"Avrian," he says. "Call me Avrian."

Chapter 30

Sunlight filters into the small cave, and I open my eyes to find Commander Wang—Avrian—gone. A brief moment of panic passes through me, but I follow his footsteps to the peak of a small snow-capped hill and find him sitting, quietly observing the landscape below. It reminds me of Mount Hikirojaro, and I'm brought back to the memory of gliding.

"I'm guessing he dragged you all up the mountain and then pushed you off?" Avrian says, hearing me approach.

I smile, remembering the excitement in Naveen's eyes. "Something like that."

"For all of his stupid decisions," Avrian muses, "he never had a lack of courage, I'll give him that. The first time he proposed gliding off of a mountain, I climbed right back down."

"Seriously?"

"Seriously."

"I never pegged you for the type to run away from danger," I say.

He shrugs. "Jumping off of a mountain with nothing but a hang glider wasn't very inviting to my twelve-year-old self," he replies.

"He thinks very highly of you, you know," I say.

I look over as a small smile reaches Avrian's face.

We sit in silence until the sun reaches its highest point and our stomachs begin to growl for food.

"We'll starve soon if we don't find something to eat," Avrian says, standing as he dusts snow off his pants.

"Don't remind me," I say.

"I have an idea," he says. "Follow me."

A little skeptical, I follow him further through the mountains.

"Where are we going, exactly?" I call out to him, pausing for a breath. "You're lost now, aren't you?" He turns back, his eyes twinkling. "You have very little faith in my navigation abilities."

"Seeing that we're still in the middle of nowhere, yes, you are correct," I say.

Avrian finds this amusing. "Not to worry. We're almost there."

Almost where? I want to ask.

It turns out that 'almost' doesn't have the same meaning to Avrian as it does to me. We walk for at least half of the day by the time he finally stops.

"We're here," he says proudly, scanning the white landscape. "I almost forgot about this place."

"Are you sure?" I say. "All I see is more snow."

He waves a hand, and I join him from where he stands at one of the mountain peaks. "If you look behind that peak, you can see it."

I follow his gaze, and to my surprise, I see a structure that looks like some kind of warehouse. It's an extremely odd place for an industrial structure, but if it can help us, I'm grateful for it.

"An old warehouse?" I ask, following him as he walks toward it. "What's it doing in the middle of the mountains?"

"You'll see."

We approach the metal building, and he types something into the keypad by the door. I'm surprised it's still functional. The door of the warehouse automatically opens to reveal a small, incredibly old biplane. It's a sleek, dark blue color with double wings and a white stripe down the body.

"Wow," I say with awe as I admire the antique plane. I've only ever seen images of them in history books. "Can it still fly?"

Avrian rummages through the storage closet and his eyes light up as he pulls out a canister of gasoline. "Let's hope so."

He fills the tank and checks all the other mechanical elements of the vehicle.

"There should be some food in the cabinets," he says.

I find a few ancient cans of preserved food and rusty pieces of cutlery in the cabinets. The labels on the cans have worn off with time, and despite every instinct telling me not to eat it, I know I have no choice. I peel back the lid to reveal some sort of green and brown slop.

"On three?" he offers, lifting his spoon to mine.

I nod, hoping I won't end up spitting it all back up into his face. "Three."

We both gulp down the mashed food and struggle to force it down. I'm almost certain it's expired, but we down the entire can, anyway.

"Lords, that's awful," Avrian says, wiping the corner of his mouth.

"How long have these been here?" I ask, the rotten taste still clinging to my tongue. I take a handful of freshly fallen snow to wash it down, and he does the same.

"Years. Decades maybe," he says. "But better than nothing."

"True," I say, but my stomach isn't so sure.

He crosses the warehouse and continues working on the plane, tightening screws and greasing the wheels. "Alright," he says, wiping sweat from his brow. "It should be all set. Here." He offers his hand.

"We're certain that it can fly?" I ask, eyeing the rusty vehicle.

"Come on," he says. "I didn't just do all that fixing up for nothing. If I want you dead, I would've left you in the snow. It would've been much easier than dragging you through the mountains, only to kill us both in a plane crash."

That still doesn't prove that the plane won't crash, I think. But we have to get out of the mountains. So, I take his hand and allow him to help me climb into the plane.

"You'll want to hold on tightly," he warns me from the pilot's seat. "This wasn't exactly built with passenger safety in mind."

"Oh, great," I say, hesitantly wrapping my arms around his waist.

I'm instantly aware of how close he is, and the warmth radiating from his body. I feel every muscle tense as he shifts in his seat.

Nervously, I shift the subject. "So instead of worrying about the engine crapping out, I can worry about getting tossed out of the plane."

"Precisely," he says, flashing me a not-so-reassuring smile. "Ready?"

I sigh and nod.

The front propellers spin faster and faster, and then the engine purrs to life.

The plane moves slowly out of the old warehouse, and my grip tightens slightly. Ahead of us, about a half mile or so, is a cliff. And we're headed straight for it.

The plane picks up more speed as Avrian drives it toward the edge.

The plane moves forward, wind whipping through my hair and small shards of ice scratching my cheeks.

"Hold on!" Avrian shouts, as the plane's wheels roll over the cliff.

My arms are like steel around him, and all I see is darkness. The sound of the engine and propellers fill my ears.

We're falling.

I bury my forehead into his shoulder, and hear his heart beating furiously as he attempts to get the plane to fly.

A few moments pass and we have yet to crash, so whatever he's doing must be working. Slowly, I open my eyes, and we're calmly flying through the mountains. The pounding in my chest slows, and I loosen my grip.

I can see for miles. The mountains stretch in all directions, and the shimmering snow gleams in the moonlight. I take in a deep breath and the cool air tickles my face.

"You haven't even seen the best part yet," he says, turning to me.

"When were you going to tell me you had a plane stashed away in the mountains?" I ask.

"Perks of being the heir to the Order, I suppose," he says. "Like I said, I almost forgot about that place."

The heir. His words remind me of the very thing I've been trying to ignore. His father is the leader, who has killed hundreds of my people in his pursuit of the Marrow. The old woman from the desert, who I've decided must have been his mother, said it was a family business.

But Avrian isn't like them, I tell myself. *He doesn't want to kill me. He isn't out hunting for anything—or anyone.*

I sigh and push the thoughts away.

Avrian slows the plane and looks up at the sky. Mimicking his motion, I look up to see the most beautiful, vibrant display of colors I've ever seen. The pitch-black sky is streaked with pinks, greens, and bright yellows, as if an artist had painted it with their brush. The colors move through the darkness like soft sheets of Imperial silk.

"Woah," is all I can find to say.

He turns the plane, and we land softly on the peak of one of the tallest mountains in the range. We can almost touch the lights.

I follow Avrian and climb out of the plane. We sit in the snow, leaning against one of the plane wings. I don't notice that our shoulders are brushing against each other until I break my gaze away from the celestial miracle to face him.

He, too, is in awe. For the first time since I've known him, he looks truly relaxed. It's possible that he reminded me so much of his father that I overlooked the boy beneath. In this moment, he looks at peace with himself, and my heart can't help but melt just a little.

He catches me staring, despite my best efforts to avert my eyes. "Enjoying the view?"

Flushed with embarrassment, I nod. "It's incredible," I say. No view from the palace could ever compare to the magic flashing across the sky.

He laughs to himself.

I scowl. "What?"

"Nothing," he says.

I shake my head in mock annoyance.

As I watch the lights move through the sky, I allow myself to forget everything else. I don't think about the war, or my mother, or the leader, or Sorin. Not even Will. Despite feeling a pang of guilt, I let the warmth of Avrian and the beauty of the lights drown out the constant noise buzzing in my ears.

Slowly, we fall asleep to the soft lull of the night.

I awake on Avrian's shoulder, but instantly sit up when I remember the cut running across it. Dawn is breaking, and I know we have to find our way to some sort of civilization. If we don't, then we'll either freeze to death or die of hunger. Neither option sounds particularly appealing.

Avrian's eyes flutter open as I stand and brush the snow from my now cold, wet pants.

"Morning," he says groggily, sitting up.

I smile a little. His messy hair and cloudy morning eyes is a version of him I never thought I'd witness.

"Come on, sleepyhead," I say. "We need to get going."

He rubs his eyes with his hand and rises to his feet. I never realized how much taller he is than me. He towers above me almost as much as Jaice does, and it makes me feel small again, like the fragile princess who was never let out of the safety of the palace.

But Avrian never treats me like that. I'm sure Jess would like him for that reason as well. As Jess crosses my mind, I remember what she said she'd do for me. With dread, I realize I may never receive her letters.

I can't worry about that now, I think to myself.

"Alright, alright," Avrian says. "Let's go."

I board the plane, with him following closely behind. "How much fuel do we have left?"

He checks the gauge and frowns. "Not very much. We'll have to get lucky."

The plane's engine roars to life, and soon we're off of the ground and gliding through the air once more. I have to admit, the feeling of flying is phenomenal. I'll never tire of the sharp winds blowing through my hair like icicles through a raging waterfall.

An hour passes, and I feel Avrian shift. He cranes his neck out the side of the plane and his face brightens.

"There," he says, pointing down to a small valley between the mountains. "The village of Kherenai. We can stop there and restock our supplies."

A wave of relief washes over me as we get closer to the village. It's small, but it'll do. There's a total of about fifty buildings, all wooden huts built from pine. In the center of the village is a clearing, but I can't make out the details.

Abruptly, the smooth rumble of the engine begins to shake and screech. The sounds come out in labored puffs, and the plane lurches forwards, rocking us back and forth.

"You've got to be kidding me," Avrian says, cursing under his breath.

"What's happening?" I ask, furrowing my brows as unease crawls inside of me.

Avrian tries to adjust the engine and manage the plane, but his efforts are in vain. "The fuel gauge just dropped," he says. "If I don't land now, we're going to crash."

He does everything he can to keep the plane under control, and he tries to lose as much altitude as he can in the little time we have. I watch as the ground draws closer, first in little increments, and then all at once.

The plane spins uncontrollably, and Avrian shouts curses as he attempts to soften the crash. My heart races and the propellers come to an abrupt halt.

Soon after, the plane is falling.

Chapter 31

"*A*vrian!" *I shout.*

The plane collides with the swooping valley below us. As we skid down the valley, Avrian takes my arm, and we throw ourselves out of the plane just before the engine bursts into flames.

Avrian curses again under his breath. "Damn it," he says, rushing over to me. "You're not hurt, are you?"

"I'm fine, don't worry," I say, sitting up.

My eyes drift to his shoulder, and with horror, I realize the impact of the fall reopened his wound. Blood trickles down his arm and turns the white snow bright red. "Your shoulder—"

"I'm alright," he says brusquely, covering the wound with his hand. "Come on, let's head down to the village."

Taken aback at his drastic change in demeanor, I follow him carefully down the steep face of the mountain. A shadow crosses his face and unease settles in my stomach. My legs are wobbly as we walk, still processing how we managed to survive.

The village is welcoming, and I insist we get Avrian to a doctor immediately. Despite his best efforts to protest, we find a small healer's hut in the center of the village.

"Just rest here for a little," I say. "The medicine will help."

"I don't need rest," he says. "We should head back."

I cross my arms and give him a stern look. "I'm not risking it," I say. "If that gets infected while we're in the middle of the mountains, we'll be in a whole hell of a lot more trouble."

I can tell he isn't happy about it, but he stops arguing and settles down on the rug. I watch as he closes his eyes and falls asleep. Or at the very least, he pretends to.

I watch as the healer presses mountain herbs into a dressing that he uses on Avrian's shoulder. The gash is deep, but the healer claims he'll be ready to travel and wield his sword again in a few days. Unfortunately, we don't have the luxury of waiting that long.

I leave the Avrian to rest in the healer's hut while I search for information from the locals. The first thing I look for is food, but the pickings are slim. I have no money, so in the end I trade one of my golden earrings for two snowshoe hares, three grouses, and a small basket of some wild berries.

As I ask around for a map, I'm directed to the Village Chief.

I step up to the hut and call a light hello, since there is no door to knock on. A deerskin flap is the only barrier between the contents of the hut and the cold winter.

A woman appears moments later. Her skin shows faint signs of age, and her dark hair is tied back in double braids. She wears the same fur pelts and leather shoes as the others, and her earrings consist of gleaming rocks and gemstones. Necklaces of the same fashion are fastened on her neck, one secured with the talon of a great bird.

"Hello," I say. "It's an honor to meet you."

The woman gives me a small smile. "Come in, my dear."

I follow her inside the wooden hut and examine the animal hide sprawled on the floor. A small fire crackles in the center of the room, providing warmth and light.

"I came here with a friend," I begin. "We're looking for a way back to the northern borders of Imperia. I was hoping you could help us?"

She nods slowly as she processes the information. "You come from the Imperia. What brings you so far out here?"

"We lost our way in the mountains," I admit, not wanting to go into the grisly details of the battle. "Our plane crashed and so, for now, we're stranded."

The woman stands and pours warm liquid from a large pot into two glasses. She hands me a glass and takes one for herself. "Drink this," she says. "It'll help calm your body. I can tell that you've had quite a shock."

"It's not anything to worry about," I say. However, I can't seem to shake the feeling of unease that continues to follow me. I know that as long as the Order has control over me, I'll never get rid of it.

"Our people have lived in the mountains undisturbed for decades," the chief says, taking a sip from her own glass. "And I'm to believe you just happened to stumble across our village?"

I nod. "I know it seems improbable, but that's correct. We'll leave as soon as we can, of course. But the crash compromised our transportation."

"And where will you go?" she asks.

"The Winter Palace," I say. "Maybe some of the others are waiting for us there as part of a rescue mission."

She thinks for a moment. "Well, I suppose my people can take you, but I hear it's a war zone. Are you sure it's safe to go?"

"I don't think there's anyone left there," I say, my voice quiet.

Her eyes soften, and she stands. "I'll have a group of my people escort you there on our sleds."

I peer out of the hut, following her gaze as she watches the sled dogs return from what appears to be a hunting trip. A few men follow and a large caribou lays limp on their sled.

"In the meantime, try to get some rest," the chief says, directing me out of the hut. "You can stay with your friend in the healer's hut, if you like, or we can provide you with a different space."

I dip my head respectfully. "Thank you. I am in your debt."

"A princess does not bow," she comments.

I look up in shock. "How do you know who I am?"

The chief laughs. "I have been around decades longer than you," she says. "It would be a shame on my honor if I could not identify the royal family. I will not ask why you are here, nor will I alert your father's guard, for I assume you have a good reason for leaving the palace. Am I correct in my assumption?"

"I'm not so sure," I say, sinking back into the sofa.

Curiously, the chief tilts her head.

I draw a breath. "I left to keep my brother safe," I say. "But it seems I only made things worse. I think I may have killed him." I haven't fully processed that hypothesis until this moment, but it seems all too believable. "I fear that everything I've done has been for nothing. "Perhaps if I had stayed, everyone would be safe."

The chief places a hand on mine, and our gazes lock. "Our reasons may seem clear in the beginning, but as time passes, you begin to see how blurred they become. Can you truly say that nothing has come out of your time?"

I ponder for a moment, letting the words of the chief sink in. "I guess not," I say, thinking back to the friends I've made along the way.

"I knew your mother well," she says. "She would be proud of you."

I don't believe her. How could my mother be proud of a traitor, a murderer, a deserter?

Standing abruptly, I give the chief my thanks. Pushing past the flap of the hut, I make my way back through the snow and find the healer's hut.

When I arrive, Avrian is stirring back into consciousness.

"I can't believe you made me take that," he says, eyeing the sedatives resting on the healer's cabinet. "What if something happened while I was out??"

I roll my eyes and sit next to him. "Quit being so dramatic," I say, redressing his wound just as the healer had shown me. "Sit still."

He grunts but straightens his shoulder so I can wrap it. I try to ignore the scars on his back from years of fighting and his toned muscles sculpted from even more years of training.

Instead, I focus on the thin black lines of his dragon tattoo and trace the shape with my eyes. It wraps around the back of his neck and the head dips low on the back of his left shoulder. The expression is fierce, and I almost find the nerve to ask him about it.

"Any news?" he asks, breaking through my thoughts.

"The chief says she can arrange a dogsled to bring us back to the Winter Palace," I say.

"Good," he says. "If my men are smart, they'll know where to find us."

"What'll happen if they don't?" I ask.

Avrian shrugs. "Well, then we'd have to find our own way back," he says. "And I'll never hear the end of it. Perovka takes any chance she can get to gloat."

The mention of Taiana reminds me of the day she fought me in training, and the air around me seems to grow stiff. I remember the coldness in her eyes, and the way she seized my throat as if to kill.

"Are you two close?" I ask, thinking of how they acted toward each other in the Mangra.

Avrian lets out what sounds like a laugh. "We have history," he says. "But that is very much in the past."

"Not so far past you wouldn't send her to do your dirty work," I say.

He tenses under my touch, and I try to ignore it as I continue dressing his cut.

"I didn't ask her to attack you like that," Avrian says. "But it was not uncalled for. And for what it's worth, I think you only stood to benefit from it."

I raise my eyebrows. "How is almost getting killed in training helping me?"

"You needed someone to challenge you," he says. "Akerman's training is fair. Real fighting is not. Perovka doesn't care for the etiquette of the ring, so you learned to prepare for the unexpected."

I open my mouth to argue with him, but a small part of me knows he's right. Jaice always stops when I need a break. A real opponent would use my moment of weakness to their advantage, which is exactly what Taiana did.

"You could've fought me yourself," I mutter. "She's not my commander, you are."

Avrian shrugs. "She was more than willing to do it," he says. "Perhaps that is because she isn't too fond of you. I can't *possibly* imagine why."

The teasing in his voice surprises me, and I almost don't register the insult.

"What's that supposed to mean?" I ask.

"Well," Avrian says, "you're quite rude, you have no respect for those of higher rank, you openly defy orders...should I go on?"

I lift an eyebrow. "Did you forget who's currently bandaging your wound?" I ask, wrapping the bandage extra tight to make my point. "I could just as easily make a mistake and accidentally leave you here to bleed out to death."

Avrian frowns and glances down at my hands. He doesn't speak as he watches me tuck the last strand of bandage to secure it.

"What, are you finally at a loss for words, Commander?" I ask.

"No," he says. "I simply chose not to validate your crude remark with a response."

I fight to contain my amusement and sit back on my heels. "I want to leave tomorrow."

"We can go now, if you would prefer," he says, lifting himself up.

"Careful," I say, trying to keep him from re-opening his wound. "If you don't let that heal properly, we'll have to stay even longer."

He rolls his eyes in frustration. "I'll be fine," he says. "I've been through much worse. We need to get back as soon as possible."

"Fine, have it your way," I say. "If you start bleeding again, don't expect me to help you."

Avrian grins. "Never."

Chapter 32

*W*e board the sled a few hours later and set off back through the mountains, this time with adequate supplies and a more reliable mode of transportation. The sled is large enough for both Avrian and I, along with two members of the village. A pack of eight dogs is leading the sled at the command of the conductor. They jump into action, and we glide across the silky ice.

The men from the village speak in their native tongue and I doubt they can understand me, so I turn my attention to Avrian.

"How did you get it?" I ask, touching the emerald pendant around my neck.

"I bargained for it," he says simply. "Varys can be a very reasonable man, with the right motivation."

"Why did you do it?" I ask.

Avrian shrugs. "He doesn't need it. And besides, it's yours, isn't it?" he says.

I nod. "It was my mother's."

Avrian raises his eyebrows and folds his arms over his chest. "Speaking of," he says. "Her documents went missing from my office. You wouldn't happen to know anything about that, would you?" My first instinct is to deny it, but he already knows. "I needed to see them," I say.

A faint smile appears on his face. "I knew you two trained together, but I didn't think he'd stick his neck out like that for you," he says, laughing to himself.

"How did you—?"

"Nav is clever, but not *that* clever," Avrian says. The familiarity in his voice is oddly endearing.

"You didn't punish him for it, did you?" I ask, my voice shaking.

"No," he says. "He came to my office the next day and placed the file on my desk. I figured he had suffered enough—between the guilt of theft and the silent treatment you subjected him to."

I wince.

"So," I say, changing the subject. "You're next in line. That must be...exciting?" The awkwardness of my question makes me wish I kept my mouth shut.

"Varys plans for that, yes," Avrian responds grimly. "But filling his role isn't exactly high on my list."

"You said it yourself that you're determined to climb the ranks," I say. "Isn't your father's position the last stop?"

He shrugs and runs a hand through his hair. "I'm fine where I am," he says. "And don't refer to him like that."

"Like what?"

"As my father," Avrian says.

"Oh," I say, turning away. "Sorry."

"There's a reason I don't share his last name," he says, his tone sharp.

I look up, waiting for him to explain.

Avrian sighs and stares out into the arctic landscape blurring by. "I grew up with my mother," he says. "Varys never wanted much to do with us until we were old enough to fight."

"Us?" I ask.

"My sister and I," Avrian clarifies. "It worked out for both of them, though. My mother never approved of Varys' ways. To her, he was always too cruel, too violent. It was a marriage of convenience and nothing more."

I watch him carefully.

"She would take us down to the shores of Cryencia," he says. "While most of it's a blur now, she did her best to give us a normal childhood. I remember climbing the bluffs and right before I could jump off, my mother would draw me away and scold me for being reckless. She would suggest building sandcastles instead, and my sister would laugh at me from the shore."

Something resembling a smile spreads over Avrian's face as he relives the memory.

"With her, I never had to worry," he says. "She cared for us in a million little ways. And now, when I think of her, I think of the sun and the beach and the tides lapping over the shores."

His expression turns grim, and he shakes his head.

"But one day, Varys showed up at our door and told us our mother was dead," Avrian says, his voice strained.

"I'm so sorry," I say softly. "That must have been devastating."

He tries to shrug, but I detect hesitation in his movements. "It was," he admits at last. "But my sister remembered Varys from before my mother took us away, so she trusted him. Naturally, so did I."

"And then he took you back to Dravkia?" I ask, feeling my heart break for him.

Avrian nods. "Yes," he says. "We were children and didn't know any better. And, after all, he was still our father. Varys never entertained our questions about our mother, so slowly, we started to forget about our lives before Dravkia."

"What changed?" I ask.

Avrian shakes his head, a sad smile turning the corners of his lips.

"Enough about me," he says.

"My mother died when I was born," I say, wishing I could find the words to comfort him. "I don't enjoy talking about her, either."

"I know," he says, to my surprise.

I furrow my brows. "You know about my mother?"

"Of course, I do," he replies. "Varys always had an irrational infatuation with your people."

"What can you tell me about her?" I ask, sitting straighter.

"Not much," he says absently. "I do know that Varys took a particular interest in her. Sort of like he has with you." His voice is full of disgust.

I imagine Varys using my mother just as he's trying to use me, and it makes me sick.

"What did he want with her?"

"I don't know the full extent of it," he says, "but from what I've been told, she was meant to marry the emperor. I can only infer that it all has to do with his ridiculous obsession with the Blood Marrow, but how, I have no idea."

The Blood Marrow.

The words send chills through my body.

So, Avrian does know about it.

Of course, he does.

I bite my lip, and I'm grateful for the harsh winds drying my eyes so tears won't fall. It was all for a mission. My mother never loved my father, and somehow, I must have been part of the mission as well. From the very beginning.

My breath catches in my throat as I begin my next question. "I thought she was killed because she broke the code and fell in love," I say. "If she did it for a mission, then what happened to her?"

Avrian looks at me apologetically. "That kind of knowledge is above my pay grade," he says.

I close my eyes, pain enveloping me as my emotions surface. "I wanted to find her, to understand what happened to her," I say. "But what's the point of searching, when to her, I was just another mission?"

Avrian remains silent, his eyes meeting mine.

"You understand the nature of our work," he says, putting a hand on mine. "My guess is, she didn't have any other choice."

"You *always* have a choice," I argue.

"You can't be sure she's dead," Avrian says, although his voice becomes nothing more than a whisper against the screeching winds.

"I'd rather believe she's dead than believe she's hiding somewhere only pretending to be," I say, an unfamiliar hatred filling my words.

I instantly regret it. At least there's a chance that she's still alive.

"I didn't mean it like that."

"No, that's alright," Avrian says.

Shards of ice pierce my skin, and my body starts to feel the harshness of the subzero temperatures. Avrian notices and gently pulls me closer to him. I rest my head on his chest and tuck my knees up to my chin to keep warm. I want to disappear, to fold into the safety of his arms and remain there.

"When we get back, I'll have Varys tell you the truth about what happened," he promises, his mouth resting next to my ear.

I close my eyes. *Do I want to know more? Do I really want to hear how, or why, Varys may have killed her?*

My mind focuses on Avrian's words.

When we get back.

Going back means the leader will once again have me in his stronghold. Once I'm back in the city, there's no way out without him knowing. If what Simu said is true, the leader could very well be looking for me. He could treat me exactly as he treated my mother: as a pawn in his game.

"We're here," Avrian says, after a few hours of dozing off.

The sled slows, and the deserted battlefield stretches before us. The agonizing cries and screams come rushing back to me. Snow covers the entire field, but I don't forget all the bodies that lay dead underneath.

Is Sorin buried among them? Is Will?

The Winter Palace stands before us. It's a tall and pristine white building with four large steeples. Most of it has been destroyed by Taiana's legion, but the left wing of the palace still stands. It's no use as a military stronghold anymore, but there's enough shelter to protect us from the arctic winds.

I take a deep breath, and we climb out of the sled, thanking the villagers. The moment our feet touch the snow, the conductor yells something, and the dogs take off, leaving us to face the palace alone.

"Think there's anyone in there?" I ask Avrian, who stands by my side, clutching the ivory sword the chief had given him.

"Stay close," is all he says before heading toward the large marble archway.

He pushes the double doors open and peeks inside. I remain at his side, my hand resting on my dagger. The inside of the palace is shambles—paintings have been torn and ripped off of the walls, and broken glass litters the floor. The chandelier that once hung in the foyer has been shot down and now lays in a sharp, deadly heap in the center of the room. Across the hall, the staircases are covered in ash, and almost every door is detached from its hinges.

"Is anyone here?" Avrian calls out, using his commander's voice.

No one replies, and nothing stirs. We continue deeper into the palace, searching for any survivors. As we round a corner into the dining hall, I spot soldiers slumped against the tables and walls. They're all dead. The ceiling of the hall has been blown to pieces, and now reveals the dark, stormy sky above us.

A screech sounds overhead, and instinctively, Avrian pulls me under his arm and adjusts his grip on his sword. I search the open sky and catch a glimpse of a red bird swooping down into the dining hall. It shrieks, and as it comes closer, I realize how big it is. The hawk's wingspan must be at least six feet, if not longer.

I look closer and see a piece of parchment attached to its foot. It's a messenger hawk, sent from Sejeran based on the royal crest wrapped around its neck. I step toward the monstrous bird, and it allows me to pluck the message from its grasp.

"Careful," Avrian warns, his weapon pointed at the creature.

"It's okay," I say. "It's just a messenger hawk. Please don't skewer it."

Avrian lowers his sword, but his eyes never leave the bird.

I open the parchment scroll and begin to read. It's a poem, I realize. One in Jess' handwriting.

Eyes of onyx may rest upon,
A wisp of smoke in a dead bark dawn,
A dove caught in brambles,
Like a butterfly in feathered silk.

Ancient answers and stolen stories,
Found in the depths of the deepest quarries.
Like a raven's cry and crow's fear,
The clock runs dry and near.

Weary of the shadows and weary of jewel,
A sunken city and vile king rule.

My dearest friend,
As a crimson fox hunts alone,

See past the deception under the sun,
Down to the bone,
Only then will your job be done.

I stand clutching the letter in my hands and I don't realize I'm trembling. I always knew she had a knack for poetry, but the prophetic prose makes my mind spin in circles. Of course, she can't say exactly what she found, for the fear of it ending up in the wrong hands, but even I can't decipher her message.

"What does this mean?" I ask, mostly to myself.

Avrian, who scans the paper over my shoulder, frowns. "This is from Sejeran?"

"The princess is my friend," I say. *Or at least, she was,* I add silently. After learning about the death of her father, I'm not so sure she still sees me as a friend. "She's helping me research the Blood Marrow, and it seems like she's found something, only I can't decode her message."

I read the letter again and again, but I can't seem to make any sense of it.

"She addressed the letter to you," he says. "I'm sure she trusts only you can fully decode it."

"But the problem is, I don't understand it," I say, frustration washing over me. I take a seat on the cold marble, trying to clear my head. "*Ancient answers and stolen stories.* She must be referring to the texts in Sejeran's library."

I shift my eyes down the page. "*A sunken city,*" I repeat. "She means Dravkia. She's warning me against it and it's *vile king.*" My breaths come in small but rapid puffs, and Avrian sets a hand on my shoulder to steady me.

"We can't be entirely sure," he says.

"What is she warning me about?" I say, half-hearing him. "What does she know?"

"It has to be here somewhere," Avrian says, but we don't get to continue reading.

Footsteps sound down the hall behind us, and we both leap to our feet. Avrian draws us both behind an overturned table and we draw our weapons. The hawk screeches and flaps its mighty wings back through the shattered ceiling, disappearing into the thick overcast of clouds.

My grip tightens on the hilt of my dagger as we wait for the figures to approach.

Chapter 33

The sound of footsteps grows near.

I strain my ears to catch their conversation. Murmurs echo down the hallways and the howling wind threatens to drown them out.

Beside me, Avrian tenses.

As the figures round the corner, their voices become clear, and I recognize them instantly. Relief washes over me as I leap to my feet.

"Jaice! Crayln!" I exclaim.

Relief crashes over them both, and I rush over and pull them into a strong embrace.

"Glad to see you're still breathing, Princess," Jaice says affectionately, wrapping his arm around my shoulders.

I can't help but laugh. "Me, too," I say. "What are you guys still doing here? I thought all the troops cleared out days ago."

Crayln pats me on the back, and for the first time since the gliding incident, I see him smile. "We went back with the rest, but then requested a striker to come back for you two." He gestures over to where Avrian is standing. "We had a good feeling the commander wasn't gonna go down that easily."

Avrian nods to Crayln and Jaice. "Mavros, Akerman," he says. "I'm glad you came."

They dip their heads respectfully. "Of course, Commander."

"It's been a crazy few days," I say.

"You have a nasty wound, Commander," Jaice says, observing Avrian's torn shoulder. "We should get you back to the city as soon as possible."

Avrian waves him off. "We'll stop and refill our supplies first," he says. "There's a hub with some of my spies down in the Imperial City."

I give him a grateful smile. We both know our packs are filled to the brim with supplies from Kherenai, but he's giving me a chance. A chance to escape. A chance to be free.

"Alright, that's fine with me," Jaice says. Then, he turns his attention back to me. "I'm surprised you aren't sporting any battle scars, Princess."

I shrug. "I guess I'm better than you thought," I say, shooting him a grin.

Jaice raises an eyebrow and looks to the commander and then back at me. "Perhaps," he says, although I know he's wondering how I've remained virtually unscathed.

I wonder the same thing. During the battle, I took my fair share of blows, but as I scan my arms and legs, I can't find any wound bigger than a faint scratch. The electric tingling inside of me grows again, and I shift uncomfortably in my seat as a warmth spreads over me. Something feels off, but I can't place it.

Crayln and Jaice both murmur in agreement. "Our plane is just outside. We'll set a course."

I watch them walk out and draw back. I turn to Avrian and ask, "Why are you helping me?"

"Who said I was helping you?"

"You and I both know we aren't in need of any supplies," I confirm.

"We're stopping at the Capital because I need to check in on my men stationed there," he says simply. "What you choose to do once we get there is none of my concern."

"If you say so," I say.

I start to follow the others, but Avrian grabs my elbow. His grip is assertive but gentle, and I meet his eyes, which are so full of emotion.

"Know that if you attempt to escape, Varys will not rest until he finds you," Avrian says, his voice low.

"I know," I say.

"Are you sure you want to try? We can't be sure what he has planned for you. Whatever the Sejeran Princess found could mean something entirely different."

I avert my eyes, contemplating my options. Either return to the city and succumb to the leader's wishes or run the risk of being tracked down and killed.

"What do *you* think I should do?" I ask him, my voice heavy with desperation.

His gaze lightens, and he drops his hand. "You should return with us."

"You say that because you're one of them," I say to him, my tone harsher than I intend. "I don't know why I even asked. Of course, you want to help him and make your job easier."

I regret the words as soon as I say them, but a part of me knows they hold some truth. Before he can speak, I turn my back and make my way across the dining hall.

"You should return," he calls after me. "Because there are people in the Order who will lay down their lives to keep you from harm. Because none of us will let him hurt you. If we're all scattered, there's no guarantee we will reach you before he does. That is why you should stay."

I stop in my tracks and look back at him, his eyes piercing into mine.

He passes me, and without another glance, he says, "The decision is yours."

I stand, dumbfounded. I knew we had gotten over whatever hard feelings there were between us, but never did I think he cared that much about me.

After a moment, I collect myself and climb into the striker with the others. Avrian is in the cockpit, and the others are on the benches along the sides of the ship. I walk over and sit across from Jaice and Crayln, a strange silence settling in the cabin.

Avrian starts the engine and it roars to life. He pauses for a second before putting the ship into motion. The last time he flew, it ended in us crashing into the middle of a mountain.

Whatever moment of hesitation he may be feeling is over in seconds, and soon we're lifted into the air.

I peer out the window, watching the Winter Palace grow into nothing more than a glistening snowflake among the vast mountain range. The High Range Sierra stretches for countless miles, and it makes me wonder how we managed to hike through it.

"How did you survive?" Jaice asks me, curiosity finally getting to him.

"Ask the commander," I reply, nodding my head to Avrian. "I was unconscious for most of it."

Avrian says nothing.

"He evacuated me from the bridge before it broke," I say. "Then, we just walked through the Sierra until we reached Kherenai. They were the ones who helped us get back to the palace."

Jaice shakes his head as if he almost doesn't believe my story. "That's insane," he says. "You guys walked through the mountain range from the palace to the village? Do you have any idea how far that is?"

"Well, we didn't walk the whole way," I say. "We found an old plane in one of the Order's warehouses."

"I feel like you're leaving something out," Crayln says with a wicked smirk appearing on his face. "Two people in the middle of the mountains, stranded, with only each other for warmth and company..."

I scowl. If I was sitting next to him, I'd give him a shove like I've seen Naveen do a hundred times. "Nothing happened," I say defiantly, my face growing hot. I don't dare risk a glance at Avrian.

Crayln just laughs, and a part of me is glad that he's slowly shifting back to his regular self. "Don't worry, I won't tell." He winks, and I chuck my bag at him, knocking him square in the chest.

"Stop arguing," Avrian calls back, and I feel the ship descend. "We have to remain as undetectable as possible. I'm sure our faces are plastered on every wanted poster in the city."

"Yes, Dad," Crayln mutters, quiet enough so Avrian can't hear him.

I hide a laugh.

We climb out onto the roof of one of the Order's skyscrapers, which I've learned are stationed in every continent. The Imperial City is enormous, to put it simply. It's at least ten times the size of Dravkia, and while I've watched the city all my life, I never realized its true size. There has to be millions of people all congregating on the streets below us.

"There's a bar down on 76th," Avrian says as we follow him down the set of spiral stairs. "If we're lucky, we'll catch some of my soldiers in time for happy hour."

The bar is packed, with people practically bursting out of its walls. We do our best to squeeze through the doorway and wait for a small space to open up at the bar before slipping through the crowd. We can hardly hear each other over the roaring sounds of drunk men yelling, but we huddle close together as Avrian scans the bar.

I drape my hood over my face to conceal my features as best I can. We're in my homelands, after all. Someone is bound to recognize me. Crayln and Jaice catch on and use their bodies to block me from the lingering eyes of others.

"Stay low," Avrian says to me, calculating and analyzing every person in sight.

He reaches up a hand and signals to a man in the far corner of the bar. My eyes follow his gesture and I see not a man, but a boy. As he nears, I notice that he's about Will's age.

Just the thought of my younger brother makes my heart ache. I'm so close to home, I could swoop in and invite him to come with me, wherever I'm headed next. But that's a silly fantasy. Stringing him along with me would only put his life in even more danger. Besides, I don't even know if he's alive. And if he is, he certainly won't want to see me. Not after what happened in the North.

The boy with sandy hair makes his way toward us, pushing through the dense crowd of drunks. His eyes are sharp, and I can already tell that he's been training for years. He doesn't miss a thing.

"Commander," the boy murmurs quietly as he approaches. He gives the official salute and stands up tall, his eyes scanning the rest of us skeptically.

"Ethan," Avrian addresses. "Any notable events to report?"

His bright eyes flick across the bar as if to ask if it's safe to share.

Avrian nods in encouragement. "They're all too drunk and loud to pay any attention. Go on."

The boy, while he seems nervous under the commander's intimidating stare, remains tall. "The Emperor's guard has been patrolling the city constantly. A curfew of 10:00 p.m. has been set for all citizens and mandatory home searches are in place," he says, and then he sees me. His eyes grow wide. "It's her! They're looking for her!"

"Shh," Avrian says, hushing him quickly. Then, straightening himself out again, he says calmly, "She's with us."

"Hello," I say to the boy.

He stares at me but doesn't offer a greeting in return. Instead, he turns back to the commander and continues his report. He details a few missions set in place in the city and explains a few other hiccups in their plans.

"Well done," Avrian says to the boy. "One last thing. Is Owens in the city?"

The boy searches his brain for a moment, but finally finds his answer. "Yes, I saw him a few days ago. He was just arriving through Xi Cross Station."

"And where is he now?"

"The Imperial Inn on 70th," the boy replies. "At least, that's where he was going when we exchanged words."

Avrian nods gratefully. "Very well," he says. "You may be on your way." Before the boy leaves, the commander hands him a small pouch of what I assume are coins, and the boy's face lights up in a wide smile.

"Thank you, Commander," he says, saluting again and then disappearing back through the crowd.

I want to ask why such a young boy is working for the Order, but I know better than to ask such a foolish question.

"Owens?" I ask.

Avrian's eyes turn to me. "To put it plainly, he connects us with the underground market," he says. "He has extensive knowledge on almost everything, but especially rare drugs and substances."

"Nav never mentioned you were one for pills, Commander," Crayln says, cracking a smirk.

"I'm not interested in buying them, Mavros," Avrian says flatly, stepping off of his barstool as he heads for the exit. "He may just be one of the few people who can give Iris some answers."

My ears perk up at the sound of my name. "Answers? As in, he knows about the Blood Marrow?"

"The what?" Crayln asks.

Avrian ignores him. "I can't be sure, but that's the thought," he says. "I figured it's better to know what it's about than going in blind."

"What are we talking about?" Jaice and Crayln ask together.

Avrian turns to them. "You'll find out soon enough."

If I can find out more about the Marrow, I'll have a clearer idea of what Varys wants with me. Then, I'll decide whether to return or run.

We walk out onto the busy street and walk toward 70th street to find Owens. Dodging all the traffic becomes increasingly more difficult, as many vehicles ignore the red stop lights all together.

"Woah there!" Jaice says, putting his hand out before a shiny black car can strike him in the leg. The car comes to a screeching halt and releases a series of blaring alarms in response.

After walking a few miles, Avrian leads us through the doors of the Imperial Inn. It's elegant, with high ceilings and gold accents scattered throughout the lobby. Our shoes click on the marble floors, and I can't help but notice how everyone's eyes seem to land on us.

I watch as Avrian steps up to the front desk and presents his fingerprint on the small machine that the concierge pulled out from behind the counter.

Another hub for the Order, I assume.

"Welcome," the woman says, saluting. "He's in room 839."

"Thank you," Avrian says, and then motions for us to follow him to the elevator.

Crayln studies the golden buttons on the side panel, his eyes gleaming. "Think it's real?" he asks Jaice.

Jaice shrugs. "Maybe. But don't even think about taking it."

Crayln frowns. "Why not? Surely, they have plenty."

Avrian snorts. "I'm still your commander, you know," he says. "I consider planning thievery right in front of me as nothing more than disrespect."

I give him a slight nudge. "Lighten up, he's only joking."

Avrian gives me a disbelieving look. "He's a thief."

"*Was* a thief," Crayln corrects, folding his arms. "And that was over a decade ago. I was only ten."

"Once a thief, always a thief," Avrian retorts.

I raise a confused eyebrow.

"Cray stole the commander's favorite sword once," Jaice clarifies. "He never got over it."

Crayln lets out a howl of laughter at the memory. "I was pretty good, wasn't I?"

We step out of the elevator and Avrian silences him with a look. "Control yourself. Owens is not to be taken lightly."

A cloud of apprehension follows me as we make our way toward the dealer's door.

Do I really want to know the truth? What if it's more than I can handle?

Jess's words echo in my mind as Avrian knocks on the cherry wood door.

See past the deception.

I need to be smart. According to Jess, I shouldn't be standing at a stranger's door. I shouldn't—*can't*—trust him.

Before I can change my mind, the door swings open, and a man hangs in the doorway with a crossbow pointed straight at us.

Chapter 34

The three of us flinch and draw our own weapons, but Avrian remains unmoving.

"Owens," he says coolly.

Instantly, he lowers his weapon, and to my surprise, pulls Avrian into a strong embrace. The man is older than us, possibly in his mid-forties, and has fiery red hair and a lean frame. He invites us all inside the room with the wave of a hand.

"You've brought friends, I see," Owens comments, still smiling and hooking an arm around Avrian's shoulders.

"It's been a while," Avrian says.

"Too long at that," Owens says, taking a swig of whatever liquid occupies his flask. "So, kid, what's up?"

I watch as Owens takes a seat on the small sofa by the windows, and while he invites everyone to sit, no one does. The room is clean, almost abnormally clean, but I assume that's to be expected. He can't have anyone tracing his fingerprints, or worse, his substances.

"Well, you're a friendly bunch, aren't you," Owens says, raising his glass to where we're all standing by the door. "I'm not going to bite. Come on, kid, you didn't tell them about me?"

"I told them enough," Avrian says.

Owens smiles, and I can tell that the two of them have a long history.

"I'll get to the point," Avrian begins. "We don't want to waste your time."

"Ah, don't worry about me, kid," he says. "I enjoy the company. Although usually they're a little nicer, or at least they threaten to shoot me. Those three are like cardboard cut-outs."

"I'll show you cardboard cutout," Crayln says, drawing a dagger.

Jaice holds out a hand and holds him back.

Ignoring his comment all together, Avrian continues. "The girl has an affiliation with one of Varys' drugs. She's looking for some answers."

Owens eyes me closely, and I feel unnaturally vulnerable. It's as if he can see right through me, and I know he recognized me immediately.

"Alright," he says slowly. "Please, sit. And tell me what this drug is all about."

I raise an eyebrow. "Aren't you supposed to tell *me* about it?"

Owens smiles. "Well, that's hard to do when you haven't even given me its name," he replies, taking another long swig of his flask. The twitching that follows tells me it's a little stronger than the common Imperial wine.

"It's called the Blood Marrow," I say.

He stops in mid-swig, and his flask falls to the carpet. Everyone watches him as he slowly bends down to pick it up with trembling hands.

"Varys told her about this?" he asks eventually, eyeing Avrian.

"More or less," Avrian says. "He expects her back in the city within a few days."

Owens leans back in his chair, running a hand through his rusty hair, and sighs heavily. "What are you hoping I tell you?"

He's scared by the name alone. That can't be good.

"I need to know how to get it," I say, trying to balance my voice. "Or at least, how the leader intends to get it."

Owens looks up again, but instead of looking at me, he exchanges another glance with Avrian.

"Tell her," Avrian says, his voice tight.

"To put it plainly, you're in real danger, kid," Owens says. "The Blood Marrow is very rare and is passed down through generations of Imperial warriors."

Owens scans me, and I don't miss the glint of recognition in his eyes.

"You knew who I was the moment I walked in," I say, my voice barely a whisper.

He nods. "Indeed, I did, Iris Wu. You have created quite a fascinating story. A princess turned rogue. Virtually unheard of."

"Keep talking, Owens," Avrian says. "We don't have all day."

"Alright, alright," Owens says, frowning. "As I said, you're in danger and I do not exaggerate. If you value your life, I suggest you never return to Dravkia."

"What will happen if I do?" I dare to ask.

I feel Jaice take my hand in an attempt to steady me, but I hardly feel him at all. I feel so far away from my body, as if I'm watching everything from outside of it.

"You are what our leader has been searching for," Owens says, his eyes dark, focused on the intricate patterns of the liquor-stained rug below him. "A daughter of a Kuyang Warrior with the marrow of legend in her bones."

"*What?*"

"You are one of the Kuyang," Owens replies. "You hold more than you know. *That* is why the leader wants you and your people."

"The massacres…" I whisper, images from Simu's textbook flashing in my mind.

"Precisely. They were all done in search of the Marrow. However, they were unsuccessful," Owens says. "Only a select few—descending from the greatest of warriors—will possess the Blood Marrow."

"But my mother wasn't a warrior," I protest. "Her village was destroyed when she was just a child."

Owens nods. "This is true," he says. "But your mother's grandfather was one of the greatest warriors of his time. *He* possessed the marrow and passed it down."

My head pounds furiously, and Jaice's hand drops with shock. Avrian closes his eyes and slowly massages his temples while Crayln stares blankly at the carpet.

"Does that mean my mother…" I say.

Owens nods. "It would be a probable conclusion," he says. "But I do not know whether your mother possesses the Marrow. You, on the other hand, I am quite certain."

"How do you know for sure?" I ask, my voice shaking.

"Tell me," Owens says. "Can you feel it surging inside of you? Can you recall times where you should have been gravely injured, yet you somehow survived?"

I can't speak, but I nod. I can think of many times where I should have borne injuries but

I didn't. The battle in the North, the Mangra, and even when I fell off the roof the night I left the palace. I shouldn't have walked away unscathed from any of those, but I did. And this explains why.

"Iris," Jaice says. "What's going on?"

"The leader isn't who everyone thinks he is," I say to him, watching horror creep into his eyes. "His family ordered the massacres of the Imperial tribes, all in search of what is known as the Blood Marrow. They're murderers, terrorists of the highest caliber."

As I say the words, I realize just how blind I've been. I thought the Order could help me, instead I walked straight into the leader's outstretched claws.

Jaice's face pales. I can tell he doesn't want to believe me, but he does.

"And what does he want with Iris?" Crayln asks, stepping closer to me.

"Varys will harvest the Marrow until there's nothing left," Owens says, his voice raspy. "I predict a shower of chemicals, so strong they will burn away all skin and muscle tissues. The operation will be fatal. He's already tried it on most of the tribes but has found none. Until you."

I swallow hard, and my throat threatens to choke me. I remind myself that I'm not in Dravkia. The leader doesn't have me. He will never have me. I'm in my city and I'm free.

"Then why hasn't he killed me yet?" I ask.

"The Marrow, as we've learned, isn't fully developed until you reach complete maturity," Owens says. "At eighteen years of age."

"But I saw the photos of the massacres. There were *children*," I say, rage and fear consuming me.

"This knowledge is recent," Owens says. "Varys was unaware, and his forefathers were even more clueless."

Hundreds dead. For no reason at all. I feel like throwing up, and then marching into Dravkia and spearing Varys through the heart.

"Are you certain about this?" Avrian demands, anger rising in his voice. "If I find out you're lying, I'll put an arrow through your skull."

"I believe him," I say, reaching out to put a hand on Avrian's arm. "Jess warned me about it, too. She must have known."

Down to the bone,
Only then will your job be done.

My job, I realize, is to provide the leader with the Blood Marrow. I'll be forced to undergo a cruel operation that will destroy me and grant the leader incredible strength. It seems so surreal. I don't want to believe it.

But if I focus, if I look inside of myself, I can feel it. I can feel the power rumbling in my bones. Bones that used to be hollow are now denser than ever; powerful, *alive.*

I shiver and turn to Owens. "How do you know all of this?"

"Yeah, how do we know it's not a trap?" Crayln says, a fire burning in his eyes. "People like him come out of the womb conniving and manipulating. I wouldn't trust a word he says."

"I want to know the source of your information," I say.

Owens shrugs. "Consider it primary. Varys needed my help with his search for the Marrow."

His eyes slide to Avrian, whose jaw tightens.

Crayln bristles at my side. "If you're so close with the leader, then why tell us all of this? I'm sure Varys wouldn't be too pleased to know that you spilled his little secret."

I watch Owens, eager to hear his response.

He cocks his head at Avrian. "Because," he says, "the kid asked me to. Despite my allegiance to the Order, if Wang came to me asking me to kill Varys, I'd do it."

"Don't be ridiculous, Owens," Avrian says. "Even a child could see through that lie."

"I'm not lying," he says genuinely. "Look, Varys may be my leader, but you're much more to me, kid. You're my family. My only family. I will not risk screwing that up."

Avrian studies Owens for a long moment, and none of us dares break the silence.

"Very well," Avrian says.

"Well, I suppose that confirms my decision," I say. "I can't go back."

"Definitely not," Jaice says, folding his arms over his chest. "I still can't believe this. I always knew our leader was…rough around the edges. But I never imagined I would dedicate my life to serving a tyrant."

I place a hand on his arm. "There's no way you could have known," I say.

He's still shaken, but Jaice nods.

"We need to hide you, Iris," Avrian says, standing up. "I know a place where you can lie low for a while."

Crayln still eyes Owens with suspicion. "And what about him?" he says, gesturing. "Are we sure he won't spill this to the leader?"

Avrian follows his gaze and watches Owens carefully.

"I swear I won't," Owens says.

"Let's go," I say, then I look back at Owens. "Thank you for your help."

"Anytime," he says, filling up his flask. "Good luck."

Crayln is the first to reach the door, and the rest of us file out behind him, leaving Owens to his own devices.

A small part of me is hopeful.

The greater part of me wonders if I've made a grave mistake.

As we leave the inn, I fall in step with Avrian. Jaice and Crayln lead us a few paces ahead. I sneak a small glance at him before I open my mouth to speak.

"So," I say, trying to sound casual, "are you going to tell me why you're helping me?" I ask.

He doesn't respond right away, and instead focuses on the buildings ahead of us.

"The only reason I stayed in the Order, tolerating the faults in our ways, is because I believed in our cause," he says. "I believed we were the good guys."

Avrian swallows, his gaze flickering to me.

"But it's not that simple," he says. "I don't agree with the way Varys runs things, and I especially don't agree with his hunt for the Blood Marrow."

"Why does he want it so badly?" I ask."Is it so hard to imagine why?" Avrian asks. "It appears the Marrow will grant him invincibility. To a man like him, it is something he cannot refuse."

I focus on the intricate cracks in the sidewalk. I don't want to imagine what Varys would do with the Marrow, or what it would mean for me if he obtains it.

Death, I think. *It would mean death.*

"Well," I say, "I'm glad you came to your senses. It doesn't hurt to have someone like you on my side."

Avrian lets out a small laugh. "Who said I was on your side?" he asks. "Perhaps I am simply using you to feel better about myself. Because the more I help you, the more I forget about the less morally righteous things I've done."

I shake my head and smile.

"How honorable of you," I say.

"Well, you asked for a reason to trust me," he says, "there it is."

He won't admit it, but I know he's in it for the right reasons. Something in my gut tells me he's being genuine.

And somehow, that's more dangerous than anything.

Chapter 35

A vrian takes us to a small, humble restaurant in the heart of the city. Past the dim lighting and crowded tables and chairs is a back room hidden from the prying eyes of customers. Miniature golden cat figurines hang from the walls and watch us as we duck into the room.

"So, what's the plan?" I ask Avrian, pushing aside the beaded doorway.

"You're going to stay here until we contact you," Avrian says, pushing aside boxes of spare cups and china. "Don't leave unless you get word from me. I'm sure Varys will try as many tricks as he can to get you back, but I trust you're smart enough not to fall for them."

I nod.

"The three of us will head to Trasylar," he continues, rubbing the back of his neck with an anxious hand. "I have allies there, so we should be able to arrange a more long-term plan."

"Can we trust these 'allies'?" I ask. "Trasylar will be under Varys' control soon."

Avrian looks uncertain. "It's the best shot we have," he says. "Besides, some of my soldiers who didn't fight in the North are stationed in Trasylarian territory. If I can get to them, I'm sure I can convince them to help us."

"That's the plan, Commander?" Crayln says. "I think we should march into Dravkia and tell everyone that their leader is a murderous lunatic. The Order won't stand with him after that."

Avrian turns on him and frowns. "You're foolish if you think a few words from you would convince the Order to turn on Varys," he snaps. "Their allegiance runs deeper than that."

"It was enough to convince me," Jaice says, folding his arms chest.

"That's because you have a personal interest in her survival," Avrian says. "The others don't care about her. They only care about what Varys has to offer them, and he's a master of spinning the truth."

"The commander's right," I say. "The others won't turn on the leader because of a few things we have to say. Besides, we don't have any proof."

None of my friends look confident.

"I don't like this one bit," Crayln says, crossing his arms. His leather jacket shines in the overhead lights as he leans against the shelves. "Why can't one of us stay here with her?"

"Because," Avrian says, "the more of us there are, the more attention we receive. We don't need to give anyone a reason to be suspicious."

Jaice lets out a frustrated huff. "I'm with Cray on this. Some people have probably already spotted her within the city and would turn her in the moment Varys advertises a bounty."

"Besides, can we even trust these people?" Crayln asks, gesturing out toward the dining room filled with families.

"I have known the owners for a long time," Avrian says, "I trust them."

Crayln laughs in disbelief and Avrian shoots him a glare.

"Guys," I say. "I'll be fine. If you think this is the best option, then I'm with you, Commander."

Avrian looks at me in surprise. Then, he smiles. "I didn't haul you across the mountains only for you to die now."

The sound of his words makes me flush, and I tell myself it's just the rising heat of midsummer in the city.

"So, it's settled," I say.

"We need to find fuel for the ship," Crayln says. "I saw a station down the road. I'll handle it and meet you guys back on the roof."

Jaice moves to join him, and they walk out of the restaurant, leaving me alone with Avrian. We haven't had a moment alone since the mountains. I'm fully aware of how close he is, and the way his shirt hugs his muscled frame.

Dim folk music filters in from a radio in the main restaurant and I'm reminded of the music I heard the first time I stepped foot outside of the palace.

Avrian's hand reaches out and brushes a piece of fallen hair out of my eyes. My skin tingles under his touch, and I stiffen.

"I won't let him hurt you, Iris," he says, his voice raw. "I know I've made it difficult for you to trust me, but I promise I'll do everything I can to stop this."

"You shouldn't say that," I whisper, looking away. "Even you can't predict what's going to happen."

"Varys will have to take every sliver of life from my chest before he can even *think* of hurting you," Avrian says. "I mean it."

"Why? Why risk your life for me?" I ask. "You used to hate me, remember?"

A low laugh rolls in his throat. "I did," he admits. "And perhaps I still do. Although the reason for it is quite different now."

"Oh?" I say. "And what's the reason?"

"I hate you because of the way you make me feel," he says. "I hate that you make me forget about everything else until the only thought left in my mind is you."

A smile tugs at my lips.

"You think about me often, Commander?" I say.

He shakes his head, almost as if he can't believe it.

"From the day you called me an asshole up until this moment, I have not gone a day without thinking of you. For better or for worse," Avrian says. "Mostly worse."

I can't help but laugh, and I try to ignore the heat creeping over my skin. He steps closer. Close enough so that my nose is just hairs away from his.

"Tell me to go," he says, his eyes searching mine. "Tell me to leave and I will. It'll make things so much easier for the both of us."

I watch him carefully, but I say nothing. I don't want him to go.

The tension between us grows tighter, pulling me closer and closer toward him. Every alarm in my body goes off, telling me this isn't a good idea. But I ignore every single one.

"Damn it, Iris," Avrian says. "You were supposed to tell me to get the hell out of here. You were supposed to tell me you'd rather slit your own throat than kiss me."

I feel the warmth of his hand around the side of my neck, pulling me closer. My heart feels as if it'll beat out of my chest at any moment, so I hold my breath.

"But then I'd be lying," I say quietly, letting him draw me toward him.

His other arm drops lower and rests on my hip, pressing me against him. My mind becomes a haze, and all I want is to be closer. I want him to hold me, to kiss me, to *want* me.

I try to reason with myself. I'm officially on the run and Varys will never rest until I'm dead and he has his Marrow. If I let Avrian get too close, there's no telling what could happen.

I pull away, just slightly, and muster the courage to meet his eyes. His beautiful eyes.

"We can't do this," I whisper. I hope my words will break this trance, but it only seems to encourage him.

His thumb brushes my bottom lip so lightly that I'm not sure he made contact at all. My hand reaches up to take his, and I slowly pull it away.

"Avrian," I start, but I can't remember what I was going to say.

"Say that again," he says, his mouth grazing my ear.

Passion swims in the depths of his eyes, and I want to melt into his arms and let him hold me. But that's nothing more than a fantasy. One that would never last. One that would leave us both hurt.

"Please don't stab me for this," he says.

I feel his hands on my waist and on my back, and then he's kissing my neck with a fierce, exhilarating passion. I draw in a breath, and all logical thought begins to fade.

I don't want him to stop.

But this can't happen.

"It was better when I thought you hated me," I say, but I don't pull away. "At least then, I wasn't so conflicted."

A smile plays on his lips. "What makes you conflicted?" he asks.

I swallow, heat flushing my cheeks. "You," I answer. "You're so damn confusing. I don't know how to feel about you half of the time."

"And now? How do you feel about me right now?" he asks.

When I don't respond, he laughs and places his lips on mine. I close my eyes and let the last of my hesitation fall away. My lips part to meet his. The heat of his touch holds me in a trance, and I kiss him back, running my fingers through his hair.

One of Varys' men could appear at any moment. We would be caught off guard and the entire plan would be ruined.

But it would be worth it.

My savior comes in the form of Jaice and Crayln, arguing as they burst through the beaded curtain and stumble into the room.

Startled, I push myself away from Avrian, but he keeps his arm around my waist. He shoots me a knowing smile, which sets off fireworks in my chest.

Clearing my throat, I look over at the two boys barging in, both empty-handed.

"No luck?" I ask.

Jaice rolls his eyes and shoves Crayln into the racks. "This bastard pissed off the entire station, and they kicked us out before I could even get a word in."

"Yeah, well, I wouldn't have said anything if *he*," Crayln spits, pointing an accusatory finger at Jaice, "hadn't told me to play servant and go gather all our supplies from the inn."

I raise an eyebrow, my face still hot. "You don't appear to have found any."

"That's the other thing," Crayln exclaims. "The blasted place was empty! I think he just wanted to get rid of me." He raises his arms in the air to exaggerate his point.

"Look, the fact of the matter is that we still need fuel," Jaice says over Crayln's complaints.

Avrian frowns. "You two are complete idiots."

He shoots me a look. His face looks slightly flustered, and I find it particularly charming.

I drag my eyes away, realizing that I'm getting distracted again. He, too, seems to notice I've been staring at him, and I see him smirk out of the corner of my eye.

"Well, looks like I'll have to do it myself," Avrian says.

"Good luck," I say to the three of them as they prepare to leave.

Jaice pats me on the back. "We'll be fine," he says confidently, and I know he means it. "Don't let them catch you until we get back, alright?"

I laugh. "Got it. I'll signal them the moment you guys are in range."

Jaice ruffles my hair, and I duck away, straightening it out before Crayln attacks me with a strong embrace.

"I'll miss you too much, so don't die on us," he says, giving me a lopsided grin.

"Same goes for you," I say. "Nav's going to need a hell of a lot of jokes when he gets out of the infirmary, so start brainstorming."

"Already on it."

I grin and watch him disappear through the wall of hanging beads, Jaice following close behind. Before they reach the doors, I can already hear them resuming their previous argument.

I nod to Avrian. "Good luck, Commander."

"I prefer hearing you say my name," he says, standing still, as if to say he isn't going to leave until I say it.

"Oh, yeah?" I say. Now it's my turn to wield a mischievous grin. "Well, you'll have to wait until the next time we meet."

He looks at me and laughs. "Until next time." His lips brush my cheek before he heads for the exit, leaving me stunned. A smile flashes across his face, and I can't help but mirror it. A glowing, raging fire ignites inside of me.

Next time. The words echo in my head.

There *will* be a next time. I'm not going to die, and he isn't going to, either. We promised each other that much.

I sink to the floor, closing my eyes. I think of so many things, and then nothing. Varys won't let me slip through his fingers easily. I need to remain sharp.

A target rests on your back, and some of us will never rest until you are dead.

The old woman from the desert had spoken those words to me.

At the time, I didn't understand how right she would be.

Chapter 36

The owners of the restaurant come to find me once they close and offer me a plate of dinner filled with steaming dumplings and stew.

I take it gratefully, not having had a proper meal in days.

"Thank you," I say, sipping the warm soup and letting it soothe me.

The old couple smile back at me as they clear dishes and sweep the floor.

"Of course, dear," the woman says. She leans on her broom, her white hair falling in thin wisps down to her shoulders. "You look so much like your mother."

"Did you know her?" I ask, stepping through the beaded door.

The woman smiles. "Not very well," she says. "But I remember her coronation day. It was a beautiful celebration. The city held parties for weeks and our restaurant had never been so busy."

I join her, taking a broom from the closet. "Can you tell me more about them? My parents, I mean."

"Your mother and father's love story is the one thing that has remained hidden from the public," the woman says, setting a tray of cups into a bucket of water. "Emperor Wu had a betrothed, she was a princess from Cryencia. But during the first few weeks of their engagement, he fell in love with another."

"My mother," I say.

The woman nods. "Yes, that's right," she says. "Your mother was a servant at the palace, but somehow, she caught your father's eye and their relationship grew from there. It's really a shame what happened to her, she was a compassionate woman and made a good empress."

I sweep the rest of the dust into a pile and set the broom against the wall. The music dies away as the old man switches off the radio.

"It's getting late," he says. "Your help is much appreciated."

"It's the least I can do," I say. They're risking more than they know keeping me here. Sweeping and scrubbing a few dishes is hardly enough to make up for it.

Every day with breakfast, lunch, and dinner, we have a cup of herbal tea. It reminds me of the palace, and I remember how close I am to it. I'm so close to my old life, but I'm hardly the same girl I was when I left.

The woman sits beside me at an empty table long after closing time, running a jade comb through my hair.

"Young love is a beautiful thing," she says, separating my hair into different sections to prepare it to be braided.

I turn my head to look at her, but she lightly guides it back into place.

"I'm sorry, I don't know what you're referring to," I say.

The woman laughs. "I am an old Imperial grandmother," she says, "It would be shameful if I could not detect such things."

I focus on the wooden floorboards, kicking around small flecks of dust.

"But that boy is not so simple," the woman warns, folding pieces of my hair together. "He has been through more than a boy his age should have."

"I know," I say, my mind flashing to Avrian. My stomach flutters as I remember our kiss and the way he makes my heart race every time he walks into a room.

When my hair is all tied up, the woman stands and touches a palm to my cheek. "I wish you all the best," she says. "Whatever may happen, do not lose sight of yourself."

As night falls, I settle back into the dark room and lay my head on the make-shift bed the woman provided for me. As I toss and turn under the thin sheet, my chest feels hollow. I think of my friends, and Avrian, and I realize how alone I am.

I hear voices from inside the parlor.

My hand instinctively flies to my dagger, and I jump to my feet. It's well past closing time, and the voices grow louder with every passing second.

Crouching behind one of the storage shelves, I press myself against the wall, hoping to hide myself from view.

The old man's voice sounds. He's yelling. "There's no one here," he says, although even the least trained member of the Order could see past his lie. "I swear on my name, we would never harbor fugitives."

I close my eyes and curse under my breath.

My fingers curl around my dagger, and I prepare to burst through the door. But a shrill scream sounds and the woman lets out a cry.

I heard a *thud,* and then another. My stomach drops. They're dead, they both are, and it's my fault.

"Check the back!" a man shouts.

Snapping back into reality, I turn and run for the back door. As guilt and anger builds up inside of me, I bolt.

Panicking, I dash through the thick crowds of people congregating on the streets. The night life in the city is still thriving and I use the masses as cover. I don't look back, but I know there are pursuers on me.

Car horns blare as I jump through the street, trying my best to dodge the rapidly moving vehicles. Adrenaline pumps furiously, and I don't slow down. I don't have a plan, so I go to the only place I can think of, hoping it can act as my safe haven.

Pushing through the grand doors of the Imperial Inn, I run past the woman at the front desk and search for the stairs. As I round a corner and find the staircase, I hear my pursuers barge in.

"She went that way!" the woman at the desk shouts.

Pounding footsteps immediately follow her directions.

Fleeing up the flights of stairs, I exit on the eighth floor, searching and trying to remember which door is his. Eventually, I come to a familiar door and bang on it with all of my remaining strength.

The door swings open on my third knock, and I practically fall into Owens' room. My knees collide with the carpet, and I use my forearms to cushion the fall.

"Shut the door!" I shout, catching my breath.

But Owens doesn't move. Footsteps sound behind me. The two men who've been chasing me now block the doorway with their enormous frames.

"You're back," Owens muses, staring down at me.

An icy wave of realization hits me.

"You didn't," I growl under my breath.

Owens only sneers, a cold flicker in his eyes.

Balling my fists, I punch Owens hard in the nose. Before I can land another hit, the two men have my arms pinned against my back and drag me to the floor. I grin with satisfaction as Owens stumbles over, using the wall to steady himself while scarlet blood pours from his broken nose.

"You traitor!" I shout.

He laughs, wiping the blood away with a kerchief. "Oh, princess," he croons. "Trust is a fragile thing, isn't it? Difficult to gain, yet so easily broken."

The look of triumph on his face disgusts me, and I want nothing more than to pull out my dagger and fight him. But the two men, both three times my weight, hold me down no matter how much I struggle.

"Why?" I demand, looking up at Owens with a hard glare. "Why did you do this?"A wry smile slides across his face and he presses a bony finger up to his cracked lips. "My allegiance is to the Order," he says simply, attempting to appear innocent. "My loyalties have never strayed."

"Enough with the act," I say. "You said he meant more to you than the Order."

Owens slowly steps across the room and takes a seat on the desk, looking down at me as one of the men presses my cheek into the carpet. I can smell the liquor spilled a few days prior.

So, it was all for show, I think to myself. *He never cared about me or Avrian. He planned to turn us in from the start.*

"The kid will come around eventually," he says. "It's not the first time I've gone against his wishes. I think it's for the best, really. If he got everything he wanted, then he'd never experience hardship. We grow the most when we experience difficult times."

I scowl. "You know *nothing* about him." *But neither do I,* I admit silently.

"Little princess," he says, a hint of warning creeping into his voice, "I raised him in Dravkia and trained him to be the ruthless fighter he is. You are in his way, and it just so happens that Varys will compensate me handsomely for your safe return. How can I refuse?"

Frustration and fury cloud my vision. I feel so helpless, but the longer I am in his presence, the more I want to claw his face off. The more I want to watch as the Order burns before my eyes.

"You're a fool," I say, trying to wriggle out of the men's grasp.

Owens frowns, looking at me as if I'm some dirty little bug who had the audacity to land on his shoe. "I've had enough of your mindless chatter," he says, his eyes drooping in mock boredom. "Silence her."

One of the men loosens his grip on my hand, and in his moment of weakness, I release my arm and reach for my dagger. The weight of it feels so familiar in my hand, like it's an extension of my body.

With a newfound strength, I drive the dagger into the chest of the man beside me, and his grip releases. Turning around, I drop kick the other, who tries to launch himself at me. My dagger meets flesh, spraying blood all over the white bed sheets.

I stand to face Owens, but he's already moved. He's too quick, and he pops up behind me, suffocating me with a rag drenched in a vile liquid. I try to force the smell out of my nose and mouth, but it's too late, and I feel myself slipping out of consciousness. No matter how much I try to fight it, my body succumbs, and I fall limp.

"Sleep well," Owens hisses in my ear. "The leader is waiting for his Marrow."

Chapter 37

The poison runs its course through my system, and I hear faint voices around me. As I open my eyes and my vision comes into focus, I know I'm in the back of a moving vehicle, ropes binding my arms and legs.

Two men sit in the front, caged off by metal bars so I can't reach them. The blaring sounds of car horns tell me we haven't left the Imperial City.

"Hey, you bastards," I call out loudly through the small window. "Are you going to let me out to use the restroom or should I do it in here?"

The two men, both unfamiliar, turn.

"Orders say we're to keep you bound until we reach Headquarters," one of them says. He's in the passenger seat, and the scars on his face tells me he's seen his fair share of missions.

"Well," I say. "Let me ask you this: Would you rather let me use the restroom properly for five minutes or spend an excruciatingly long period of time cleaning the back of this truck?"

The driver shoots me a worried look. He's young, and by the way sweat beads on his forehead, he must be new to this.

"Shut your trap, girl," the passenger barks. "One more word and I'll come tape that big mouth of yours."

"Oh," I say loudly. "My apologies, good sir. I merely forgot how sensitive you men can be."

"Stop the truck!" he orders.

The young driver slams on the brakes, and I'm thrown into the metal side of the vehicle as it rocks forward. I hear the slam of the truck door, which means the man has stepped out and will be coming for me next.

"Sir," the driver says. "We don't have any tape."

The passenger scowls. "Then get a rag for all I care!" he shouts. "I just want her to quit yapping. We have a long trip ahead of us and if she doesn't stop, I'll throw her out into the street."

The driver looks worried and starts rummaging through the small compartment under the dashboard. "I'll find it, sir."

The man stands impatiently outside of the vehicle, tapping his foot against the black asphalt.

Perfect.

I take a chunk of my shirt in my mouth, and I clamp down. Then, I press my wrist to the bottom of the truck, and I press down with all of my strength. I hear a *pop* and pain shoots through my hand.

I grunt into the thick folds of my shirt, but my broken hand allows me to twist out of the ropes. The electric buzzing, which I know is the Marrow, starts to heal my broken bones. The pain that follows doesn't go away so easily, but I push away the feeling.

"Finally," the man mutters.

I hear his heavy footsteps approach the door, and the lock clicks. Without waiting for him to unlock the doors, I kick them open, slamming the heavy metal into his face. He falls to the ground.

I spot the blue tint of my dagger sticking out of his belt, and I reach down and take it.

Racing to the truck door, I slip in and reach across to set my blade against the driver's throat.

"Get out," I say.

"Wait, wait," he says hurriedly, fear pouring out of him. "I can help you!"

"I highly doubt that," I say.

The driver's eyes dart around nervously. "I'm serious!"

I narrow my eyes. "Would you really betray your own so easily?"

"I know where our ship is," the man says, "That's what you want, right?"

My eyes narrow, but soon the other man will regain consciousness, and I have to move out before he does. "Why should I trust you?"

His gaze flickered from me and to his unconscious comrade. "More are on the way. You won't get far without my help," he says, his voice just above a whisper.

I narrowed my eyes, but I know he's right.

"So, you can get me to a striker?" I ask,

He nods, fumbling with the pedals. "Yes."

The truck takes off, but I don't lower my weapon. The streets are emptier than usual, but we dodge every passing vehicle.

"How many of you are there?" I ask him.

"A few more of us are waiting, guarding the aircraft," he says.

I think for a moment. "You'll have to call them off."

He shakes his head. "I can't," he says. "They're my higher ups. I have no say in their affairs, especially since they have direct orders from the leader."

I bite my lip, scanning my head for a plan, anything that could help me. I look over to the driver, who's still terrified but has managed to collect himself a little. "I have an idea, but I need your cooperation. Will you do it?"

"Do I have a choice?" he asks quietly.

"Look," I say, trying to sound as nonthreatening as possible. "I don't want to hurt you. I'll let you out here if that's what you want. But I can't go back."

He furrows his brow and never meets my eyes.

"Please," I say, sheathing my dagger.

The man looks more confused than ever. "Why is going back so bad? From what I heard, you chose to join the Order. You pledged your loyalty, did you not?"

I gaze out through the windshield, thinking of all the ways the leader could kill me. "I'll die if I go back."

A heavy moment of silence passes.

"Alright. I'll help however I can," he says. "I was a member of your guard once and I swore an oath to protect you at all costs."

My eyes widen in surprise.

"I'm Feryn," he adds, his gray eyes finally meeting mine. "Your Highness, it's an honor."

I smile a little. "Iris," I say, although he already knows who I am. "You can forget the formalities. I'm not a royal anymore."

We climb out of the van and take a flight of stairs to the rooftop. My hands are bound with rope again, and Feryn leads me through the doors leading to the outside. He takes a deep breath, and I know he's trembling, but I do my best to play the part.

A black striker rests on the landing strip, and four men in black suits stand at its base. I assume they're waiting for me. They're all armed with swords strapped to their backs and daggers concealed under their jackets.

"Commander," Feryn says, his voice loud. "I have the girl."

My eyes trail over to the man he addresses as 'Commander.' I know there are three regimes, but I've never seen the head of the third until now. And I wish I hadn't. He's tall, and with his broad shoulders and deadly weapons, he's extremely intimidating. No wonder Feryn is afraid of displeasing him.

"Very well. Put her in the ship," the commander says with cold eyes.

Feryn tugs me up the ramp and three other soldiers accompany us, along with the commander.

This is going to be more difficult than I predicted, I think to myself, but try to keep a cool face.

"What do you want with me, anyway?" I say to them, trying to wriggle out of my binds. It's all part of the act.

"Silence," Feryn says, shoving me into the seats.

I scowl at him and shoot the others a glare. I have to wait for Feryn to make the first move, and that's when I'll rip myself out of the bonds and fight for control over the ship. But he doesn't move.

My eyes make a dangerous glance at him, but he remains focused on his commander.

"Wang's regime must've gone soft," the commander growls menacingly, his silver hair nothing more than stubble on his head, "if it only took my most inexperienced soldier to catch her." He lets out a cold, deep laugh.

Feryn smirks proudly. "It was nothing."

Then the commander frowns. "What happened to Watson? You didn't run into any trouble, did you?" Feryn's mask breaks for a moment, but then he straightens. "Of course not, sir. He said he received direct orders from the leader to scout the city for the princess' allies."

I let out a nervous breath, waiting for the commander's response.

"I heard nothing of that sort," he says, rubbing his chin. "A new development?"

Feryn nods. "The leader radioed in just a few moments ago, and Watson was dropped off at the bar."

The bar seems to be a common meeting place.

To my relief, the commander shrugs and seems bored with the topic. He rises from his seat and heads toward the cockpit, his back facing us.

Feryn reaches for his crossbow and points, but the arrow never comes. Before he can shoot, the two other men sitting across from us lift their weapons.

My ropes fall harmlessly to the ground and Feryn tosses me my dagger.

"Shoot!" I tell him.

Feryn does, and he hits someone in the shoulder, knocking him back while the other man draws a sword. I kick him square in the chest before he can stab me, but the commotion gains the attention of the commander.

I watch him reach out and grab the radio. Panic consumes me, and I race over to him as he opens his mouth.

But I'm too late.

Chapter 38

"We're being compromised," is all the commander can force out before he collapses under the weight of my fist.

No, no, no.

Those words are enough to alert the leader of the situation. The commander lays motionless on the ground.

The pilot turns, but Feryn drives his head against the side of the ship, and he's knocked unconscious.

I curse under my breath, my first slamming into the wall. "He knows," I say.

Feryn sighs, and his eyes never leave the bodies of his fallen commander and comrades.

I pick up the radio and try to signal Avrian's ship, but there's only static. I tap my foot against the floor, waiting.

They could be out of range, I reason. *Or they could be dead…No, they can't be.*

"We need to head for Trasylar," I say.

Feryn nods and eventually draws his eyes away. He punches in some coordinates, and I take a seat in the cockpit.

"I'm going to hell," he whispers.

"That makes two of us," I say, glancing down at the blood on my own hands.

Feryn shifts uncomfortably.

"How'd you get roped in with them?" I ask, trying to change the subject as best I can.

Feryn takes the seat next to me and thinks for a moment. "I wanted more," he says. "I wanted more than to be a palace guard. While yes, it's brave work, I never felt fulfilled at the end of the day. I was scared I would feel that way for the rest of my life."

"So, you joined the Order?"

He laughs a little. "Well, I was a bounty hunter first. But I was careful to do my research and only went after people who deserved it." Even though he tries to defend himself, I can hear the shame in his voice. "My mother never looked at me the same way after."

"I'm sorry," I say.

"No, I shouldn't have said that," he says. "I'm lucky to have gotten the chance to know my mother."

"It's alright," I say. Of course, Feryn knows my mother died before I was born. The entire country knows that.

"If you had the chance to meet her, would you take it?" he asks me.

The question surprises me, but the answer was easy. "Yes," I say. "But it's complicated." I feel that everything in my life is the same. *Complicated.* "She did terrible things, things I'm not sure I can forgive. But at the same time, I want to hear it from her."

Feryn nods slowly in acknowledgement, but I know that he doesn't really understand. How could he?

"This is yours, right?" Feryn says, holding up the sapphire hilted dagger.

My heart tightens at the sight of it and the comfort it brings me. I take it and palm it in my hands. "Yes, thank you."

Naveen gave me this.

We fly for hours, and I distract myself with the towns and cities below, thinking of all the people leading their own separate lives. I make up stories for them, trying to think of anything but my own life.

There's a woman down in the village with three kids and a loving husband. She walks to the well every day to gather water for her children's baths and for their tea water. Her husband works the rice fields from dawn until dusk and they sit together as a family for supper. She leads a modest life, yet she's happy. Much happier than any princess could be, even with all the riches in the world.

Then there's a man, about fifty. His children have left for the city, for a better life, while he remains alone in his village. He's never left that village and never will, although he dreams of it. He dreams of cloud surfing and diving into the depths of the sea. But he'll never make it there.

I allow these stories to fill my mind as I fall asleep.

Just look at what happened last time you trusted a member of the Order, I scold myself, jerking my thoughts back to reality. I think back to Owens and my jaw clenches at the thought of him.

"Your Highness, please wake up!" I hear Feryn say, shaking my shoulders.

My eyes fly open, and my hand reaches for my knife. "What is it?"

"A call for you," he says darkly, his eyes trailing to the cockpit's radio system. "It's the leader."

I take a deep breath and pad over, picking up the microphone as if it's made of delicate glass. My entire body goes rigid as I hear his voice.

"Miss Wu," he says. "You have taken over one of my planes, it seems."

"That's correct," I say, finding my voice.

I hear him chuckle through the crackling mic. "I understand you may be upset by the battle in the North, but I encourage you to see the bigger picture. Everything has been done in an effort to unify. I do not want war."

I can only scoff. He wants to rule Trasylar. With that much power, he would burn this world to nothing but ash.

"I hear you've met Owens," the leader says. "Taking you against your will was never my intent."

Not wanting to play his game, I remain silent.

"Besides, he's known for spreading the dirtiest of lies," he continues. "Don't believe what he's told you and rest assured, I will give him the harshest of punishments. I invite you to aid me in it, Iris. Surely you would like revenge?"

He's lying, I remind myself.

"I'll pass," I say tightly.

The leader sounds displeased, and that gives me a surge of satisfaction. Did he really think it would be that easy?

"The choice to return to us is yours, as it's always been, Miss Wu," he says. "But I'm almost certain you will find your way back."

"You're wrong," I growl. "And you can drop the act. I'll never set foot in that underwater hell again. I know you want the Marrow."

"Not even to visit your friends?" he asks.

My thoughts shift to Naveen, and my stomach turns to lead. He's going to use Naveen as a bargaining chip. He's still wounded in the infirmary and there's no way I can get him out without Varys knowing.

"I have no friends," I lie, although my voice sounds faulty. "Your soldiers mean nothing to me. Do with them as you will."

"Well," he says, his voice smug. "If not my soldiers, then how about the supplier? I hear you two have grown quite close. It would be a shame if anything were to happen to Simu Gong."

The intercom slips through my hand like a wad of butter, and I watch it sway back and forth as it hangs from its coiled cord.

I swallow hard. Simu is in danger. Simu, who has done so much for me. He taught me about the Marrow, about my mother. And Varys will kill him for it.

"Don't hurt him," I say, gathering the courage to pick up the microphone again. "Varys, I swear, if you hurt him—"

The leader laughs. "His fate is in your hands, Ms. Wu," he says. "Your choice will dictate whether or not he lives."

Feryn sets a hand on my arm. "You can't possibly trust him," he whispers to me. "He'll say anything to get you to go back."

"Well, Miss Wu?" the leader asks.

"Go to hell, Varys," I shout. "I don't give a damn what happens to anyone in the Order. I'm done."

I slam the radio off in a furious rage and rip the microphone from its cord, throwing it against the wall. It shatters, and concern rises in Feryn's eyes.

I feel hot tears swell in my eyes and I run my hands through my hair, trying to calm my pounding heart. The world is spinning fast, and soon it becomes impossible to breathe.

Simu is at the leader's mercy, and it's all my fault.

I can't let Varys get to him.

"Your Highness," Feryn says softly. "What are you going to do?"

He doesn't need to ask. It's clear from the look in my eyes, and that's what frightens him the most.

"We're going back," I say.

"Hold on," he says. "You know that you're walking into a trap, right?" His voice is desperate, and I know he doesn't want to go back either.

"I know. That's why I need to go alone," I say. "I'll drop you off wherever you want, and then I'll head for the city."

His face twists with conflicted emotions. "My duty is to protect the princess," he says. "I can't let you go alone."

"I'm not the princess anymore," I say. The title has dragged me down for my entire life. It feels nice to leave it behind.

Feryn doesn't look convinced. "You can't just expect me to let you walk in there by yourself," he insists.

"Why do you suddenly care so much?" I ask, regretting the harshness in my voice. "Just a few hours ago, you were completely fine with letting them take me back. What's changed?"

"Nothing," he says.

"You're hiding something," I say.

Feryn gives in and sighs. "He wanted me to keep you safe," he says in a low whisper. "My one job is to keep you safe, and that's what I intend to do."

I pause. "He?"

"Wingate," he says reluctantly. "Sorin Wingate of the Emperor's guard."

My eyes grow wide in shock. "Sorin's alive?"

Feryn's eyes look wary. "That part I do not know," he admits. "But before he left for the North, he asked me to watch over you for him. His return was never promised, and he knew that. *That's* why I joined the Order. To follow you."

So, the whole bounty hunter thing was just a cover up.

My thoughts trail to Sorin. My friend, my best friend. Or at least, he was. He never stopped trying, he never stopped protecting me. And I turned him away. I chose the Order over him.

He didn't understand, I try to tell myself. *He was going to turn me into my father.*

But I don't need Feryn to lay his life down for mine. I can't let him do that, no matter if it's Sorin's dying wish or not.

"Alright," I say. "We have to stop somewhere for food, but we'll head out for Dravkia first thing in the morning."

"Of course, Your Highness," Feryn says, dipping his head.

We find a small restaurant in a town on the outskirts of the Imperia. It isn't very busy, so we don't run the risk of being detected.

Feryn gets up to use the restroom, and that's when I bolt.

By the time he returns, I'm already heading toward the depths of the Dark Sea.

Chapter 39

*When I approach the swamps above Dravkia, the sun has al-
ready begun to sink below the sea.*

The twilight sky stained with dark blues and purples masks my
ship and I pray no one has spotted me. If I'm lucky and Varys believed
what I said, I'll have bought Simu a little time.

I think of everything that could go wrong with my plan and try to
work out a strategy to avoid it. By the time I land the striker just south
of the entrance, where it'll remain hidden in the swamp, I'm feeling
more confident. As I wade through the murky water, away from where
my ship threatens to sink, I detect voices.

Ducking behind a large mud bank, I watch and listen.

I spot Taiana, and I stiffen. She'll have no problem killing me and
turning the Marrow over to Varys on a silver platter. I can't let her see
me.

"That girl is nothing but trouble," she mutters to her two companions.

"At least Varys will have her back here soon," one of them says. "I
heard he needs her for one of his projects."

"How does he expect to bring her back? The old loon apparently
threatened her if she ever dared to return."

"The two of them are close, apparently."

"Ha, well that's fitting," Taiana says.

A beep sounds and the door swings open. As soon as they descend in the elevator, I dart toward the heavy metal door. Before it closes, I wedge a stick into the crack to prop it open.

My first shot of luck.

I wait outside the elevator until I'm certain no one's inside. Clutching my dagger in one

hand, I press the button for the elevator.

To my relief, it's empty, and I step inside.

I'm back in Dravkia. Now, I'm entering as an enemy.

The city opens before me, and the once welcoming lights now act as spotlights, capturing my every move. I throw my hood over my head and duck through the streets. I run deeper into the city, past the library and down the dark corridors and alleys I know so well.

With every stride, my heart rate accelerates. I pray that Simu is safe, calmly scanning over his scrolls lit by the dim candles of his lair.

I round the corner, and I see the familiar run-down building. It's quiet, strangely quiet. Everything seems untouched.

Varys hasn't arrived yet, I think.

Drawing a deep breath, I push past the sheets of metal covering the doorway and the familiar smell of old parchment hits me. Crossing the messy room, I start toward the basement.

"Simu?" I call out into the darkness.

My voice echoes through the space, but no answer follows. Unease clings to me as my feet hit the smooth floor. I walk through the shelves, running my fingers over the leather books and the boxes of tools as if they could comfort me.

"Simu?" I say again.

No answer.

The floorboards above my head creak. I fight a gasp and press myself against the cold iron shelves.

The owner of the footsteps continues, and I hear the squawk of the door hinges as he finds his way down the basement steps.

As the figure reaches the bottom stair, I can see the faint outline of black cloth and the gleam of pristine white hair.

Alistar.

What is the spy doing here? I ask myself. *Did Varys send him?*

Anger heats my blood, and I tighten my grip on my dagger. As he walks down the rows, I emerge from the shelves.

"Don't take another step," I say.

He stops abruptly, and his eyes flash with surprise. "Iris?"

"Who sent you here?" I demand, taking a step closer. "Was it Varys?"

"What's more important is, what are *you* doing here?" he says, barely taking notice of the dagger pointed at his head. "Aren't you supposed to be in the Capital?"

My confusion must be visible, because he clears his throat. "Jaice messaged me. He told me everything, more or less."

"Where's Simu?" I ask.

Alistar drops his gaze, and an unsettling air surrounds us.

"Alistar..." I say. "What's going on? Am I...Am I too late?" My voice breaks, and I look at him, desperate to hear him tell me Simu is alive and well and safe.

But he doesn't.

"Iris," he says, "Simu is dead."

His words come crashing down on me like the weight of a thousand suns. I feel myself shaking, and my dagger clamors to the floor. Simu is gone.

"This is all my fault," I say as tears fall down my face. "He put himself in danger because of me..."

"No," Alistar says, placing a hand on my shoulder. "Simu has been working on his research since long before you arrived. But for a while, he gave up. You *reminded* him of why he set out to do this in the first place."

I look up at him through blurry eyes and I see the pain straining his face. I don't understand the reasoning behind his grief.

"Did Varys send you?" I ask, stepping away.

Alistar shakes his head. "No," he says. "I came on my own. To mourn."

Then, it makes sense. Alistar Drakos, the Order's most notorious spy, works for Simu. Worked. *That's* how Simu always seemed to know what was going on. And that's why Alistar is here.

"Do you wish to see him?" he asks me, his voice quiet.

His question takes me by surprise, but I nod and wipe the tears from my face.

"He's outside."

I fly up the stairs, tearing through the mess of papers. I trip over a stack of candles, but I keep going. As soon as I emerge from behind the metal scrap, I see him.

My breath catches in my throat.

Simu. He's bound to a tall pole and his face is frozen in a mask of pure terror.

I sink to the ground, the bones in my knees clashing as they meet the hard earth. Alistar stands beside me a moment later, closing his eyes.

"How could they do this...?" I whisper.

Alistar lets out a shaky breath. "The leader killed him because he knew the truth about the massacres and everything else regarding the Blood Marrow," he says. "He was ready to expose Varys and his true motives to the rest of the nations. Trasylar would never follow a king like that."

"Alistar," I say. "Alistar, this is *my* fault. I should have handed myself over to Varys. I should have let him kill me."

He turns to face me, and I expect to see hurt and betrayal and anger, but his expression is calm.

"Simu would never expect you to do that," he says. "And neither do I. You are here now, that is what matters. You tried."

I laugh out loud and point. "Are you kidding? Look at him, Alistar! He's *dead,* tied up like a damn animal."

"He didn't want to leave you like this," Alistar says. "He had so much more to teach you. I hope you know that."

I squeeze my eyes shut and cover my face with my hands. "This was never supposed to happen."

After a long moment, I finally collect myself, and Alistar helps me to my feet. My stomach twists as I look over at Simu, and I force myself to approach him.

With Alistar's help, we untie him from the post, and I look away from the deep gash along his neck from where Varys must have struck him.

Alistar carries him to his lair, and I light the candles that he loved so much.

I set a hand on his as I kneel beside his body. "This is not the end," I whisper to him.

Varys will be brought to justice. You will not die in vain.

I force myself to rise from the ground, and one piece of paper flies away and catches my eye. My smile fades as I pick up the loose sheet of parchment. On it is a message written in Simu's messy, frantic handwriting.

My eyes spread wide, and I clutch the paper with both hands.

"What is it?" Alistar asks, reading over my shoulder.

"He did it," I say in disbelief. "Simu found her."

"Found who?"

I set the paper down, shaking. "She's alive," I whisper. "My mother, she's alive, and she's here in the city."

Alistar meets my gaze, and he seems to understand.

"Go," he says. "You have to find her."

Chapter 40

The elevator takes me below the city, and I keep myself focused on finding my mother. I tear through the doors, still furious, and make my way through the dark, cavernous hallways.

A few soldiers make their rounds, and I fight my desire to attack them.

They aren't Varys, I remind myself. *They're soldiers, just like Jaice and Crayln and Naveen. They don't know what Varys has done.*

When they're gone, I follow an empty hallway into darkness and round the corner. Two guards occupy the space, bickering with each other.

"I helped you out last week!" one of them says. He has a large mustache under his nose.

The other one, a short and pudgy man, rolls his eyes. "Yeah? Well, why don't you be a pal and do it again. All I'm asking is for you to watch the post while I go have a smoke. Haven't been outside in ages."

They both sound grumpy, and I sit in the shadows, waiting.

"What's in it for me, eh?" the one with the mustache challenges.

The short man smiles. "I'll get you a date with that girl you've had your eye on," he says, laughing to himself. "How about it?"

The man thinks to himself through narrowed eyes, and I resist the urge to tap my foot impatiently.

"Deal," he says, his shoulders slumping with defeat. "You gotta promise you'll do it, though. Not like last time."

The shorter man is already on his way down the hall, laughing in triumph.

When the remaining soldier is alone, I take my chance. I creep up behind him and bring him down with a forceful strike to his neck, just like Jaice taught me. He isn't dead, just unconscious. I have to move fast.

Down the dark hallway is a small inlet made of rock. Boxes of supplies fill the space, and I manage to find some tape and tie a makeshift rope out of loose fabrics and rubber bands.

I pull us both behind the safety of the rock and quickly put on his uniform. His black hood hides most of my features. I snag his keycard and dagger and stuff both into my pockets.

Before leaving, I make sure he's tied securely with a thick mound of tape covering his mouth. I know he doesn't deserve it, but someone will find him, eventually. I just need to buy as much time for myself before that happens.

I stick my head out and scan the hallway. It's empty.

Continuing down the hall, I hear footsteps. They grow closer, and I see two soldiers ahead of me, both with long, intimidating swords strapped to their backs.

"You there," one of them calls out, and I freeze in my tracks. I keep my head down. He steps closer and peers down at me. "Where's your partner?"

I hesitate but force myself into the role.

Don't blow it.

"Out for a smoke," I say, making my voice deep. "You know how stuffy it can get in here." I smirk, trying to sell the act.

Luckily, they eat it up and laugh along. "That man's a genius," they say, glancing at each other. "Say, got any smokes on ya now?"

I shake my head and scoff. "Bastard, took 'em all with him."

"Well, damn," one of them says, disappointed.

"We'll find some more next time we're out," I say casually, and start to walk again.

The tip of one of their knives stops me.

"Hey, have I seen you before, soldier?" the man asks.

"First day," I say. "Got any advice for a rookie like me?"

They look at each other, and the man lowers his weapon. "Rule number one: the leader's word is law. No one defies him and lives to tell the story."

I nod but keep silent.

"And second," he continues, getting lost on a tangent. "If women are your thing, just know that half of them are crazy and the other half aren't interested, so save yourself the trouble and don't even try." That tip sounds like it's more directed at himself than at me.

"Good to know," I reply. "But I ought to get back to my post now."

The man steps aside. "Alright," he says. "Good luck. You'll need it."

"One more thing," I call, and they both turn around. "Where is it I'm supposed to go? The commander assigned me to guard the prisoners, but without my partner, I'm not sure how to get there."

One of them raises an eyebrow. "Not knowing where your post is on the first day? You ain't gonna last long."

I wince. "Sorry," I say. "But my partner said he'll meet me there, and if I'm late, he'll turn me into the leader." I hope they can hear the desperation in my voice.

"Fine," one of them says after a while. "The leader keeps his prisoners on the city level, behind Headquarters. Through some kind of tunnel at the back of the building."

I give my thanks and head back into the elevator. This time, I'm accompanied by a few other soldiers, two women and two men. We ride in silence.

The five of us get off on the city level, and I can feel eyes on me immediately. Not human eyes, but the eyes of the city. It's as if Varys knows I'm here.

I keep to the side streets and the outskirts to avoid as much traffic as I can.

Eventually, I reach Headquarters. It feels like years have gone by since I first arrived, but it's really only been a few months. I remember how Taiana had stormed her way past security, but I know that won't work for me.

I spot a group of soldiers walking toward the gate, IDs in hand. Despite every instinct warning me against it, I go up to one of them, a girl who can't be more than a couple of years older than me.

"Hey," I say to her. "Do you think you could help me? I'm supposed to meet my partner inside, but I'm new here and haven't set up my security identification yet."

The girl looks startled, almost surprised that I'm addressing her. "Oh," she says. "I don't know how I can help you. What's your name?"

"Alex," I say, looking down at the identification badge I carry. The card doesn't include the man's photo, but I know it would only take one quick search in their database to find him.

"Well, *Alex*," she says, although there's a strange tone in her voice, as if she can see through my false pseudonym, "I suppose you can slip in with me. You can be my apprentice."

"You'd do that?" I ask, almost too hopefully.

She lowers her voice. "Of course, I would. Your bravery is commendable," she says, and I know she's identified me straight away. "I didn't think you'd have what it takes to come back."

If she recognized me that quickly, a woman I don't even know, there's no telling how easily the leader could pinpoint me.

I give her a small smile, most of my vision still shaded by the hood. "Apologies, but I don't know what you mean."

"That uniform is much too big for you," she says, laughing. "Next time, steal from someone your own size."

She grins and takes my arm in hers. As we near the gate, she steps up to the machine and swipes her card and punches in a few passwords.

"Miss," a guard says, stepping forward before we reached the stairs. "She didn't go through the mandatory security checks. We'll need to stop you both right here."

I swallow but keep my head down.

"She's my apprentice," the woman says, almost too cheerfully. "Just appointed her this morning. We're headed in to get her initiated by the leader right now, and we would hate to keep him waiting."

The guard clears his throat, but the woman gives him a stern look, and he steps back. "Apologies, my lady," he says, dipping his head. "I didn't know it was you."

I turn to her, an inquisitive look in my eyes. Just who *is* she?

She senses me staring and laughs as we walk up the marble stone staircase. "The leader is my father," she says. "It comes with its perks."

My eyes widen.

Despite her eagerness to help me, I stiffen as I realize exactly what her being the leader's daughter means. She could be taking me directly to him. It could be a trap. It most definitely *is* a trap, one I stumbled right into.

Her father killed Simu, I think to myself. *She may have even helped him.*

I try to tug my arm out of her grip, discreetly at first and then with all of my strength. But she doesn't budge. Her grip is abnormally strong. She pulls me down the hallway, ignoring my struggle.

"Shh," she says, pulling me to the back of the building. We pass multiple guards on duty and I do my best to look nonthreatening, but she's the leader' daughter. No one would be foolish enough to stop her in her own city.

"Let go of me," I say through clenched teeth.

Ignoring me, she brings me before two great metal doors. Before I can speak, she punches a code into the keypad and leads us both inside.

It's dark, save for a few lamps lighting the way down a long, narrow passageway. All signs of industrialization are lost, and we're surrounded by a rocky, barren cave. The sounds of the water echo through the tunnel, and I see glistening pools along the sides of the path.

"What are you doing?" I hiss, reaching for my dagger.

Her dark golden hair glitters as she releases her ponytail so that it falls in light waves down her back. She smiles, her bright hazel-green eyes sparkling, and I see the resemblance between her Avrian.

"I'd prefer it if you didn't stab me," she says, her tone oddly light. "I'm just trying to help."

My eyes narrow. "The last time one of you 'tried to help,' I ended up in the back of a truck, arms bound and on my way back to Varys. So, sorry if I come off a little cold."

She doesn't seem to take offense at my tone, and instead beckons me to follow her down the illuminated tunnel. "It's safe, I promise. I arranged for the cameras to be disabled in here for the next hour. Thought you might like some privacy. And, you know, avoid my father finding out you're here."

"How did you know I would come?" I ask.

"I didn't know for sure," she says. "But my brother has told me about you. He says you're stubborn."

"No more than he is," I say.

She laughs. "Anyway," she says, "I figured that meant you weren't going to stay away forever. Especially not when your mother is being held here."

"She's really here?" I ask.

She nods.

Still wary, I follow her further into the labyrinth, which is much longer than I anticipated. We walk down a few flights of stairs, and the glowing moonstones continue to light our path. I never drop my guard, and my dagger rests in my hand.

"Why are you helping me?" I ask, careful to remain a few paces behind her, which would give me both a running start and the higher ground.

She pauses and looks at me, a shadow crossing her face. "Because I know what happens to people like you," she says, her voice heavy.

"People like me?"

"Yes. The Kuyang," she replies, her face contorting as if she had just witnessed a terrible crime.

I look away, unsure of how to respond. She's Varys' daughter. I can't trust her.

"He's going to try to kill me," I say, simply confirming what I already know.

She looks down and swallows. "That's his plan, yes." She grimaces. "But it won't happen on my watch, of course. I can give you twenty minutes with your mother, but after that, you will need to leave as quickly as you can. I know a way out through the prison that should leave you undetected."

I watch her closely, trying to sense any hints of deception or scheming, but I can't. She continues down the stairs and we reach a door made of tall metal bars. Two bright torches sit in iron holsters on each side, and she motions for me to take one.

We've made it to the prison.

"What's your name?" I ask her.

She holds her torch in front of us, her beautiful features illuminated in its warmth. "Astoria," she answers.

We approach the door, and I draw a deep breath,

"She's the only one here," Astoria says, unlocking the door. She offers a smile that gives me a hint of courage, and I maneuver my way through the darkness.

Along the walls are cells, blocked off with heavy metal bars. I don't want to think of the people who may have once occupied them. Taking a deep breath, I prepare myself before rounding the corner.

When I do, a shiny glass wall reflects the orange light of my torch, and I see a faint reflection of myself as I draw closer.

My chest tightens. Then, I see her. She's there, on the other side of the glass. The woman who I thought was dead. The woman who worked for the Order.

The woman who, no matter what she's done, is still my mother.

Chapter 41

*T*he cell is dark, but I know the figure huddled inside of it is my mother.

Apprehension rises inside of me as I creep closer, my footsteps lighter than Imperial silk. A tsunami of thoughts comes crashing through my mind as I remember the rumors, the stories, the lies.

I need to hear it from her own lips.

"Mother?" I whisper, my voice barely audible. "Mother, it's me. It's Iris."

The figure shifts, and I come face to face with my mother, whose features are almost identical to my own. The only difference is that hers are painted with age and weariness, while mine only display the latter.

She has the same almond-shaped eyes and the same soft nose bridge. Her hair is dark, like mine, and the resemblance warms my heart. Pushing aside the dirt and grime, she's beautiful.

"Iris," she croaks, her voice hoarse. "Iris, what are you doing here?"

My heart falls at the brashness of her tone, one I was least expecting.

"I'm here to speak with you," I stammer, thrown off. "And to get you out of here."

Her eyes shine with what I can only assume are tears. "My child," she says, her voice breaking. "There is no escaping for me. You must know that by now, if you have made it this far."

I shake my head adamantly. "I planned this perfectly," I insist. "There's a passage leading out of the prison. The cameras are down. He won't know until we're far away from here."

She smiles sadly. "I'm sure they've told you the most wicked things about me," she says pensively. "And yet you still risk yourself to come here?"

"I don't care what they've said," I tell her, although that's only half true. "I want to hear it from you."

"And if I confirm everything you already know? What if it's all true, the stories?"

"It doesn't matter," I say. "No one deserves to be a prisoner here."

"They will kill you," she says. "You're almost eighteen. You don't have much time."

"I won't leave," I affirm. "Not unless we leave together."

She stands, and I watch as her tall, dark figure rises above me. "Look at me," she orders, her voice strong.

I obey, and I see her clearly.

Her skin is caked with dirt, and thin scars line her frame. Along her back lies a rope of tangled, unkempt hair. I realize she's almost nothing but bone.

"I don't understand," I breathe. "Why did they do this to you? You were one of them..." My voice breaks.

She stares into my eyes, regret twisting her face. "I'm dying, my child," she says. "Stringing me along will only burden you further, and I think I've contributed to your suffering enough."

Tears burn in the corners of my eyes. "That isn't true," I say. "I need you, Mother. You refused to give me up to the Order, didn't you? You *saved* me."

"I had you intending to give your life for mine," she says darkly. "That alone is enough for me to deserve the most severe punishment hell has to offer."

"It doesn't have to be like that," I say, putting my hand on the glass. "What if I say I forgive you?"

"You can say it, but could you ever fully mean it?" she asks. "You will always resent me because of what I've done, and I deserve to live with that knowledge."

"Let me take you home."

"Home?" she echoes. "And where, my child, is this home you speak of?"

I bite my lip. "We'll find it," I promise. "Staying here isn't an option anymore."

She sighs and leans against the wall. "Do you have any idea how I kept them from taking you the moment you took your first breath?"

I shake my head softly.

"I remember it clearly," my mother says. "That day. Your birthday. From the moment I held you in my arms, I fell in love. I felt the bond of a mother and child and I knew I wasn't going to let Varys take you from me.

"So, I did what I do best. I lied. I'm not proud of my actions, yet I would choose selfishness over losing you without hesitation," she pauses and stares at the floor, her eyes hazy.

"How did you manage it?"

"One of the palace maids had a child a week before," she says. "I told her everything. I don't know why, maybe it was my guilty conscience. But then she volunteered to sacrifice her own child for mine. I was scared, and I refused to let her do it. But she insisted.

"Eventually, there wasn't any time left. I received a message, and they told me they were coming. So, the maid took you and hid you deep under the palace while I..." her voice trails off.

I gasp. Could it have been...*Myra*? No wonder she was so terrified of the Eye.

"Varys took her child instead of you, but word soon got out about your existence. Somehow, Varys knew you lived, and he was furious," she says, pain flashing across her face. "I knew I had to flee once the warning arrived at the palace."

"The Eye," I say.

She nods. "It destroyed me to leave you behind. But believe me, it would have ended worse had I taken you with me. Varys' men caught me just south of the border, before I could escape."

I furrow my brows. "Why do they keep you here?" I ask. "Varys knows you must have the Marrow, just as I do, right? Why didn't he kill you for it?"

"For the same reason they didn't kill my brother," she says.

I blink. "Your brother?"

"You've met him," she says. "I know you have. I don't expect he told you much, though. He was always quite cryptic."

My eyes widen.

"You don't mean..." I say, my voice faltering. "You don't mean *Simu,* do you?"

My mother's face lifts at the sound of his name, and my stomach drops. Simu was my uncle. He's my *family,* and I never knew.

"Yes," she says. "My brother came to find me many years after we got separated. He told me you were here, and I tried to convince him to drive you away." She shakes her head, as if disappointed. "He saw too much potential in you to let it go to waste."

I blink. The first time I met him, he told me I should not have come. That was my *mother's* doing. She was warning me even then.

"Mother..." I say, not sure if I can bring myself to tell her the truth of what happened to Simu.

She holds up a hand. "I already know," she says, her voice soft.

"I'm so sorry," I say, guilt rising inside of me. "I tried to stop it."

My mother shakes her head. "He did not finish preparing you to wield the Marrow," she says. "This puts you in even greater danger, and it will only increase the chances of it falling into the wrong hands."

"What do you mean, 'preparing' me?" I ask.

"The Marrow holds secrets and powers even I do not understand," she says. "With every generation, the Marrow's power grows. There is no telling how it will manifest inside of you."

"I don't understand," I say, stepping closer to the glass. "I hardly understand the Marrow at all."

"In time you will come to know it and its power," my mother says. "But the more power you draw from the Marrow, the more it takes from you. There is a limit, and once you surpass it, the Marrow will restore the natural order, and your life will be given back to the earth."

"You mean...I'll *die*?" I ask.

My mother nods, her expression grave. "The Marrow represents life," she says, "and with life there must also be death. This is how the world maintains order."

I swallow and think of every time I've used the Marrow without even knowing it.

"So, every time it heals me, the Marrow is actually *killing* me?" I ask, my heart beginning to race.

"It is not as linear as you make it seem," my mother says. "The Marrow responds uniquely to each individual who wields its power. Your body will tell you when you are approaching your limit, but ultimately it is up to you whether it is worth pushing past it."

I want to ask her more questions, but Astoria's voice cuts down the corridor.

"We need to go soon," she calls.

I turn back to my mother and plead, "Please come with us."

"I will not," she says.

Frustrated, I shake my head. "Why not? Why do you insist on remaining a prisoner here?"

"I'm not going to watch you die before my eyes, Iris," she says. "If we're caught together, Varys will bring a wrath upon both of us worse than anything you could ever imagine."

I clench my fists. "You say he'll make our lives terrible, but hasn't he done that already?"

My mother's gaze is hard. "Varys and I have a history that made him show mercy," she says, as if she's ashamed. "But that will not hold for a second time."

I narrow my eyes and step closer so I can see the faint lines around her mouth and in the creases of her eyes. "A history?"

She takes a step back, staggering. "He was my first love," she says.

My breath stops in my throat with horror.

"He wasn't always the man he is today," she says. "His father was the one who began the search for the Blood Marrow. *His* generation unleashed the massacres against our people, slaughtering them in hopes of finding it. That day, when they came to my village, Varys saved me. He prevented them from testing on me."

I listen intently as my mother recalls her story.

"By the time the Order had won, I was the only child left in the tribe," she says, her face haunted. "I supposed that helped. They took pity on me, so convincing them to spare me wasn't hard."

"Did any of the others make it?" I ask.

"I choose to believe that some did," she says sadly. My mother sighs. "I'm not proud of the things I've done or the people I've worked with. But I loved him, and that's what made me stay. He made me believe there could be some good in this world."

"What changed?"

"Varys' father took over," she says. "He gave his son a choice: either I would be harvested for the Marrow, or I would bear a child to stand in my place."

A tear falls from her face, and she doesn't meet my eyes.

"I need you to know that I was never planning to give you up," she says. "We just needed to buy time. But by then, it was too late. Varys' priorities shifted, and power became his true love."

"He's a coward," I mutter, imagining the pain my mother must have gone through. I don't even feel angry anymore. Instead, I pity her.

"I should've known to escape then," my mother says, her voice cracking a little. "But I was a foolish, love-struck woman. I clutched onto the hope of changing his mind." She shakes her head disapprovingly. "I pray you are not so blind."

"I'm not," I say, making a silent vow to make sure what I say holds true.

A smile reaches her face. "Good," she says. "Now, I will not ask you again. Go now and avoid making my mistake. There is nothing left for you here."

"I'm not leaving until I kill Varys," I say to her. "And I'm certainly not leaving without you."

"Astoria!" she calls. "Take her away."

Chapter 42

*A*storia is at my side in an instant, but I resist her urges for us to *leave.* My mother disappears deep into her cell, and she seems to morph into the darkness.

"Mother!" I call as Astoria takes me by the arm and drags me away. "Mother, please! Let go!"

"We have to get you out of here *now*," Astoria says quietly. "Your mother cares about you more than you know. Listen to her. Escaping will be the best thing you can give her."

I don't want to listen. Raw emotions boil through my body, a mix of anger and sadness and helplessness. I'm so close to helping her. She's alive. I *talked* to her. But I can't save her.

"Iris," Astoria says, shaking my shoulders and rocking me back into reality.

We're standing outside the prison, the metal door locked shut. My mother is just out of reach. How could I let the opportunity to save her slip away?

"Why won't she come?" I ask, sounding like a child. "Why won't she let me help her?"

Astoria's eyes don't meet mine, and I know she's conflicted. "She's set in her ways. It would be easier for her to stay in her cell than to risk your life escaping. She knows you'll understand someday."

"How can you be so sure?"

She shrugs. "My father appointed me a prison guard, but mostly, I just talk to her. We've had years of conversations, and the vast majority are about you, Iris. Not one day goes by that she doesn't think of you; that she doesn't wish things had been different."

My eyes are clouded, and I feel a small weight lift from my chest. I allow Astoria to lead me back through the rocky tunnel, the echoes of my mother's voice repeating in my mind. I won't let her sacrifices be in vain. Varys will never get the Marrow.

"I'm going to kill your father," I say aloud in a murderous tone that seems foreign to me.

Astoria doesn't look back at me. "Revenge is a dangerous ambition, but a powerful asset all the same."

Ahead of us, harsh voices sound, and Astoria flattens us against the wall, tucking me as far out of view as she can. The soldiers are approaching quickly, torches in hand.

"They should be this way," one of the men says, and I recognize him. I'm wearing his clothes.

"Stay here and stay low," Astoria whispers, pushing me into a small groove in the rock. "I'll get rid of them."

I nod, but my suspicion grows. She said she's helping me, but maybe it's just some cruel, wicked game the leader created.

"Soldiers," she says from down the hall, her voice radiating authority. "State your business."

"My lady," Alex says, and I flinch. "We have good reason to believe that there is an infiltrator in our midst. A girl, not more than eighteen. She's been scurrying through the ground level and has been attacking us."

"Yeah," one of them says, and I assume it's the man with the mustache. "She's dangerous. Doesn't look it, but we think that an internal lockdown should be in order."

"That won't be necessary," Astoria says, her voice very persuasive. "I've already found her and I'm dealing with her."

Shocked gasps ripple through the crowd. "Are you sure it's her?"

"Where is she?"

"You dare question my judgment?" she says, her voice icy. "I'm having her brought to my father as we speak. If you have an issue with my authority, feel free to take it up with him directly."

They all murmur quick apologies and seem to grovel at her feet for forgiveness.

Cowards, I think smugly.

"Our sincerest apologies, my lady," one of them says. "We will be returning to our posts, and please, let us know if there's anything we can do for you."

"Tell the guards at the south wall to re-station themselves to the front. If that girl infiltrated our city, then what's to say she doesn't have more following her?" Astoria says. "I want at least double the amount of soldiers guarding the main entrance."

"Yes, my lady," they say in unison.

The metal clanking of boots fades up the rocks and echoes down the cavern. Once I hear the slam of the metal door, Astoria returns to my side.

We head down the path Astoria set us on and slip through a small door ingrained in the rock. Had I not been following her, I would have completely missed it.

"We'll head out through the back entrance," she explains as we walk down the long hallway. It appears that we're back on the ground level. "I had them direct the guards in the south to the main entrance, so we should be able to avoid trouble."

"And you think it will work?" I ask her.

"It should," she says, and to her credit, she doesn't try to convince me that her plan is completely foolproof. She knows the risks and the odds and doesn't hide it from me.

"Okay," I say as we travel into the main area of the ground floor. There are already less soldiers patrolling around and more lined up to ride the elevator to the main entrance. Astoria works fast.

We walk hurriedly to the back of the cavernous room, and I keep my head down, trusting Astoria to guide me adequately. There's a large set of oak doors and she unlocks them with the digital keypad.

"Once I open the door," she says, "run. There is a tunnel that leads to the surface. It's long, but you'll make it out just fine."

I look at her and nod. "Thank you."

"Don't thank me until you're safe," she says, almost wincing as she opens the doors.

My heart stops.

A dark shadow blocks the entrance, and behind the door stands the leader.

His large frame looms over us, and three men stand behind him. His Elites.

Astoria whips around to face me, her face twisted in pure shock. "Iris..." she says, her voice breaking. "Iris, I didn't know, I promise."

I almost don't hear her, blood roaring furiously in my ears. I was so close, so close to freedom. But I was foolish.

Why do I keep doing this? I demand. *Am I so desperate that I still can't see through the most obvious deception?*

"Miss Wu," the leader's cunning voice sounds. "Back so soon, are you?"

Astoria stands, blocking me from her leader's ravenous glare. "Father," she says. "Please, you have to understand. I ran the tests again. She isn't who you've been looking for."

Varys is hardly interested in his daughter, his eyes barely glancing at her.

"She doesn't carry the Blood Marrow," Astoria insists.

"And what makes you say that?" the leader says, stepping closer.

Astoria shrinks back, pressing me against the wall. "Keeping her here is pointless. She's useless to us."

"You're insignificant to me right now," Varys says. "I'll deal with you later. But for now, I think I'll begin calling my clients. We're finally near the harvesting day." A malevolent grin stretches across his face. One more step and his toe crosses the threshold.

Astoria slams the heavy door shut before he can cross. "RUN!" she yells, barricading the door with her own body.

Varys will break through in no time, but I do as she says and I run. My legs carry me across the floor, and I do my best to outrun the other soldiers who pick up the chase. When I approach the elevator, I know there's no escape.

Metal footsteps grow louder behind me, and two Elites seize my arms.

I try to scream, to run, but I can't.

I feel as if an invisible cage has fallen around me, and I can't help but feel that everything has been for nothing.

All of my strength slips away from me as my knees collide with the stone ground. A heavy boot digs into my spine, and I fall limp in defeat.

Powerless.

I'm utterly powerless.

Chapter 43

The Elites haul me to my old room in the soldiers' quarters, stripping me of my weapons. They slam the door shut and leave me alone to realize the weight of my failure.

Slumping against the wall, I close my eyes and lean my head back. I tried to save Simu, but I was too late. I finally found my mother, but I failed to escape with her.

I sigh and hang my head in my hands, knees tucked up to my chest. I wish I was back in the palace, before the Order became a part of my life. Despite being locked up, I was safe, and I didn't have to worry about watching my friends risk their lives for me.

I drag myself over to the base of the tall floor to ceiling windows and I lean against the cool glass. Tears slide from my cheek and run down the windowpanes, blurring the lights below. I try to focus on the beauty of the city, to distract myself. But in every light, I see the eyes of Varys watching me. In every striker that races by, I see my friends who are unaware that the plan has already been foiled. In every soldier running toward the Needle, I see myself.

I feel small and insignificant, filled with false hope, only to be crushed under the weight of this city and all the horrors that swim in the waters surrounding it.

After hours alone in my room, I hear a faint rattle coming from the bookshelf in the corner. I angle my ears toward it, wiping tears from my eyes as I stand. Walking over to the buzzing, I search for the source of the noise. Under piles of books is a thin, wrapped object. It looks like a book, but it's much lighter and thinner than one. There's a small note taped to the back.

"If you need me, I'm here," I read under my breath. "I hope this makes it to you in time." Avrian's signature is printed below.

My heart skips a beat as I run my fingers over his name.

I unwrap the paper and discover a smooth stone slate. It looks ordinary, just stone. But it buzzes again, and writing appears on its face.

The message reads, *We're coming.*

I gasp, almost dropping the tablet.

Quickly, I search for a pen and begin to write on the smooth stone. As soon as I finish, the message disappears. *Who are you?*

Did you read my note? the tablet says.

How do I know you are who you claim to be? I reply back. *How did this thing get in my room?*

I had one of my men drop it off, he writes back. *But that's not important. What's important is that you lay low and wait for us to reach the city.*

Don't. He'll kill you, I message back.

A response appears moments later.

You promised a next time.

My eyes widen, and my hands quiver under the cold stone.

Avrian. It's really him.

Consider the promise broken, I respond.

A moment passes.

Your guard friend is here too, is all the stone says, before going blank.

My mouth hangs open, and I don't know if I believe him. Is it truly possible that Sorin is alive?

No matter how many times I message, no matter what I say, he does not reply, and the tablet remains dormant. Frustration consumes me and I throw it at the window. The tablet shatters.

An alarm blares the moment the pieces hit the floor, and two soldiers file into my room, assessing the scene.

"What's going on in here?" they demand. Their uniforms harbor the official crest of the leader: a silver emblem of two conjoined rings, cracked and splintered. They're Elites.

"It fell," I say.

One of them walks over and clears the glass shards to prevent me from using them as weapons. They then proceed to remove all other glassware and cutlery from the room, eyeing me skeptically.

By the time they finish removing things, my room is bare. All that remains is a sofa, the bed, and a desk in the corner that's bolted to the wall.

As I watch them move in and out of my room, I think about how easy it would be to slip out while they weren't looking, or how I could take them both if I played my cards right, but I don't. I know that even if I get past them, I won't be able to escape the city. I have no choice but to wait.

I spend two days in my room before the guards return and handcuff me. They lead me through the hallway and duck my head into the back of a black car.

We travel the length of the city, and the shame of defeat keeps my head down.

Once the car comes to a stop, the men drag me out and lead me into an elevator. Moments pass in a stiff silence, and they take me to a small cave-like room. All four walls are made of solid rock, and two Elites guard the entryway. The only light comes from the moonstones embedded in the rock walls, and I recognize the leader standing a few feet away. A smaller man stands at his side.

"So good to see you again, Miss Wu," the leader says. "Happy Harvesting Day."

My arms are still bound by the two soldiers, and I have no choice but to step inside.

"Stop this now, Varys," I say, using his name as if it diminishes the power he holds over me.

He chuckles. "It's Harvesting Day," he replies. "To stop now would make all our efforts for the past few centuries in vain."

Centuries. I shiver.

I stomp my foot hard on my guard's foot, and he grunts in pain, loosening his grip slightly. Twisting, I step out of their grasp and pull a dagger from one of their holsters.

Before they get the chance to grab me, I rush towards Varys.

He draws his own knife and grins.

I don't waste a moment, and my dagger passes through the air just inches away from his chest. He dodges me, but I call upon every combat maneuver Jaice taught me, and I meet him blow for blow.

His knife nicks the tip of my ear, but I slice mine across his calf and he grunts. With one hand, he throws me to the ground, and I throw the dagger at his stomach. To my horror, he catches it in midair and drops it harmlessly to the floor.

The Elites are on me in an instant, and Varys stands back, ignoring the blood dripping from his leg. They pin me to the ground, holding me with a firm boot to my back.

"You didn't think it would be that easy, did you?" he asks.

I narrow my eyes but I don't respond, angry that I allowed myself to be bested so easily.

"I heard my son's aircraft is headed here, and according to him, you're on board," the leader continues, crouching down to stare me in the eyes. "Interesting, isn't it?"I swallow.

"He says he rescued you from a prison down in Trasylar," he muses.

"I have no idea what you're talking about," I say.

Varys laughs, his piercing eyes fixated on me. "Clever girl. My son is not so easily swayed. How you got him roped into this, I do not know. But consider me impressed."

I wonder the same thing, but I don't give Varys the satisfaction of knowing that.

"No matter," the leader says. He turns to his men. "Prepare her for the harvest."

His men haul me up and heavy metal chains clamp around my wrists despite my best efforts to protest. One of the Elites shoves me against the wall and sharp rocks collide with my spine. The chains tighten, and I can no longer move my arms.

"Your fate is a shame, really," the leader says. "A mind like yours would thrive in the environment I have created. You could have become a powerful asset to our cause."

"I would never do anything to help you," I say through gritted teeth.

"But you already have," the leader counters. "You've done so much to help us."

He's right, and I know it. Hatred burns inside of me, but it's not all directed at Varys. I *chose* this. I chose to help them. I chose to be *one of them.*

The short man beside Varys walks over to me and begins assembling tools from a small cart. A pit forms in my stomach as he draws out a knife and polishes it with a velvet cloth.

I'm trapped. No one will hear my screams. No one will come.

Varys *won.*

Chapter 44

"*You are a miracle,*" *Varys says.* "And today, on September twenty-fourth, we will share this miracle with the world."

The medic steps forward and peels back my sleeve. His gloved hands are cold, and I shrink away under his touch.

"Together we will be an unstoppable force," Varys says.

I almost laugh.

"Together?" I echo. "You're going to *kill* me."

"You will live on through the Marrow," he says. "Your power is what will allow me to change this world for the better."

One of the medic's assistants appears and hands him a small glass filled with what I only assume to be the mixture Owens talked about. The smell is powerful, and I feel lightheaded as the odor floods through my nose.

The medic takes the beaker and holds it up. "A mixture of acidic properties originating in the caves of Trasylar," he says. "It is capable of burning straight through to the bone. It will open up the tissues and allow for the extraction of the Blood Marrow."

I try to break out of the chains, but no matter how much I struggle, I know they won't give. The Elites are another issue.

"Do you truly think this will even work?" I demand. "The Marrow was a gift to Imperians, sent from the gods. It was never meant to be harvested like this!"

"It is a gift to be shared with all," Varys says. "I will bring the reign of selfish kings and emperors to an end."

I want to tell him he's a tyrant, but I can't find it in myself to argue. My words would only fall on deaf ears.

"Continue the extraction," Varys says to the medic.

"No!" I shout in protest.

The medic's icy hands touch my skin, and with horror, I watch as he pours a small portion of the liquid onto my arm. Instantly, pain surges through my body and I let out an ear-splitting shriek.

My skin is burning, bubbling away as it succumbs to the acid. With every passing moment, my body tries to repair itself, but the acid is stronger. I can't escape. I can't even speak.

Simu warned me. Jess warned me. Even Owens warned me.

I should never have come back.

Black spots cloud my vision, I fight against the pain, against the iron chains binding me to the rocks. But it's not enough. Tears of agony burst from my eyes and I feel the acid tear closer and closer to my bone.

I'm as good as dead.

But I should know I won't get off that easily.

Pools of light flood my vision and I feel my nerves buzzing back to life. The stone wall digs into my spine, but the chains that bound my wrists are on the floor in a broken heap. Someone pours cold water over my arm, dimming the pain.

I blink, expecting to see Varys, but he's nowhere to be seen.

I look over to see a flash of blond hair. My vision is still blurring in and out of focus, but I know that face. Sorin flinches, his pale eyes locking with mine. He presses a thick wad of cotton pads onto my arm to stop the bleeding.

"It's going to be okay, Iris," he says to me. "We got here just in time."

I gasp for air and I feel my heart rate slow. The bright moonstones overhead amplify the throbbing pain in my head, and I struggle to keep my eyes open.

"Sorin?" I choke out. "You're here...how?"

Sorin helps me to my feet and offers his shoulder.

"I had to come back for you," he says. "Some of the Imperial soldiers dragged me from the snow, but we were taken back to Trasylar as prisoners."

"Then how...?"

"Some of your...comrades found us in Trasylar's stronghold," he says. "One of them—the one from the Mangra—recognized me and agreed to take us to you."

"Us?" I echo.

"Me and Will," Sorin says. "He's waiting outside with Astoria."

I blink, head still spinning.

Footsteps sound to my left, and I turn. Astoria stands in the entryway, offering me a comforting smile. Will stands behind her, his hair still cut short in a military style. But he looks like the young boy I left that night. The soldier in him is gone.

"Will..." I say.

Will takes a step closer, and before I can speak further, he throws his arms around me, and I instinctively do the same.

"I'm so sorry," he says, his eyes swollen with tears. "I don't know what I was thinking. Joining the battle was stupid. So stupid. When you left, I was so angry."

"I know," I whisper.

"I missed you so much," he says.

"I missed you, too," I say, fighting back tears. "I'll never leave you like that again, I promise."

He wipes tears from his face and steps back, looking up at Astoria.

I follow his gaze, and my stomach churns. "What happened?" I ask. "How did you lure them away?"

"They were called to the city when the fighting started," she answers.

"Fighting?" I ask.

Astoria lowers her eyes. "My brother took Mavros and Akerman to the city, along with a few others he picked up in Trasylar. I've never seen him act this way," she says, her voice dark. "The plan was for it to be a simple, bloodless coup. But I fear it is turning into much more."

At least the three of them are still together, I think.

"This isn't going to end well," I say, my voice shaking.

"I know," she says. "But I couldn't stop him. I don't think anyone could have. Either way, he was successful in luring my father away. That's what matters now."

"We have to help them," I say, stepping forward on wobbly legs. "The Elites are almost an entire regime in themselves. Avrian and the others can hold their own, but only for so long."

"You're right," Astoria agrees. "But my brother has a loyal regime. Once they learned the truth...well, they agreed to stand against my father. They are not alone."

"And the Second and Third Regimes?"

Astoria bites her lip. "The Second remains neutral. Largely because most of their soldiers are out on missions."

I lift a surprised eyebrow. I would have expected Taiana to leap at the opportunity to kill me.

"The Third is siding with my father," she continues. "When soldiers are left without a leader, they will naturally turn to those in power. My father is the obvious choice."

"How can we help Avrian and the others?" I ask urgently.

Astoria takes my other arm and hoists me onto her left shoulder, aiding me out of the room.

"You can help by getting to safety," she says. "There's a ship this way. You need to take it and leave as soon as you can. Wingate, I'm assuming you can fly?"

Sorin, to my surprise, nods. "Yes."

"Since when?" I ask him.

He winces a little. "As a part of the guard, I had to learn to fly the emperor's airships. The strikers here work similarly."

"I'm not leaving without our friends," I say.

An approving smile slips out of Astoria's stoic expression.

"Iris, you can't fight in your state," Sorin points out.

"Yes, I can," I say, stepping out of their grasp to prove my point. "I think I can devise a plan if I can survey the situation. Can we get up to the Beacon?"

"The Beacon?" Sorin asks.

"It's the tallest building in the city," I explain. "If we make it up there, we'll have a clear view of the entire city."

Astoria and Sorin exchange worried glances, but before Sorin can argue, Astoria nods. "It's possible, but there's fighting outside of Headquarters. Breaking in will be near impossible."

"If you can get me up to the Beacon, I'll figure something out," I say, as confidently as I can manage.

Sorin takes my arm. "If you get caught, everything the others are doing will be for nothing," he says.

"You don't think I know that?" I say quietly. "I have to help them. If they die because of me, I'll never be able to forgive myself."

Without waiting for him to argue, I turn to Astoria. "Let's go."

She nods and we head for the elevator. Sorin is at my side in an instant, his expression shifting from fear to determination.

"If you're sure about this, then I'll stand by you," he says. "You know I will."

Sorin draws one of his swords and hands it to me.

Astoria raises an eyebrow. "A sword?" she says. "That doesn't really seem like your speed."

I open my mouth to form a retort, but she pulls out a beautiful, familiar dagger with a sapphire encrusted hilt. My eyes widen.

"Is that mine?"

She smiles. "My brother said you would want it, so I swiped it from my father's office before I came to get you."

I take it gratefully and send a silent thank you to Avrian.

"Also," Astoria says, "please don't be angry, but I sent for your friend. The moment I learned your little brother was coming too, I knew we had to get him out."

"Who did you call?" I ask, my eyes falling on Will.

"The Princess of Sejeran," she answers. "My brother told me you two were close. I had a feeling you would want to stay and fight, but we both know this isn't a place for children."

Jess. She's coming here, to Dravkia, I think, horrified.

"You did *what*?" I say, trying to keep my temper in check. "It's incredibly dangerous for her here!"

Astoria places a hand on my arm. "I know," she says. "But the princess is clever. She is probably here by now."

I don't know if I should be angry or grateful.

"Let's find her before Varys does," I say.

We head towards the elevator, and to my relief, we don't run into any guards. Astoria and Sorin must have dealt with them before I awoke.

The elevator doors slide open to reveal a familiar figure, and I smile. She's safe.

"Jess," I exclaim, still in shock that she's here.

She grins in greeting, but the energy she once had is gone. "Iris," she says. "I came as soon as I got the call."

"I am forever grateful you did," I say. "But it's not safe here. You can't stay long."

She nods. "I know, but you needed my help."

I smile gratefully.

"You never wrote back," she says. "Did you get my hawk?" Worry shines in her eyes.

"I did," I say. "But you're right, I didn't get a chance to write back. We were pretty short on supplies."

Jess shrugs it off. "Are you sure you still want to fight? It's madness up there. I've never seen such a sight. I'm lucky I slipped by unnoticed."

"I have to," I say.

I look over and see Will trailing behind us, as fragile as a leaf in a hailstorm. Even though he trained to be a soldier, he isn't ready for this kind of combat. The Order plays dirty, and he's not used to that.

Jess' eyes soften as they rest on my brother. "I'll take him now, then. He'll be safe with me in Sejeran. I can make sure he's well protected."

"I can't thank you enough," I say. "You've been a much better friend to me than I have been to you."

"I have no doubt you'll return the favor," Jess says, giving me a wink. Then she leans closer so I'm the only one who can hear her. "I don't blame you for what happened. I know it wasn't your fault."

I almost ask her how she knows we're responsible for the royal advisor's mysterious death, but she draws away.

"Take the path hidden in the rocks," Astoria instructs, directing them towards the same tunnel she tried to help me through. I can only pray that Varys isn't blocking it this time. Astoria seems to know what I'm thinking, and she throws me a knowing glance. *I promise he's not there.*

Will throws his arms around me one more time before I send him off with Jess. He'll be safe with her. Much safer than on the battlefield.

I draw in a deep breath and board the elevator.

The ride up is quick and the heavy metal doors open up to the flickering lights of the city. The front half is nearly deserted, and the streets are deathly quiet. I can only imagine the chaos occurring outside of Headquarters.

I follow Astoria down the back alleys, and we make our way to the Beacon. It's an enormous structure made almost entirely out of thick glass. Any guards stationed around it must have joined the fight, because we're able to slip in with ease.

I do my best to massage my shoulder as we wait in the elevator. The thick padding on my arm keeps the bleeding at bay, and the Marrow works quickly.

"I'm predicting we have ten minutes before my brother's regime gives out," Astoria says. "They've already been at it for a couple of hours. I can't image the casualties."

"Hours?" I say as we reached the observatory deck.

Astoria sighs. "You were out for quite a while, but I don't blame you. Considering the treatment you went through, it's a miracle you're walking."

How could I let this happen?

I press my head against the glass.

From across the city, I spot Headquarters instantly. The grounds surrounding the marble building are covered with soldiers, dead and alive.

I use the tower viewer stationed at the edge of the observatory deck to get a closer look. The magnification is astonishingly powerful, and I can make out the individual shapes and features of each soldier.

Avrian is easy to spot. He's in the front of his regime fighting as if that's all he knows how to do.

As soldiers battle around him, he draws a long double-edged sword from across his back. I've never seen him wield it before, but it's clear this isn't his first time. He skillfully slices through at least two of the Elites with one swift jap of his arm and deflects attackers with the other end.

I force myself to pull my eyes away from him, trusting that he can hold his own for a little longer. I spot Jaice next, sword in hand. To my relief, he seems to be managing. But as I look closer, I see blood running down his cheeks and arms. I'm too far away to tell if the blood is his.

Crayln takes longer to find, but eventually I spot him on the roof of a nearby building. Next to him sits a large crossbow, but he hardly takes interest in it. What really holds his attention is the laptop propped up on his knees.

"Is there any way to contact them?" I ask.

Astoria peers out of the window as well, the gears inside of her mind cranking. "They took radios with them, but I've tried. The signal's been cut."

"We need to head for Crayln," I say, directing them to where he sits on the roof. "The guy down there with the computer."

"What's he doing?" Sorin asks, taking a turn at peering through the tower viewer.

"He's in charge of our Cyber Division," Astoria replies. "It's likely he's attempting to hijack my father's communication panels. That way, he can't give out orders from the safety of his office."

I nod. "Exactly. We have to get over to him and regroup. Maybe we can buy him some time."

"I like the sound of it," Astoria says, retrieving a spear from a compartment nearby. The staff is made of a white marble, and the tip is clear. It must be diamond. "Fill us in with the rest of the plan on the way."

Headquarters is still at least three miles down the road, and as we draw near, the avenue becomes dense with traffic. Some people are rushing to get to Headquarters and join the battle while others are fleeing. Occasionally, a soldier will dart in front of our car and Astoria has to slam on the brakes, causing us all to fall back into the seats.

"Idiots!" Astoria shouts, the car honking as she furiously pounds on the steering wheel. "We're never going to get there in time."

I grip the handle of the car door, holding it for a brief moment in contemplation. "We'll take it on foot," I say, pushing the door open before they can protest.

"Iris, wait up!" Sorin calls after me.

I slow my pace and wait until they're at my side. Then the three of us bolt down the crowded avenue. Adrenaline courses through me as we pass honking cars and continue towards the battle.

I clear my throat and yell over the blaring sounds of the city. "We'll get to Crayln first," I say. "Then we'll split up. Sorin, you can stay and guard him while Astoria and I break into Headquarters."

"The last part worries me," Sorin says.

"I have an idea, though," I say, still working through the plan in my head before telling them. "We'll drop in through the roof undetected." I lift my chin and focus my eyes on the nearing battle.

"How?" Sorin asks.

"Just trust me."

"And once we're in?" Astoria asks.

"Then we make our way to Varys and we corner him," I say. This part of the plan will take a miracle and then some, but I continue. "We'll need to take out the Elites guarding him, but we may be able to lure them away. And then, we'll force Varys to retreat his forces and we get him to surrender."

Astoria purses her lips but doesn't speak as she runs alongside me, keeping the quick pace with ease.

They remain silent for a moment, no doubt running the plan through their own minds, working out the kinks and calculating the odds of it succeeding.

"We have no other choice," Astoria says. "Wingate, take this radio and give it to Crayln. Notify us when you're able to break through. We're going to need some help with the cameras and alarm systems."

He nods and catches the radio, tucking it safely in his pocket.

"Stay safe," I say to him as he veers towards Crayln's roof.

"Right back at you."

I watch as he turns and disappears into the crowd, worry nagging at my stomach.

He'll be okay.

He has to be.

Chapter 45

A hand takes my arm, and Astoria shoots me an impatient look. "We have to hurry," she says.

"Right," I say. I motion for her to follow me.

"Iris," she says, falling into pace beside me.

"Yes?" I ask.

She sighs. "I'm so sorry," she says. "I have hardly given you any reason to trust me, but please know that I will help you no matter what it takes. I know that what my father is doing—what he's *done*—is wrong."

"I believe you," I say.

"I've always wanted to stop this," she says, almost apologetically. "But I've never had the means to do it. Not until you came along."

"Well, it's not too late," I say. "We need to make sure the hunt ends now."

I lead Astoria to the apartments, and we make our way to Naveen's room. His room is exactly how he left it. His bags are in a pile on the floor and I rummage through them, searching for our gliders.

"What's the plan, exactly?" Astoria asks, inspecting the gliders carefully.

"We'll never get inside Headquarters through the front doors," I say. "So, we'll go through the roof."

She still looks skeptical but doesn't protest as we make our way back to the Beacon. We take the elevator and shoot up to the top. Once we're standing on the deck, we unfold the wings.

"And you're sure this will work? I've never done this before," Astoria says, pulling back her golden hair.

"It will," I say. "Follow my lead."

We exchange glances. Headquarters lays directly before us, still swarming with soldiers.

"He has no *idea* what's coming for him," I say.

We jump.

The air lifts us, just as it had when we were gliding off of Mount Hikirojaro. Only this time, we have to dodge the tall buildings looming in front of us and avoid being seen. I look back to make sure Astoria is following. She grips on tightly to the bar, and to her credit, she keeps her composure.

I direct my gaze to the battle below and my heart sinks. More and more of the Elites file out from Headquarters to join the fighting. I spot Avrian, still battling but now soaked in red. Fear claws at my stomach, but I tell myself repeatedly that the blood isn't his.

We land on the roof. The guards are distracted by the fighting and don't seem to notice.

Astoria lifts her radio to signal the others. "Mavros, any luck disabling the alarms in the north wing?"

Crayln's voice comes on the radio and relief washes over me. "Where have you *been?*" he demands. "We've been worried sick."

"A slight detour," I say, hoping that he can't hear the sadness in my voice. "Not to worry, we're back on track now."

"Give me one minute," Crayln says after a moment, the furious typing of keys sounding in the background. "Once I turn off the alarms, you'll have thirty seconds before I'm locked out again, so work fast."

"Understood," Astoria says. She holds her hands above the vent, prepared to lift it out. We run the risk of triggering the alarms and spoiling the entire operation, so we wait for Crayln's call.

"Now," Crayln says.

Astoria reaches for the iron bars and using her blade, she lifts the vent from its screws and a hole opens up before us.

I drop down, and she follows close behind me.

A breath of relief escapes her lips, and we pad softly down the stairs, surrounded by the haunting glow of lights. Astoria drags me into a small storage closet, and once she decides that it's safe, she radios Crayln again.

"Did you find him?" she asks, her voice still low.

"No," he says. "I can't find him anywhere."

Astoria frowns. "Then where could he be?"

"He's not on the field, I can tell you that." It's Sorin's voice this time.

"You don't think he went back to find me, do you?" I ask Astoria. "If he figures out I'm gone, he'll know what we're up to."

"Unfortunately, I think you're right," she says. "He wouldn't want to let you out of his sight for long."

"Then who's managing his Elites?" I ask. "Someone has to be giving out orders."

Crayln sounds again through the radio. "It's Owens," he says darkly. "I found him in the central control room. I always knew he was a snake."

"That bastard," I say, clenching my fists. "Leave Owens to me. Astoria, I'll leave finding your father up to you."

She shoots me a glance. "He knows I helped you," she says.

I look away. "Then I'll go to Varys and you can take the control room. I don't want to cause you any more problems."

Astoria shakes her head. "Yeah, right. And then my brother will kill me for sending you right into my father's grasp. I'll talk to my father. You can stop the fighting here."

"We don't have much time," Crayln says from the other side. "We need to act now."

"Alright," I say to him. Then, I look at Astoria. "Take the radio and call them if you run into trouble." As much as I want to trust her, I'm not sure if she has what it takes to fight him.

She hesitates but knows that it's for the better. "Don't do anything stupid, alright? Don't be afraid to play it safe. We don't need a martyr."

"I know," I say.

Slowly, I open the closet door and peer out into the hallway. It's dark, but still empty. Astoria heads back to where we cut the hole in the roof, and I follow her instructions to the central control room.

It's on the front side of the building, in one of the offices with a large window overlooking the carnage below. I imagine Owens sitting in a chair, watching the chaos with glee.

Four Elites guard his door, armed to the teeth with protective armor. My knives won't be able to hit them unless I aim for the head. Even then, I would have to get lucky.

An alarm blares at the far end of the hall, and I wonder if Astoria accidentally set it off, but I realize that it's the fire alarm. The floor begins to flood as the overhead sprinklers spring to life. Three of the Elites run down the hall to check out whatever tripped the alarm, leaving one to guard Owens.

I know Crayln has given me an opening, and without wasting a second, I dash for the door. The Elite aims his sword as soon as he spots me, but I'm faster. My arm hooks around his and I flip him over my back. He lands roughly on the floor. He slashes, but he misses, striking the wall instead.

"Close, but not quite," I huff, landing a punch to his cheek. I watch as his helmet rolls on the floor. He's unarmed but still dangerous, and using his weight to his advantage, he easily throws me off and my head snaps back into the wall.

A shock ripples through me but I'm not finished. He's already standing and lands a heavy blow to my abdomen. Before he can strike again, I kick him in the shin and then drive my knee up with a force that causes him to crumple to the ground.

Jaice had strictly ordered me not to use that move on him during training, but in this situation, it works beautifully.

I tie the Elite outside the door with a piece of his shirt and hope that it will buy me enough time.

The door is locked, but I fish the key from the guard's pocket and steady myself before inserting it into the keyhole.

Chapter 46

The control room is small and the far wall is made entirely out of glass. I can see the battlefield clearly. Cars are being used as shields and barricades, and the firing of arrows and clashing of swords seem to have no end. Some of the soldiers resort to hand-to-hand combat while others simply flee. It's absolute chaos.

My stomach turns to lead as my eyes fall on Owens, his rusty hair neatly combed back as he lounges in a black swivel chair. He smiles upon my entry, as if he's been expecting me.

"The moment my cameras cut out," he says, "I had a hunch you'd appear. And here you are. Call me a soothsayer." He smirks at his own feeble attempt at humor.

I start toward him and step on top of the conference table. Without hesitation, I draw my dagger, my blood boiling. I'm close enough to hit him without fail.

"I'll only say this once," I say. "Call off your dogs. *Now.*"

His face remains infuriatingly calm. "Iris," he says. "Why so hostile? After everything I've done to help you." He gestures with his hand to the soldiers below. "If you really want this to stop, then give yourself up. Be a good little girl and surrender."

I scowl and shove the metal to his chest. "The only reason you're still breathing is because I want to make sure that your death is as painful as you deserve," I say. "But if you choose to act like a fool, then I might just speed things up."

Owens grins.

"Tell me where Varys is hiding," I say.

A voice comes on the radio behind Owens, causing us both to turn.

"Sir," the static voice says. "They're retreating. The First Regime's soldiers have surrendered."

My jaw tightens and I step closer, my dagger hovering above his chest.

Owens shoots me a smug grin. "You wouldn't."

"You severely underestimate me," I say.

I take a step back and I throw it.

Only the dagger doesn't penetrate him.

The impact throws him against the window, his chair wheels spinning furiously, but there's no blood. Owens does not scream in agony. Instead, he laughs. A psychopathic, bone-chilling laugh.

"You didn't think I'd sit up here completely unprotected, did you?" he says. The dagger sticks out of his chest, and he plucks it out like a toothpick, tossing it to the floor. "Thank the lords for armor. What would we do without it?"

From under the control panel, Owens draws the same crossbow he had in Imperia. "Now it's your turn to choose: either go back to Varys and give him the Marrow or die here, and then we will *take* it."

He presses a button on his radio system. "Attention, soldiers," he announces.

The fighting outside of the building seems to freeze. All eyes turn to Headquarters, even though I'm sure they can't see us.

"It is my pleasure to announce that the cowardly attempts to overthrow our leadership have failed," he says. "We, the honorable and rightful members of the Order, claim a victory. Not only in protecting our family, but in capturing the vessel of our miracle. Long live the Order of Alabass."

The crowd is stunned, but after a moment, they cheer. The Elites remain in a droid-like silence, but the Third Regime howls in triumph. On the side of the lawn, wounded soldiers of the First Regime limp away from the building, but not before being rounded up and captured. They're prisoners now.

My heart aches. Avrian remains untouched, but he's no longer fighting. Instead, he stands in a group of his soldiers, tending to the wounded and fending off advancing Elites. Jaice stands by him, but he's clutching his shoulder and blood trickles down his arm.

"See, kid?" Owens says. "We always win. That's how it is, how it's been, and how it always will be. Those with power will always win, and those without it are destined to fall."

I turn to him, a fire burning inside of me. "Then you should know," I spit, "that I don't give up power that easily."

He opens his mouth to laugh, but I draw one of the throwing knives strapped to my waist and take the shot, aiming at his exposed shoulder where I know the vest doesn't reach.

It's a clear hit, and he stumbles. Owens shouts, swearing through the pain as he folds in on himself. Excitement flutters through me. I take another shot, this time aiming at his leg.

"That was for Simu," I say.

Owens crumples to the ground, and he glares furiously. "And tell me, how do you plan to escape?" he chokes out, clenching his teeth. "I have every exit blocked, and everyone in the city is setting out to kill you. If you think your three lone deserters will come to save you, then you really haven't learned anything."

"You don't have to worry about that," I say coldly. "You won't be around to witness it."

Out of the corner of my eye, I see his finger squeeze his trigger, but I catch it too late. A blast of metal erupts from his crossbow.

Agony rips through me like a hurricane, and my dagger slips through my fingers. I reach down and grip my thigh, biting down on my teeth to keep from crying out. Pain pulses and snakes through me and soon my hands are covered in blood.

I know I have to leave. The guards will be back any minute, but I can't move. A pool of blood grows beneath me, and I can't find the strength to crawl to the table to hoist myself up.

Owens isn't faring much better than I am, and he struggles to his feet. I watch as he spits blood from his mouth and stumbles toward the door. He casts a glare at me as he holds onto the wall for support.

"I'll be back," he says. "And when I return, you will lose."

He disappears into the hallway, and I let out a shaky breath.

Moments later, I see a new figure enter the room. Blond hair whips past me and soon, Taiana is standing over me. She isn't dressed for combat, and I remember Astoria telling me her regime was remaining neutral. I don't miss the knives hanging at her waist.

She's finally going to kill me, I think. *It's what she's been wanting since day one.*

To my utter shock, she bends down next to me, her pale eyes fixated on my leg.

"Tear off strips of your shirt," she orders. "I need them to make a bandage."

I blink, dumfounded.

Without waiting for me to respond, she does it herself, ripping off two cotton strips from my shirt. I'm in too much agony to protest. She bunches up one of the strips and stuffs it into my mouth.

"What are you...?" I make out, forcing my eyes to stay open.

She frowns, and I can tell she isn't happy about this arrangement. So why is she helping me?

"Bite down on it," she says. "It'll muffle your screams so you don't alert every single guard in the city."

I do as she says, and her fingers work the arrow out of my leg. A searing pain tears through my body and I scream into the cloth, hoping no one can hear me. It's more agonizing than the acid that had eaten away at my flesh, but I manage to stay conscious. To my relief, she retracts the hot metal tip from my thigh, but removing it only amplifies the pain.

"Calm down," she snaps. "You're making it worse."

I want to tell her she's being unreasonable, and she has no *idea* the pain I'm experiencing, but I keep my mouth shut. Mainly because I can't seem to form words through the pain, but also because I'm grateful for her help. Even if she's always made it clear how much she despises me.

"I'm not doing this for you," she says matter-of-factly. Taiana takes the remaining strip of cloth and ties it tightly around my leg. It instantly turns red as my blood soaks it through.

"Then for who?" I say, pulling the fabric from my mouth.

She looks at me with her typical disapproving glare. "Wang would never speak to me again if I let you die," she says at last. "I will not risk losing my oldest friend."

Her words shock me. I always knew there was some history between them, but I never imagined their relationship ran so deep. I ignore the pang of jealousy in my stomach, and it's soon replaced by a ripple of pain as Taiana tightens the bandage.

The fabric is securely in place now, and the blood slows. My leg grows numb. A faint buzz ripples through me, and I can almost feel the tissues in my leg slowly repairing themselves.

"Thank you," I say to her.

A pit forms in my stomach.

Taiana stands, staring distastefully at my blood on her hands. She turns her head toward the hallway, and I notice her shoulders loosen. "I'm certain you can handle it from here," she says, and turns away.

She disappears down the hallway. I consider calling out to her, to tell her not to leave me here, but my body doesn't obey.

Then, I hear footsteps outside of the doorway, and I stay low, watching as a figure enters the room. I realize she wasn't talking to me, but to whoever is now walking toward me.

Dread forms in my stomach. Was this all a trick? From my vantage point on the ground, all I can see are two black boots and I figure Varys has finally come for me. Taiana only wanted to keep me from dying so Varys could kill me himself.

Chapter 47

y heart rate quickens, and I throw myself behind the table and shield myself from the approaching figure.

But the figure isn't Varys, or an Elite, or even a soldier.

"Avrian," I gasp, trying to push myself up as he rounds the table.

His head snaps at the sound of my voice, and he comes running toward me. When his face comes into view, I notice countless bruises and cuts on his face, but nothing looks too serious. He keeps knives strapped to his belt, and his double-edged sword rests in its holster across his back.

"Iris," he breathes, collapsing at my side. He pulls me toward him and takes me in his arms. I can feel his entire body shaking, and I know he's been through hell and back, possibly even more.

"My gods, what happened? What did they do to you?" His voice, despite everything, is steady and gives me a strong sense of security.

"It's okay," I manage. "Taiana—Commander Perovka—she helped me bandage the wound."

"And it's a good thing she did," he says, examining the blood-soaked cloth around the wound. "Gods, I'm going to kill him."

"You're so reckless," I say, wiping blood from the corner of his mouth. "What were you thinking—running up to Headquarters like that? A rebellion?"

He smiles so wide I can see the deep grooves of his dimples appear. "I have a good track record of keeping promises. Couldn't let this one slip by."

I can't help but grin back at him, but as I do, everything else comes crashing down on me. I think of the old married couple from the restaurant in the city, and tears flood my eyes.

"Avrian," I say as tears run down my face. "Avrian, they're dead...I'm so sorry. I'm so, so sorry." Guilt resurfaces, and I can't meet his eyes. He asked them to protect me, and they gave their lives for it. "I wanted to help them, I *really* did—"

Avrian pulls me to his chest and buries his face next to mine. "This isn't your fault, Iris," he says.

"Simu's gone too," I hear myself say into the fabric of his shirt.

My breathing comes in ragged puffs, and I wrap my arms around him, holding on to him as if it could solve everything. As if holding on to him could mend all of my wounds.

Still surrounded by his warmth, Avrian brushes the tears from my face and forces me to look at him. The understanding look in his eyes grounds me, and I steady my breathing.

"We have to get you out of here," he says, his voice turning serious as he glances down at my leg.

I nod, finding the strength to collect myself.

His jaw tightens, and he hooks my arm around his neck and hoists me up.

"The others are on the roof of the old warehouse," I say, breaking the suffocating silence.

Avrian nods, and as we turn the corner of the hallway three Elites race toward us. He unsheathes his throwing knives, and in the blink of an eye the three Elites slump to the floor.

We make our way to the building harboring Crayln and Sorin, and I suddenly feel self-conscious as Avrian hauls me up countless flights of stairs. He's injured, too, and I can't imagine the pain he's experiencing.

"I can walk the rest," I offer as we reach another landing.

Avrian raises an eyebrow. "It'll take twice the amount of time and cause you three times the pain. I don't think that's a good idea."

"Really, it's fine," I say, attempting to wriggle out of his arms.

He keeps me secure and continues climbing. "You don't have to continue to prove your strength to me," he says softly. "Besides, if I were Varys, I'd be running for Trasylar by now." He flashes me a grin. "An angry Iris is something I don't think anyone wants to get in the way of."

"Real funny," I say. "Next time, I'm carrying you, alright?"

He laughs but doesn't get the chance to reply.

We approach the door at the top of the building and walk out onto the cement roof. Crayln and Sorin lean against the ledge, blood flecks present on their faces and clothes, but otherwise they're unharmed.

Three Elites lay motionless on the ground a few feet away.

Jaice, to my surprise and relief, is with them. He's injured, bleeding heavily from at least a dozen flesh wounds, but he's alive.

"Iris!" they say in unison as they spot us. "Commander!"

Crayln rushes over. "I'd hug you, but I fear it would only cause more pain," he says, cracking a half smile.

"You're probably right," I say, but I embrace him anyway.

My entire body tingles as the Marrow pulses through my bones, spreading into my flesh and blood. An electric buzz fills me, and I can feel my body slowly mending itself.

Sorin smiles, and I hug him next. "Thank the gods you're okay," he says.

Assisted by Avrian and the others, I limp my way over to Jaice. Patches of scarlet cover his face, and a long gash runs down his side.

"Are you alright?" A stupid question, but I don't know what else to say.

Jaice, to his credit, manages to smile. "Never better, Princess." He motions his head toward my leg. "And what happened to you? Decided to ditch your shirt, I see."

I look down to see that less than half of my shirt remains, exposing my bruised and bloody midriff. I shrug coolly, as if it's no big deal. "Got shot," I say. "Nothing I can't handle."

Jaice snorts. "You got your revenge, I hope?"

I look down. "No. It's not enough until Varys is brought to his knees," I say. He's the ringmaster. As long as he's loose, we will never be safe.

"I like your thinking," Jaice says.

I look over at Crayln. "Have you gotten any word from Astoria?"

Crayln shakes his head. "Not for a while. Last thing I heard was that she located Varys and followed him to the surface."

"Where are they headed?" I ask.

"I don't know. I need to get into the control room," Crayln says. "From there, I'll be able to access the information for all of our air-craft."

I bite my lip. Surely the Elites are filing back into Headquarters. Breaking in again won't be as easy. And Owens is still crawling around in there.

Avrian walks to the edge and scans the scene below, the gears in his mind turning. "Varys couldn't have gone far—he's not stupid, he won't risk losing track of Iris. We need to lure him out into the open. Here in the city he's too powerful, but if we can get him to reveal himself at the surface, we may stand a chance."

The others nod, and I remember that he's still our commander. Jaice and Crayln are trained to follow his lead and will do so without question. Sorin, on the other hand, is taking his time to analyze the pros and cons of Avrian's proposal.

"How can you be so sure?" Sorin challenges. "He could be halfway to Imperia by now. Or to any other region, for that matter."

Avrian's gaze falls on Sorin. "I know him very well," he says. "He will not leave, not when his valuables are here in the city."

"We can't leave Naveen," I cut in. "The moment we leave the city, Varys will have him killed, I'm sure of it."

Jaice and Crayln agree immediately.

"He's a liability," Avrian warns.

"You wouldn't leave him here," I say, remembering the way Avrian talked so fondly about him the night we visited the infirmary.

His eyes soften, as if he's saying, *of course I wouldn't.*

"I'll carry him on my back if I have to," Jaice says. "Whatever it takes to get him out of here with us."

"Then it's settled," I say. "We're going to need to split up. Sorin, Crayln—you two will go up to the surface and track down Varys. Once you do, get him to land in the marsh."

"How, exactly?" Crayln asks. "We can't just wave our hands and expect him to listen. He'll know it's a trap."

"I'll go," Avrian says. "He'll probably have a word or two for me, anyway." Although his voice is firm, I can sense the confliction on his face.

"And what about Taiana?" I ask Avrian. "Owens saw her helping me. She'll be a target, too."

Avrian shakes his head. "She can hold her own," he says. "I trust she will make it out just fine."

"Alright," I say, still surprised that Taiana came to help me. "Then Jaice and I will find Naveen and meet you at the surface."

Avrian looks uneasy. "And if the Elites catch on?" he asks. "If we're up at the surface, we won't be able to get back in time to help."

"We'll manage," I say, exchanging a confident look with Jaice.

Jaice grins. "I didn't spend months training her just for the fun of it," he says proudly. "We've got this covered."

Still, the others look worried.

"In your state, one hit and you'll be down for the count. No offense, big guy," Crayln says, eyeing Jaice and his injuries.

Jaice scowls. "How am I supposed to *not* take offense to that?"

"Crayln has a point," I say. "You've been through a lot today. No one expects you to be invincible."

"Then let me come with you, too," Sorin says.

We don't have time to debate any further, so I nod. "Okay, then. Let's go."

Crayln salutes me as he throws his crossbow over his shoulder.

"See you on the other side."

Chapter 48

*A*fter *making sure we're well armed, we head through the streets toward the infirmary.*

The entire plaza is crowded, and a mob of soldiers gather at the doors. Hundreds of victims from the battle file in. Many of them are part of the First Regime, so they're familiar to me.

Guilt rises inside of me, but I try to push it away.

"We have to get through a different way," Sorin says. "If we try the front doors, someone is bound to alert Varys of our whereabouts."

I nod in agreement, spotting several Elites mingling in the crowd, weapons drawn to keep order.

"I'll create a distraction," Jaice says. "Then you two can go through the door on the west wing. If you take that stairwell, it should take you straight to Nav."

I'm hesitant, but I know there isn't time for a better plan. "Meet up with us back at the elevator when you're done," I say. "And don't be stupid. If they try anything, get your ass out of there, alright?"

Jaice smirks. "You say that every time."

I shrug. "Yet you always seem like you need the reminder."

Jaice tucks his sword into its sheath and heads out, merging into the amorphous crowd of injured soldiers.

Without wasting a moment to watch Jaice, Sorin and I round the infirmary and head for the back entrance. Two guards are waiting outside of the door by the time we arrive, but Jaice must have pulled through because a call comes through on their radios that draws them away.

The door is unlocked, and Sorin follows me up the stairwell until we stop on the seventeenth floor. I'm winded and my leg is throbbing, but I push the pain aside and make my way toward Naveen's room.

To my relief, he's there.

He's sleeping.

Sorin stops short beside me. "I should never have pressured you to come back to the palace," he says, leaning against the wall. "I'm sorry I didn't take the time to understand everything that you were going through. This whole thing with the Blood Marrow, if I had known—"

"It's alright," I say softly. "I still imagine I'm back in Imperia sometimes. But not within the palace walls. I see us visiting the city, like we always talked about."

"I think of that too," Sorin says. "One day we will."

"Nav," I say, shaking his shoulders. "Nav, can you hear me?"

Groggily, he opens his eyes and pushes himself up. "Iris?" he says. "What's going on?"

"There's a lot happening right now," I say. "We'll fill you in, but for now, we need to get you out of here."

He blinks and rubs sleep from his eyes.

"We gotta go, *now*," a voice sounds behind us. Jaice stands in the doorway, panting. A nasty wound spills across his forehead.

"What happened?" I demand.

He shoulders through us and makes his way to Naveen. Hoisting him onto his shoulder, Jaice says, "Long story short, they're onto us."

"Hey!" Naveen protests. "Put me down."

"It will go a lot smoother this way," Jaice says. "We don't have time for you to fall behind."

"By now they've probably blocked off all the doors, so we'll have to take the window." I glance over to the tall windows and frown.

"Iris, we're on the *seventeenth* floor," Sorin says, peering out.

Jaice doesn't hesitate and slices through the window with his sword, sending broken glass everywhere. "There's a building right next to us," he says. "We'll have to make the jump."

"You're joking," Sorin says, stepping away from the obliterated window.

I fight the urge to cringe away from the edge. "Alright," I mumble, watching the chaos of cars and soldiers below. "Hopefully, I've still got some luck left on my side."

"It's not far," Jaice says.

"I swear, if you drop me, I'll kill you," Naveen says.

The next roof is only a couple feet away, but I still don't trust myself to make the jump.

Jaice goes first, darting across to the next building with Naveen securely on his shoulder. Despite his injuries, Jaice lands perfectly on the roof and motions for us to follow.

I glance at Sorin. We exchange a look of mutual concern and count to three. Then we leap in unison. I feel the wind on my face for a brief moment before crashing onto the concrete roof below.

"There's a small striker on the landing pad," Jaice says from the other side of the roof.

Sorin and I follow his voice around the corner to the miniature striker. It's designed for two people, but somehow, we manage to squeeze in four.

"It's only for a few minutes," Jaice says, his cheek pressed up against the window.

"Someone's sitting on my leg," Naveen says, wincing.

Sorin takes on the role of pilot, and soon enough, we're flying above the city. I feel as though my lungs are being crushed by the weight of Naveen's body.

We land outside of the elevator and the moment the doors open, we all tumble out. Jaice takes Naveen, and we climb into the elevator, prepared to face whatever is waiting for us at the surface.

"Is someone going to fill me in?" Naveen demands.

"Uh, let's see," Sorin says. "Your leader is evil, he wants to kill Iris, and we're trying to stop that from happening."

Naveen takes a moment to process this. "I don't even know what to say to that," he says. "Damn."

"Yeah," I say. "A lot has changed in the past few days."

The elevator stops, and the doors draw open to welcome bright morning light. Streaks of pink and orange stain the sky as we step out of the elevator. Along the swampy horizon, I spot the small shape of what looks like a plane.

"There!" I say, directing the others toward it.

"Hold on," Jaice says, chasing after me. It's his turn to be the rational one. "We need a plan. If they're stalling him, we need to get close without him knowing and assess the situation."

My instincts urge me to race toward Varys and pin him to the ground, but I hold back, Jaice's calm rationale keeping me grounded.

"Fine," I say.

I follow him through the murky water until we reach the edge and rise out of the water, only to dart behind a tall cypress tree. Its gnarled bark and thick, outstretched roots provide enough cover to keep us hidden. Ahead of us in the marshy wetlands stands the leader, shielded by a team of five Elites.

And Astoria kneels in front of them, held at knifepoint.

Chapter 49

S orin sets a steady hand on my arm. "He won't kill her," he says. "Keep your cool."

I press my lips together but remain hidden, watching intensely.

Across the field I find Avrian and Crayln, both bristling with visible rage. They're engaged in a heated conversation with the leader, but we're too far away to make out their words.

"We have to help them," I say.

"Just tell me what to do," Naveen says, squaring his shoulders.

Jaice laughs and sets him down against a large tree trunk. "Sit down and rest," he says. "You're in no condition to fight."

Naveen looks Jaice up and down, examining his injuries. "And you are?"

"Enough," I say, pushing them apart. "If we play this right, neither of you will have to fight at all."

"What do you propose?" Sorin asks, loading his crossbow anyway.

"One of us needs to take out the Elite holding Astoria, then we can take out the others. But the first shot *must* take him out," I instruct, taking in the scene.

"Problem," Jaice says. "There are five Elites and only four of us. Well, three and a half. I doubt Nav can shoot properly in his condition."

Naveen scowls. "I'm the sharpest shooter in the Order," he says. "I could shoot a rattlesnake upside down from five hundred feet away. This is nothing."

"You haven't so much as walked across the room, let alone aimed a crossbow, in *weeks*," Jaice counters.

"He's got a point," I say. "But we do need you in order to make this work."

Naveen's eyes brighten, and Sorin hands him the spare crossbow. Turning it over in his hands, he grins. "I've missed this."

"One of us still has to take two shots," I say. "I can do it."

I glance around and no one objects.

I load my crossbow with one iron-tipped arrow and the others do the same. We crouch in the stalky marsh grass and slowly make our way toward the line of Elites backing Varys.

Astoria is still on her knees, with the Elite in the center holding her bound wrists with one hand and pressing a knife to her temple with the other.

The three of us press our stomachs to the ground and aim our crossbows at our respective targets. We're in earshot to catch the conversation.

"I'm proud of you, my son," Varys says. "You've proved your strength and your worth. Soon, the rebels will be dead, and you'll realize where the true power lies. I have no doubt you'll come back to take my throne."

Avrian scoffs. "I have no desire to assume a position built on lies and murder," he growls back.

Varys chuckles. "Is this all because of that princess?" he asks. "Never did I imagine my son would one day turn on me because of a *girl*."

Sorin clenches his jaw but doesn't risk taking his eyes off of his target to look at me.

"Funny how things change," Avrian responds flatly.

"Think for a moment," Varys says. "Are you so willing to throw all of this away?" He gestures with his arms. "All of this, and for what? Friends? Pathetic. Men like us do not have friends. When they discover who you are on the inside, they will vanish from your life without a trace."

Avrian lifts his chin. "I'm tired of your games," he snaps back. "I've waited far too long, but I'm not afraid to leave anymore."

"You're foolish," Varys says. "Just like your mother."

I see Avrian stiffen.

"She thought she could hide you from me," Varys says, "so I eliminated her. If you choose to stand against me, I will have no choice but to do the same to you, my boy."

Avrian's trembling now.

"No..." I hear Avrian say, his voice low.

A few paces away, I see Astoria bristle.

"Father," she calls out, still held at knifepoint. "Please, please say it's not true!"

The desperation in her voice makes my heart break for her. Even after everything Varys has done, even though she's willing to help us, she still loves him. He's her father, after all. And she doesn't want to believe the one thing that could sever their bond forever.

"He's not lying," Avrian says, and I know everything is starting to make sense for him. "He's exactly the kind of man who would do such a thing."

Pure hatred drips from his mouth like venom, and Avrian unsheathes his sword.

"Your mother tried to block your potential," Varys says. "By raising you two away from the city, she was making you weak."

Tears roll down Astoria's face and fall into the grass below her knees.

"You made us into murderers," Avrian shouts.

"Very good ones, at that," Varys says, lifting his chin. "You should thank me."

Avrian advances, but as he does, the Elite holding his sister presses the knife against her neck, making him stop.

I suppress a gasp, and turn toward the others, signaling.

"We have to make our move *now*," I whisper to them.

Jaice nods, locking in on his target. Sorin and Naveen do the same, and the determination in their eyes gives me the confidence I need to start the countdown.

Three.

Two.

One.

We fire. As soon as my first arrow releases, I prepare the next and fire it.

Four of the Elites, including the one standing above Astoria, collapse to the ground. One of them remains standing.

"Damn it, it's jammed!" Jaice curses.

"We have to move!" I say.

We push ourselves up off of the wet ground and make our way toward the others. In the moment of chaos, Astoria gets to her feet and retrieves her spear from the ground.

As we near, Avrian's green eyes meet mine, and relief transforms his face.

"You have come to kill me, I presume," Varys says, unflinching.

I step forward until I'm only a few feet away from Varys.

This man is the source of so much pain. He's ruined so many lives, innocent lives. Hatred for him burns in my veins and I can hardly bear the sight of him. Keeping my finger off of the trigger of my crossbow proves to be much more difficult than I expect.

"You're a spitting image of your mother," Varys says. A cruel grin tugs at the corners of his lips. He knows exactly how to get under my skin, and I hate it.

My body goes rigid with rage. "You have no right to speak as if you know my mother," I snarl. "You gave up that right the day you betrayed her."

"She was a fool," he shouts. "Refusing to stand by my side led to her downfall."

"You're outnumbered, Varys," I warn.

He lets out a horrifying laugh. "My daughter will come around," he says, glancing at Astoria. "And do you truly believe my boy to be on your side?"

My gaze flickers over to Avrian, who, to my surprise, drops his gaze.

"Why don't you tell her about our missions in Imperia?" Varys says to Avrian. "I'm sure you remember. After all, how could you forget your first taste of victory?"

"There was no victory in killing them," Avrian says, his voice dangerously low.

Chills run up and down my spine, and I tell myself he's lying.

"Their blood will remain on your hands forever, my boy," Varys says. "You can't lie your way out of this one."

Avrian swallows, his face twisting in painful regret. To my horror, he doesn't deny his father's accusations. Somehow, he finds the strength to lift his chin. He holds my gaze, looking at me as if his father has disappeared.

"I do not ask for forgiveness, Iris," Avrian says, "but I'm done hiding behind excuses. I killed for the Order. I killed for my father. But I regret it with my entire being."

My breaths are shallow, and I can hardly control my body. I keep telling myself that he's wrong; that he didn't kill them.

The sharp knife of betrayal mercilessly carves through my heart. He might as well have ripped it out with his bare hands.

Avrian takes a step closer.

"Iris," Sorin says, a hint of warning in his voice.

Ignoring him, Avrian continues. "I wish I had left the Order a long time ago. I have gone to sleep every night regretting the things I've done. That is, up until the point I met you. Getting the chance to meet you made everything else worth it, Iris."

Before I can respond, Varys cuts in.

"Such sweet words coming from such a cunning mouth," Varys says. "You enjoy the kill, boy. I've made sure of that. Do not turn away from your destiny."

Avrian's eyes grow into slits as he pins his father with a stone-cold glare. But Varys is done talking to him.

His amber eyes latch onto me.

"You think you can corrupt my son but let me tell you something: Everything that happens here is decided by me, and I have decided that your time is up," he says.

His sour breath makes my nose wrinkle, and before he can speak another word, I fire.

My arrow hits square in the leg, and he roars in agony. He's still mobile enough to grab his own throwing knife and point it at me.

"No!"

I whip my attention toward Avrian. Before I can stop him, he steps forward and uses his body to block the path connecting me to Varys.

Varys' dagger rips through the air, and I hear the agonizing sound of metal tearing into flesh.

Chapter 50

"No!" I scream, rushing toward Avrian. He's still standing, but the dagger buries itself deep into his stomach.

"Avrian!" I say, looking back and forth from the dagger's hilt to the pained expression he's trying so hard to conceal. "Avrian, oh my gods. What the hell were you thinking?"

He smiles at me. "I wasn't."

Nervously, I steal a glance over at Varys and watch as Jaice and Crayln advance on him, blocking him from aiming another knife at us. Jaice draws his sword, and Crayln makes sure he doesn't get a clear shot at me.

"Avrian, you're..." I say, my breath catching.

I feel his arms on mine. His grip is strong, but I can tell he's struggling to stay upright. "I'll be fine, Iris," he says.

He swallows hard and blood trickles from the corner of his mouth.

My gut twists and I wipe it away, but when I look down, I see blood dripping from his wound, and I know he's in danger of bleeding out.

"Ave!" Naveen cries, starting toward us, but the last Elite blocks his path.

In his state, Naveen can't fight, but he loads his crossbow anyway. Astoria moves to join him, spear in hand.

"Someone needs to call for help! Find Taiana!" I shout.

"I'll go!" Naveen shouts back.

"Your leg—" I say.

"It's fine," Naveen replies, already moving back toward the city's entrance. "You can count on me for this!"

Sorin moves to take Naveen's place and circles the Elite.

With one last glance, Naveen shoots across the field and heads for Dravkia, running faster than ever, despite his leg.

"That's not necessary!" Avrian shouts after him, but nothing will stop Naveen now. Avrian turns to me and frowns. "Perovka is the last person I want seeing me like this. She'll never let me forget it."

"Nevermind that," I say. "Your pride can take a hit if it means you'll survive."

He scoffs.

"Sit," I say. "Standing will only make things worse."

Avrian tries to protest. "I can still fight," he says. "We can't stop now, not when we're so close." Despite his words, he winces and his hand flies to the dagger's hilt.

"No, don't," I say. Frantically, I unbutton his jacket and use it to apply pressure to the wound. "We can't remove it, not yet."

"Stop fussing over me," Avrian says.

I look up and glare at him. "I'm not going to let you die," I say. "Especially not in my place."

"I have absolutely no intention of dying today," he says, but I hardly hear him.

Too many people have given their lives for me, I think. *I will not lose Avrian too.*

Even though I'm angry, even though I hate that he helped Varys hunt for the Marrow, all I want is for him to be okay. I'll yell at him later. But now, I just can't lose him.

I guide him to the ground, using the tall grass to shield us from where Varys stands with Jaice and Crayln. Their weapons are drawn, but I force myself to turn away and focus on Avrian.

"I have something to give you," he says. "It's a shame I couldn't find a more appropriate time."

Avrian shifts, and he draws a thin black box from his pocket. A messily tied bow clings to the frame, and I spot my name written in ink along the side.

"Happy birthday, Iris," Avrian says.

Confusion and shock hit me all at once. Here he is, bleeding out on the field, and the one thing he wants to do is wish me a happy birthday. Even *I* forgot that today is my birthday.

"Avrian, *what*?" I say.

"Take it," he says. "Please."

A heartbeat passes, but I take the small box from his hand and open it. My breath catches.

"I know it isn't much," he says. "And I know it does not begin to compensate for the hell of this day. But I wanted to give it to you."

"It's perfect," I breathe. "Avrian, it's perfect."

I take the small rose in my hand, careful not to damage the beautiful purple petals. It's unlike anything I've ever seen before. The stem is smooth, and I bring the flower to my nose to take in the crisp, sweet fragrance.

He remembered.

Not only did he remember that I love roses, but it's a purple *rose.*

"They are said to be the rarest," Avrian says, his voice growing fainter. "But also the most beautiful. I believe it is quite fitting for you, wouldn't you agree?"

Tears slip from my eyes and roll down my cheeks.

The jacket I'm holding on his stomach is drenched with blood, and it's as if I can feel his life force being drained out of him.

"Why did you do this?" I whisper.

"Isn't it obvious?" he says, the corner of his mouth curling into a grin. "I didn't want to fall for you, Iris. I did everything I could—I convinced myself I hated you and that you were nothing but a liability to my regime." He lets out a small laugh. "I even hoped Perovka would scare you off and you would run back to the palace. But you never did. And it only made me fall harder."

Every word is an effort for him to say, but he does anyway, his eyes locking onto mine in a way that makes me melt.

I didn't want to fall for you. Which means that Avrian Wang, the son of the cruelest man I've ever met, has fallen. For me.

"I knew it was only a matter of time before you found out what I've done, how I've helped my father," Avrian says through ragged breaths. "And I knew that forgiving me would be near impossible. I just wish I was the one who told you."

My heart twists at his words.

"That's enough," I say softly. "I don't blame you. I don't blame you for it."

Avrian swallows, and I can tell he's thinking of arguing, so I lean down and press my lips to his, stealing away his protests and excuses. He kisses me back, and with each passing moment I feel the beat of his heart slow.

His hand brushes hair from my face and his gaze meets mine. "Gods, you're so beautiful."

"How could you...?" I whisper, my vision blurring. "How could you do this?"

How could you be so caring, so honorable, so sweet...and be dying in front of me? I demand silently. *How could you be so cruel?*

"Because I'm in love with you, Iris," he says. "So dreadfully, so helplessly in love with you."

"Then don't leave me!" I close my eyes, shutting out the clashing of metal and the shuffling of boots against earth. The fighting around us becomes nothing as darkness envelops me. All I can hear is the pounding of my own heart.

"Avrian, gods help me, *don't go.*"

I can feel him slipping away.

"I love you," I say. "I love you and I can't bear losing you."

Please don't go.

He's falling through my fingertips, and every heartbeat is fainter than the last. He's dying. And I'm powerless to stop it.

Completely and utterly powerless.

His eyes fall shut, and I cry out again and again, trying to keep him with me. I scream until my throat burns, holding on to him with everything I have.

"Iris!" I hear Sorin shout.

I draw my head up, following his gaze, and I find my friends locked in a battle they can't win. Jaice's sword lays in the grass a few yards away, and Varys knocks Crayln to the ground with a strong punch to his jaw. Jaice is bleeding heavily, and he won't withstand it much longer.

The Elite lays unconscious on the ground with Astoria's spear protruding from his shoulder. Astoria races over to me and drops to her knees beside her brother.

"Is he okay?" she demands, setting her hand on her brother's chest, feeling for a heartbeat. "Iris...oh my gods."

No, no, no.

"Look at what you've done," a voice says.

My blood turns cold as Varys approaches. Jaice lays in a bloody heap and Crayln struggles to his feet with Sorin supporting him.

Astoria bristles by my side, and I stand, shielding Avrian from view.

"This ends *now,*" I say, tightening my grip around my dagger. "I'm done playing your games and I'm done letting you take everyone I care about away from me."

Varys laughs. "I do not fear death, girl," he spat. "Unlike my son, I have no regrets."

"You're lying," I say. "Everyone has regrets. Only cowards choose to hide from them."

"Try me," he sneers.

"I bet you regret throwing that knife," I say, my voice colder than it's ever been before. "Your son could *die.* Will you stand here and do nothing?"

His mask cracks, and he steals a glance at Avrian. Pain flashes across his face.

"He was foolish," Varys says, attempting to hide his grief. "He chose this for himself. I regret nothing."

"You're sick," I say, stalking closer.

Without responding, Varys darts forward and lunges. I dodge his first attack, throwing myself out of the way, but he's fast. His massive fists threaten to crush me, every swing more dangerous than the last. He knocks the crossbow from my hand and I stagger, wiping blood from my lip.

I think back to when I fought him right before they chained me up, and I remember his moves. The way he widens his stance tells me he's waiting for me to strike, only to use his weight to knock me to the ground. I brace myself for it, and when he lunges, I move to the side and dig my dagger along his back, drawing scarlet blood.

He rears back, breathing heavily now.

Sorin starts forward, but I put out a hand.

"No," I say.

Varys snickers, taunting me. "Do you honestly think you are a match for me?" he asks. "Deep down, you're still the weak princess who ran away from her palace. Do not forget it."

I clench my teeth. "She died a long time ago," I say. "I am nothing like her, Varys. She would be afraid to kill you. Unfortunately for you, I don't share the same fear."

His face spreads into a wicked grin, and he removes the black crossbow from his back and loads it.

He shoots, and before I can move, the arrow pierces through my leg. I collapse onto one knee, and Varys wastes no time. He takes my head in his hand and forces me down into the dirt, sending a shockwave of pain through my body.

I feel Varys' heavy boot on my back, and I struggle under his weight and the blaring pain pulsing in my leg. Frustrated, I try to twist away from him, but he hotels me firmly in place.

He will not kill me.

I grunt, and my vision pulses furiously. He's shouting something, and the others are running toward me, but it comes in broken fragments.

Using the last of my strength, I reach out and take hold of the crossbow in the grass beside me and I shoot.

The arrow hits him deep in his stomach, but something sharp and cold strikes through my body and I jolt. Pain overwhelms my senses and I fall limp.

I shot him.

But he shot me, too.

Chapter 51

I *don't know how long it's been, but I feel my senses buzzing back to life.*

There's a fierce pounding in my head, but I'm alive. I look down at my arm, which is almost fully healed. And the cut on my leg has left nothing more than a small scar.

Then, I notice the bandages wrapped around my stomach covering the wound from where Varys shot me. Carefully, I peel back the white cloth, and to my surprise there's only a faint mark of where the tip of the arrow pierced my flesh.

The greatest change is the feeling inside of me. The Marrow has reached its maturity. I can *feel* it, and it's powerful. It feels different with every passing second. It's a growing, living entity that flourishes with electrifying power.

I find myself in a beautiful room, and to my right is a large marble arch-shaped door that opens to a balcony. At first, I think I'm back in the palace, but the blend of vivid teals and pinks and yellows are far different from the golden and scarlet colors of Imperia.

Sunlight pours into the room through the glittering skylights above my head, and I find the strength to push myself out of bed. On the nightstand, a neatly folded stack of clothes awaits me.

I walk out onto the balcony, and the sight before me is nothing short of breathtaking. I'm up high on a cliff, and down below, spread out before me, is a town full of houses of every color. Some are a bright sky blue, while others take on a canary yellow color or the shade of white peaches in spring. Past the cliffside is the vast cyan colored sea, stretching for miles in almost every direction.

"You're awake!" a voice says.

I turn to see Naveen, his face glowing in the sunlight.

I smile, and he pulls me into a strong embrace. "I'm so glad you're okay," he says. "We were all so worried about you."

"Same goes for you," I say.

Naveen smiles, but his expression is solemn, and the memories of what happened back in Dravkia come flooding back to me. As I remember, I'm overwhelmed with a sense of dread.

I pull back, frantically searching his face for any clues. "Nav," I say, "Where's Avrian?"

Please don't say he's dead, I pray. *Please, please, please let him be okay.*

"He's alright," Naveen says. "He hasn't woken up since Dravkia, but he's alive. It's a miracle, really."

I feel my shoulders drop as relief pours over me and I close my eyes, thanking whichever divine being has chosen to take pity on him.

"Come on," Naveen says, gesturing for me to follow him, "I'll take you to him."

He still keeps most of his weight on his left leg and I notice him limping slightly. I follow him down the corridors of the house, gazing out through the open windows overlooking the water. We round a corner and come to a room higher on the cliffside and Naveen pauses.

He glances at me and opens the doors to reveal a room similar to the one I woke up in, only the curtains are drawn to block out the sun.

"As I said," Naveen whispers, "he hasn't woken up yet, so don't get your hopes up."

I touch his arm gratefully. "Thank you."

He nods and heads for the door. "I'll leave you," he says. "The others are gathered in the common room, I'm sure they'll want to see you."

I smile. "I won't be long."

When Naveen disappears, closing the tall glass doors, I finally find the courage to walk over to Avrian's beside. His chest is bare, and bandages cover the lower half of his torso, covering the wound from Varys' dagger.

I trace his dragon tattoo with my eyes and set my hand over his. Something makes me nervous, but I force myself to sit on the small ottoman beside him. Bruises and scrapes cover his face. I take a cloth from a small porcelain dish and dab it over the cuts.

Brushing my thumb over his cheek, I imagine him waking up. I imagine seeing his green eyes finding mine and seeing that smirk of his spread across his face.

I place my hand on his chest and close my eyes, focusing on the slow, even beat of his heart. I concentrate in silence, listening to only the blood pulsing in my ears. His muscles twitch under my hand, and I can feel him under the layers of bone and flesh. It's as if he's drowning in the sea and I'm just inches away from reaching him.

Avrian, I say. *Avrian, if you can hear me, wake up. Come back to me.*

For a while, nothing happens, and I think I'm imagining the faint aura of his presence. He's trapped behind the thin barrier of consciousness, and if I can only break through that barrier, I'll be able to bring him back.

Come back to me.

I concentrate harder, squeezing my eyes shut as I call upon the power within me. I feel the electric buzzing grow more powerful until it pulses throughout my very being in strong waves. Focusing on Avrian just below my fingertips, I call out to him.

His presence is faint, but it's him.

I hold on to him with everything I have. I focus on the steady beat of his heart and the rise and fall of his chest. Every aspect of his life is within reach, and I force it to the surface.

As power courses through me, I remember what my mother said about the Marrow's limits. Despite her warnings, I shove the thought away. No matter the risk, no matter the consequences, I will save him. The Marrow can take everything from me if it must, but he *will* wake up.

A shockwave shoots through my veins, powerful enough to make me gasp. I open my eyes as the pulse inside me releases, and a bright purple and white light sears my vision. Around me, the room lights up, blowing away the curtains covering the windows. The blast shakes the room and the porcelain bowl on the nightstand now lays in a broken heap at my feet.

I look down at my hand to see light pouring out from under my palm.

Avrian's heartbeat grows faster and faster and I watch as his hand twitches, and then his jaw. The light around us persists, and I feel him stirring.

"Avrian," I say, calling out to him. "Avrian, can you hear me?"

As the light around us dies away, replaced by sunlight, I watch as his eyes flutter open.

"Gods, I love hearing you say that," he murmurs, smiling.

I let out a breath and can't help but return his smile as I take him in my arms.

"You're okay," I say, mostly to convince myself.

He pulls me closer, and he buries his nose in my hair.

"I told you I had no intention of dying," he says.

I laugh and cup his cheek with my hand. "I'm glad you didn't," I say. "I'm really, really glad you didn't."

"I suppose this only means that I'm further in your debt," Avrian says. "After all, this is, what, the second time you've come to my rescue?"

"The first time didn't count," I say.

He grins. "It did to me."

"Come," I say, pulling away. "I'm sure the others will want to see that you're okay."

"I still don't understand how you did it," he says, marveling. "You're incredible, Iris."

"It was the Marrow," I say as he lifts himself up out of the bed.

Avrian shakes his head. "No," he says, resting his hands on my waist, "it was *you*."

My stomach flutters as he pulls me closer.

"You are quite possibly the most powerful being in this world," he says. "You have the power to bring me to my knees, to bend me to your will. And perhaps the worst part is… I enjoy every moment of it."

He tilts my chin up to meet his gaze and kisses me with a fierce, fiery passion. I kiss him back and wrap my arms around his neck. As I melt into his warmth, I finally feel the tension in my muscles fade away.

"I will never deserve you," Avrian says, pulling back just enough to speak. "But I have never been one to run. Unless you tell me to leave and that you never wish to see me again, I will spend every waking moment of my life making up for what I have done."

I shake my head, smiling. "I look forward to it."

"My heart is yours, Iris," he says. "It will only ever be yours."

"Good," I say, "because you have been the keeper of mine for quite some time, and I expect you to take good care of it."

He grins and places a light kiss on the top of my head. "Always."

Together, Avrian and I find our way through the labyrinth of marble balconies and corridors to the common room. Tall arches come together to create an intricate structure made of stone and glass windows overlooking the coast. The coast of Cryencia spreads before us, and the ocean glitters in the setting sun.

I spot Astoria sitting cross-legged on a long sofa with a book in hand, and she immediately drops it to the floor when she sees us appear. On the opposing sofa, Naveen, Crayln, and Jaice sit and play a game involving cards and a crystal dice. Sorin stands with his back facing us, looking out over the horizon.

They all turn when we enter the room and jump up to greet us.

Jaice's left arm is covered in bandages, but he pulls us both into a strong embrace, and even Avrian allows it. Naveen smiles at me and then smothers Avrian in a hug.

"Man," Naveen says, "I don't know what I would do if you didn't pull through."

Astoria comes next to greet her brother, ruffling his hair. "Well, then it's a good thing we didn't leave him in the swamp," she says.

Avrian ducks away, smiling. "You wouldn't dare."

Crayln appears next to me and laughs. "Well, you did it," he says to me. "I don't know how you pulled it off, but you did it."

"Hey, don't talk about that yet," Naveen scolds, jabbing Crayln in the ribs.

"Cray's right," Jaice says, nodding to me. "You did good, Princess."

I grin. "It was all of us."

I see their smiles fall a little as a new figure appears in the archway. I turn, following their gaze, and see the last person I would expect.

Taiana stands in the doorway. Her hair falls loose at her shoulders, and she wears a simple white dress. I've never seen her in anything but her black commander uniform.

She leans against the wall, arms folded over her chest.

I look at Naveen, lifting an eyebrow.

"She's the reason Ave's still here," Naveen explains quickly, sensing tension in the air. "Some of her soldiers specialize in medicine, and they were able to keep him alive. After that, we couldn't leave her back in the city."

"I can speak for myself, Khan," Taiana says. Then, she turns to me. "But yes, he's right. I could not stay in the city after that."

"Thank you," I say to her, remembering that she bandaged my wound *and* managed to save Avrian's life. "Really, I can't thank you enough."

Taiana smirks a little, but I see the glint of amusement in her eyes. "I don't plan on staying here forever, so don't get too attached."

"Well, she's finally come around," Crayln says. "I never thought I'd live to see it."

"I have no idea what you're referring to, Mavros," Taiana says, rolling her eyes. "I still wouldn't want any of you in my regime."

Sorin joins us moments later, and I notice a few new scars across his face and arms.

"Lieutenant," I say, grinning.

"It's been a long time since anyone has called me that," Sorin says. "A lot has changed, hasn't it?"

"I suppose it has," I say, glancing around the room. Everything about this, the place, the people, it's nothing like our old lives in Imperia.

"I'm glad you're here with us," I say to him.

Sorin smiles. "I will go wherever you go," he says, "for as long as you'll let me."

"Alright, alright," Crayln shouts above the chatter. "Reunion's over. I'm *starving*. Let's eat!"

We all exchange amused looks, but we follow him out onto the patio suspended over the cliffside and the town below.

I pause as I take in the figure standing beside the table.

"Mom?" I ask.

My mother crosses the balcony and draws me into her embrace. Around us, my friends file past and settle down at the table.

"Mom, you came," I say, not quite believing it.

She smiles, her eyes brighter than they were when I saw her in the prison. Her hair is smooth and untangled, and her skin is softer. She looks alive again.

"I am so proud of you, Iris," she says, cupping my face in her hands. "You have grown so strong. I only regret that you have had to do it on your own."

"Will you stay with us?" I ask.

My mother drops her hands, but her face is calm. "I have been away for a long time," she says. "There are many things I must tend to, but I will always be with you, Iris. Whenever you need me, I will come."

She takes my hand and leads us to the table. I settle in the seat between her and Avrian. As the warm ocean breeze hits my face, I notice the lightness in my chest. For the first time since I left the palace, I can finally breathe again.

As night falls over the town, I join Avrian on the balcony. We lean against each other, watching the stars as they blink across the dark blanket of sky.

"Is this where you grew up?" I ask him.

He lets out a breath and nods. "Yes," he says.

"I see why your mother chose this place," I say. "It's beautiful."

Avrian turns to look at me, his eyes reflecting mine. "I never imagined I'd find the strength to come back here," he says. "But I'm glad we're here, and I'm honored that I get the chance to share it with you."

I smile and reach out to take his hand in mine.

The crashing waves below us fill the silence, and I focus on the salty air and the glow of moonlight illuminating the town below us. As we sit overlooking the edge of the world, I realize I believe everything will turn out alright.

"Whatever comes next, we're in this together," I say. "All of us."

THE END

Acknowledgements

When I first came up with the idea for *The Blood Marrow* in the spring of my sophomore year of high school, I never imagined it would grow into a published, full-length novel. Yet here we are, and I could never have done it alone.

First and foremost, thank you to my parents Cory and Donna Gabel for putting up with my crazy writer-brain that never shuts up. Your continued support through my highs and lows means the world to me and more. Special thanks to my dad for reading the messy scraps of draft one and keeping my wild ideas in check. Thank you to my aunt, Jessica Cino, for dedicating hours to reading my very first manuscript from when I was twelve. And to my extended family, thank you for always believing in me and for listening to me rant about pesky plot holes in my manuscript.

Thank you to my friends, you know who you are, for your unwavering support. Thanks to all of you, I can look back on high school with fond memories of the good times we had while bonding over stressful AP classes.

Lastly, I would like to thank you, my readers. The community of readers I have been blessed with is truly amazing, and for those of you who continually support me on social media or by simply reading my book, thank you.

Kiera Shen Gabel is a young writer based in New England and has been writing stories ever since she could pick up a pencil. As an award-winning author and artist, she can be found typing away in her room or bringing her characters to life visually through art. For a glimpse at her current works in progress, updates, and more, visit www.kierashengabel.com.